Clara
A Good Psychopath?

Clara
A Good Psychopath?

ANNE E. THOMPSON

The Cobweb Press

Published by The Cobweb Press
www.thecobwebpress.com
thecobwebpress@gmail.com

A CIP catalogue record for this book is available from the British Library

ISBN 978-0-9954632-5-7

Cover design and typeset by Geoff Fisher

Printed and bound in Great Britain by CPI Antony Rowe

For David

Foreword

Imagine for a moment that you can see through time. Pretend you can see through the curtain separating your past and future, and consider what that might mean.

There are some events in life which are more important than others. You would agree? So, I have a question for you: If you could look ahead, to the consequences, do you think it would change your actions?

Would the fourteen-year-old boy refuse to take that first drag on the ciggy behind the bike sheds, *if* he could glimpse his sixty-year-old self, gasping for breath through a breathing tube as cancer ate his body? Or would the allure of mocking teenaged friends still be too strong?

Would the slim prom queen make eyes at the rugby team captain, *if* she could glimpse her swollen body stuck at home with screaming kids, in a greasy kitchen with the telly blaring? Or would the urge to prove she was the most attractive, desired, girl in the school still be too strong?

In short, do you think we would alter our present if we could see the future? Or sometimes, is something worth the price that we pay?

Is now *always* more important than later? Would we shut the door on that future sight, ignore consequences, because actually, the urgency of now is too great. We *cannot* resist what we gain in the present, for fear of what it will bring in the future. We want money in our pocket, not in the bank. Because, after all, how much is anything worth anyhow?

I think so. It might be different if we could jump back, if having withered in a hospice we could then return, choose again, take a different path. But looking forward? Nah, I think not.

Introduction

My new Gucci sneakers were definitely out of place. They had looked very white as I walked towards the flats, the embroidered bee emblem shining as it caught the sun. They were excellent shoes. They looked great, were a joy to wear and shouted to the world that I had money and knew how to dress. Of course, not everyone would be listening. Not everyone would recognise quality for what it was. Like Sam. I doubted he would know a Gucci shoe if it rose up and hit him on the nose.

It was several weeks ago that I had decided to visit Sam Whittaker. I knew he was known as a wise old man, but it wasn't his wisdom I was after. No, what I needed was a bit of renewed credibility, someone who could inspire a little trust in me. I knew I had 'burnt my bridges' as Michael would have said, what I was hoping was that Sam might build me a few new ones.

I didn't bother to phone before I went. He was old; I figured that his life would be mainly empty, centred around church activities and outings to the shops. It was Wednesday afternoon, the shops in the village would be closed and the oldies group met Tuesday mornings. I parked in the little layby next to the flats and walked up the stairs to the second floor, I didn't fancy the foul-smelling lift. Mind you, most old people's flats smell like toilets, so I wasn't going to be taking deep breaths while I was there.

The steps were concrete, probably as smelly as the lift, the harsh tang of disinfectant mingling with something worse, assaulting the nose. Not that it bothered me, smells rarely did. But I noticed. Made me wish I wasn't there. Added to my unhappiness, my discomfort at the necessity of the whole thing. I wasn't used to needing people, asking for help.

My hand hurt too. I had hidden it inside my pocket, a sort of attempt to keep the bandage clean, to protect it a bit. The thought of something banging against it made me feel slightly queasy. I could feel it rubbing against the lining of my pocket, raw, the nerves exposed and screaming. My feet stomped up the steps, loud, angry, resentful. I wanted choices and I knew I didn't have any. Not anymore. No choices, just one slim chance and it depended on the decision of an old man who should have died decades ago.

I knocked on the front door – three loud knocks so he would hear me – there didn't seem to be a bell. I heard the bang of a door inside, heavy steps as he walked down the hall, the scrape of the chain being put in the slot. The door opened all of three inches. I smiled down at Sam, my best, 'please trust me, looking slightly contrite' smile. He frowned up at me, surprised but not necessarily antagonistic. Perhaps I did have a chance.

"Hello Mr Whittaker," I said, loud enough that he would hear me, old people are usually deaf. "It's Clara Oakes, I hope you don't mind me popping in. I was hoping you could give me some advice."

"Oh yes?" he said. He didn't move, didn't open the door and invite me in. That was a bit unexpected. Perhaps he had more sense than I'd assumed. Never mind, I could do this, I could persuade him that I was harmless and humble and needed his help. The help bit was true anyway.

"You see, I've made some…" I paused.

I didn't know how much he knew and I didn't want to make things worse by admitting to things that weren't public knowledge. On the other hand, if I didn't appear sorry for things that he knew about, it would go against me. I needed this old man to trust me, to speak for me.

"I've made some big mistakes. I've hurt a few people. But I'm sorry, I realise I was wrong and I want to change. Can you help me? Will you give me some advice? Tell me what I should do?"

I did not, of course, expect that I would be listening to his advice. It was the me talking bit which was important. But I thought that if I appealed to his 'wise old man' image, he was more likely to let me in and to listen to my side of things.

He stared at me for a full minute, those watery blue eyes with milky whites and damp lashes looked right through me. He made his decision and nodded, shut the door so he could unhook the chain, opened it wide enough for me to enter.

"Alright, come on in. I'll hear what you have to say. Don't take me for a fool though, I'm old but I'm not stupid. I know people like you. Go on," he gestured with his head, that I should go first, "second door on the left. You can sit in there."

He followed me down the narrow hall, past his greasy kitchen, old fat smells mingling with damp carpet and dust. I led the way, interested that he had positioned himself so he could watch me. Perhaps he was right, perhaps he wasn't a fool. That was okay though. Most of my story was true, and I really did need his help.

The carpet was thin, stained in places. I turned in through the doorway he'd indicated. It was a sitting room, small, too much furniture and too much heat. I did a quick scan of the room, from habit as much as anything. A quick evaluation of anything with value. There were some old frames on a sideboard that might be worth something, the photographs inside faded now, one a sepia print of a young woman, one a wedding photograph. The rest was rubbish, would go straight into a tip when the old man finally died. Unless there was something worth having in the sideboard itself of course, but I doubted it. Perhaps a medal from a long-forgotten war. Maybe some kind of heirloom. But Sam Whittaker had never been rich, anyone could see that. I've no idea why he was held in such high esteem really, especially in the church. But church people are a bit weird, a bit twisted in their priorities.

I took a seat on a hard chair next to the electric fire. I considered asking if I could turn it down a bit, maybe open a window, let in some air. Decided to keep things simple. I would tell my story, hope for the best.

I wondered if he would offer me some tea. Not that I fancied any, not from that kitchen. Probably catch something, nothing in that flat looked like it was cleaned very regularly. But he didn't. He just lowered his stiff bones into the chair opposite, leant his stick against the chair arm and looked at me. He didn't speak, didn't make it easy. He just waited. Watching me all the time with those faded eyes. I had no idea what he was thinking. I struggled out of my jacket and shoved it behind me, buying myself a bit of time, trying to get my thoughts properly sorted. Then I began to speak.

I must've talked for over an hour. Sam got up at one point — raised his hand so I paused, then heaved himself to his feet, told me to wait, left the room. I sat there, listening to his heavy footsteps as he went down the hall, into his bathroom. I waited, stared at the sideboard, the yellow patterned curtains at the window, the faux fur rug lying in front of the electric fire. I heard the flush, his heavy steps as he came back, then lowered himself into his seat, and nodded for me to continue. It was a bit rude really, treating me like he was deigning to listen to my story, like he was better than me. But I swallowed it down, took it all in my stride. It's always important to keep the final aim in mind, and I knew I had to take whatever he threw at me, had to appear humble and patient. Otherwise he wouldn't believe me.

By the time I had finished talking, my throat felt sore and I might even have accepted a drink, had he offered one. But he didn't. He let me finish and then he sat there, for what felt like ages. Thinking I suppose, deciding what he was going to say. I wasn't sure what I'd do if he decided to not help me, to not persuade the others that I had changed, was someone they should continue to accept. There wasn't anything else I could say, I had told him everything. Well, not about my hand, that was just embarrassing, not something you want other people to know about. But I had told him everything else, the whole unbelievable story, which I hoped, because it was true, he would actually believe.

So I sat there, waiting. I could hear the clock ticking away the seconds, some kids swearing outside, a door bang in another flat, Sam's breathing, slow and wheezy. Then he cleared his throat, a great rattle of rearranged globs of phlegm, helped along by a thump on his chest with his gnarled fist. He nodded. I took that as a good sign, meant he was accepting what I'd told him.

"Alright, I believe you. Reckon some people need a sledgehammer and that's what you seem to have got. No real options left for you young lady. You're right, you do have to change.

"I don't know why he would bother with you actually. Perhaps you can do something the rest of us can't, I don't know. Not really my place to say why. But I can tell you one thing, your place isn't here anymore."

I started to protest at that. The whole point of coming was so that he would speak on my behalf, make it possible for me to stay. I had not sat in his pokey stinky flat for the fun of it, nor for any sort of need for penance. I wanted him to help me. I began to wonder if I had wasted my time. He raised a hand, indicating I should settle down, let him finish.

"No, just listen. You came for advice, now listen to it." (Actually, I hadn't, I'd come so he would help me, but he didn't know that. I listened. Wish I hadn't now.) "You have something to do. I don't know what it is, maybe you do, maybe you'll find out later. But it isn't here. You need to move away, leave the folk here in peace."

He looked up at me, those ancient eyes staring into mine. Not unkindly, perhaps even with sympathy.

"Do you know where you should go?"

I hadn't known, not until he said that. But as soon as he did, as soon as he asked the question, it was obvious. Everything fell into place and I found I actually wanted to go. It was even quite exciting, and I like exciting, bit of a risk.

I was going to India.

Chapter One

Several weeks later – it takes longer than you might think to sort everything – I was at Heathrow airport. I will explain, of course, you won't be keeping up with all this, will be wondering what is going on. So I will go through it all, right from the beginning, so you understand. I thought about it all myself actually, right there in the airport. I was travelling Business Class, and I thought about it all in the lounge, while I was waiting for them to call my flight.

Are you surprised I was flying Business, did you think I might save the money, use it for someone more needy or something? That just shows how little you know me, how much I need to explain. If I had to go all the way to India, I sure as hell wasn't going in Economy. I had savings, I might as well use them. If I was being taken out of my comfortable world and was going to have to cope with goodness knows what in the future, then I figured I deserved a little luxury. And it *was* luxurious.

First of all, I was picked up from home. They call it a limo service, but actually it's just a rather nice car with a driver to lift your bags. Which is lucky, because mine were heavy. My hand had mostly healed, though the skin was pink and delicate. But I didn't like using it, still felt the need to protect it, so I was glad to have help.

The phone rang as I was leaving, and I paused in the doorway, deciding whether to answer it. It wouldn't be work because I'd told them I was going on holiday (I'd decided not to resign, just in case – better to keep my options open). If it was my parents the call wouldn't be worth listening to, they had said all they needed to and

I didn't need to hear it again. My friends were irrelevant now, I was moving on. If it was related to the house sale, my lawyer could handle it, it was what I was paying him for. So I ignored it, slammed the door behind me, and climbed into the back seat of the limo.

We drove straight to a special entrance at the airport, with staff waiting as the car stopped. They took my bags from the car, right through to my own check-in desk. I even had my own security lane, passing the rabble who were scrabbling to separate liquids and computers while the rest of their bags disappeared into the x-ray tunnel.

I joined them briefly the other side of security, walked past their tense faces as they searched for a spare plastic seat, or queued for food, or wandered around shops, while they waited for their gate to appear on the board. I made my way to the lounge, up a short flight of stairs, past the shoe-shine man. I tell you, that lounge was another world.

I was greeted with piped music and hushed voices. There were heaps of complimentary magazines on a shelf and bays of easy chairs around a giant screen showing the football match. The overall impression was of bright lights, leather seats, mirrors. They even had little screens flickering with images of fires, so you could pretend that you were somewhere other than in an airport, waiting for a long flight. The floor was wood, so it was easy enough to roll my cabin case to a seat, though there were patches of carpet in the seating bays. We were meant to be comfortable, to feel cosseted. There was a dining area, a whole menu of restaurant food waiting to be served, not that I was very hungry. Everything was included in the extortionate price of the ticket – so 'free' really (unless you thought about it for ten seconds).

I decided to eat Eggs Benedict. It was served within minutes, the yolk mingling with the thick sauce. Comfort food.

I ordered a gin, and took it to an easy chair, hidden behind the snooker table, somewhere I could be quiet. That's where I started to think, to go over everything that had happened; everything that had brought me here, to this unreal corner of luxury in a busy airport. I went over it all in my mind. My whole life really. The ice chinked against the glass as I sipped. I cast my mind back, as far as I could remember, and thought, evaluating everything that had brought me to this point. Sit a while and let me explain.

***

My earliest memory is of Aleksander holding my ankles and spinning me round. One minute I was lying on the grass, green and warm from the afternoon sun, the next I was watching the garden spin past me: path–hedge–sky–flowers; a whirl of colour and fuzzy images. It was 1995 and I was three years old. I loved it.

Aleksander was my cousin. He was ten years older than me and was the most exciting person that I knew. He was the son of my father's brother. There were no cousins on my mother's side. No family at all, actually, but we will come to that later.

My earliest memory ended abruptly. My mother's legs interrupted the path, hedge, flowers sequence. Her voice, a cry of alarm, interrupted my squeals. I was dumped back on the grass. The world continued to spin. That was it, end of game. My mother often spoiled my games; that sad fact continued well beyond my third year.

Another memory, one that is clearly in my mind, is a birthday. I think I was five, though I'm less sure of that, I may have been six – certainly I was attending school at the time. I was born in the summer, so my parents had decided I would have a party outside, a big picnic in the garden. I wasn't too bothered about having a party at all, I do remember that. There wasn't anyone in my class who I particularly liked, I didn't really have friends when I was growing up. People are generally boring. There was a group of girls who I liked to organise and a few boys who laughed at my jokes, but I didn't especially want to spend time with them.

But my mother insisted that I should have a party, had forced me to think of names and had written them with a red felt pen on some little cards that she made into invitations. On the day of the party, my parents spent time decorating the garden. They had blown up balloons and strung them from the post at the end of the driveway, and there were ribbons in the trees. My mother spread a blanket on the lawn and laid it with cutlery, jellies in fluted cardboard dishes, bowls of crisps, plates of chocolate biscuits and muffins. I stood, under the apple tree, and watched her. I could see that she was trying, wanted it all to look nice. Which was irritating because I didn't want a party, I didn't want a bunch of children coming into my garden, enjoying food that should have all been for me.

I waited until she had nearly finished, until the first children were beginning to arrive, clutching gifts and wondering where I was. I was in the shed, getting my bike. As my mother greeted children and showed them into the garden, I rode my bike towards them, whooping loudly and pedalling hard.

I rode fast and purposefully. Straight to the blanket, over the food and cups and napkins. I had to stand on the pedals to turn the wheels as I ploughed through the food, splattering jelly across the lawn, spraying cake crumbs over the blanket. Everyone watched. No one spoke. Until my mother did. She made a sort of cry and chased after me. Which made it more fun, added a bit of danger to the mix. I pedalled faster, ignoring her shouts, laughing at how stupid she looked, chasing after my bike as I rode round and round the apple tree.

My father stopped it. He came to see what the noise was about, stepped into my path, lifted me from the saddle, carried me into the house. That was end of my birthday. I was sent to my room with legs sore from a slap and no supper. I had to listen to those other children playing the games my parents had planned, laughing while they ate the remains of the food.

But I didn't really care. I had never wanted a party in the first place.

My mother was always trying to instigate friendships, often asking her own friends to bring their awful offspring to the house. Then we would be put in a room together, a few games suggested, followed by a horrible gap when the mothers went off together for a cosy chat in the kitchen over coffee. We would stare at each other – me and whatever stray kid had been forced to visit. Sometimes they would smile, try to start a game, begin to look at my toys. My toys. That's the thing, they were mine. Not for sharing. I would have to teach them that. Perhaps shout or spit to make them stop touching. Or let them touch, for a little while, then shout loudly, find the doll with the broken leg that I'd put under the bed last week, go crying to the kitchen, explain to my mother that Sarah or Jane or Carol, hadn't been careful. They had been rough with my things, had broken my favourite toy. Please could they go home now?

There would be some embarrassed conversation between the adults, the kid's mother apologising, offering to pay for the damage, the girl protesting her innocence, saying she hadn't even touched the doll. Which was fine, I didn't care whether they believed me or not. The main thing was that the harmonious afternoon was shattered, they would leave as soon as they politely could and never be tempted to return. People only ever brought their children to play once.

Of course, sometimes it was us who did the visiting. I remember going fairly regularly to visit some friends of my parents; people who they'd known for years, had been to each other's weddings, both had children about the same time. They had three daughters and lived in a large house, much nicer than ours, arranged over three storeys. I liked that house. One of the daughters had a room on the third floor, right up in a converted attic and I liked to go up there, away from the others, to stare out the window at the sky and to look through her things.

Her toys were better than mine. She had lots of dolls and a huge dollhouse with miniature furniture which even had a stable attached. The stables had toy horses in them, and those horses had real hair for their manes. I had toy horses too, not that I ever played with them, but they were made completely from plastic, their manes and tails moulded and solid. These horses almost looked like tiny real horses, the way their tails swished when they were moved. It didn't seem fair that her toys should be so much nicer than mine.

There was a little desk in the corner of the room, with a lid that lifted up and paper and pens and scissors inside. Scissors that were sharp. Sharp enough to cut through hair.

I decided to use them on one visit, trimmed each tail to a stub, watching the hair fall to the carpet like dandelion seeds. I hid the spoiled horses behind the linen basket on the landing, where they wouldn't be discovered until well after we had left. The hairs I scooped up and held out of the window, opened my fingers, watched them blow away in the breeze. It still makes me smile to think of it, watching those strands of hair released onto the wind, while the rest of the children played in the garden below.

My parents did their best. I wouldn't want you to think they didn't try or didn't care. I can see that now. I grew up in a good home, full of love and discipline. It's just that the discipline didn't manage to quite change me. Or maybe it did. Maybe if they hadn't tried, I would've been different – 'worse' some would say. Though that's a fruitless discussion, we never know what we *might* have been.

I do remember them disciplining me though. Mother would stand in front of me, explaining why I shouldn't behave in a certain way, why lying was wrong, why people were hurt when I stole, or said cruel things. And I would listen. I would look right into her eyes and try to concentrate. But I wasn't really interested. I didn't care. She would talk, her voice getting louder until she was shouting, losing control. I sort of liked that, it felt like a small victory to see her break down over something I had done.

Sometimes my mind would wander, I would think about something unrelated, sometimes something funny, and I would find my lips curling into a smile even while she was shouting at me. Of course, then she would get really angry, would assume I was laughing at her, not taking the reprimand to heart. Sometimes she would smack me, a stinging slap across the legs or bottom. Designed to hurt but not damage. They did hurt too, I remember crying, when I was very young. As I grew slightly older, they just made me angry and I would beam whichever parent had hit me with eyes of hatred. Or laugh in their face, tell them it hadn't hurt, now could I go or did they want to abuse me some more?

Thinking about it now, as an adult, I expect they would have sought some kind of help, a counsellor or something. I probably wasn't the same as other children. I always thought I was special, the rules didn't really apply to me. But if I'm honest, if I try to look at all this dispassionately, through your eyes, I was probably a difficult child to raise. They probably would have involved some kind of external help. If we'd stayed in the same place for long enough. Or if the twins hadn't been born.

Ah yes, I haven't mentioned the twins yet have I? They were born when I was four.

I don't think my parents planned more children after me, in fact, given our family history, I'm not sure that they ever actually planned me. But when I was four, my mother fell pregnant and then discovered it was twins. I have never understood why they went through with the pregnancy, especially after having me. Perhaps they figured the odds were on their side, they couldn't possibly produce two of me. Maybe they felt they deserved a 'normal' child this time, one that would be easier to manage. Or perhaps they had some sort of moral qualm that made them go through with it. I've never asked, and I doubt they would tell me the truth anyway. Everyone has their own brand of dishonesty.

So, my mother gave birth to twin boys, Edward and Michael. Both had hair so blond it turned white in the sunshine and eyes as dark as chocolate buttons. They weren't identical but they were inseparable.

Before the birth, my parents did all the things that the magazines and elderly relatives suggested. My mother tried to involve me in the pregnancy, taking me with her to the antenatal clinic, referring to the bump as *"your* baby brother or sister," which later became, *"your* brothers."

When the babies were born, I was taken to the hospital to see them. There was my mother, sitting on the bed in a pink nightie, two plastic crates on wheels next to her. I thought they looked like square fish tanks with giant red squids inside. Next to each baby was a gift, wrapped in blue paper.

"Your brothers have bought you presents," said my father, and lifted me onto the bed next to my mother.

One of the babies started to cry, and I saw my mother look at Dad. He shook his head, telling her to leave it to cry. For that one minute, I was the centre of their attention, I took precedence over the babies. They needn't have bothered. I had no interest in the boys. Not until they were about three, old enough for me to influence them.

Like I said, the boys were inseparable. They were however, very different, Michael being right-handed and serious, Edward being left-handed and loud. Michael always enjoyed English and art,

Edward always excelled at mathematics and music. My every memory of them has them together, in the same room, playing or arguing or watching telly. They even slept together, long after they were given separate rooms, they would drag their duvets into one room or the other, sleeping on each other's floors when they grew too big to share a bed. Even now we are adults, if I meet one of them without the other, it feels odd, like meeting half a person. Not that we do meet very often, not after everything that's happened. I think they would like to write me out of the family tree if they could, forget that there ever was a third child.

I had no opinion about them at all. They were boring. I found their demands on my mother's time irritating, but I was at school by the time they were born and I think she always made sure I had her attention in the evenings. I wonder though if it stopped her seeking professional help for me. She simply didn't have the time or energy. Then we moved to the US. This is hardly significant – we returned to the UK for my most important years. But I should include a few snippets from my time stateside, otherwise you won't have the whole story; and it probably did alter me a bit, allowed me to develop some of my skills.

I was aged six, so it was after the escapade with the picnic party. My father worked in the city and had been asked if he could do a secondment, relocate for a few years to the US. I'm not sure what my mother thought. Perhaps she was glad to start afresh, thought that a new start would be good for me. I was already making my mark at school, she was used to the teacher calling her back when she came to collect me. I really don't remember much of what went on, but I do remember spending a lot of playtimes in the headteacher's office. And for some reason I was never allowed into assembly, but for the life of me, I cannot remember why.

**

My gin was finished, so I placed the empty glass on the table, thought about getting another. It would make me sleepy though and I needed to stay reasonably alert until I was on the plane, probably better to wait until after we had boarded. I checked the time. Still ages to go. The chair was comfortable but a man had arrived on the chair opposite. He was talking loudly on his telephone, telling someone called Bill that they "needed to sign off by next Friday." It was too loud, intrusive. I wanted to think.

I scowled at him – talking so loudly in a public area was selfish. I collected my bag from the floor, walked past him slightly too closely so the sharp edge of my pull-along clipped his shin. He started, but before he could complain I was gone, wandering through the lounge, looking for somewhere quiet. There was a business room, separated from the main lounge with glass screens. It was probably quiet, but the chairs were all upright ones, arranged around desks with telephone points and computers. I fancied a bit more comfort than that.

There were some hanging chairs, next to a place where you could book a manicure. I would skip the manicure, I don't like to be touched; it always seems very odd to me, some strange woman holding your hand while she applies nail varnish. The chairs looked comfy though, and no one else was near. I took one, swung gently backwards, closed my eyes and returned to my thoughts, the evaluation of my life. I hope you're listening, taking note of who I was. It will help you to understand who I became.

***

I remember my parents preparing for the move. They would stare for hours at photographs that estate agents had sent through, checking where places were on the map, deciding where they wanted to live. We had a succession of men walking through the house, looking in all our cupboards, giving quotes for transporting all our belongings. I only remember because I was constantly being told to tidy my things, that strangers were coming to inspect my bedroom. Of course, I hated that. I would wait until I heard my mother go to answer the door, then go and tip over as many toy boxes as I could.

My mother spent hours on the telephone, arranging everything. This frustrated me, sometimes I wanted her attention. She would lock herself into the study (all our doors had locks on them, it was like living in a prison, though I don't recall ever being locked *in* a room). I would bang on the door, sitting on the floor outside and kicking at it with both feet, a steady *bang, bang, bang.* She never appeared, she had grown too good at ignoring me by then.

My other tactic was to create as much mess as possible, to punish her for resisting me. I'd go upstairs, empty my cupboards and fling everything down the stairs. A pleasing trail of shoes and clothes and toys and books. The heavier items fell with a thud, bumping from stair to stair, pages scattering from books, mud dislodged from boots. If the twins were also up there, safely in their playpen, I'd reach through the bars, try to pinch them so they screamed. She usually came then, whisked me up and plonked me in a different room. Occasionally I would also receive a stinging slap, but I think she was trying to limit how often she smacked me by then. Probably my behaviour resulted in more than an 'acceptable' level of physical discipline.

I don't remember much about the actual move. I know the packers arrived while I was at school, so I returned home to find my bedroom empty, all our possessions squashed into a steel container on the back of a lorry. I vaguely remember the flight, being bored and making splatter patterns on the seat in front with the tray of plastic-wrapped food that appeared at regular intervals. And being worried every time I used the washroom, in case I was sucked out of the plane when the toilet was flushed.

We moved to New Jersey. Tall trees, the highest sky you can imagine, wide roads and huge cars.

The house we rented was all on one level, with steep stairs down to the basement and garage. The door to the basement was kept locked. I tried to open it every so often, but I never found it unlocked. My parents were careful.

There were trees and deer, which meant ticks and Lyme disease. I only remember this because my mother smothered us in insect repellent whenever we went into the garden. I didn't much like deer, seeing them as the cause for being covered in slime. I collected rocks and sticks, kept them in a pile by the air-conditioning unit, and threw them whenever a deer wandered into the garden. I never hit one. One night I went into the kitchen and collected all the knives from the kitchen drawers, thinking I would make a trap. I have no idea now what my plan was, but it involved a pit and knives and I had visions of slashed necks and death. I don't think I planned to also harm my brothers, but should one of them wander into my trap by chance, that would've been an added bonus.

But my father heard me, found the knives and put them all back. The following night, when I sneaked back to the kitchen, all the drawers had locks on them. They must have been fitted while I was at school.

School in the US was not much better than in the UK. It was not designed for people like me. When we first arrived, my parents asked for the school to test me. The English system started earlier than the American one, so I read fluently and understood some mathematics, whilst American children of the same age were still learning their letters and numbers. Academically, I was two years ahead of my age. Physically, I was tiny. Emotionally, I was probably bit of a nightmare. I think my mother worried that if I was put into kindergarten, with children my own age, I would continue to manipulate my classmates and cause trouble. If I were the youngest

12

in the class, which was allowed because academically I was equal, then perhaps I would be less of a leader. It didn't work.

The school compromised, and I joined a class one year ahead of my age.

Actually, my class had a mix of ages. The US system tended to list students according to ability, which many parents thought was detrimental to self-confidence. If they had a boy who was immature, they decided it was better for his overall development, to start school a year later, when he had matured slightly, so he wasn't listed at the bottom of the class. This meant that I was in classes with children who were sometimes two whole years older than me. They were huge. Of course, this didn't worry me, I don't recall ever being frightened by anything. I did use it to great advantage though. Who would ever blame the tiny English girl when fights were started or protests instigated? I found that I could persuade those children into all kinds of trouble, then let them take the blame.

Each day we were all driven to and from school, either by our parents or by the school bus. No one walked in our town, I do remember that. There weren't even paths along the roads, the gardens went right up to the tarmac.

I went to school by bus. It waited outside our house every morning, the lights flashing so all the traffic on both sides of the street knew they had to stop. I liked the power of that, thought that when I grew up, I might be a school bus driver, make the traffic stop. I always walked very slowly to the bus, climbed the steps inch by inch, as if unable to move my legs. I would see the cars stopping outside and count how many had been brought to a standstill while I wandered to my seat. On a good day, I would have eight cars waiting. The bus driver would shout at me, tell me to hurry. I ignored him. He wasn't allowed to start moving until I was seated, the power was all mine.

The next memory that really stands out is at the end of a school semester. The mothers all decided to take us to Dairy Queen after school, a little treat to welcome in the summer. My mother collected me from school and we drove the short distance to the ice-cream parlour. The twins were left strapped into their car seats, the doors open so they could see us. I chose a chocolate dipped cone, stood licking it before it melted, the ice cream dripping in a long line down my arm. All the kids stood in a group, bragging about their grades or comparing which summer school classes they had signed up for. Lots were taking classes in crafts – pottery or sewing. A few were being forced into academic classes, to improve their grades. I stood off to one side, not wanting to talk to anyone, waiting for my mother to finish chatting so we could leave. I knew she wouldn't be too long, she would want to get back to the twins, shut the doors and get the air on to cool down the car.

I was at the point of causing a disturbance, doing something so we could leave immediately, when the dog ran into the road. I have no idea where it came from, one of the houses I guess. It shot out, like it was chasing something, straight under the wheels of an oncoming car. The car screeched to a halt, the driver raced to the front to see if there was any damage, us kids all ran up to see if the dog had survived. We crowded round, a shuffling group of onlookers. It was alive, but only just. It lay there, on the side of the pavement, where it had been thrown up after the car hit it; its leg at a funny angle, its eyes glazed. One of the kids started to cry, a few looked like they might be sick. The driver was muttering about his car being damaged, it not being his fault, did anyone know who owned the dog and he hoped they had liability insurance. The mothers were reassuring their kids, leading them away, not wanting to be involved.

I went right up to the dog and knelt down. I knew my mother would try to drag me away too, so I pretended I wanted to help it.

"I won't touch," I promised – probably she was worried that we might get sued too as everyone was trying to apportion blame. Or perhaps she was worried about rabies, unsure if the dog had been vaccinated. I just sat there, out of reach, watching.

The dog was in pain, it kept shuddering, trying to move the damaged leg, attempting to raise its head. After a while it stopped, it lay still, the breathing became more shallow. I watched. When my mother looked away, checking the twins were still happy, I put out my hand and poked the hurt leg, wanting to see if the dog had enough life left to react. It made a noise, a sort of whimper, but very faint, more a snuffle of expelled air. The breathing got less even. I stared at the eyes. I watched the wildness leave them, saw them glass over. I felt I was watching the actual life slip out of the animal, could almost say the exact moment it became dead. It was the most interesting thing I had ever seen.

I became aware that my mother was watching me and looked up. Her eyes were hard to read, but she looked worried. Young as I was, I knew that profound interest in something dying was not how one is supposed to react. I gave her a wan smile, tried to look sad, told her that I didn't think there was anything we could have done. In the car on the way home, I talked about the dog some more, said it had made me want to be able to help when things were injured, that I might try to be a doctor or vet. I knew my mother was listening intently, that she wanted to believe me, to see my interest as something positive. I think my mother has always wanted me to be normal. But normal is somewhat tedious, don't you think?

Chapter Two

The music in the airport lounge changed to some kind of piano solo, reminding me of church. I was certainly comfortable now. The waitress came over and I ordered a tonic water – didn't want to be too dehydrated on the flight. I picked up a magazine to flick through while I thought about that first church. I mention it, because church has been another great source of followers for me.

I realised early on that churches tend to be packed with gullible people, whichever side of the Atlantic they happen to be on. It was while we were living in the US that we started to attend church and I realised what a wonderful place for influencing weak people it was. All you need to do is learn some jargon, some facial expressions, and the possibilities are limitless. If things had been different, perhaps I would have started a sect of my own. Most people are weak, they need a leader to tell them what to do, and they would be happy to pay for the privilege, to keep that leader comfortable.

We started to attend simply because, in New Jersey, just about everyone attends church of some kind. It's a bit weird really. The schools are completely separate from all religion, so even little kids don't make Christmas cards or do a Nativity play. They wish each other "Happy Holidays," and talk about "spring break," not Easter. However, apart from that, religion is much more acceptable than in England. People will often talk about praying for people, even at the park or in shops: if two people are sharing news, one will often round up the conversation by promising, "I'll pray for you," or "Catch you later then, God bless." And as I said, the churches on Sundays are pretty full.

My friends (not sure if 'friends' is an accurate description, but I can't think of a better one) seemed to fit into three categories. There were the Catholics. These tended to be of Italian origin, and many were, I think with hindsight, probably connected to a 'family'. I remember even some of the toughest, most unruly boys, talking about their First Communion, being forced to buy a suit and having aunts and uncles arrive to celebrate. Then there were the Jewish children. They were mainly noticeable at Christmas time, because they all received gifts *before* we did, as part of Hanukkah. Then there were the protestant churches: the Methodists, the Baptists, the Lutheran or Pentecostals. Where we lived, there were mainly Baptists.

We attended a large white church, surrounded by a car park of expensive cars and filled with pews of manicured people. It was very professional. The singing was led by a group of proficient musicians, the words appearing automatically on great screens above their heads, peaceful images projected in between verses. There were Sunday schools for every age group – even the adults attended one, with a coffee and donut break before the main service. Those people were committed, you have to give them that. Quite *what* they were committed to, I am slightly unsure. But the impression they gave was a good one, especially if you are into plastic smiles, trouble free lives and pseudo-concern for the less well off. They all liked to conform to an image. This has proved invaluable over the years as I have manipulated people.

My parents got quite into the church thing. They started to attend every Sunday and we got dragged along with them. I soon found it was more fun than school. Before the Sunday School class I would agree with the other kids some kind of cue word or action, perhaps a word that the teacher was bound to say at some point during the session. Then, when the cue happened, we would all act in a prearranged way. Sometimes we all dived under the table

17

and refused to come out, or we fell to our knees or started to chant a rhyme. I was never punished. Church is all about forgiveness, and that is jolly useful for someone like me. All I ever needed to do was stare at the floor (mainly so they couldn't see the glint in my eye) and tell them I was sorry.

"Gee Miss Alyssa, I'm real sorry. I didn't mean to upset you, I guess I misread the situation."

For those leaders, forgiveness meant lack of punishment (dodgy theology, but even today, as an adult, I wouldn't hurry to point that out). Someone appearing contrite could expect to get off with a sharp word and a frown. I was already learning that churches are a good place for someone like me. So much fun to be had, so many people waiting to be led.

To begin with, I bribed the other kids to follow my lead. I took money that I had acquired from various purses, or candy bars taken from our larder. Later, when my leadership was established, I threatened anyone who preferred to not join in. I was too small to fight, but I was friends with Bobby. He was big.

Bobby was also in my class at school and I realised his potential early on. He was big and he was dim. Really dim. I met him when I was in first grade. The other kids were mean to him, teasing him, calling him names. We had a weekly spelling test, and Bobby always scored the lowest. In break time, the other boys would laugh at him, throw sticks broken from the trees in the play area, call him Bobby Booby. He would stand there, not retaliating, looking forlorn.

For a few days I watched from the edge, deciding whether to get involved, which side would be most fun to join. I realised that Bobby was much stronger than every other boy in our grade, probably because he was older. I felt this could be used. So on the third day, I left the edge of the circle and stepped forwards. I picked up one of the sticks, a fairly large branch, and stood next to Bobby.

"Why don't you all just leave him alone?" I said, in my best English accent. Americans listen to English accents. "Go on, get out of here."

They stared, gaping mouths in loose smiles. I was tiny. Any one of them could have picked me up or knocked me down. But I wasn't scared of them and they knew it. They knew that if I got hurt, a teacher would take a dim view of it. They also recognised that I was tough. I might not win a fight but I wasn't going to be afraid to land a few punches and they weren't sure I was worth the effort.

Swearing and laughing, whooping that, "Bobby has a girlfriend," they left. I turned to Bobby.

"Gee, why do ya do that? Why'd you always let them beat up on you?" The English accent was less clear now, I could slip between both accents, and this was a time to sound American, familiar and safe. I was young, but I had an intuitive grasp of what people responded to.

Bobby shook his head, not able to think of an answer. I'm not sure Bobby ever thought much about anything. He became my friend. I cultivated the friendship with gifts of stolen candy and a quick defence when the bullies came near. In return, Bobby would do pretty much anything I asked. He was strong and big, and even though I don't think I ever actually put it to the test, the threat of him punching kids at church was usually enough for them to comply with what I wanted. I began to learn how useful people can be. My skills at manipulation were also being honed. I was foreign, the girl with the funny accent. I learned that if you mimic people, copy their speech patterns and body language, they are more likely to listen to you. Of course, at the time, this was all subconscious, a child's desire to fit in with a new culture. The kids at school spoke with an accent, so I copied them. At home, I spoke how my parent's spoke. I didn't realise it at the time, but I was learning to be a chameleon.

I was never expelled from school, and I think I probably did rather well while we lived in New Jersey. Much of the work was a direct repeat of what I'd covered in the UK, with a heavy emphasis on presentation. We would write stories, full of punctuation errors and spelling mistakes, but they were rarely corrected. Our offerings were then typed onto the computer by an adult, and printed and bound into books. They looked lovely, even though when I look at them now I'm amazed no one attempted to improve the content.

We also gave regular spoken presentations. At the end of a project, all the parents would be invited into the classroom. We stood at the front, with some sort of visual aid – perhaps a spaceship made from old boxes, or a painting, or a chart we had drawn. Then, using 'prompt cards' we had made during lessons, we gave a short speech about our work. Most kids stumbled through their presentation, either reading their cards directly, or gazing at the ceiling while they fought to remember their planned sentences. I was a natural public speaker.

I looked at my audience, made jokes, used my hands to point out various things of interest. As I looked around, I could see the other parents staring at me, wishing I was their child. My mother was at the back, a half smile, half frown on her face. She was pleased to see I was excelling, but I could tell she was worried too. Perhaps she thought all the attention was bad for me. My mother is the only person I know who can smile and frown at the same time. It was her almost perpetual expression in those days.

Whatever she thought, I can now see how useful those presentation skills were. I have put them to good use, and it was a good lesson. Content rarely matters if it is presented well. Just look at some of our politicians...

As I said, during the long summer break, everyone attended some kind of 'summer school'. My grades were pretty good (not through hard work, my English education had set me in good stead,

20

plus I was naturally a fast learner). I, of course, would've skipped all summer courses if I'd had the choice, but my mother decided I should be the same as the other kids. I think she wanted to spend long hours improving her tan at the town pool, she didn't want me around more than was necessary. She signed me up for a variety of courses – all of which were a disaster, because my main aim was to cause as much disruption as I could whilst never being spotted as the instigator. Except for clarinet lessons. That was different.

Parents like to brag about their children's accomplishments, and my parents were no different, so they decided I would learn a musical instrument. I chose the clarinet, because those shiny keys looked expensive and I didn't think my parents would be willing to pay. My parents bought a second-hand instrument for an exorbitant price, and I started to meet Miss June every week. She was a tall thin woman with very bad breath. We never bonded.

I did however, bond with the clarinet.

At first it was impossible, and I opened the case only when at lessons. Miss June would ask if I had practised and I would assure her I had, knowing that me playing scales was never going to happen. I unpacked the clarinet as slowly as possible, often breaking a reed so as to waste even more time. Miss June attempted to explain how to read music, chanting stupid rhymes about good boys deserving fudge, while I gazed out the window. I then attempted to make some sort of sound from the wretched instrument. Usually it emerged as a loud squeak, while Miss June told me to loosen my mouth, and tighten my diaphragm, and stand up straight. I disliked her intensely. I think this would've continued indefinitely, had she not signed me up for a beginner's concert. I was furious.

The letter was sent directly to my parents, explaining that at the end of the summer course there was to be a concert and all beginners would have the opportunity to showcase their achievements. The audience were requested to be understanding of the students' inexperience, but it would help them to have a taste of playing to an audience before they decided whether or not to continue with their lessons through the year.

Now, I did not care what other people thought about me, but I did not like to look a complete fool. I explained to my parents that I was unable to perform. My father explained to me that unless I performed, the cost of the clarinet would be deducted from my allowance for the next year. The thought of standing up in front of a group of parents and producing some sort of dying buffalo scream was intolerable. I decided to practise.

I set the alarm for 5 am, thinking that if I woke the entire family every morning, my father might relent and decide I should stop having lessons. He didn't. Each morning I forced myself from bed, grabbed the clarinet from where it was balanced on the open case, and squeaked my way through scales and exercises. Gradually, I began to improve. The squeaks became less regular, and tunes began to emerge. Miss June was impressed. My family were all lacking in sleep.

By the time of the beginners' concert, I was ready. I played some simple tune, which I can't even remember now, while Miss June rounded the sound with a clever piano accompaniment. The audience listened, the clarinet behaved, and I discovered I rather enjoyed performing. When I finished, I gave a sweeping bow, being careful to keep the clarinet horizontal so the spit didn't drip out and ruin the look. I knew my rendition was the best, the other beginners had clearly not put in the hours. I like to be the best. I decided to continue with the clarinet. It was a good decision.

During the hot summer break, my mother would often take us to the town pool, then lie there, improving her tan, while we amused ourselves. Even when we were fairly small, she didn't really want to be bothered by us. Looking back, it's a wonder one of us didn't drown. We would arrive, struggling from the car with heavy bags of snacks and towels, and choose a place to sit. Then my mother settled down, started to apply lotion, or dug into her bag for the novel she was reading. She would jam her sunglasses over her eyes and that was it, the sign to us children that she had finished with us for a couple of hours, we were dismissed. I was supposed to watch the twins, which always gave the lifeguard some action, as without fail I would entice them towards the deep end of the pool and knock them in. They learned to swim at a very early age, and I like to think that was thanks to me. Even if one of them needed to use the washroom, my mother wouldn't stir.

"Do it in the water," she would say. Or, "Ask Clara, she can take you."

Well, Clara didn't do things like that, so the pool it was. Not especially hygienic, but I don't think anyone noticed. I did query it with her once, tell her that she should take the twins, but she told me they put disinfectant in the water, we were meant to wee in there and the washrooms were dirty. I was young. I believed her.

It was my father who would come into the water with us, tow us in inflatable boats or play ballgames. My father would make toy farms with us, or camps in the garden.

I was learning other skills. When I went on playdates to friends' homes, I always sought out the older brothers, sidled into their rooms and announced I had candy to share, or a copy of some computer game that I knew would appeal to an older boy, the sort of game responsible parents banned. (It was easy enough to slide them into my pocket in the rental store, while my mother spent time choosing Disney crap for my brothers.)

Some of the boys knew the code to their parents' safe. This tended to be where the gun was kept. Most homes had a gun in those days, though I assume the parents thought it was safely locked away out of reach. Some kept the bullets in a different location, perhaps a high shelf in the garage, or a locked box in the wardrobe; but the gun was usually in the safe. I'd persuade the boys to show me they knew where it was, then taunt them into teaching me how to use it. Usually, we would 'practice' using an empty gun, aiming at imaginary targets in their basement. I learned the feel of a gun, the way different triggers pulled – some smooth, some stiff as if they needed oiling.

I do remember one boy, Daniel, actually loading the gun. His mother had 'run to the store for some milk' and us kids were left alone in the house, with Milly the maid to 'watch over' us. Milly was quite happy for us to do our own thing, she used the opportunity to read Daniel's mother's magazines while lying on her bed in the front of the house, headphones clamped to her ears. I stood in the doorway, silently watching her, then sneaked off to find Daniel. He was lounging on his bed, and I persuaded him to show me the family gun.

"Do you know how to load it?" I said, using a voice that told him I doubted he was capable. Males always like to prove they can do everything, have you noticed that? Daniel was no exception.

"Sure I do," he said, "but we better go into the yard. I can show you how to shoot."

The backyard was big, probably about an acre of land, mostly woods with an area of grass near the house. We ran into the trees. It was a revolver, looked like something his grandpa had used in the war. Most families owned semi-automatics, neat little guns that would fit into a glove box. (I had seen quite a few by this time, was becoming something of an expert.)

Daniel swung out the cylinder and slid five bullets into the holes before clicking it back into position. He held the gun in one hand, as if feeling the weight of it. I looked up at him. He was quite tall, with dark bushy hair that needed a cut. Whenever he was nervous, he would blink repeatedly, as if he had something lodged in his eyes. He was doing that now, his nose wrinkled, his eyelids batting.

"Go on, shoot at the tree or something. Or aren't your fingers strong enough now there's bullets inside?"

He looked at me, his eyes still, then shrugged.

"Sure. But don't go squealing at the noise, little girl."

He stood with his feet slightly apart and faced a tree, raised the gun with straight arm, screwed up his face while taking aim, then fired.

I didn't squeal, but I did jump. It was so loud!

We stared at each other, both waiting to see if anyone would come, wondering who had heard. I figured we had about two seconds until Patsy, his sister, would come charging from the house. But she never came. We were undisturbed.

Daniel grinned at me.

"Pretty cool huh?" he said.

I held out my hand.

"Now my turn. I want a go."

He stepped back, shaking his head, thinking we had taken enough risk already. But I was insistent, this might be my only chance.

"Come on, you can't wimp out now. Give me the gun quick, before your mom gets home. Otherwise I have something on you, don't I? I can tell everyone you messed with your parents' gun. If we both fire a round, we're equal – I can't tell and you can't tell."

I could see him thinking about this, it made sense. Slowly, he raised his arm, offered me the gun.

I took it in my hand and immediately dropped it. It was hot! We both stared at it as it lay on the ground, looking heavy and evil somehow, even though I knew it was just metal, just a thing to be used. We were lucky that dropping it hadn't fired off another round, and I felt my heartbeat speed up. This was the most exciting playdate in a long time. I grinned at him, leaned down and picked it up again, careful to only touch the grip panel.

I knew how to ease back the trigger, but it was stiff, I needed to use both hands. I was trying to keep the gun still, but the weight was too much for my weak wrists and it was waving from side to side as I tried to aim at the trunk of a tree. I pulled the trigger towards me, nearer and nearer to the grip panel. It fired. The recoil pushed my arms back and up, and I took a step backwards, before looking to see what I'd hit.

I hadn't hit anything. We found a hole in a trunk that Daniel had hit, and found no trace of my bullet at all. But it didn't matter. The experience was exhilarating. It was the first time I ever fired a gun, but it was a lesson I never forgot. It would return to me later, of course, when I was beginning to view guns in a rather different light. But as a child, they were all about excitement and forbidden joys and power. It was the power more than anything else that I really remember.

Many of my daydreams in those days were violent. If I was handed a glass of juice, I would imagine the glass shattering, the blood spurting from the hand. If I saw a pet, I would calculate the amount of pressure I might need to throttle it, to squeeze the neck until it couldn't breathe. I'm not sure why my brain followed these paths. And I never acted on them. I think I never saw a way to actually do them without being caught. And I didn't trust my mother not to punish me, to turn me over to the police. I always felt she would like a reason to be rid of me, so I was careful not to give her one.

I think those are the only salient points from our time in the US. We returned to the UK in time for me to begin senior school.

The building was Victorian, lots of tall walls and brown stone and corridors which looked damp but weren't. It resembled a workhouse in my mind, a place where cruel overseers forced poor people to labour. I found ways around the system though, there were always people to exploit and persuade.

Up until then, I had largely ignored the twins. In fact, my memories of them in New Jersey are almost non-existent. By the time we returned to the UK they were just beginning to be interesting, to be old enough for me to influence. My mother would watch me speaking to them, the frown more dominant than the smile then. I didn't understand at the time, had no idea the impact her own sister had made on her life. But I'll tell you about that later.

There's nothing else in my childhood which I think will interest you. A few 'wild parties' I suppose. We used to keep a close eye on Facebook, once it appeared. If we happened to see happy family photos in a foreign country of someone who we knew, we would send round a message and meet at their house the same evening. Usually there was some kind of alarm, and we would restrict ourselves to the garden, perhaps swimming in their pool if they had one.

Occasionally though we got lucky, if there was no sign of an alarm on the outside of the house, we would risk going inside. I was usually first, most of my friends were followers rather than leaders. It was fun, I can tell you! The sheer excitement of choosing a window to break, waiting, poised to run, in case an alarm sounded or a neighbour stirred. Then climbing in, taking care to avoid the broken glass, finding my way around the dark home, searching for keys – which were usually conveniently left in doors. Laughing as my friends entered, their faces white, some of them nervous, but all excited, all looking for a laugh, something forbidden.

We rarely stole anything (other than a few drinks of course, but that doesn't count.) I was quite strict on that, wanted the police to dismiss the incident as 'kids' not criminals. If there was cash lying around I might help myself to some, but mostly we just enjoyed our departed hosts' hospitality, had a laugh, were gone by morning. Nothing OTT, just normal teenage stuff.

I did steal from other places, but again, it was small, normal stuff that any kid would do. Chocolate bars from the harassed shopkeeper when all the kids arrived after school, flooding his shop while we waited for the bus, pushing to the front, a dozen hands reaching out at once. It was easy enough to help myself before squirming to the back of the pack and sidling from the shop. I was never caught, I wasn't stupid.

So, what do you think? Nature or nurture? The nurture aspect probably had some part to play. From my mother's side, at least (and as I am about to tell you, the 'nature' side of things from Mum was definitely warped.) I don't think she was really the maternal kind. As I said before, I'm not entirely sure why she ever had children. She did try, she would set rules, make us help with chores, discipline us.

My mother kind of did her own thing, mostly she just wanted us quiet, not to disturb her. Or else to help her. We did seem to do most of the housework in those days – at least the boys did, I was rather good at avoiding chores, hiding under a bed with a comic or disappearing into the garden for hours, only reappearing when I was sure all the washing up would be finished, the carpets would be vacuumed, everyone else would have done the work.

Even when we were adults, having my mother's undivided attention was rare. If I attempted to meet her in a coffee shop, or went to visit her, she would chat and listen until something better came along. If one of her friends happened to pass, or a favourite show came on the television (which was never turned off), then she would turn away, even if I was mid-sentence, and become absorbed in the more interesting choice. As a child, I demanded her attention by making a scene, being rude or loud. When I was older, and had more skills, I simply turned her friend's attention to me, amused both of them, or left. When she started to watch the television, there was no point in staying really, easier to just get up and go.

I think she did her best, I think she loved us. Certainly she loved the twins, but they were easier to love, more compliant. I guess she didn't have whatever is necessary to love unselfishly. Almost as if something was missing inside her. Which again, could be due to either nature or nurture. Perhaps both. I'll tell you about her own childhood, it will help you to understand.

Chapter Three

I didn't even know my mother had any family until I was eighteen. We knew she had been raised by Ralph and Jean, an elderly couple we were forced to visit sometimes. They had fostered my mother when she was young, and they pretended to have a continued interest in her and in us, but it was all for show really. They never let me have the things I wanted, and it felt like everyone was acting whenever we visited. Uncomfortable.

Then, soon after my eighteenth birthday, I found my mother sorting through a box of rubbish. It was stuff she had saved from her childhood, looked like old school books, things like that. She shooed me from the room when I went in, obviously didn't want me to see. So I waited until she had gone out, it was probably a week or two later, and I was in the house on my own. I decided there might be something interesting in there, something I could use in an argument or when I was trying to persuade her to do something. Mainly I was just curious as to what she didn't want me to see.

My parents' room was in the back of the house, overlooking the garden. They didn't encourage us to go in there, and even when we were tiny, I don't remember ever sleeping with them – they weren't the sort of parents to take us kids into their own bed if we were having trouble sleeping. It was their private sanctuary. I expect my mother had read somewhere that this was good for a marriage, to have a private room, away from the family. Most of her rules were based on books (she was an avid reader). It was as if she wasn't capable of formulating ideas herself, perhaps she didn't have the confidence to decide things because her own upbringing was so erratic, or maybe it was just her personality. Either way, some leader type – usually religious – would make some pronouncement from the pulpit or in a book, and that would instantly become my mother's view. Sometimes, when I challenged her, she couldn't even remember why she held the view, or what had caused her to form a certain opinion, but she held onto them rigidly anyway.

So when I pushed open their door, it felt like trespassing, a forbidden zone, even though I was an adult and lived in the house. They had a deep red carpet and green curtains and a blue duvet. My parents weren't really into interior design. And it smelt of them. My father's aftershave mingled with my mother's deodorant, bound together by that smell, the deeply familiar smell, of my parents. I paused in the threshold for a second, absorbing it, enjoying the sensation that I was somewhere I shouldn't be, knowing they would disapprove if they knew I was in there uninvited.

It was late afternoon. I had taken the afternoon off, knowing everyone would be out, and the sun was streaming through the window and reflecting from the mirror on my mother's dressing table. She had an old fashioned handheld mirror, not that she ever wore makeup, but she used it to see the back of her hair after brushing it. It was now casting patterns of stars onto the ceiling, and I had an urge to pick up the mirror and cast the reflections around the room, to watch the puddles of light dance. I didn't though, I walked past their bed, on my mother's side.

I first went to the top of the wardrobe. People always put their valuables in high places, have you noticed that? Jewellery will be kept in the top drawer in a bedroom, money hidden behind the corkscrew and tea-towels in the top drawer of a kitchen, keys on top of cupboards. I reached up, felt behind the hatbox and suitcase and old teddy bear, and there it was, as expected, the shoebox she had been so keen to hide. I pulled it down. It was a bit dusty, despite being opened fairly recently, so I brushed it off before setting it on the bed. I made myself comfortable, legs tucked up beneath me, leaning back against my mother's pillow, and removed the lid.

The box was packed full. At the top were a few letters, their blue envelopes jagged where they had been torn open. I started to read.

Dear Miss Brooks,   25th April 1998

I hope this reaches you, as I have asked social services to pass it on (they were reluctant to give me your contact details.) My name is Margaret Smith, and since 1982, I have been the foster mother of your sister, Joanna.

I'm not sure if you've been keeping up with the news, but if you have, you will know that Joanna has got into trouble, and is currently undergoing a trial in London.

I wondered if you planned to attend the trial or visit your sister, and if so, whether we could meet. There's something I would like to discuss with you, and it would be easier face to face.

Best Wishes,
Margaret Smith

I paused, holding the letter and staring at the ceiling. So, my mother had a sister. Odd she had never once mentioned her, she might as well not have existed for all we knew of her. Not that she ever really talked about her past anyway, just occasional snippets about growing up in care, how much she had hated having to share everything all the time, never having anywhere that was her own, lots of moving schools and so never having long term friendships.

To be honest, I always felt she used it as an excuse, it was a convincing sounding reason to avoid the things she didn't like. She didn't want to move house because, "I moved so many times as a child." She didn't want to bother making this house look nice because, "I'm not used to owning things, I don't know how to look after them properly – you decide John, you're better at it than me, having had a normal upbringing." Dad had made nearly all the decisions in their marriage, she always claimed her unsettled childhood made her unable to do things, decide things.

She also made it an excuse for her failings. So, if she'd slapped me harder than she'd meant to, or not repaired my school uniform in time, or not helped with homework, she'd say, "I'm sorry Clara, but it's hard for me to know how to be a mother, not having had one of my own." Not that she sounded sorry. Her eyes always said that Clara had deserved the slap, or shouldn't need help with things because she was quite capable of doing things for herself. But the words were there, the ready excuse, as if it made everything better.

I suppose she must have had a mother, at some point, though she always claimed she couldn't remember her, had been put into care when she was very young. I wondered now if that was true. Was she also going to claim she couldn't remember her sister, this Joanna?

I sometimes wondered why my father stayed with her. She was pretty useless really. They had married quite young – he was only twenty-five, which is young for a man. Maybe he liked to look after her, made him feel important or something. He was older than her, so maybe that was it. I wasn't born until 1992 – two years later –

so he couldn't blame me for having to marry her. Who knows? Perhaps he loved her.

I wanted to discover who this Joanna was, and whether my mother had met Margaret or not. Carefully folding the letter, I slid it back into the envelope and took the next one.

Dear Mrs Oakes,   Sunday, 17th May 1998

May I call you Lisa? Thank you for replying, and congratulations on your marriage. Now I know you are married, it probably makes it even more important for us to speak, but I will explain a little more in this letter, and then you can decide. I would really like to sort things out between the two of us, if I can, rather than going to the expense of lawyers and things.

I completely understand that you don't want to see Joanna again. I'm sorry to hear she hurt you when you were children, and I hope you have been able to recover from that. Although I love Joanna (you can't help but love children who you care for I find), I know she's not an easy person. I'm afraid though that there isn't any money, that isn't what this is about. If there was any money due to you and Joanna, I would certainly let you know, but as far as I am aware, there never has been and Joanna herself does not have money (and in fact was still living with me). She does have a job, but only in a chemist's, it doesn't pay very much. So even though I understand that you feel as if you're owed money, I'm afraid there isn't any.

My main reason for writing, apart from making sure you knew the situation in case you wanted to visit Joanna, was to let you know she has a daughter. Emily is now 8 years old. She has always lived with me and Joanna, and I have raised her. As it looks as if Joanna will not be returning home after the trial (there seems little doubt that she was guilty) we obviously need to make arrangements for Emily. I love her, and I can provide a good home for her. I would very much like to adopt her and continue to raise her. But I am aware that as Joanna's sister, you are her next of kin, and you might feel uneasy about this. If the situation worries you, please could we meet to discuss it? I would so much rather deal directly with you if possible, rather than have a nasty situation later. If there are any problems, I'm sure we can sort them out between the two of us, so the adoption can go through smoothly.

If you want to see Emily I can send you photos, or of course, you would be welcome to visit.

Best Wishes,
Margaret

Another surprise. I had a cousin. Well, another cousin, there was already Alexsander of course, my hero from childhood. But he was Dad's side, the side of the family we knew about. This was more interesting. I checked the date and did the maths, she was two years older than me. Where was she now, and what was she doing?

Always the possibility that she might be rich of course, or useful in some other way.

And what had happened to this Joanna? I reached for the last letter, not bothering to put away the opened one first. This was getting interesting. What exactly had Joanna done?

Dear Lisa,   Monday, 1st June, 1998

Thank you so much for your letter. I was delighted to hear you have a family – gosh what a lot of work one-year-old twins must be! I completely understand why it is difficult for you to meet me.

I will happily continue to care for Emily. Don't worry about the money, I wouldn't dream of asking you for any, that was not my reason for writing at all. I just wanted to be sure that you wouldn't decide Emily should live with you. I wanted to avoid any problems before they happened. I'm not rich, but I have enough savings to look after Emily properly, and I will not ask you for any help at all. It sounds as if you have your hands full with 3 little ones as it is.

I am sorry to hear you are still angry about how Joanna treated you, though I do understand. Emily is not like her mother, she is a lovely little girl (I enclose a photo) though she does look like her. If you ever change your mind about never meeting her, and decide you would like her to meet her cousins, do let me know. Otherwise, I will

respect your wishes and not mention to Emily
that we have made contact.

I won't contact you again. I understand that
speaking about Joanna brings back painful
memories. Thank you so much for being clear that
you are happy for me to adopt Emily. I wish you
well.

Best Wishes,
Margaret

It wasn't the letter that shocked me. It was the photograph.
There, smiling in her school uniform, hair pulled into a ponytail,
was a girl who looked unexpectedly like me. She was sitting, one
shoulder angled towards the camera, in the classic 'sit down quickly
and smile because I've got 172 other children to photograph' pose.
But it was a clear shot, you could see her features – the brown eyes
staring straight into my blue ones, but the same shape, above the
same snub nose, under the same wide forehead, which was easy to
see because it wasn't hidden by a fringe like mine always was. She
even rested her front teeth on her bottom lip and showed too much
gum, just like I used to when I was her age. Weird, really weird.

I doubted my own mother would have described me as "a lovely
little girl" though, so perhaps the similarity stopped with our
appearance.

Had my mother ever met her? Was her reason for not attending
the trial due to the twins being so young, or would she have
avoided it anyway? And what had Joanna done?

I was impatient to get my computer, start to search on Google.
But I looked through the rest of the shoebox first, looking for
answers.

Under the letters were more, in white envelopes, and older. They turned out to be from my dad to Mum while they were seeing each other. Lots of lovey stuff and rude innuendoes. I didn't do more than skim those, looking for Joanna's name, but it wasn't there. Did my dad even know about her?

There were some photos too, some of Mum and Dad when they were young, a wedding shot of her laughing at something, with a mouth full of dinner (not one for the album), a baby photo of each of us kids. There was a brochure from a hotel in Spain, where I knew they'd gone on their honeymoon, and below that was rubbish from Mum's childhood – a swimming badge, a diary with a picture of a goat on it (which turned out to be all about the food she ate each day when she was seven), a necklace that looked like it was made of tin, a ring she probably won at a fair and a list of names. I looked at the names, but they didn't make any sense, there were about twenty names, man and woman, printed one after the other. The pens and writing were different, so perhaps they were a record of all the people who had fostered Mum. Some had crosses after them – maybe they were the ones she didn't like. No way of knowing.

I stuffed everything back into the box, in roughly the same order it had come out. I wasn't too bothered if she realised someone had been through it, at some point I would ask her about it anyway, ask her why she had been keeping secrets. Who this Joanna was. I put the letters back into the envelopes, put them on top, and replaced the lid. My legs were stiff now, so I stretched them a bit and yawned, before returning the box to its not very good hiding place. Now for some online research.

My bedroom was at the end of the landing, next to the bathroom. It was my space, and I liked it. It wasn't exactly cosy, I was no more a home-maker than my mother was, but it was comfortable.

I liked to keep things private, so I had lifted the carpet in one corner and pulled up the floorboard using Dad's claw hammer. It couldn't be seen, I had put the carpet back, and below, the nails in the floorboard had been knocked flush, so the board rested there unsecured but level with the others. It was my hidey-hole. I'd had a phase of taking things from the other kids. Nothing much, you know the sort of thing, watches left in changing rooms, purses balanced invitingly on the top of full bags, money from my mother's housekeeping, small items lifted from shops. The sort of little things all teenagers take, for when they need some extra cash or a bribe. The hidey-hole was well used in those days, a safe place. I seem to remember that at the time we're talking about, when I first found out about Joanna, there were a couple of rings in there, taken from one of the 'empty' houses we'd 'visited' earlier in the week.

There I was, perched on my bed, pink laptop open (no idea why it was pink, must've been a phase) and I typed "Joanna Brooks" into the search bar. At once, before I'd even finished typing, the page was filled with information.

There was a box to one side, with photographs and bullet points giving the facts, and lists of links to news reports, television websites, newspaper headlines. For news that was a decade old, Joanna was still a top story.

It turns out, she had killed a bunch of people. No idea why. There were some boring links, psychologists spouting about her reasons, people making statements, but the basic facts were all in the little box of bullet points.

Most of it was dated about ten years previously, around the time of her trial. There were a couple of later reports, saying she had changed prisoner categories, or discussing her because her case was like a more recent story, but nothing interesting, nothing from her. Lots of regurgitated news, making something out of nothing. Aunty Joanna must be behaving herself. Probably hoping for an early release date or something.

The thing that was really interesting, was what *wasn't* there. No mention of her kid. No mention of her sister. I tried doing searches for just them, Emily Brooks, or Emily Smith (in case she'd taken that Margaret's name) but nothing much came up. Just one solitary statement, that Joanna had a young child, repeated in several reports. I reckoned they must have put a gag order on the media or something, she must've been in school, there must've been people who knew about the kid.

More relevant, 'Lisa Brooks' came up blank too. Perhaps they'd been apart too long and social services never released their old records. I was surprised none of their old foster parents, or other kids from the care homes ever said anything though. There were, to be fair, a couple of articles that mentioned "a sister" (Joanna and a sister were brought up in care until... blah blah blah) but nothing specific. Nothing that would link my mother to her sister. Of course, she was married by then, so the name was different, but journalists aren't stupid. I was surprised they hadn't found her.

This was big. Not because the media hadn't found my mother, but because she hadn't sought them out. She hadn't cashed in on a front page headline, sold her story to some rag (and it's not like we couldn't have used the money). Nothing. Which made me smile. Because it left me with two rather delicious options. Either I could go to the press myself, because they had not yet covered the 'sister' angle. Or – and this was better – I could use the information to influence my mother. She must've *really* not wanted to be linked to Joanna to have kept quiet for all this time. I wasn't yet sure of her reasons, but I expected to find out, and then it would be gold dust.

There was of course, the problem of my new cousin. There was always the chance that she knew about my mother and would have the same idea, would spill the beans before I had my chance. But I thought it was unlikely. If she wanted to sell a story, her own would be much more valuable, so she too must be living below the radar for some reason. Maybe she was just like her mum, and was out there bumping off the neighbours or something. I also thought it possible she didn't even know about us. That Margaret had obviously been worried my mother would mess up her adoption plans, I didn't think she would want to risk any changes to that outcome. I thought she would have kept to her word, not told the kid she had an aunt and cousins. No reason for her to provide a possible alternative living arrangement if she wanted to keep the kid.

No, I thought the Emily factor was insignificant. I decided to wait. To bide my time and watch. At some point this information would be high value stuff, and when that time came, I would be ready. Of course, I didn't know then just how high the value would be, or how it would set off a whole lot of other explosions. But I was just a kid then, everyone makes mistakes at that age.

I clicked once more on a photo of Joanna. She stared back at me, full face, defiant. Then I shut down the computer, watching the screen fade. My own sunlit face stared back at me, reflected on the black screen. My face, uncannily similar to Joanna's. Better hair but same features, same expression. A whisper of Joanna. Even back then, I recognised that we were alike, I could see the echo of her in my own appearance, feel the similarities in our character. Perhaps what I discovered that day influenced me, led me to my chosen career. The aunt I never met. The sister my mother forgot.

Chapter Four

It was soon after this that I chose my career. I chose well. I had for a few years been working part time in the local cafe. Initially, this wasn't by choice, as I've explained, if I needed more cash there were easier ways to get it. But my parents (mostly my dad) were pretty insistent that earning your way through life was an essential part of adulthood, and arranged for an interview with their friend, who owned the cafe. I would've ignored them of course, but it came at a time when I was desperate to be allowed to go on a post GCSE trip with my friends to Magaluf, and I needed both their permission and their funding. I decided to take the job and then leave later, when the holiday was sorted. As it turned out, I quite liked working there, so I actually stayed for a few years. I even worked there during the uni holidays when I was a student.

There are a lot of perks to working in the catering trade, especially if you're as gifted as me. Some are the legitimate perks. It's warm, you get to eat free food, and you can invite your friends to eat there and give them a discount, which means they owe you a favour later.

You get to meet a whole range of people, and The Toasty Bean, despite its daft name, happened to attract a lot of rich customers (or guests, as I was supposed to call them). Knowing rich people is in itself an excellent thing. You can smile, chat, be efficient, and most of them will tip well.

You also have regular customers, those with too much time and money. If you treat them like they're special – stop what you're doing to welcome them, keep their table clean, tell them when something's nice and fresh or getting a bit stale – they will start to chat. It's easy enough to give them free stuff when the boss is away, so they see you as on their side, generous. In reality, the 'free' dessert isn't really yours to give. But people don't like to think about that, if they're getting something for nothing, they don't tend to examine the morality too closely. If you act as if you like them, they will start to like you in return. They begin to see you as someone safe, someone they can be less guarded with; even though they actually know nothing about you at all. So they'll be more casual with both their possessions and their information.

I remember one particularly lucrative day. Mr Wilczynski liked us to take phone numbers if we took a telephone booking. Then, if the customer was late, we could phone to check they were still coming. We didn't get many bookings – it was more a teashop than a restaurant, but we did get the occasional one if it was a birthday or a large group coming. I was always sure to take both the number and the address. The address I wrote in my own book of contacts, ready for a rainy day. On this day, we had taken three separate bookings. In between the calls, I waited tables.

"Good afternoon Mrs Brown, table for three? How about the one by the window. You make yourselves comfy and I'll be over in a sec to take your order."

Mrs Brown and her two overweight guests squeezed their way to the table. I had chosen the window table purposefully. They would like it, and think I had treated them well, but mainly I liked to watch heavy people try to negotiate between the other chairs. It was funny to watch, and it also meant people en route had to move slightly so they could pass. Which in turn meant all those carefully stowed valuables were dislodged slightly. People tended to be careful to hide their bags when they first sat down, they forgot to check again if they had moved to let someone pass.

A Mulberry handbag was slightly exposed from behind a jacket, and a man's coat had swung on the back of his chair, giving easy access to the inside pocket. I would be sure to keep the Brown table well supplied with drinks. When one of them got up to use the washroom (big bodies did not produce strong bladders I had noticed) there would be another upheaval, which would make for a nice distraction.

Sure enough, after about twenty minutes, one of the men got up and waddled towards the back of the cafe. I made my move and walked from the table I was clearing, past the slightly exposed wallet, which slid easily onto my full tray, and into the kitchen.

The kitchen was always frenetic: surfaces being wiped, Mr W checking fresh pastries in the oven, Fred loading the dishwasher and wiping surfaces. I took the tray straight to the dishwasher, unloaded it onto the surface while slipping the wallet behind my apron. I grinned at Fred, told Mr Wilczynski the pastries smelled wonderful and filled a milk jug from the fridge. In the corridor outside the kitchen, where I could only be seen if someone looked from the main doorway, I removed half the twenties from the wallet (I knew it would be full, you get a feeling for these things) and placed them in my pocket. On my way back to table four I returned the wallet to the jacket pocket, bumping the chair slightly to cover any movement the occupier might have felt.

"Here you are," I said, arriving at table four with a smile, "I've brought you some more milk. Those jugs are tiny, they never hold enough, do they?"

The customer smiled, confused. They had plenty of milk. But it was kind of me to care.

The man who was missing the twenties had readjusted his chair, but not looked in his pocket. He probably wouldn't check his wallet until he and his friend left, by which time the money would be safely in the Tampax box at the bottom of my handbag.

Even if he made a fuss, tried to prove the money had gone

44

missing while they were in the cafe, they could hardly start accusing everyone. And if they did, my purse was almost empty and I didn't think a man, especially Mr Wilczynski, would want to look through personal hygiene stuff. No one ever did comment though. If anyone ever noticed, they must've assumed they'd lost it somewhere else.

Another perk was the information gained through chatting. I had the ability to learn where someone was going on holiday, if they were taking the whole family, how much hassle it had been to find somewhere to kennel the dog, how long they'd be away. All you needed were a few interested questions.

"Oh, sounds lovely, so we won't be seeing you here for a few days then? You're going for two weeks? That's really nice, you deserve a nice break. Will you be back in time for the carnival? Ah, not going until the day afterwards – well, I hope you have a great time." And of course, if they had ever phoned to book a table – and had their address entered into my contacts book – I had a great time too, having an impromptu pool party with my friends, catered for courtesy of Mrs Chatterbox.

Michal Wilczynski both owned and managed The Toasty Bean. Even in jeans and sweater, he looked like he belonged to the crew of the *Titanic*. Something stiff and correct about him. He liked things done properly, and was a stickler for hygiene. I didn't mind too much – I ate there often enough, and I wanted my snacks to be safe – until he told me I needed to attend a Hygiene Safety course. This was not so good. I knew I was clean enough, I didn't need some poxy certificate. I started to argue.

Mr Wilczynski told me I had to go, it wasn't optional.

"This is necessary. I am inspected, the Hygiene Inspector will come, and he will ask me, have I trained my staff? I can say yes, of course I can, but if he wants to know how I trained you, what can I say then? I need proof you see, always we need proof.

"This is not just you. Anna must be trained also. Both together."

He paused, nodding his head as if agreeing with himself. He knew I would resist anything that involved effort, but he wanted to keep me. I was good for business, customers liked me.

"We will not make it an effort. Sometimes, you prepare food, yes? So you have to attend an official course. I must pay for this. The authorities, they run the course, but the cafe owner, he is the one who must pay. You go, you listen, you answer some questions, then it will be finished. Very easy. I will keep my thumbs crossed for you.

"I will pay you," he said, keen for me to comply. "I will pay you as if you were working, though really you should pay me. You will have a certificate, will be qualified. You will train on my time, and I will pay you. It is a good deal, no?"

So I did it. I sat in a stuffy office on an orange chair with a wobbly leg, and watched a DVD, and listened to a man who fancied himself as some kind of academic. I was told things I knew, like that I should wash my hands before handling food; and things I didn't know, like that food can be kept hot for two hours and should then all be thrown away. We sat in silence, me and Anna.

Anna was another waitress. She was a big woman, thin blonde hair stretched over a swollen head and forced into a tight bun. I wasn't sure the plastic chairs would be strong enough to hold her – perhaps it was her weight that had bent the leg of the chair I was sitting on. She was nervous, I could tell from the way the rolls of fat under her chin wobbled, from the little gasps as she breathed in through her open wet mouth and from the putrid aroma that gradually pervaded the room.

At the end of the film, we were given a sheet of questions and half an hour to complete them. It wasn't brain surgery. I had filled my answer sheet with ticks well before the time ended, and it was checked by the bored man with the battered briefcase. I had passed, which wasn't surprising. Anna had not, which was also expected.

Mr Wilczynski told her she could try again, another time. But she left soon after and was replaced by Josie, who was slimmer. And had a brain. I think the strain had been too much for poor Anna.

Which all leads me to the decision I made about my future career. I liked being in the catering trade because of the fringe benefits. I was also interested by the whole hygiene training. Watching Anna sweat away while she attempted to pass an exam, knowing the whole kitchen team went into overdrive if we thought a health inspection was due. When the health inspector called in, usually unannounced, he was treated like a king. No one but Mr Wilczynski was allowed to speak to him unless we were asked a question, everything must be perfect, all was high tension, big pressure. The man had power. Power is something that appeals to me.

All I needed was five GCSEs and a couple of A levels (one in science) to get me into uni. I chose a BSc in Environmental Health as the easiest option. I was ready to become a food hygiene inspector.

Chapter Five

My father had one brother, William Oakes, born 1955, grand protector and patriarch of the family.

Forgive my sarcasm, but he was like that, completely besotted by his own importance. According to my father, he was always the favourite and when my grandparents died, their estate hadn't been split equally, so William had managed to come off rather better than my father. He now lived in the familial home. The brothers were not close.

When I was little, we used to visit each other once a month. Uncle William and Aunt Susan lived in the next town to us, they were older than my parents, and even as a young child I was very aware the relationship wasn't equal. Aunt Susan seemed to be always trying to teach my mother how to do things better, I can still hear her whiney voice in my head.

"Now Lisa, next time you cook Yorkshire puddings, if you heat the tins to a really high temperature first, you'll find they're much better. Those ones have hardly risen at all, have they? And I'm not sure how you're going to get those tins clean. Perhaps if you soak them overnight…"

My mother would smile, tight-lipped, and make some remark about how she "didn't know things like that, not having had a mother to show me."

Actually, I think Aunt Susan would have rather liked to have been my mother's mother, she certainly couldn't have done a worse job than she did with Alexsander. She would lower her bony bottom onto a chair, as if worried it would contaminate her, and look around the room, inspecting it for signs of dust. When my mother left the room, she would stand, and cross to the bookshelf, running her finger along the edge of the top shelf, checking if it was clean. Any signs of dirt, she would shake her head and smile, as if proven correct about something important.

Of course, she never took the slightest bit of notice of me, nor of the twins when they came along. We were children, and she didn't 'do' children. Not even her own. I think that's what caused Alexsander to be such fun. He did pretty much what he wanted, and as long as he could cope with a few disapproving sighs, or being shouted at because his shoes were dirty, he lived as he pleased. Which when he was thirteen made him great fun, and by the time he was twenty meant he was experimenting with hard drugs. When I say 'experimenting' , I don't mean in the harmless, have a laugh with some magic mushrooms in Magaluf sort of way; I mean completely screwed up by them.

Perhaps that's why we stopped seeing them, except at Christmas for the obligatory Christmas Eve drinks in their overheated conservatory. Maybe the lank-haired skeleton with blackened teeth sitting in the corner wasn't something they wanted people to see anymore. I remember I tried to chat to him, when I was about eleven and we were living back in the UK, for old times' sake really, but he couldn't focus, his blank eyes stared through me. And he twitched a lot. I dislike when people twitch, so I gave up and went back to trying to persuade the twins to mix vodka into their orange juice. After a few years he simply stopped being there at all, and we heard he'd moved 'to London'. I don't even know if William and Susan knew where he was.

Perhaps that's what killed her. When I was in my early teens, I was told Aunt Susan had breast cancer. Can stress cause cancer? Seems likely to me. I didn't really know what that meant at the time, just that it was horrible and she would soon be dead.

We didn't have drinks that Christmas Eve. We had them the following September instead, after her funeral. Alexsander didn't put in an appearance. Perhaps no one knew how to contact him, assuming he was still alive himself.

The funeral was a dismal affair, but I guess that's appropriate. And it was Aunt Susan's funeral, after all. It was never going to be jolly. We filed from black cars into an empty church and sat on hard pews while the vicar described someone who none of us recognised. There were a couple of hymns, which the choir sang while we all looked embarrassed and hid behind our order of service sheets. The twins were giggling, I think one of them had farted, and my mother was trying to keep them quiet. I was next to my father and I could almost hear his thoughts, his resentment of his brother, the feeling that he'd deserved to be unhappy by keeping all the family money.

We were all glad when it was over. Stuck in a room with people we'd never met, everyone awkward while they balanced plates filled with food they didn't want to eat. The overly loud voices of the people who'd drunk too much, the whispers of the people who hardly knew her but were trying to appear like they had a right to be there. And us. None of us liked her or would miss her. We were there because it was our duty, was what you had to do. I smuggled a slug of vodka into my juice and walked around smiling at people. The twins stuffed egg rolls into their pockets to avoid having to eat them, while our parents stayed until it was not impolite to leave.

It was when I first began to properly notice Uncle William though. I think I realised his potential, even then. He was horribly grateful to us for going (like we'd had a choice). He saw us to the door when we left, tried to shake hands with the twins and kiss me and my mother. He held me in his mothball stinking arms, pulling me close while his face scratched my cheek. I pulled away, stared at him as he slurred how touched he was that we'd come, that perhaps we could all stay in contact a bit better now, now he realised how important family were, was all that really mattered in the end, wasn't it?

I saw my father stiffen at that, he was thinking about the money again, I could tell.

He almost said as much afterwards, when we were driving down the gravel driveway, away from the fat red-bricked house with the leaded-light windows.

"For all their money," he said, "I wouldn't change places. Seems to me it's brought them nothing but misery. I've no idea what Bill will do now, but he's hardly been lucky in life, has he?"

He stopped then, held in the rest of the bitterness, but we felt it, filling the car and altering our own views. My mother reached out, put her hand on his arm while he drove. And I gazed out the window, pretending I didn't understand.

***

Actually, I didn't see my uncle again for several more years, not exactly sure when, but I know I had finished uni, and passed my Higher Certificate in Food Premises Inspection. I was doing my six months of 'practical training', working towards my interview so I could be registered with the Chartered Institute, and one of my trips took me to a community centre in my uncle's town. It was mostly boring work, but necessary, and I did enjoy the freedom of having several centres for work, because if I wasn't at one, people would assume I was at another.

I happened to be passing right by my uncle's house, so I thought I would pop in, see how he was, if Alexsander had resurfaced, if any of Aunt Susan's jewellery was going spare that would be nice to 'keep in the family', that sort of thing. You never know when a good deed like visiting an old man might turn to your own

51

advantage. He was getting on a bit now, must have been well over sixty. As I said, we didn't see him anymore. The Christmas drinks had never been resumed after the funeral (thank goodness) and although I think my father phoned his brother occasionally, I'm not aware that they ever met. They had never really liked each other, I guess they just stopped pretending after Alexsander disappeared and Susan died. No point really.

I turned my car into the familiar gravel drive and drove up to the house. There were lawns on either side, and a large cedar to one side. It used to have a swing from one branch, Alexsander used to push me higher and higher, until an adult saw and told him to be careful, I wasn't a toy. It was a good place to escape to when you'd had enough of adult conversation and wanted some time to yourself. When the twins were big enough, I used to try and entice them onto the swing too, offering to push them. But they were always wary, knew I wouldn't stop when they wanted to get down, so they never would. The swing had gone by the time Susan died. Someone must have taken it down.

The back of the house had a high wall that ran all the way around the garden. It was mostly covered in ivy, and while I stood on the doorstep, I noticed it had crumbled in places. Perhaps Uncle William wasn't managing the upkeep of the house.

I rang the bell, heard it trill inside the house. I thought he must be out, there were no signs of life, and was about to turn away, when I heard a cough, and heavy footsteps came to the door.

"Hello Uncle William," I smiled into his surprised face. "It's me, Clara, your niece."

"I know who you are," he said, frowning, "but I wasn't expecting you. Is something wrong? Has something happened to your father?"

"No, nothing's wrong," I said. "I was working in the area, thought I would pop in, see how you are. Haven't seen you in ages – are you keeping well?"

"Can't complain," he said. Which was either a lie or else he had changed a lot, because he was one of the most complaining people I knew when I was a child. "Well, you'd better come in, as you're here. Do you want tea? The milk might be off."

I followed him towards the kitchen, chatting as we went. I was beginning to enjoy myself. The house had an empty, underused feel, as if one old man wasn't quite managing to fill a house intended for a large family. It smelled the same though, a sort of dank floury smell mingled with clothes detergent, which brought back lots of childhood memories. Racing along the hallway with Alexsander chasing me, watching my mother writhe at Aunt Susan's sarcasm, slamming doors in an attempt to make my parents finish drinking coffee and take us home.

We walked along the dark hall, past oil paintings that you could barely see in the gloom, into the light of the kitchen. It was a big space, with windows into the south facing back garden. Aunt Susan had loved her kitchen, it was always light and warm, and she had filled it with all the latest gadgets. My heels clicked on the flagstones and I crossed to the large oak table in the corner. It was sticky and littered with crumbs. I didn't sit.

"Why don't I make the tea, Uncle William," I said, "you sit down and be looked after for a change while I tell you about my job."

He sat, obedient, elbows on the dirty table, head resting on hands. I guessed he had grown good at obedience, living with Aunt Susan. He watched me as I moved around the kitchen, comfortable in a space I had visited many times as a child. It was a mess now though, my aunt would be turning in her grave. Perhaps no one had yet filled her place. That had potential.

I washed a cloth, avoiding the grey ring that clung to the edge of the sink, and wiped the table and a couple of the surfaces.

"Don't you have anyone who cleans for you?" I asked.

"No, not now. I did have a woman who came in, Mrs Grimley,

but she stopped last year. Said her knees were bad or something. Not sure I want anyone else, you hear stories, don't you? People being robbed blind by cleaners, conmen using it as cover to exploit you. Can't trust anyone these days. And I'm alright, it's only me here, I manage fine on my own."

"You do very well," I said, keen he should lose the whole defensive attitude. "Not many men would manage on their own like you do, especially with such a big house to run." (He clearly wasn't doing well, actually, the place was going to ruin. But I wanted him to think I was on his side.) "But it's a lot for you to do. I'm surprised my parents don't help more, seeing as Dad grew up here and everything."

That was a mistake, I saw him stiffen at once. I had touched on a sensitive topic, and I was cross with myself for being so clumsy. I wanted him to know I was on his side, against my parents, who should've been helping him. Instead I had made him think I was having a dig, bringing up the whole 'eldest son inherited the family home' issue. I kept talking, trying to get back on track.

"I guess they're too busy with their own lives, they can be a bit selfish that way. But we haven't forgotten you. Well, I haven't, anyway. You and Aunty Susan were always very good to me when I was little." (Another lie, but people don't tend to spot lies if they are being flattered by them.)

The kettle was boiling, so I opened a few cupboards to find teabags, sterilised the teapot first, then threw a couple of bags into the pot and topped it up.

"Are you still working?" I asked, pulling cups from the cupboard. They both had brown rings around the top, so I washed them under the tap and found a not too dirty tea-towel in a drawer to dry them with. My uncle was droning on about cutting down his hours, the mood of the office changing now all these young people had come on board. I didn't really know what he did, to be honest it didn't

54

interest me very much. Some kind of management, I knew that, in an IT company I think. It must've paid well, though he'd never struck me as especially clever. I carried the teapot and cups to the table and went to the fridge. There was milk, but I didn't need to smell it, the lumpy fat floating on top showed it was well past being off. I poured black tea into the cups and added some sugar to disguise the taste. Uncle William nodded his thanks and took a loud slurp. His manners had gone to pot along with the housework it seemed.

I sat next to him, nodding as he spoke, asking the occasional question. I could see he was uncomfortable with me being so close, that he was seeing me as an adult, not his niece, so I settled back in the chair, leaned away from him, allowed him a bit more space. I wanted him to like having me there, to be completely at ease. I was good at listening. Or at least, at appearing to listen. Generally, what people say is a boring waste of time. I have always felt that, but I also noticed when fairly young, that if people know you're not listening to them, they are quickly irritated and dismiss you. So I had learned to appear attentive. I would make frequent eye-contact, nod, keep my hands still. My thoughts were usually elsewhere, but my body looked as if it was enrapt, and people talked. Uncle William was no exception. I guessed he didn't get many opportunities to talk these days.

He told me all about his job, the pain in his side which woke him at night, the book he had been reading and his views on the latest saga in parliament. I watched his mouth (too stretchy) and his eyes (green like my father's) and his hair (white, but nice and thick for someone his age). He tapped the table as he spoke, his sleeve rolled back to show a gold watch on his thin wrist. After an hour, I glanced at the big clock ticking above the window and said I ought to be going.

I cleared up the tea things and washed them. There was some

Flash under the sink, so I cleaned that too, wiping away the grey ring. Then I threw away the cloth and draped a clean one from the drawer across the now shiny taps. Uncle watched me, absorbing it all.

He saw me to the door and opened it. There was a slightly awkward moment then, him not really knowing how to say goodbye appropriately. I leaned up, gave him a quick peck on the cheek and pretended to not notice his blush of confusion. He wasn't really one for affection, but it's good to keep people a bit off-guard. Especially men.

"Thanks so much for the tea, Uncle William," I said, opening my bag and looking for my keys. "Perhaps I could pop in again sometime? It would be nice to keep in touch."

"I'd like that," he said. "But only if you're passing, I wouldn't want to be any trouble."

I gave him a cheery wave and climbed into the car. He watched me, waving from his doorstep, until I reached the road.

I drove away smiling. That had been most successful. I felt like the character in my favourite story, the one about boot soup. Do you know it? I first heard it at infant school, and even then it had appealed. It's the one about a tramp, knocking on an old woman's door, asking for food and she refuses to help him. Until he says he can make her some soup, using just an old boot. So she brings him a saucepan and some water, and he puts in his boot and boils it up. Then he tastes the soup, and tells her it's delicious, it just needs some salt and pepper. So she brings him the seasoning, and he tastes it and tells her it just needs an onion and it will be perfect. The story goes on, with the old woman bringing him more and more ingredients, until finally, the tramp has made a nice bowl of soup and they both settle down to eat it, with the old woman having no idea that actually she has provided everything necessary.

As I said, it impressed me as a story when I was about six, and

I've never really outgrown it. I like the idea that you can trick people, make them give you exactly what you want, and if you're clever about it, they think it's you who's done the favour. So I drove away from Uncle William's thinking of that story and smiling. I figured we might be able to make some soup together.

***

I started to pop in to see Uncle William fairly regularly after that. I had been assigned a few businesses in town which were Category E, so grocers, the community hall, a couple of off-licences. They were considered very low risk as they didn't serve food to the public, but they needed to be visited occasionally, to keep the local authority's books up to date as much as anything. They were given to me as ideal places for me to practice, where I wouldn't do any harm if I missed something, and I could develop my 'dealing with the public' skills. I was making the most of it.

Most people, especially those running small businesses, have very little idea about the law and local authorities. Any sort of inspection fills them with dread. This is extremely useful. I would walk in, clipboard in hand, looking all official and ask to speak to the manager. I had a quick checklist to complete, but it was easy to spin it out, to check behind the bins and ask about how often they cleaned the sink, where were bottles stored, did they know how to watch for pests. As they gave me their answers I would sigh, and jot down things on my clipboard. Occasionally I would even tut, or shake my head. By the end, they would be sure I was about to stick a penalty notice on them, close them down, ruin their business.

That was the time to change track. I would then become their best friend, give them a nice smile and ask if we could talk somewhere privately. Speaking quietly, I would lean in and explain that things weren't quite running as they should be, I had noticed quite a few problems. But I respected that they were an honest bloke working hard to run a decent business. The last thing I wanted was to cause them any grief, making enough to live on was hard enough as it was. So, perhaps I could ignore a few things, not put them into my report.

I left it there. I never hinted they might like to offer me a little something, a small gift to seal our friendship. I didn't need to. It was rare that I left without a bottle of something nice, or a box of chocolates. For which I was always extremely grateful and very surprised. There was never any suggestion that this was expected, was a bribe. I wasn't stupid.

The off-licences were the best, I was building up quite a decent supply of bottles at home. But after I started to visit Uncle, I found the grocer's more helpful. I would pop in, just for a chat because I was passing, and tell them how I was visiting my uncle, that he was very fond of those luxury biscuits, or decent filter coffee, or some fruit. I found the grocers to be most obliging. I think Mr Singh even quite liked me, he would give me a huge grin when he looked up from his till to see me standing in the doorway.

"Hello Miss Inspector, how are you today?"

"Hi Mr Singh, I'm good thanks. Not doing an inspection today, just thought I'd say hello. I want to take my uncle some fruit, do you have anything nice? Is it okay if I pick a bag of things to take? What do I owe you? On the house? Well, thank you Mr Singh, that's very kind. You're a good friend to me. Give my regards to your wife. I shouldn't mention it really, but I'm due to come back again in the summer. Probably July. Keep it between you and me.

"Nice to see you. Bye"

Ah yes, all very pleasant.

So when I arrived at Uncle William's, I was always bearing gifts. After a while he grew used to me coming. I gradually cleaned up his kitchen, wiping cupboards and sorting crockery. The biscuit tins were refilled with fresh cookies, the bowl on the kitchen table had fruit, and by the time I left, the house would smell of percolated coffee. He began to look forward to my visits.

At first, I confined myself to the kitchen. I didn't want to start cleaning the whole house, and I couldn't bear to sit in a mess. I did once follow him into the lounge, but you could see the dust dancing when we sat on the gold cushions, and the surfaces were thick with it. I felt dirty just being there, and washed my hair when I got home. No, I knew I could keep the kitchen clean enough for my weekly visits. The rest of the house could wait until I was living there.

I knew I needed to go carefully if I planned to move in. The suggestion should come from Uncle William, not me. The idea of how to move things along a little presented itself one afternoon.

We were in his kitchen, as usual. He was at the table, reading out snippets from the newspaper while I baked cupcakes. Baking was new development – I hoped it would remind him of the good bits of Aunt Susan, perhaps prompt him to want to see more of me. I was quite a good cook actually, it was a school subject I had always enjoyed and cakes were easy enough, even in a foreign kitchen. He folded the newspaper and sighed.

"Those smell nice. Susan was always a great baker, I do miss her food. She only used white cake cases though," he said, watching me fill a bun tin with paper cases. "She said it was a waste of money to buy coloured ones when plain ones were just as good. They're only thrown away afterwards." He gazed out of the window for a moment, lost in thought.

"We could use you at our church," he said, turning back to me. "There was a tea last Sunday, in aid of our missionaries, and the food was awful. I don't think anyone cooks anymore. It was all packets of crisps and shop bought cakes. Hardly worth going out for."

"Are you still going to the church in Marksbridge?" I said.

He nodded. "Been going there since Susan died."

"I need to find a new church," I said. "The one we go to doesn't really have anything for someone my age, and to be honest," I licked some mixture from my fingers and reached for a spoon, "I'm not sure how sound the teaching is." I began to spoon the mixture into the paper cases. I had found them in the grocer's shop and they were rather nice, with pink edges. I ignored the dig about cost, he was a rude old man.

Uncle William took the bait about church at once.

"You should come with me one Sunday," he said, "you might like it."

Now, I didn't actually attend church very often. I tended to go when I needed to persuade my parents about something and wanted them to be feeling pleased with me. But Uncle William didn't know this. He had been attending church regularly since Susan died, for the company I suppose. I figured it would have quite an influence on him, an influence which I could use to my advantage. So I appeared all reluctant, and let him persuade me to go with him that Sunday. Just for a look, to see if I liked it.

I thought it would help my plan you see, help to ease me into Uncle William's life. It was a good idea, a nice way to make it easier to manipulate things the way I wanted them. I didn't know then that it wasn't just my plan. I thought I was in charge.

Chapter Six

I wore smart jeans and a new pullover for my first Sunday at Marksbridge Baptist. The car park was fairly full when I arrived, and I didn't want to get blocked in, so I drove past the church and parked on the road. By the time I had walked back, the service had started.

There was an old bloke welcoming people at the entrance, and I could see he was excited to see someone new walking in. Churches are like that – always keen to entice new people through the door. They're great places if you want a bit of attention, try it some time. Of course, I knew all about how to behave, the language these people speak, so I fitted in right away. We went through the whole welcome handshake (really, who actually shakes hands in real life these days? Churches are in some kind of time warp). I explained I was meeting my uncle, and slipped through the open door (better not shut it, all those hordes of unsaved people who turn up will be put-off if they encounter a shut door) and looked for Uncle William.

He was sitting near the front, wearing a navy blazer and a tie. Old people like to be smart for church. Young people like to prove 'it's what's inside that counts' so tend to come scruffy, regardless of who they might offend. The church was fairly full, but I was lucky, they were about to start singing, which meant they would all stand up. I slipped into the place next to my uncle, walking with my head bowed, like I was shy. Churches like people who are a bit unsure of themselves, someone they can help. Of course, if you actually want to be spoken to, you need to make eye-contact later, give someone a nice smile.

Uncle William glanced down at me, and I smiled up at him, and looked at the screen to join in with the words.

I have never understood why churches like to sing. I mean, why *everyone* has to sing. Singing is something that either should be kept private, for showers and cars when no one can hear, or else done by people who can manage to follow a tune. Where, other than churches, are you forced to stand and sing some song that no one has ever heard before? (Who likes to keep standing up anyway?) It is very odd. But then, there's a lot about churches that's odd. This one wasn't as bad as some, because at least they had a band. There was a woman playing keyboard, a couple of blokes with guitars, a flautist and a cellist. It was mostly not too bad. Though they needed a clarinet. Obviously.

I looked around as we sang. The church had quite a good mix of ages, a few young families, a smattering of people who looked about my age, some oldies. There was one bloke who might be interesting, he had sandy hair that stuck up at the back, and was very tall. He wore a leather jacket and I assume, from the way she was leaning towards him, had a girlfriend. But that didn't matter. She wouldn't last long if I decided he had potential.

We sang four songs, back to back. *Four songs.* Exhausting. They had simple tunes and idiotic words. That's the thing with churches trying to be modern, they want everything to be about feelings and love and themselves. Mostly themselves. The songs all follow a basic "me, me, me, me, God" structure. The words are about "I want this, and to feel this, and to have this – and wow, God loves me."

If you analyse it, people always lie. So although Christians today will *claim* they believe in some sort of great big, creating God, what they *actually* believe in is a pocket genie who can help them find their car keys and will heal Aunty Sue's cancer if they ask. A God who makes *them* feel better. It comes out in the garbage they sing every week. Although God was not a myth I bothered to think about, I was fairly sure the pocket genie variety was a modern fabrication.

We sat. The chairs were all arranged facing the front, with a wooden lectern and microphone to help the speaker hide and be heard. There was a small table with a large vase of flowers. English churches always have a flower arrangement, with accompanying rota pinned to the wall in the foyer somewhere. It gives the women something to bitch about.

Someone called Sam Whittaker was invited to the front to lead the prayers. He moved bow-legged to the front, leaning on a frame. Several people smiled, you almost felt a ripple of affection spreading through the church as he made his way to the lectern. Interesting. This was someone with influence. He stood at the front and looked around, taking in his people, holding onto the lectern for support. When he spoke his voice was clear and deep, a strong west country accent blending his words so they had an almost storybook quality. He prayed for a long time.

Someone else who caught my eye was the minister. Rob Pritchard, old enough to be my father probably, but not without attraction. He had good hair, grey at the temples, and nice eyes, but mostly it was his manner. You could tell from how he spoke that he was used to being liked, getting on with people. I thought it might be interesting to discover how close he would sail to temptation before he pulled away. If he pulled away. I like a challenge, and a clergyman would certainly be something unusual. Perhaps I would start with Master Leather Jacket and move on to Rev Nice Eyes once I was more established.

There was a Bible in the back of the seat in front. I pulled it out, and flicked through, looking for something to distract me. Uncle William glanced down, so I turned to a page and followed the words with my finger, as if absorbed by what was being preached

63

and searching for further evidence in the book. I felt him nod his approval. In the last song (there is always a last song, finishing at the end of the talk would be far too radical) I closed my eyes. I stood there, eyes shut, swaying with the music. I was letting them all know I was already 'saved', they could accept me as one of their own. When we went into the third repeat, I raised a hand too, reached for the ceiling like I was searching for a lightbulb to unscrew. Absorbed by holiness, I was. (Why sing it more than once anyway? In case someone has forgotten what the words mean and catch it third time round?)

After the service there was coffee. There's always coffee. Usually it's that nasty instant stuff, though some places have started serving something more palatable, probably as an attempt to not appear as weird as they are. It doesn't work. Even decent coffee is usually served in mugs that were bought about a hundred years ago. This was no exception: mass-produced coffee in a smoked glass mug. I wondered how they were stored, if the church was careful about looking out for rodents, and if they were dried by a dishwasher or a germ-ridden tea-towel. I decided to risk it though, all that singing had made me thirsty.

Of course, there was a queue to receive it. Churches like queues. Uncle William settled at the back and tried to introduce me to someone called Mavis. I smiled politely, and said I needed the washroom. I left the coffee hall briefly, then re-entered and walked to the front of the line. Feigning ignorance, I spoke to the person at the front, asking if there was a charge. Of course, they assured me it was free, asked if I was new, and ushered me into the place at the front. I don't queue.

A woman with tired eyes approached, and introduced herself as Esther. We went through the normal, hello, who are you, how did we manage to ensnare you in one of our services, routine. Then I discovered she was married to Rev Nice Eyes. That made her more interesting. She could introduce us. I gave her some attention, turned the conversation back to her.

"Have you been here very long then?"

"Yes, actually, since our children were small," she said.

"How many do you have?"

People just love to talk about their children, have you noticed that? It's like they haven't noticed the rest of the world has no interest whatsoever in their offspring. She had launched into an explanation, so I adopted my listening face.

"We have two boys. Samuel's at uni, Exeter, he's reading English. I think he's hoping to do journalism, but it's not an easy job to get in to. We'll see though, he's doing very well with his English and he writes for the student newspaper.

"Joseph is in the sixth form, studying science. He hopes to go to uni next year, to Nottingham, where his girlfriend also hopes to go. So then we'll just be two again."

I nodded. "Do you work?" I said.

Her eyes clouded at that. There was a story there, but she just shook her head.

"No, not now. I used to teach. I'm busy with the church now, there's always loads to do."

I watched her as she spoke. It wasn't just her eyes that were tired, her hair and clothes all looked like they had been rushed, made tidy as quickly as possible. She wasn't bad looking, could've made something of herself if she'd tried. But she hadn't tried. She was dragging herself through the day, maybe not even bothering to look in a mirror. I thought the Rev would probably like to look at someone who had taken a little more care of themselves, someone who wasn't old before their time, someone like me.

She was asking if I had enjoyed the music. I hadn't, but I told her it was lovely, so nice to have a proper band rather than just a piano. It's always important to like the music in a church – they link it to spirituality. If you like silly choruses in a Baptist church, it shows that you are modern and evangelical. If you like old fashioned hymns in a C of E, it shows you are 'deep' and not 'liberal'. They never seem to realise that actually, it's a matter for taste, not religion. I don't actually like much music at all, but if pressed, I would opt for a bit of Wagner.

"I play myself, actually," I said. "I used to play my clarinet at my old church, but there was some trouble with the music director, so we went back to just having hymns, and they're not as suited to a range of instruments."

I could see her eyes lighting up at that one, seeing a use for me. Churches are always on the lookout for fresh blood, people who can help in some way.

"Let me introduce you to Sadie," she said, "she organises our music. I'm sure she'd love to meet a clarinettist." She scanned the hall, and waved over a woman who had been about to join the coffee queue.

"Ah, Sadie, this is Clara. Clara Oakes. She's William's niece and is thinking about joining us. She said how much she enjoyed the music this morning. She plays a clarinet."

Sadie was a dumpy woman, probably mid-thirties, rolls of fat under her chin and over the waistband of her too tight trousers. She smiled, showing large teeth with a smudge of red lipstick on the front left one. I recognised her as the keyboard player. The leader of the band was always the keyboard player.

"Hello Clara, lovely to meet you. Where were you before? Oh, the Anglican church. Right...

"Well, I'm glad you enjoyed the music. You play a clarinet? Do you play often? Right.... We've got a practice lined up this Wednesday actually, if you wanted to join us? You'd be very welcome, the more the merrier. We don't all play every week," (This was to let me know that if I wasn't good enough, my playing would be confined to the practice sessions) "but you can come down and jam with us if you want."

Esther had melted away, off to search for some more gullible new people I expect. (You can take that sentence either way – both are true.) Sadie had been passed the responsibility of securing my second visit, and in fairness, she didn't do a bad job. Even if I hadn't had other reasons, I might have gone to their practice. Though I'm not sure I would describe it as a 'jamming session'. I took the details (which made her eyes light up, she was earning her Brownie points in Heaven) then went to find Uncle William. I had been watching him while I spoke to Sadie, looking to see who he spent time with. There was a thin woman with wispy hair who gave him lots of attention. But I didn't think she'd be a problem, he hardly looked at her while she was talking, looked a bit bored if anything.

I also looked for Master Leather Jacket. He was leaning against the wall, hand around his mug of coffee (real men don't use handles) staring into space while his girlfriend and someone in a flowery skirt giggled and chatted. He glanced up, as if he could feel me looking. I looked away quickly, then looked back. He was still looking at me, so I lowered my eyes and smiled. When I looked at him again he was staring openly and grinning. It always worked – the sweet, I'm shy but approachable smile – men can't help but smile back.

Of course, girlfriend noticed and turned to see what he was smiling at. I gave her my innocent smile, and she turned back to boyfriend. They wouldn't be coming to say hello. Never mind, he could wait for another day. I didn't think I cope with any more eager Christians, it was time to thank my uncle for the invite and leave.

I left via the main door, hoping to encounter Rev Nice Eyes. He was there, shaking people's hands as they left, checking his flock were all okay. I watched him for a moment. He was talking to an elderly woman, holding her hand as he spoke, nodding when she answered. He was comfortable being tactile, a caring man. I grinned to myself, thinking my little experiment was actually going to be fun.

When he was free I moved forwards, looking as if I planned to slip out unnoticed. He stopped me, of course, said how nice it was to see me, he hoped I had enjoyed the service.

"Yes thanks, it was lovely. I came with my Uncle, William Oakes, do you know him?"

"William? Yes, yes, know him well. He's one of our regulars," he said.

"Well, I really enjoyed the service. I might come again, it has a nice feel to it. In fact, Sadie has invited me to come and play on Wednesday, with the music group, so I'll try to come to that."

"Really? Great! What do you play?"

"Clarinet."

"Hey, that's great, lovely mellow sound when it's played well. I might see you then, if you do decide to come. I play guitar – not very well, but they allow me to come to the practices. Well, they have to – I'm the minister!"

I smiled up at him, letting him know I appreciated the joke. I decided he was really rather nice looking, those dark eyes, nice even teeth, and tall. I like tall.

"That will be nice," I said, "does your wife play too? Esther isn't it?" I decided against the flirty smile, better to mention the wife, keep everything legit. If I tried to move too fast he'd back away, better to appear safe.

"Yes, that's right, Esther. No, she doesn't play now. Well, she can, she plays the piano, but we don't have one at home, so she can't ever practise. Perhaps she'll go back to it one day, she was quite good once.

"It will be good to see you, if you can make it on Wednesday. We could do with some fresh input."

'Fresh talent,' I thought, 'but you can't say that, it wouldn't sound proper...'

I waved, smiled and walked away. I took care to walk well, hips swaying slightly, head up. Just in case he was watching. But I didn't turn back to check. If I was going to play this game, I couldn't make any mistakes. It had to be him who came to me. Which would take time, but I wasn't in a hurry, there was Uncle William to sort first.

***

When I arrived at the church on Wednesday, I could hear the music before I opened the door. Scattered notes and laughter drifted into the night. I tried the main door, but it was locked, so I made my way to the side. There was no outside light, so I walked slowly, looking for debris so I didn't trip. I didn't want to damage my clarinet. The path wasn't well maintained, with uneven paving and a stray brick. I wondered what the church liability insurance was like.

The side door was slightly ajar, yellow light seeping out and cold night oozing inside. Not good for their heating bills. I left it open and went into the main sanctuary.

There was a small group huddled around the keyboard, an elderly woman removing a violin from the case balanced on a chair. Sadie glanced up as I entered and waved me over.

"Hey, great to see you. Right, come and join us, we've only just started."

She had forgotten my name, I could see from her eyes. I smiled back, deciding not to help her but Rev Nice Eyes came to her rescue.

"Hi Clara, glad you decided to brave us again. Let me introduce you. Sadie you know–" She nodded, curt and boy-like.

"Then we have Melissa on violin–"

She was ready to play, and drew down the bow, giving a

welcoming few notes. Then beamed at me, like it was something clever. Twee.

"John and Brian on guitar—"

John was tall, young, bald. Not bad looking apart from the lack of hair. Brian was short, dark, with the sort of flexible mouth that reminds you of a frog – no lips and too much movement. Both men grinned, strummed a few notes. This was a group that liked to copy each other. Fine. They would be happy to have a leader, and that could be me.

"Led by, and kept in order by, Kimberly."

Kimberly was fat. Short dark hair, big grin. I guessed she would be the comedienne of the group, someone who hid a lack of self-control with the cookies, by pretending she didn't care and was happy with her size. She didn't strum in welcome, so not as easily led as the others. Instead she smiled, said, "Hi", then moved across the hall to the music stand in that careful way that people who have always been overweight sometimes have. She might be big, but she wasn't clumsy. She did, however, have a rainbow-coloured strap on her guitar. I doubted this meant she was gay – her eyes had assessed me as a potential rival, not a possible lover. She had probably bought the strap because it was pretty. Which says a lot in itself. She was now busy placing sheets of music on the stands that were arranged to the side of the keyboard.

Rev Nice Eyes was still going. "And last but not least, we have Jennifer on flute. And me, of course, Rob. Julie can't make it tonight. She plays cello. Glad to have you with us Clara."

Jennifer was taller than me and slim, with very short blonde hair. She smiled, but not with her eyes. Either shy or snooty, hard to tell. I smiled back at her and began to unpack my clarinet. I needed to warm it up a bit before we began, otherwise when I started to play it would sound flat, losing its tuning as the tube gradually lengthened due to the room's temperature. It wouldn't blend with the other instruments. I began to blow gently into the mouthpiece, letting the warmth from my lungs steadily heat the tube from the inside. You can't hurry instruments.

The rest of the group were laughing, choosing the order of the songs, chatting about their week. They were friends, and this was as much about relationship as it was about music. I prepared myself to be the 'slightly shy but very sweet' Clara that occasionally appeared. I wanted to fit in too, to edge my way in, blend into an established group. Easier to alter things from the inside. Some things are better taken slowly.

I was interested that Esther-the-dutiful-wife wasn't in attendance. If she played the piano, I couldn't see why she wouldn't come, to spend the time with her husband if nothing else. It's not like they had kids to worry about. Sadie was probably unwilling to share the keyboard, but there was an old piano in the corner, she could've played that. I doubted this was going to be a very tuneful session, a few bum notes on an out of tune piano were unlikely to spoil it.

Kimberly was showing Brian and John some picks she had made with a special cutter bought online. Rob and Sadie were discussing songs, when she looked up, saw the time and coughed loudly.

"Right guys, we need to get started. We'll start with 'All Across the World'. Clara, you play in B flat right? Can you transpose? I don't have any other music." She sounded doubtful, like this was something she should've thought of before she invited me. She probably had something on her computer at home to change music into different keys, but that would be no good for now. If I played the same notes as the others on the clarinet it would sound awful, we would clash. She looked worried, I knew she was wondering how to tell me I couldn't play, while still sounding welcoming to a new person.

But I was adept at transposing, playing a note higher than the

71

one marked. I glanced at the music and it was very easy, a kid could've played it.

"It's fine," I said, "I think I can manage, I just need to raise each note by a couple of semitones. I should be able to do that as I play. I'll just listen to the first run through though, watch you all for a minute."

She looked relieved and turned back to her music. "Right, let's start. One, two, three…" She began to play the introduction, the others joining in as soon as they could. Not exactly all in unison, but they caught up pretty quickly. John was a head-nodder, his shiny crown keeping pace with the music. Kimberley swayed, her guitar resting on her stomach at a slight angle, her eyes glazed. She knew this song well. Rev was managing to keep up, but I could see it was a struggle for him, a slight frown appeared and he kept licking his lips. I guessed the guitar was a new hobby. Perhaps he fancied Sadie. Brian was grinning, he was enjoying himself. He began to mouth the words, his too big mouth stretching into shapes, wet and ugly. Melissa was not bad. Her music was younger than her appearance, and she didn't produce that horrible scraping sound you often hear from a violin. She was playing the melody, keeping pace with Sadie, whose timing was slightly irregular. I really couldn't hear Jennifer at all. There was something very angular about her. I wondered if she was even blowing, or just fingering the flute so people thought she could play.

I moved next to the vacant music stand, next to Melissa, and joined in when they started to repeat the verse. The clarinet added texture to the music, deepening and rounding the sound. I played well, and added notes to the music I had been given, so it sounded much better. We arrived at the end and everyone stopped playing. They all turned to look at me. There was a pause.

"Right…" began Sadie. "Right. Well, you can play, can't you?"

She looked surprised. They all did. As if they had expected a squeaky novice rather than an accomplished musician. They didn't know me yet. I don't do things unless I'm the best.

"Clara, that was beautiful, really beautiful," said Rob. "You are going to make us all sound so much better."

Melissa nodded. "Yes, that was lovely Clara. How long have you been playing?"

"Oh, since I was little," I said. "We used to live in America, and I started learning there. I think they start younger over there, I've heard in England they don't let kids start learning until they're older. Something to do with their teeth I think." I kept my voice low, pretended I was shy to be talking about myself and was trying to make the conversation more general, less about me.

"My mother plays too, so she taught me at first."

(No, you didn't miss something. My mother wouldn't know which way up a clarinet went. But it made her sound slightly more middle class. These people were not a group of labourers, and I wanted them to accept me. Of course, if they ever met my mother, they would know at once that she had no education at all and was extremely unlikely to be able to play anything musical. But why would they meet her? Uncle William didn't much like her, and I certainly wasn't going to be inviting her.)

Rob looked interested. "You lived in the US? For how long? You don't have an accent at all – are your parents American? No, wait, William is your uncle, so at least one of them is English…"

I opened my mouth to answer, but Kimberley began to strum loudly and Sadie shuffled her music and announced the song we'd be playing next.

We played through a couple more songs. The sort of bouncy rubbish that evangelical Christians love so much, with simple tunes and daft words. The kind of song that might as well be 'The Wheels on the Bus Go Round and Round' for the amount of theological depth they contain. Each time, Sadie counted us in, started playing, and by the end of the first line, everyone else was playing. I was holding back on purpose, I assume everyone else was just unable to start on time. I wasn't sure about Melissa, she might have been coming in late on purpose too. I didn't sense much love between her and Sadie. Couldn't hear Jennifer at all.

"Right," said Sadie, "last song. This time, try and come in on the count guys, okay? Are we ready? No John, 'You Are King' – got it? Right, after two. One, two…"

She played the first few notes, then stopped. No one had started with her. "What's the deal here guys? Are we all going to play the intro or just me? You can either start with the verse, or all begin the intro when I do. But don't be late, it sounds awful when we start at different times."

"Ooops, got it wrong again boys!" said Kimberley. "Slapped wrists all round."

"This is quite a reflective song isn't it?" I asked. "Something that might come before a time of silent prayer?"

Sadie nodded. "Yes, what were you thinking?"

"Well," I said, pausing as if hesitant to be speaking so soon after joining the group. "Does anyone else ever play the introduction? Perhaps have a change of instrument, to make people notice. So, as it's a slow, thoughtful song, could Melissa lead us all in with the violin?"

"That's a nice idea," said Rob. He was obviously keen to encourage his new recruit.

Sadie looked less certain. She was the band leader. She played the introductions, set the pace, played the first note of the verse loudly so the congregation knew when to start singing. "I'm not sure," she said, searching for reasons to refuse. "Our church is a bit hard to lead sometimes, they might not know when to come in."

"Well," said Rob, "how about if we have a play through first? So Melissa plays the entire song once, sets the mood, then we all start

74

to play as per usual, and the congregation start singing. That might be nice, for a change."

"I'm not sure if the violin has enough volume," said Sadie. Which was a stupid thing to say, because there was a sound system and microphones and the sound desk could turn up Melissa's mic.

"Perhaps if Clara played too?" said Melissa. I could see she liked the idea. She was probably more musical than Sadie, but was older and therefore not deemed 'with-it' enough to lead the music. Churches like to think someone 'young and groovy' will attract more young people if they're involved with the music. The very fact that they still use the word 'groovy' shows where the main problem lies, but there we are. Melissa was too old to be more than background accompaniment, unless they were desperate.

Of course, me playing the introduction had been my plan all along, but I looked suitably worried. "Oh, I'm not sure if I should…" I said.

"Of course you should," said John, "it would sound great."

"Yes," said Rob, "let's give it a try at least. All right with you Sadie?"

She nodded. They were supposed to be making the best music they could, to honour their God, use their gifts, help lead the worship – crap like that. She could hardly refuse to let us try, could she?

It sounded much better, of course. Two decent musicians, playing music suited to their instruments. I kept very still while I played, looking humble and worried. But the sound I produced was brilliant, and Melissa kept up well. When the others joined in, they spoiled it, but the rest of the church would be singing, so it was going to sound awful anyway. There was no further discussion at the end. The tune would be played through by clarinet and violin, the guitars and keyboard would then play the introduction, so the people knew when to start. Jennifer could do what she liked frankly, her instrument seemed to be of the silent variety. Sadie made a note on her music. Things were already moving in the direction I wanted.

The practice session ended. I sat on a chair at the end of a row and began to dismantle my clarinet, taking care to remove the reed and wipe it before clipping it into its plastic holder. Reeds were expensive, especially when you got to play at a decent level. They were easy to split, to snag on a sweater, or catch on the ligature when sliding it over the mouthpiece to hold the reed in place. Or, more commonly, other people touching the instrument. This always irritated me intensely. People seemed to think it was okay to handle instruments and it wasn't, it was akin to searching through a handbag. Rob and John came over as I began to pull apart the upper and lower sections. I dried them and placed them in the case.

"Beautiful instrument," said John, "and you play really well Clara."

"Thanks." I said, hoping to get rid of him.

I slotted the ligature over the mouthpiece and covered both with the cap before putting them into the case. The two men watched.

"Is it ebony?" asked Rob.

"No, just looks like it," I said. "I think this one's African Blackwood, though I started with a plastic one of course. Cheaper." I shut the case and snapped the clips shut. I couldn't stop them looking, but I didn't want this to lead to them touching, or asking to "have a go". I stood. John began to move away, realising the conversation had ended, so I smiled at Rob and rested one leg on the chair, looking more relaxed, willing to chat.

"There're all sorts of clarinets actually, a whole range of different qualities. I used to play in an orchestra." I didn't mention I only played in it once. The audition was easy, but then they expected you to turn up on time, to play when told, to be part of a whole with very little opportunity for solo playing. I couldn't even be heard, was just part of the general sound. Not for me.

I continued, "Some musicians had really fancy clarinets. One even had gold keys. Well, they wouldn't really be gold, just a gold plate. The keys are actually made of German Silver, then covered with something more interesting, to make them shiny."

He was doing his best to look interested. I went on to tell him that German Silver wasn't really silver, it was a brass and nickel alloy. My keys were covered in nickel, so they looked shiny, and I was lucky not have developed an allergy to it, which lots of people did. I figured he didn't want or need that much detail, but it was important for him to realise I was intelligent, someone he could talk to at his own level. I was telling him details he wouldn't know, showing I was more than a pretty face.

I put the case back on the chair. It involved bending, so he had a nice view down my top while I showed him the different sections of the instrument, pointing out the barrel, that could be repositioned slightly when I tuned the clarinet, the bell which increased the volume, the metal ring which stopped the wood splitting. As I spoke, I ran my finger along each piece. A manicured nail running along the length. A caress. The clarinet was a sexy instrument. He needed to make the connection. My words were factual, informative, safe. My actions were suggestive, dangerous. Together, they were acceptable, the words toning down what I was doing. When I looked up, he didn't look bored any more.

"Right everyone," said Sadie, wanting to make a final announcement before we drifted away. "That was a great practice, we got lots done. Am assuming you can all play this Sunday – with the exception of Rob, of course." She gave him a smile. "We need to practise before people arrive, so 9 am sharp please folks. Clara, is that okay for you? Can you get there then? We need to do a complete run through and be ready before people arrive."

We didn't. I knew my part already, it was easy. I did not need to get up early just so I could listen to the incompetents struggle through their parts again.

"Yes, that's fine," I said, "I'll be sure to be here for then."

"Right. Great. Thanks everyone. See you all Sunday."

I smiled up at Rob. My big smile, with shiny eyes. The one men notice.

"I really enjoyed that," I said. I closed the case again and stood. He stepped back. "See you Sunday," I said, and walked, with style, to the door. The evening had been a success.

Chapter Seven

I visited Uncle William again on Thursday. I wanted him to know how helpful I had found his church, so he would invite me again. It was important for him to feel in charge, to be the leader who was helping his young niece. I also needed to let him know I had joined the music group, so he would be expecting me to be there on Sunday. I would have to be careful to present it properly, so he felt in control.

I arrived with the ingredients for some cookies. I doubted if he liked cookies, old people eat things like fruit cake, or shortbread. But they were quick to bake. And I liked them. I would make his kitchen smell homely and give him some attention. I wanted him to be used to me being there, to look forward to my visits. To be worried when I mentioned I might have to move away, and be prepared to step in and try to keep me near. But all in good time. For now, it was cookies and a chat about the church. His church.

"I really enjoyed it on Sunday," I said, pulling the scales from the cupboard. "I thought the preaching was very good, he's interesting, isn't he?" I began to spoon the brown sugar onto the scales, watching the dial creep forwards. I added some white sugar. These were going to be sickly.

"Rob Pritchard? Yes, he can be alright. Bit too long sometimes. Tends to explain the obvious too much in my opinion. And he repeats himself – gives you a message, than says it all again. I don't know, perhaps some people need that. Really, you wouldn't know he was black, not to listen to. He's been well educated I think."

Uncle was racist. Oh, did you not realise Rob was black either?

Perhaps you're racist too. I guess I haven't mentioned it – but it was one of his attractions. I've never been with a black bloke before, I thought it would be interesting.

I didn't say that to Uncle of course. He was sitting at the table, tea in hand, watching me. He liked to watch me. That was fine, I could use that.

I moved a pan of melted butter from the stove, poured it over the sugar, and began to stir the mixture. There was something relaxing about watching sugar dissolve, smelling that warm sweetness. For a while, neither of us spoke, both watching the ingredients blend. Uncle William was contented, I decided to mention the music group. I cracked an egg, separated it, and slid the yolk into the mixture.

"I went to that music group practice last night," I said, reaching for another egg. I banged it hard on the side of a cup, opened the shell, and dropped the insides next to the yolk.

"Oh yes?" said William. "Didn't know you still played. Saxophone wasn't it?"

"Clarinet," I said. "It was okay, though I was very nervous. They've said I can play on Sunday," I said, measuring vanilla and beating it in with the wooden spoon. The alcohol from the essence evaporated, filling the kitchen with vanilla fragrance. It was very strong. You needed to add very little to change a very large amount of mixture. It gave a whole new flavour to something, hugely effective.

"They've said I can play this Sunday," I continued, "but I'm not sure… What do you think? I'm worried I'll spoil it…" I lowered my head, concentrated on stirring flour and bicarb into the mixture. The dough started to form, thick and greasy, clinging to the spoon. I could feel his eyes on me.

"Well," he said, "you don't want to make a fool of yourself…" (By that, he meant himself. He did not want his niece to let the side down. Pompous old man he was.) "But if you think you can keep up with the others, perhaps you should." (He was obviously thinking that if I pulled it off, it might earn a bit of glory for himself.)

I pulled open the bag of chocolate chips and tipped them all into the bowl. Then stirred quickly. You had to be careful with some ingredients, and I didn't want them melting before they were in the oven. That's the thing with cooking, it's important to know just how each ingredient will work, what its key traits are, so you can handle them correctly and manipulate them to be just what you want.

I opened the cutlery drawer. "Do you have a cup measure?" I asked, "Or an ice-cream scoop – ah yes, got it." I pulled out the scoop and used it to measure amounts of the dough onto the greased paper. Little dollops, well-spaced, or they would spread in the oven and join up. It was important to keep them separate, so they would be the shape I wanted later. Baking was all about preparing things properly. I glanced at my uncle and smiled.

"Thank you Uncle William. You're right, I probably should. You're very good for me," I said, as I slid the baking tray into the hot oven. "I wouldn't be brave enough to do anything without your support."

I went over and kissed his cheek. He pulled back momentarily, surprised. Then he smiled.

"It's a shame you don't have more backing from your parents," he said. "I always felt your mother was inadequate. Not sure what your father saw in her. But you can rely on me now. That's what families are for, isn't it."

When the cookies were ready, I waited for them to cool slightly – you can't hurry things if you want them to turn out a certain way. When they had hardened, I eased them from the tray and put them on a rack to cool completely. I moved the dirty bowls and dumped them in the sink. Uncle could wash those later. Then I put a few cookies onto a plate for us to eat while I told him about my day, and settled next to him at the table. I decided I would listen to his pompous drivel for another half hour, then make my excuses and leave. I was meeting friends at the pub later.

"Here you go Uncle," I said, holding his hand steady with mine and passing him a still-warm cookie. I watched him take a nibble. They were good. I knew how to bake.

***

Friday, I was due to meet a colleague at a small cafe. This counted as part of my training, was something I could write up for my log book as evidence. I wasn't yet deemed qualified to visit alone, so was shadowing an experienced inspector. This was always boring, and limited my opportunities. Necessary though.

My log book was something I must complete before I could be accredited and do inspections on my own. I had to prove I had covered all the skill areas – things like inspecting a shellfish plant, importation of food, seizure of unfit food, things like that. I still had to be accompanied, which was tedious and lowered the scope for fringe benefits. I was hoping the log book would be signed off soon, then I could fly solo.

We met at the office, and went together in his car. He was called Gary, Gary Curry. A name which always reminds me of ageing footballers, though I'm not sure why. He didn't look like a footballer, more an accountant, with thin grey hair and a pretentious manner. I had met him before. We weren't friends.

"Good morning Clara, you're late, I was hoping to leave at nine o'clock."

I had set the alarm for the right time, but last night had been fun, and I couldn't be bothered to get up early, so I'd turned it off again. I didn't tell him that though.

"Yes, traffic was bad. Is it The Bistro this morning? The one next to the station in Craddock?"

"Yes, that's correct. I'm not expecting any problems, the manager there is pretty good, knows all the rules. I thought you could concentrate on food temperatures, check they're keeping to the hot hold rules, calibrating their equipment. I know they have a food delivery on Fridays, ready for the weekend. I was hoping to be there when it arrived, so we could check the perishable food temperature was being maintained. We'll be rather late now. Unfortunate."

He picked up his briefcase and led the way to his car. A small white Fiesta. It fitted with his general mean spirit I thought. I opened the passenger door, and sat as far from him as was possible in such a confined space. He had one of those hanging deodorants, and the interior stank of chemicals. I wound down my window slightly. He glanced across, but decided to not say anything. I knew I was annoying him, but I doubted he would direct his irritation at me. He was a coward, he would instead be tough on the cafe owner, be as pedantic as was possible. Which I could work to my advantage, be the 'nice one', the one they would give free drinks to next time I visited.

Craddock was a fairly large town, unusual in that most of the shops were individually owned ones rather than the ubiquitous chains that littered most High Streets. There was a Boots, and a Factory Shop, but other than the supermarkets, the rest were boutiques or jewellers or stationers, all owned and run by small-time shopkeepers. There were also a surprising number of hairdressers and charity shops. I assumed the residents of Craddock all had nice hair and crumpled clothes. Or were rich enough to actually buy stuff from the over-priced boutiques. We parked, and I spent some time putting on my white coat and hat. They weren't strictly necessary, though had been provided free of charge, so I might as well look the part. Plus I was enjoying watching Curry squirm with impatience as I slowly buttoned the coat, peered into the wing mirror to adjust the hat, tucked in a stray hair.

"I don't want to go home smelling of fried food," I said, "easier to wash the uniform than my cardi – it's new. Do you like it?"

Curry scowled at me and looked at his watch.

"If you're ready now?" he said and strode off towards The Bistro.

The Bistro (not the most original name, but that kind of fitted with Craddock) was a glass-fronted cafe. It was on the corner of the High Street, and faced the station on one side and a bank on the other. It was full of blond wood tables and uncomfortable chairs and the menu reminded me of The Toasty Bean. It was managed by Sam Chapman, a very tall, very black, very thin man, with a strong East London accent. He was waiting for us and came to shake Gary's hand when we arrived.

"Mr Curry, nice to see yer. We're all ready for yer eagle eye. Ha!"

"Good morning Mr Chapman. We're later than I anticipated, has your food delivery arrived already? Ah, I was afraid of that. This is Clara Oakes, she is assisting me today. Perhaps you could show her what has been delivered so she can record the core temperatures? Though they won't be accurate now, of course, as they will have started to adjust to your own storage conditions." He sighed.

I ignored him. He could harp on about the time as often as he liked, I doubted it would've made any difference anyway. I followed Sam Chapman to the kitchen and washed my hands in the round sink next to the door. It was well labelled as a sink designated for hand washing only, and they had the hygienic soap and drying facilities. This guy knew the rules.

"Here you go Clara, take a butcher's at them lot," said Sam, gesturing towards the fridges – one for raw produce, one for storing cooked food. "All delivered fresh this morning."

I removed my probe thermometer from my bag, and some disinfectant wipes. I needed to check the core temperatures, to ensure all the food had been kept at below 5°C.

Most food poisoning cases were linked to 'temperature abuse', where the food had been stored for a period of time between 5°C and 63°C, giving opportunity for pathogens to multiply. Even if the food was then refrigerated, the bacteria wasn't killed, and unless it was thoroughly cooked later, it would make people sick. It wasn't always possible to keep food below the correct temperature, especially when travelling from shop to fridge, but if the time was less than four hours, it was still considered safe. So you see, checking temperatures was an important, if boring, part of the job. I checked with flourish, making sure Curry was noticing.

I plunged the probe into various cheeses, vats of butter, and a few lumps of meat. I was careful to disinfect it thoroughly between each food, because Sam was watching. Everything seemed fine. I asked him how often he checked the temperatures.

"When it first arrives, course. Then every day, first fing when I gets 'ere in the mornin'. Got me own fermometer in the fridge, see? Don't just trust what the fridge says. Then we check stuff when it cooks, make sure it's hot enuff."

"What do you heat it to?" I asked, making notes on my form.

"More'n 70°C for least two minutes," he said, quoting from the food safety manual. "Usually nearer 90 though, least for some cuts. We keep the hot cupboard at 65, for food that has to wait a bit. And we only keep stuff hot for a couple hours, then we chuck it all away." He grinned, happy to be showing he knew the rules.

I smiled back. It never hurt to have a friend who could feed you for free.

"And how often do you calibrate your equipment?" I asked.

His eyes flickered at the innuendo, but he kept things professional.

"Every week," he said. Which I suspected was a lie, but didn't bother to challenge it. "We shove the fermometer into boiling water for a few secs, then later into ice. Check it measures at 100 and zero."

"And if you need to cool and store food you've cooked?" I asked, moving down my list. "How would you do that?"

"Cool it to less'n 5 degrees, in less'n two hours."

He knew his theory, I had to give him that. I could see why even Mr Mean Curry gave him a five-star hygiene rating each year.

Curry joined us, and began to examine the handles of cupboards, behind the rubbish bin, checking everything looked clean. There were a stack of coloured chopping boards in the corner, with a large sign next to them, explaining what each colour represented – white board for cheese and dairy, brown board for vegetables, red for meat. He checked they were washed at the correct temperature to sterilise them, and opened the square dishwasher to peer inside.

Eventually, he was satisfied. The Bistro exhibited strong management and good procedures. They could keep their five stars. We shook hands with Sam again, told him the next inspection would probably be a random, unannounced one, and left.

As we drove away, Curry said again what a shame it was that we had missed being present for when the delivery arrived. I hummed a tune until we reached the office and I could get back to my own work.

***

The following Sunday, I arrived at the church a few minutes before the service started. The rest of the music group were there, of course, and I joined them at the front.

"Right, glad you made it, Clara," said Sadie. "Did you forget we were starting at 9.00? To practise?"

She was working hard to keep her voice even, to not snap at the new recruit. But it was obvious she was cross. If I hadn't been the newbie, she might even have said I couldn't play as I hadn't been there. She had something steely about her, under that 'I'm a good Christian' exterior. She wasn't used to being messed with. I wondered how far I would need to push for her to explode completely. Probably not very far at all.

I considered looking upset, so she felt bad. But I really couldn't be bothered. I shrugged and began to unpack my clarinet. She sighed, I'm guessing the whole church heard it, but she didn't say anything more.

"Lovely to see you Clara," said Melissa, keen to cover the awkwardness, to let me know that it was okay, no one else was cross. Like I would have cared. "Are you feeling confident, or do you want me to do a quick run through with you in the hall, before we start?" she offered.

I told her I'd be fine.

When the clarinet was assembled I chose a chair in the front row, right in the middle, and sat down. I held my clarinet on my knee, and bowed my head. Anyone watching (which would be everyone, I had chosen my spot deliberately) would assume I was praying. A humble soul, asking her God to help her play her best. Actually, I was reciting songs and doing my best to keep still until I could be certain most people would have noticed. I ran through the names of the group in my head – it looked caring to remember people's names, and they were the sort who would remember mine. I didn't want to look less caring than them. There was tall, blond Jennifer, with the silent flute. Chubby Kimberley with the rainbow guitar. Brian bendy mouth. Ancient Melissa. Bald John. The large girl with curly hair and a cello must be Julie. Yep, I had them all clear in my head. I counted to thirty, then raised my head, walked humbly (if such a thing is possible) to my position next to Melissa. I figured they would now all know I was a holy being, one who was serious about her religion. Important to play games according to the rules. At least initially.

The service was long and boring. Uncle was right, Rob Pritchard did go on for too long. But I was good at patience, and playing the music helped to break up the service a bit, made it less boring. I looked at the congregation while I played, sorting out who was married to who, looking unsuccessfully for Master Leather Jacket, and wondering why so many people brought such young kids to a church service. Hardly the place for kids, I'd have thought.

Though at one point we did have the religious equivalent of a Punch and Judy act. I've been in other churches where it happens, it is very weird. There were some words said by Rob: "Praise the Lord," followed by a response from the audience: "Hallelujah, God is good". Rob then smiled round, told us that we "could do better than that" and we all repeated the charade but much louder. This obviously appealed to a couple of dodgy types, who pretty much shouted the words, most people just repeated them slightly louder, feeling embarrassed. No idea what the point was. Did they think God was a bit deaf? Or perhaps it was intended to whip the crowd into a frenzy of emotion that would then carry on through the service. It didn't work. Like I said, it felt like a religious version of a puppet show, and I was tempted to shout out "He's behind you!" But I didn't, too early for jokes. It was very bizarre.

Of course, with hindsight, I can see how that particular sentence would actually have been appropriate, rather than a joke. But I didn't know that then. Back then the whole thing seemed stupid and meaningless.

Halfway through the service, there were notices of events, given out in a similar way to a town crier would have done a hundred years ago. These people obviously didn't trust themselves to read emails or a news-sheet like normal people do. The person speaking droned on for ages, telling them what events were planned for the week ahead. Most were boring meetings, like coming to church once a week wasn't enough (am guessing these people had no social life beyond the church, their only contact with other humans was with those who shared all the same beliefs as they did). They also tried to entice people into some 'do-gooder' activities. So you could help make cakes for old people, or provide a meal for someone who had come out of hospital, or go on a rota to clear gardens for the elderly people in the town. I suppose it made them feel good, to be seen to be doing stuff in the community. Sort of free advertising for the church. It did show the potential of the place though. Perhaps later, when my plans started to come into fruition I would request help for clearing Uncle William's garden. Would save some money.

When it came to my duet with the violin, I stepped forwards slightly, so I was easily seen. I played beautifully, with eyes shut, so everyone could see how sincere I was, how moved by the emotion of the music. They didn't clap at the end. Perhaps too early for that. But as I finished, I smiled at Uncle William, who was basking in the knowledge that his niece was the best musician. It was a good start.

The service ended with prayer. I stayed in my seat, head bowed, until most people had left to find coffee or go home. I felt someone sit beside me, and looked up to see Rob had joined me. Result. I kept my face lowered, but smiled up at him.

"You okay?" he asked, all vicarial charm and concern.

I kept my voice very low, so he had to bend closer to hear.

"Yes, thanks Rob. I just found that service very moving. It really spoke to me." (I was hoping he didn't ask me to elaborate, to say which particular part. I hadn't been listening that intently.) "I have lots of question though. Could I talk to you sometime? Go through a few things?"

I figured he would have time set aside for private conferences, probably a nice quiet study tucked away somewhere. Perfect for getting to know each other better.

"That's great Clara," he said, "and it would be great to talk some more. We have a discussion group actually, on Tuesday evenings. Perhaps you could come to that? I know you'd find them a welcoming bunch. It's a safe place for people to ask questions and sort out what they believe. 'No question too dumb.' Why don't you come along, give it a try?"

Because that was NOT what I'd had in mind. But I couldn't say that. Not yet. I smiled my thanks, and told him I would try to be there (whilst knowing there was no way I would attend such a group of losers. Ever.) Then I gathered my things and left.

Chapter Eight

I guess it was about three months later that I began to see some results, to move things on a little. I had been regularly visiting Uncle William, usually baking, or taking gifts of fresh fruit, flowers – things he would be missing since Susan died. He was becoming used to me being there, I could tell because we didn't talk all the time, he was beginning to feel comfortable just sitting, being in the same room as me. Sometimes he would read the newspaper when I was there, giving his view on the articles. Sometimes he would tell me about his bowls club, or some news from the town. I think he was saving up things to tell me – when something happened in his narrow world, I was the person he told. It was boring, but I was good at keeping quiet, looking like I was interested.

Church was also progressing nicely. I played regularly in the services, and up until then, had also attended the midweek practices. This was unnecessary, and I was planning to stop as soon as I was sure they relied on my skills for the Sunday sessions. Sadie was a bitch and wouldn't like it, but I figured I could get rid of her and lead the music myself. That would take a little more time though.

Master Leather Jacket had never reappeared, so I was concentrating my efforts on Rev Rob. We could probably be classified as friends. I was still seeing other blokes of course, it's not like I was limiting myself. But enticing Rob into a clandestine relationship would be a lot of fun. A test for my skills, if you like. It was time to move that on a notch. I decided I needed to make some sort of commitment to the church, so I was seen as 'one of them', lower his guard a bit. The solution seemed to be membership.

Now, you might think, as I did, that if you regularly attended a church, you were a member – same as with scouts or a football team. But no. There is another stage. To actually be 'on the inside', you have to go through a formal process and be voted in. Yes, a bit like running for a political party! First you have to let someone already on the inside know that you want to be a member. This makes them all very excited, as it proves they are doing everything right. Then they select two people to interview you in private. They wanted to invade my house, and talk to me there. Well, I wasn't having that – goodness knows what my family would've told them. I explained that it was very difficult, my family weren't sympathetic, perhaps I could be interviewed at the church? They weren't satisfied with that, obviously wanted to nose into my private life, which confirmed I had made the right decision. They asked if they could perhaps arrange to meet me at Uncle William's. That seemed to solve the problem, and helped me move things along nicely with him, so I said I would ask. I asked him when I visited the following Tuesday.

I had called in after work, taking fish and chips and a bottle of whiskey. Uncle was rather partial to whiskey, though he rationed himself very strictly, and I'd never seen him drink more than one tiny glass at a time. He didn't much like fish and chips, but I'd told him I would bring supper and I couldn't be bothered to cook. I didn't pay for fish and chips. On a previous visit, I don't remember now who I'd been with, I had spotted a delivery of fish in a bucket on the floor, and even though it was in a washable container and was fine, they obviously didn't know that. They quickly moved it – with all the bacteria on the underside – onto the clean work surface. Which made it not fine, and I had seen. I told them not to worry, I wouldn't mention it to the person I was shadowing, it needn't be included in our report. Of course, that meant from then on, we were friends, the owner and I. Fish and chips were free whenever I wanted them. The whiskey had come from the little corner shop I told you about earlier. A good value supper all round.

I warmed a couple of plates in the oven and set the table. No need to be sloppy, just because the food was easy. Uncle William was talking about politics, ranting about some new tax they were planning to introduce. Something that would eat up all his savings, which he'd already paid tax on when he earned it, so hardly fair. I nodded from time to time, not really listening. I found ketchup in the fridge, and searched the cupboard for vinegar. It was right at the back, and looked pretty old, but I figured it was a preservative, it would be okay. His salt and pepper sat on the table, but the salt mill was empty, so I refilled it with crystals from the cupboard. Then I filled two glasses with water, sat them next to empty tumblers for the whiskey, and carried the food to the table.

The grease had seeped through the paper, and the chips were soggy. But it was okay. It was hot and filled us up, and made him stop talking briefly. He ate with his mouth open, which was disgusting, but I never mentioned it. Even when he stored food in the side of his mouth, like a chipmunk, so he could carry on talking. I absorbed all his disgustingness. I was biding my time.

"That wasn't too bad," said Uncle, spearing the last tiny chips with his fork and dunking them into the ketchup. "It's a long time since I had fish and chips. Your aunt Susan never liked them, said they were too full of saturated fats."

That didn't do her much good, I thought, but I smiled at him and nodded.

"Actually Uncle William, there's something I wanted to ask you," I said.

"Oh yes?" he said. He sounded defensive. Annoying, I had hoped we were past that by now.

I lowered my head and fiddled with my napkin, as if embarrassed to be asking.

"It's the church, you see. I would like to become an official member. But they have to interview me first, and I'm not sure about them coming home. You know what Mum and Dad are like, they're bound to try and join in. And they don't understand about church, not like you do."

He nodded. "No, they don't. The trouble with the Anglican Church, is it encourages too many people who attend out of duty. They go because they think they should. It's lost its way rather, it stands for tradition and stability, but it's not about God anymore."

I didn't disagree. Nor did I point out that the Baptist Church was also not about God anymore (if it ever had been). It was about social interaction and being part of the community and having friends who all believed the same things. It was about singing jolly songs and pretending everything was brilliant. It was about ignoring old traditions and rules and making up new ones, which were adhered to just as strictly. It was about scalp-hunting, trying to entice as many people into the building as possible, to prove to themselves that their way was best. But it wouldn't have helped my cause to say that. Uncle William thought his was the right way to approach God, and I would go along with it while it suited my plans. Doesn't every religion think theirs is the *right* way? That everyone else has missed the point? They're all the same in my opinion. They're for people who can't cope on their own, so have decided the idea of a greater power, a God, is true. Then they make up rules and traditions, pretending this will please the God they have created. But their gullibility is useful, they just need the right person directing things. And eventually, that would be me. Eventually.

He was still talking. "I'm delighted that you want to be a member Clara. That's lovely. They will need to interview you, you're right there, to be sure you're joining for the correct reasons." He looked up, towards the window, as if thinking. "And of course, they will contact your previous church, to ask for a reference."

This was news to me. My previous church would be hard put to remember who I was, which did not give the impression I was trying to make.

"Oh, do they? What if someone doesn't have a previous church?"

"Well, that is often the case, of course," said Uncle. "If someone comes into the church for the first time, and becomes a Christian, makes a commitment for the first time. Then they become a member on the strength of that alone." He turned to look at me. "But I thought you had been involved at your parents' church?"

I needed to think fast. This changed things a bit, but wasn't something I couldn't solve. People are often vague about what you've told them, if you change the story they assume they misheard or were muddled. I am rarely accused of lying.

"No, not really, Uncle," I said. "As I said before, I never found St Peter's to be particularly inspiring, so I didn't go very often. It wasn't until you took me to Marksbridge" (Good to make him responsible, the one who saved me) "that I realised what it was all about."

He looked surprised. "So, you made a commitment recently? Became a Christian in the last few weeks?"

I wasn't quite sure what he meant by making a commitment. Surely I was making a commitment by becoming a member? I was quite good at 'church speak', having been dragged along from an early age, but sometimes even I wasn't quite sure what they meant. He knew I was a Christian. My parents had taken me to church since I was little. He knew that. I decided to just agree to everything. It was good practice for my interview.

(I was, to be honest, still coming to terms with the interview. It seemed completely bizarre, and it wasn't as if they were going to ban me if I didn't pass, so I wasn't sure what the purpose was. I understood why universities had interviews – to check the wannabe student was suitable. I knew my interview with the Chartered

Institute was imminent, before they would accredit me as an inspector. But a church? Were they deciding who could get into Heaven? Totally weird.)

I looked up at Uncle William and nodded. "Yes."

He reached out, squeezed my hand.

"Well done, dear, I hadn't realised. How lovely." His voice wasn't quite steady, and I was surprised to see tears flood his eyes. He gave me a watery smile.

I smiled back. Silly fool.

Of course, Uncle William was totally up for letting me use his house for the interview. It even made him look good, like he was the one responsible for returning the lost sheep to the fold, all that stuff churchy people like to think about. I phoned Rob (only the church office, hadn't managed to get his mobile number yet) and arranged a time.

***

They interviewed me a week later. Rob came himself, which showed promise, and one of the deacons. (The deacons were sort of like under-managers, they helped run things, and were mostly old men. I hadn't yet worked out how much power they had, but if it was significant, I might decide to join their numbers. Easier to mould things from the inside.)

I met them after work. Uncle William was waiting when I arrived. He led me to the kitchen, and pointed to a rectangular parcel on the kitchen table. It was wrapped in paper covered in pink spots, and had one of those shiny adhesive bows stuck to the top.

"That's for you," he said, pointing. "I was very touched by your news, and wanted to mark the occasion. I wasn't sure if you had one."

It was a Bible. As if I needed another one. I had one from when

I was little, a prize from one of the groups I'd been forced to attend. Though I wasn't sure where it was now.

"Oh, Uncle William, that's very kind." I said, and moved to kiss his cheek. That always made him awkward – though actually he was looking uncomfortable anyway, giving gifts wasn't really his thing, mean old man.

"Yes, well, as I said, I wasn't sure if you had one, or what translation it would be. There are different kinds, you see. They all have the same message, but some are rather difficult to understand as they were translated centuries ago and the language is unusual. This is a more recent translation, I think you'll find it easier.

"You should read it often Clara. It will help you. Don't start at the beginning, that's the Old Testament – some bits are rather difficult. You should begin reading the New Testament. Perhaps the Book of Luke. I have marked it for you, look." He took the book from me, showed me a bookmark placed towards the back.

The book opened, showing rows of tiny print on thin paper. It would make for good cigarette paper, should I ever take up smoking and decide to roll my own.

I assured him I would read it. Then suggested I should prepare for my interview.

I had taken some smart clothes to change into, because I wanted them to think I was serious, and I asked Uncle if I could change in one of the bedrooms. He told me to use Alexsander's old room.

I went up the wooden staircase, dusty since Susan had died, and along the landing to Alexsander's room. I hadn't been in there for more than a decade.

The room smelled musty, I doubted anyone ever went in there now. Dust motes danced in the evening sun that streamed through the window and I stood and looked around. His bed was pushed against one wall, unmade but covered with a cream counterpane. Next to it was a small chest of drawers, the top covered with tiny plastic soldiers. There was a wardrobe, which proved to be still full of his clothes, and a larger set of drawers, also full. I had a quick rummage, but didn't find anything of value, not even a few coins. Socks neatly folded into pairs, underpants lying flat. Shorts and sweaters and tee-shirts. All clean and folded, I assumed by Aunt Susan after he left.

There was a desk, but no useful information. It had the sort of things my aunt would've deemed suitable for a desk. A globe, a pot of pens, a notepad, some paperclips. No old receipts, no screwed up notes, no books with corners folded down. I wondered if it had ever been used. Alexsander would've been more into porn than notebooks. I doubted I would find any of that – Susan would have burnt it all, or thrown it out, double-bagged so it couldn't contaminate her rubbish.

There were no clues to where my cousin was now. Nothing. I wondered if he was even alive. I changed into a skirt and top. The skirt was short, it would show off my legs nicely, which would be useful if I needed to distract them. The top was modest, high-necked and long-sleeved and unpatterned. But it clung rather nicely, they would see my shape, curves in the right places. I stared in the mirror for a while, decided against makeup. Then I sat on the bed. I didn't really want to go down before they arrived, I didn't want to have to talk to Uncle. It was okay when I popped in with something to do, when I could more or less ignore him and get on with something more interesting. But to sit for ten minutes while he droned on, just waiting? Not really me.

I sat on the bed. You could smell the dust, the stale, shut-away air. I had flung the book there that Uncle had given me, intending to leave it in the room. He probably never went in there, it would save having to take it home. For want of anything better to do, I opened it at the chapter he'd marked and skimmed the words. A story caught my eye, of a shepherd looking for a lost sheep. I remembered that story – I expect you know it too, it was one they liked to tell to children, the one about some negligent shepherd, searching for a sheep that was lost. It was with a couple of other stories about lost things, a coin and a boy. The boy reminded me of Alexsander, though I'm not sure they used drugs in those days. I also doubted he'd be arriving back home either, or that Uncle William would be delighted to see him if he did. Perhaps I could include it in my interview somewhere, show I was a Bible scholar.

I closed the book with a slam. I had forgotten how simplistic it was, stories for kiddies. I guessed Christians were basically like kids, they took things at face value, which would make them beautifully easy to mould. Like sculpting butter, but so much more fun.

I went downstairs when I heard the doorbell. Uncle William was in the hall, welcoming Rob and a man I recognised from church. He was the town crier substitute, the one who read out lists of events each Sunday. His name was Kevin Matthews.

Uncle William suggested we use the study. It was a little room at the end of the hall, overlooking the garden. Another underused dust-covered room. He really should've employed a cleaner but was too stingy. That would change when I lived there. We sat in chairs facing each other. Uncle left, closing the door behind him.

I smiled at the two men, keeping my chin ducked down, as if I was shy. They started the meeting with a prayer. Christians liked to pray before meetings I found. I guess it was sort of invoking their God, passing responsibility. Then they could say and decide whatever they liked, and blame it on God afterwards if it went wrong. They had prayed about it, so surely God would direct their thoughts, and anything they consequently decided must have divine authority. People are good at self-deception. As Rob prayed I made 'churchy' noises, whispered "Yes Lord" at regular intervals, so they both knew I was agreeing, was holy. It also saved me the trouble of having to make up a prayer myself, I was thoroughly involved in Rob's.

I won't bore you with the interview details. They asked about why I wanted to join the church, what I believed, when I'd made a commitment, things like that. It was easy, because I'd had the practice session with Uncle.

I changed my mind about the whole 'recent conversion' thing though. If Uncle thought it was important enough that he would actually go to a shop and spend money, I was guessing other people might also make a big deal of it. I didn't want to be told I needed to attend some kind of beginner's group or something. I wanted to look experienced. So I told them I had 'made a commitment' when I was very young, but had never found a church that had sound teaching. (Quick smile at Rob when I said that, let him think I admired him.) I fuddled the names of which churches I had attended. If they did decide to check, it would take them a while, by which time I would already be a member. I thought that if things didn't add up later, they would be unhappy about making a fuss, asking me to clarify. I couldn't believe they would ever throw out a member, not for something as insignificant as being inventive with the truth during an interview. It would be dismissed as evidence of nerves.

They wanted to know what I had been involved in, in the past. I told them my favourite story was the one about the lost sheep, about how it must've been hard work for that shepherd to carry it all the way back into the flock. I rambled on for a while. It wasn't what they'd asked about, but they were too polite to interrupt me, and it used up the time nicely and made me appear knowledgeable and affected by their silly book. We skimmed over my family, what my parents thought, my involvement in other churches. I had attended churches often enough to blag my way through, and I concentrated on things I was confident about, my clarinet playing and how much I wanted to use my gifts in the church. I told them

I had led the music in one of my previous churches, and when they asked which one, I talked about the style of music and the difficulty of introducing different instruments. It was easy to muddle them, to speak for long enough that they forgot what question I was meant to be answering. It may have come across as muddled, but again, they would put that down to nerves, and the general impression was that I was an established church goer, who had knowledge of their Bible, and I wanted to join their membership. That was all they needed.

I told them about my job, about how important it was for people to prepare food hygienically. Their eyes lit up at that, I could see they were putting me on their catering committee, another worker for the church anthill. I brushed over the question about whether I was in a relationship. It was none of their business and might have disrupted my plans for Rob. They hardly wanted to hear that I'd had a very nice night last night with a bloke called Rory, and that last week I'd been sleeping with Tomas from the corner shop while his wife was away. I looked down when they asked, said I hadn't found the right person yet. They moved on.

The interview lasted longer than I'd expected, but eventually they left. They thanked me for my time, told me they'd be recommending me to the membership and would let me know what was decided. There had to be the vote, of course, but they were hardly likely to reject me. Like I said before, scalp-hunting was a feature of Baptist churches, and they liked to add to their numbers, it showed success.

***

When I next saw Uncle, I was crying. Well, okay, I wasn't *actually* crying, I hadn't done that since I was tiny. But he thought I was. Crying is easy, a simple matter of biology. It helps if you have some time to yourself, and can scream or shout for a bit, which strains the vocal chords and gives you a nice husky voice. Or you can just lower it a bit, try to speak an octave lower, which also makes you sound gruff. The tears bit are also simple. Stare at something, preferably a light source, for a few seconds without blinking, and your eyes will water. You don't need many tears to look convincing. Then you just sniff a lot, turn away like you're embarrassed, apologise for being a nuisance, and there you have it. Someone who's upset enough to cry is always listened to and usually believed. You can't use it too often of course, but a few well-placed tears can save a lot of time and are a huge help when wanting to win an argument or persuade someone into something.

I felt the whole emotional, Bible gift-giving advice stuff had been a good sign. I thought I could probably begin to move my plan along a bit.

So, after the next music practice, when he wouldn't be expecting me, and would therefore be slightly off balance, I called round to see Uncle William. I banged on the door, rather than using the bell, which would also give him a shock, add to the air of upset. He took a long time to answer, and I wondered if he'd gone to bed already. He fiddled with the chain before opening the door, but removed it when he saw it was me.

"Clara! I wasn't expecting... are you alright? Whatever's the matter?"

"Sorry, Uncle William," I said, sniffing, "I didn't have anywhere else to go..."

He drew me into the house, closed the door behind me, then stood there, awkward. He wasn't given to physical contact, and he wasn't quite sure how to react. Here was his niece, who had shown herself to be useful and good company, crying in his hall. He had no idea what to do next. It was easy to take charge.

"Can we sit somewhere for a bit? Would you mind?" I said,

walking towards the lounge. We never went into the lounge, I wasn't sure even he used it now. But it was comfortable and meant I could curl up and look forlorn. The kitchen was a bit too well-lit for my acting abilities.

I curled up on one of the ghastly gold sofas and pulled out a tissue, pretending to blow my nose.

"What's happened my dear? Are you hurt?"

"No, no, nothing like that," I said. I looked away from him as if embarrassed, stared hard at the lamp, ignoring the sting as my eyes fought to blink. The tears formed quickly, easing the itch and adding to my performance. I turned back to him, sniffing again, letting him see my wet eyes. "It's my parents," I whispered, as a teardrop toppled from my eye and slid down my cheek. "I don't think I can live there anymore, and I don't know where to go. I don't have enough money to buy anywhere myself."

I was speaking quietly, so he had to bend towards me to hear.

There was a pause. He was thinking.

"You need a drink," he said at last. "Wait here."

He came back with two glasses and the whiskey bottle. It was still almost full. He poured single measures, and passed me a glass. "Drink that, you'll feel better."

We didn't speak while we drank. When his glass was empty I leaned forward and refilled both glasses, pouring a generous measure into each. He didn't stop me.

"I don't know what to do," I whispered, adding a shudder for effect.

"Tell me what happened," he said.

This was the tricky bit. If I got it wrong, he would insist on phoning his brother, telling him to take me back. Which would ruin everything completely, as my father wouldn't have the first idea what he was talking about, I hadn't seen my parents for about a week. I needed to play on his emotion, to pull at that bit of him that saw me as useful, as his own, as someone he wanted close. So he would devise a plan that suited him, a way to keep me conveniently near. I needed to appeal to the big brother who liked to be in charge, who would solve the problem his younger sibling had failed with so completely. It must be me and him on the same side, against a common foe. So I started with the church.

Speaking at barely a whisper, so he was leaning close, and topping up his drink so he relaxed, I explained what had happened. How being part of the church was changing me, how my parents were rejecting everything I now believed in, how they were angry I had joined a church different to their own, which they said was verging on a sect with the things it was teaching. I talked about my brothers, who frequently invaded my room, so I had nowhere quiet to work, to read, to pray. How they ridiculed my faith and tried to change my mind. How I wasn't strong enough to cope with their attacks, how I could feel myself slipping back into the old way of thinking.

"I just don't know what to do," I said. "They want me to move out, but I don't have anywhere to go. Not even for a few days, until I get sorted…"

Clumsy and unsubtle? Yes, I know. But as I said, a few tears add a lot of credibility. Plus, he was an old man, it was time for him to go to bed, and he was drinking more than he was used to.

He stood, taking his whiskey with him. He stood facing the empty fireplace. I watched his back, could almost feel him thinking, deciding what to do. He turned.

"Well, of course, you could stay here for a few days. Until we've decided what's for the best…"

I shook my head. "No, Uncle. That is very kind of you, but I couldn't put you to the bother. Don't worry, I'll find something. There's a friend in Birmingham, he might let me crash on his floor for a bit. Or I can go to a hostel, or something."

"Clara, I insist," he said, frowning. If I moved away he would lose his companion. And I wouldn't be joining his church, which had raised his status a bit amongst the other fogeys. And what would he tell the leadership? That my parents had thrown me out and although he lived in a mansion, he had allowed me to go and live on a friend's floor? That wouldn't make him look good. Not very Christian.

I smiled up at him. All humble gratitude and relief.

"Thank you Uncle William. That's so kind of you. I won't be any bother, I promise."

***

I moved in the next day. No point in waiting. I persuaded Rory (the one-night stand) to give me a hand with his van, and loaded my stuff into it during the morning, when everyone else was at work. I was meant to be checking a place in East Gramstead, but no one would know I hadn't, I could even submit a report from memory and if everything was marked as fine, no one would query it.

Uncle William was a bit shocked when he opened the door, I could see by his face. But there wasn't much he could say, especially not with a stranger standing there. He suggested I used the spare room. It wasn't the nicest bedroom, but it would do temporarily. I thanked him profusely, and told Rory to put all my stuff up there while I made tea.

Chapter Nine

Everything was falling into place nicely, though there were a few problems along the way. The next few months passed smoothly enough. I had my interview with the Chartered Institute of Environmental Health and obtained my accreditation. This enabled me to inspect premises on my own, which was hugely beneficial. I found my identity card to be of tremendous use, even if I was in an area not covered by my authority. I would show my card as soon as a restaurant showed me to a table. I would explain that I wasn't there 'for business', but I was due to inspect their premises in a few weeks, and thought I would eat there first, to check things from the customer's side. I asked the waiter to not mention this to the management, knowing that of course, that is the very first thing they did. I then received excellent service, and usually a vastly reduced bill. Of course, if I spotted anything at all that could be mentioned in a report, I would ask to speak to the management, suggest that I could ignore it and not include it when I did my report in a few weeks' time. I never suggested this would mean my meal was free, but they weren't stupid. I never paid.

I expect you're wondering if I ever helped things along, took a cockroach in a matchbox, something like that. To be honest, I couldn't be bothered, and I wasn't prepared to risk losing my job. It would've been too obvious, they may have got shirty and made a fuss. Best to keep people sweet and pretend you're playing by the rules.

This didn't work so well with Sadie. Things came to head sooner than I would've liked.

My first problem was her insistence that she should have my mobile number. I do not give that to people like Sadie. She had asked for it, after that first rehearsal, so she could "let me know if there are any changes." Of course, I gave her the wrong number. She cornered me after the service a few weeks later, said she had been trying to contact me, but the number she had didn't work.

"Here's *my* number," she said, passing me a slip of paper with her number scrawled across it. "Why don't you put it into your phone now, and then send me a text? That way I'll get the right number."

We were standing in a group, other people were listening as they sipped the awful coffee the church served. I couldn't see a way to refuse, not without everyone noticing.

I typed the number into my phone, and sent a text. Sadie checked, but nothing arrived. Nothing was going to arrive, I had typed a different number. I began to move away.

"Texts seem to get stuck en route sometimes, " I said. "I think they go via the moon some days! I'll just get a coffee, then come back and see if it's there."

"No," said Sadie.

I turned. She was staring at me, her eyes shrewd. I stared back. I was unwilling to make a scene, that would've ruined a few other plans. But I decided at that moment that she would no longer be leading the music group.

"No," repeated Sadie, "I'm concerned you might be having trouble with the numbers. Here, give me your phone, let me see what you typed.

"I really think this is important Clara. If ever I need to change the schedule, it's important I can get hold of you. Right? You get it? I don't want you to turn up if we've changed things, stuff like that."

She reached for my phone. I was not going to give it to her. I showed her the screen.

"Right, well that's not my number," she said. "Here, I'll read it out, you type it in. Zero, seven, seven, one...." She watched, checking each number as I typed.

I sent a text. Her phone pinged. She grinned up at me.

"Right, well that seemed to work. Good. Now we can contact each other."

I moved away. If we hadn't had an audience, I could've behaved differently, but she had managed to trap me. She would be sorry.

My next problem with Sadie was when I stopped attending rehearsals. There was no point going unless it was going to further my game with Rob, and there were no opportunities to be alone with him.

I had tried a few things, like feigning a broken car. I made sure I was out of petrol as I arrived at the car park, inching it along as the petrol gauge turned past the red empty mark, nursing it as it choked at junctions, just making it into the church car park.

At the end of the practice, I had walked out with Rob, and was chatting to him as I got into the car, was still laughing at a shared joke through the window as I turned the engine, listened to it cough and die. He had no option but to come over and offer to help. We could've got to know each other better after the others had left, possibly he would have driven me home, or to a garage if he worked out what was wrong. We'd have been alone, I could have flirted more openly, strengthened the bond between us.

But John turned out to be a mechanic. He saw I was having problems, hurried over, and was only too happy to help. I soon realised the rehearsals were not the place for private chats, so I stopped going.

Sadie phoned me.

She said she was concerned that I never attended the rehearsals, and she didn't think it was a good idea for me to continue playing in the services, as it wasn't fair on the rest of the group. I was livid. I ended the call.

I continued to play, of course. I didn't think she would want a big public debate, so there wasn't much she could do about it. Each Sunday, I turned up just before the service began, unpacked my clarinet, and took my place next to Melissa. Sadie scowled, but never said anything. I'm sure she was muttering behind my back, telling everyone how difficult it was that I didn't attend the rehearsals, that I wasn't a team player. But there wasn't much she could say publicly. I was the best musician. I didn't need to rehearse.

I often took the lead during services, sometimes stepping forwards as a song ended, playing an extra melody. I would stand there, eyes shut, swaying gently, as if lost in the moment. Sometimes I played something complicated, that I had practised at home during the week. Something to impress. Occasionally Melissa or Julie would join in – they were both accomplished enough to keep up, but I was clearly the leader. I was the one lost in the Spirit, leading the church, building the emotion. Sometimes I played for several minutes, messing up the timing for the rest of the service unless they cut something they had prepared. I looked very holy. I liked everyone to see how spiritual I was.

Sadie didn't say much. Occasionally she would try to be gracious, to tell me I had played beautifully. But her eyes gave her away. Inside, she was fuming. I know she wished she had never invited me to play in the first place.

The other person who was beginning to have regrets was Uncle William. He was not happy with the living arrangements. I think he started to have doubts a couple of days after I'd moved in. My father had phoned him while I was work. He mentioned the call when I got home.

"Clara, your father phoned me this afternoon," he said.

"Oh yes?" I said, filling the kettle at the tap. I wanted tea, I was tired. I added enough water for one cup. If he wanted some, he could make his own, lazy old man. He got home from work before me, he should've been offering to make me a drink, not sitting at his table watching me, like I was some kind of servant. There would need to be some adjustments.

"Yes," he said, "and I am somewhat confused. Your father phoned to ask if I knew where you were. He knows, of course, that you often pop in, I've mentioned it before. I'm not sure he realised how frequently, but it was an obvious place to begin searching. He was surprised you had left. Your mother went into your room and found it empty. Clara, did you not tell them you were moving out? I thought they had asked you to leave?"

This was a conversation I wasn't having. I poured boiling water over a teabag and stirred it, watching the dark liquid ooze out, discolouring the water, changing it almost instantly. I flipped the bag into the sink and added milk to my mug, then walked out the kitchen.

"He lies," I said as I walked away. "You know he does."

***

As time passed, Uncle became increasingly unhappy. Gradually he began to suggest that I should look for somewhere else, said the arrangement wasn't working. It was working fine from where I was standing.

I had moved into Alexsander's old room. It was bigger than the spare room, and had its own bathroom. I had shoved all his stuff into black bags, and put them out for the dustman. Uncle William had seen them, looked inside and acted all distraught, like he believed his son might come home one day. That wasn't going to happen, even if Alexsander was alive, which I doubted. I think Uncle moved them into the loft. They weren't by the bins next time I walked past them anyway.

I had been living there about eleven months, when Michael came begging. I only mention it because it was such a cheek! We'd never exactly got on, the twins were too young to bother with really. But when he heard I had moved in with Uncle, he saw an opportunity for himself. I was just getting settled. Alexsander's room was much better now I'd added an easy chair and some bookshelves, and Rory had promised to help me install a few extra power sockets.

Anyway, I was just leaving the office one afternoon, when Miranda told me a man was waiting to see me. I asked her to get his name. Sometimes I have trouble with the odd bloke who thinks a one night stand means I owe him something, that we're in a relationship. I don't do relationships. It was fine though, she came back and told me it was Michael. He followed me to my car.

"Hi Sis, thought I'd drop by to see you. How're you getting on with Uncle William?"

"Fine thanks," I said, throwing my bag into the boot.

"Yeah, well, I was wondering if you could put in a word for me."

I looked at him. He was tall, much taller than me. His blond hair had darkened to a light brown, and it tended to stick up at the back, especially when he was nervous. This was because he had a tendency to run his hand up the back of his head and over the top – a sort of reverse 'hair smooth'. He'd always done it, since he was tiny. He was doing it now, stroking his hair, up the back, across the top, smoothing down his fringe. I wondered what he wanted.

"What sort of word?" I asked.

"A 'please can I move in too' sort of word? – No stop, don't just walk off. It would help you too, I could help with the whole keeping Uncle Bill company thing. And I'd pay rent, help with housework.

"The thing is, I don't want to stay at home. Mum and Dad are driving me nuts to stay on at school. But I just want to paint. I'm good, really I am. I just need the right break, get an exhibition together and–"

I climbed in the car and slammed the door. I shook my head as I turned the key, starting the engine.

"Can you give me a lift?" he shouted through the door.

I waved as I drove away.

Honestly, what a nerve! I don't know why he thought he deserved a cushy number. Or why he thought I might help him. And an art exhibition? Him? He was just a kid.

Besides, I didn't think Uncle was exactly enjoying my company any more, he'd hardly want to extend his hospitality further. Now I had moved in, I'd stopped bothering with all those homely touches – if he wanted fruit or flowers, he could buy them himself. I wasn't his servant. He was also grumbling about the things I'd moved, and that my music was too loud. And I woke him when I came home late. And I didn't replace the milk if I finished it. And my friends made a mess when they visited.

Actually, Uncle William should have been grateful. The house was already much cleaner. I had employed an agency from Marksbridge. They had their own keys, and came every Monday to clean. At the moment, I was paying. Well, sort of paying. I did have my wages, of course, and now I was living with Uncle and eating mainly for free due to helpful clients, my costs were minimal. But I didn't think it was my place to pay, it was his house.

I'd had bit of a search one afternoon, when he was at work, and found Aunt Susan's jewellery box. She had left a few pieces in a drawer, and they were still there. I don't know why Uncle hadn't moved them, perhaps he liked to pretend she might come back too. Anyway, there were only a few pieces, the things she had worn quite often. The best bits, pieces I had never seen her wear, were in a box, on the top shelf of her wardrobe. Her clothes had all gone, but that shelf was stuffed with things Uncle had decided to keep. Their wedding album was there, and an old pair of shoes, a bag of greetings cards, things like that. Stuff someone might want to keep as reminders. Though why anyone would want to remember Aunt Susan was beyond me.

Her jewellery box was one of those inlaid wooden ones. Rather posh. It had a key, kept in the lock (not that the lock would've been hard to smash) and when you opened it, you smelled her. I guess the silk lining had absorbed her perfume over the years, and when you opened the box, even now, you were reminded of that citrus smell she'd always worn. I think it was grapefruit. But if you ignored that, the actual jewellery was worth having. There were rings and necklaces, a string of pearls, a couple of bracelets. Some looked old, perhaps she had inherited them. Some were newer, perhaps gifts from Uncle.

I had sold them at the pawn shop in Craddock. It wasn't called a pawn shop, they pretended they were a jewellers who bought second-hand stuff, but that's what they were. The price wasn't great, I probably got ripped off because I don't know much about jewellery. But I got enough to cover the cleaning, and plenty more to keep for myself. I thought I might treat myself to a nice holiday somewhere warm. And it wasn't even stealing, because by rights, that jewellery should all have been given to me. I was her niece. It was only meanness that stopped Uncle William giving it all to me when she died. It wasn't like Alexsander would wear it, was it? Even if he did show up.

***

When Uncle noticed the missing jewels, he was furious. It was a Monday. I have never seen him so angry. He was waiting for me when I got home, standing in the hall. As I went to put my key in the front door it opened. There he was, in the hall. Shaking.

"We need to talk, young lady," he said. "Please go into the lounge."

I walked in, and sat back on a chair next to the hearth. I kicked off my shoes, tucking my legs under me and moving the cushion so I could lean against it. I might as well be comfortable while he had his rant.

"Perhaps you could explain this," he said, placing the empty jewellery box on the side table.

I stared at it, as if confused. To be honest, I was surprised it had taken him so long to discover it was empty.

"It's a jewellery box," I said.

"I know that," he shouted, losing control. "What I want to know, is why is it empty, and where is the jewellery?"

I looked at him. "Er, I don't know? When did you last check it? Perhaps Alexsander came home and borrowed them."

He stopped at that. Thought about it for a minute. It was possible. Unlikely, but possible. He shut the box and sat down, as if deflated. For a few minutes, we sat in silence, him thinking, me waiting.

"No," he said at last. "No, I don't think so. Alexsander was never clever when he took money. He was always caught, never really cared. I think he was so desperate for his next fix he didn't think about anything else. If he had come here, into the house, I would have known. He would have been messy, left things in the wrong places. And he wouldn't have taken jewels, they would be too much trouble to dispose of. He'd have taken money, emptied my wallet." He shook his head, and I knew he was thinking about his son. There was less anger, more sorrow. It was like he had shrunk slightly.

He took a breath and looked back at me.

"No, Clara, I don't think we can blame Alexsander for this one. If he's..." he paused, not wanting to say it. "If he's still alive, then I don't suppose he's in a good way. I don't expect things have improved at all. He wouldn't be capable of doing something subtly.

"No Clara, I think you need to explain. You can explain to me, or we can involve the police. Please don't make the mistake of thinking that I wouldn't involve them. I spoke to them about my own son, I wouldn't hesitate to do the same with you."

He sat back and folded his arms, waiting for me to speak.

"Well, Uncle William, I don't think we want to involve the police," I said, smiling. "You see, by rights, that jewellery should've been mine. Aunt Susan always said she would let me have it.

"And besides, I have used the money for you, to make your home more comfortable. I've used it to pay the cleaners. I felt you had let the house go a bit. Now I'm here, to look after you, I wanted it to be comfy, nice and clean."

For a moment, he looked confused, I thought he had believed me. Then he shook his head.

"No Clara, you will have to do better than that. Susan would not have given you anything, certainly not those jewels. They had been in her family for generations, some of them were very valuable. Taking them was theft. I don't feel I have any option but to involve the police. Unless you can recover them, return them all to me by the end of the week, then I shall take matters further."

He stood. He had finished his prepared speech.

"And please find alternative living arrangements. I have spoken to your father, you can stay with your parents until something is sorted. I shall expect you gone by the end of tomorrow. You certainly moved in fast enough, it shouldn't be difficult doing the reverse."

I stood too. I was angry now. This was unacceptable.

"No Uncle William, I don't think you will be contacting the police," I said. "Not unless you want everyone to know the family secret. I'm sure all your work colleagues would be terribly interested, not to mention your church friends."

He frowned. "Not many people know about Alexsander, it's true. But Clara, I will not be threatened. If you decide to tell people, then go ahead. It will embarrass me for a few days, but it reflects badly on you, not me."

I laughed. "Not Alexsander! Joanna! I bet you've never mentioned her, have you?"

He was seriously confused now. "Who?"

I giggled, this was funny. He didn't even know! I sat back in my chair, enjoying myself.

"Sit down, Uncle. I have a story to tell you. One that I think you'll find rather interesting. But first, I have something I need to collect, we'll need it in a minute."

I jumped up, walked past him and went up to my room, taking the stairs two at a time. This had arisen earlier than I'd planned, so it was lucky I was prepared. I went to the back of my cupboard, behind my clothes, and pulled out the papers.

When I returned to the room, I don't think he had moved. He was just sitting there, looking confused.

I told him. I told him all about Joanna, about my mother growing up with her sister in care, about them being separated when they were still young.

I told him how I had discovered the letters and read about Joanna's crimes on the internet. I told him how she was still sometimes mentioned in the news, how the papers would love a little more gossip. How her story had never died.

I told him how I looked very like her, people would know I was telling the truth as soon as they saw me. And if he threw me out, I would need the money. I would go to the press, tell them about my mother, make up a few juicy details, create something they wouldn't be able to resist. It would all come out, including the relationship with my uncle, my wayward cousin, the bad genes on my mother's side.

"Now then, Uncle William," I said, turning to business. "I need you to sign these."

I moved the box onto the floor and spread the papers across the table. There were several of them, all in neat legal print. I had prepared them a few months ago, just in case. Of course, I hadn't expected to use them yet, possibly for years. But things had come to a head rather sooner than expected.

"What's all this?" said Uncle.

"Your Will," I said. "Or at least, your new one, I assume you have an old one, tucked away somewhere. I just need you to sign it for me. You'll see it has already been witnessed, I dealt with that part myself, but that will be our little secret. If you could just sign, and backdate it, to the same day as the witnesses. To keep it all legal…"

He glanced at the Will, shaking his head.

"I'm not signing that," he said, "I'm not stupid. Yes, you can tell the world your horrible story, and yes, it will embarrass me. It will be very awkward at work for a while I expect."

He leaned forwards, staring at me. His voice was hard.

"But Clara, it will fade. People will gossip, I will find it embarrassing. But it will pass. She isn't even a relative of mine, your poor mother will be the one who suffers the most.

"I retire soon anyway, and although it would be nice to leave with some dignity, I can cope. I am certainly not signing this– " he flicked the papers with the pen I had placed on top. "Not now, not ever."

"Of course, I would spice it up a little," I said with a smile. "What exactly would our relationship look like to the outside world, dear Uncle William?"

I ran my tongue across my lips and undid a button on my blouse. I leaned back on the chair, lifting my hair in my hands.

"Those bad Joanna genes, passed on to her niece, who was seduced by her evil uncle…" I smiled at him, then leaned forward, whispering in his face.

"Perhaps I could confide in someone, tell them how I was just a girl when you started to make advances.

"People would listen – especially with the Joanna link. It makes for a nice juicy story, one the tabloids would love. I'm betting I could make a nice little profit.

"So you think carefully, Uncle Dear, before you start making threats, because I don't think you would do so well out of it. People have very long memories when it comes to child abusers....

"Especially if they have religious connections, people are very keen to start talking about sects, deviant behaviours covered under a cloak of respectability...

"I have no intention of moving out, I'm very comfortable here. You need to sign those papers, or I will talk. I will go to every newspaper and television station I can find. I will get their interest by showing them the Joanna link, then go on to tell my own story. You will be seen as nothing but a dirty old man, scum. Everyone hates a child molester. Everyone. Don't think they won't believe me, I can be very convincing."

He stood. Then he sat.

For a while we both just sat, listening to the clock as it ticked away the seconds. It seemed very loud, a heartbeat.

Finally, he picked up the pen, and scribbled his name. I turned the paper and checked. He had signed his name.

He stood again. His eyes were shiny and his cheeks were purple. Small beads of sweat began to seep from his skin, making his face look as shiny as his eyes. I thought he might be going to vomit, but he didn't. He drew a breath, ragged and strained, as if his lungs were refusing to accept the same air as me. He staggered from the room. I heard him collect his coat from the hook in the hall, the rattle of keys as he picked them up from the table, then the slam of the door. He was gone.

I guessed he would drive around for a while, let off some steam.

Perhaps he would visit one of his church buddies, ask for some advice. But I doubted it. He would be too afraid of what they might think, of them not entirely believing his story. Mud always sticks. I knew, I had thrown enough in my time, and my aim was good.

I collected the papers and took them upstairs.

Of course, I soon realised I had made a mistake. I had acted in the heat of the moment, and possibly ruined my long term plan. As I calmed down a bit, I realised that already Uncle would be planning to visit his lawyer, probably phoning for an appointment while he drove. Tomorrow, he would draw up a new Will, making this one void. He might even take some legal advice, ask how he could evict me.

But I thought probably, that was okay. I figured I had managed to scare him into letting me stay, even if he did void the new Will. I had needed him to take me seriously, and I didn't think he would try too hard to evict me now. He would be too worried about the consequences.

It was a shame; I had been rushed into using the papers I had prepared so thoroughly, before I was properly ready. That happens sometimes – you make a good plan and then someone causes you to rush into something and ruin it. The Will would've worked if he'd been on his death bed, if in a few years' time I had played the devoted niece again, nursed him as he got weaker. The plan had always been to bide my time, to be patient until his health failed. Now it was wasted. Never mind, I would think of something else. I had plenty of time.

Chapter Ten

Now, I know I have done some terrible, terrible things. And I am not making excuses, truly I'm not. But please believe me when I tell you that I did not expect the next day to go as it did. I will admit, at the time, I felt nothing but elation, a bubble of disbelieving joy, a laugh-out-loud start of surprise. But I hadn't intended it. I hadn't even considered it a possibility.

Uncle William never came home.

I was woken soon after midnight by someone banging on the front door. I didn't move at first, I figured Uncle could answer it, it was his house. I was still sleeping well in those days, like most people I went to bed, slept, didn't expect anything untoward to happen. So I was thick with sleep and just wanted the noise to stop. But the banging continued, so I threw back the covers, grabbed a cardigan from the back of the chair and went on to the landing.

I could see the light through the window. Blue, flashing, like the whole landing was pulsating with some alien light. There was more banging, and another ring, as if someone was leaning on the bell. I turned on the landing light, so they could see I was awake, and went downstairs.

There were two of them, a man and a woman. They asked if they could come in, and I took them into the kitchen. I thought it might be a bit warmer in there, my legs were cold. We sat at the table, and once they'd sorted out who I was (as if Uncle might have been keeping a sex slave in the house or something) they told me what I had already guessed.

They suspected Uncle William had suffered a heart attack, while

120

driving at speed along the B2028. His car had wrapped itself around a tree, killing Uncle. No one else was involved.

Of course, that wasn't strictly true, but I didn't feel inclined to enlighten them.

Instead, I did my little girl shocked face. I stared hard at the ceiling light until I managed to get some tears, and pretended my twisting mouth was trying not to cry, rather than trying not to laugh. The shock bit was easy, because as I said, I really hadn't been expecting it. The policeman made some tea, the woman asked if I wanted her to call anyone. I shook my head, decided not to make the joke about getting people round for a party.

They asked lots of questions: when was the last time I'd seen him, was he worried about anything, had he been behaving normally. All the while, I was thinking about those papers in my bedroom. I would have to move them as soon as they left, try to find Uncle's keys for the safe, put the papers in there. It would be better if someone else found them, might look suspicious if it was me. It was easy to answer their questions, to explain everything had seemed normal, my uncle was happier now I was living there, now he had company and someone to cook for him. I explained how I was trying to keep the house a bit nicer, and gave them the name of the cleaning agency, just in case they decided to check. The timing would look good, make it seem like I had cared about him and was trying to help.

I asked where his body was, and they gave me the phone number. There would have to be a post mortem, as it was an unexpected death. Possibly an inquest. They would be in touch. It all sounded like a lot of hassle to me. Shame he hadn't waited until he was lying in bed, would've attracted a lot less attention. They told me I had to register the death, so I gave them my father's details. He was next of kin, he could do it.

Eventually they left. I went straight upstairs, found the papers

121

and hunted around for the keys to the safe. They were usually in a drawer in his desk, and this time they were next to his bed, but it didn't take long. The safe was full of pocket files, all neatly labelled. I had been in there many times before. I put the papers into a big brown envelope, sealed it, and shoved it in a section marked 'Private'. It was where his previous will had been. Seemed appropriate. Then I went back to bed. I was tired, and there was work the next day.

***

When I arrived home from work, my father was waiting. He was sitting in his car, and came across as I drew up. I nodded in his direction and went to unlock the house. My house. Though I would have to behave as a guest for a little longer. He followed me into the kitchen.

"You heard the news then?" I said.

He pulled out a chair and sat at the table. I wasn't intending to offer him tea, but I was thirsty, so I filled the kettle, then went and sat opposite him. He wasn't looking good. His eyes were heavy, and his skin had a grey tint to it. I wondered if he was going down with something. He looked at me, searching my face, trying to read my mood.

"I came to see how you are," he said.

"Me?" I was surprised. My health was fine, I hadn't lost my job or anything. "I'm fine. Why?"

He smiled, but it wasn't a happy smile. More a 'this girl never ceases to surprise me' smile.

"Clara, William died yesterday. You have been living here, I thought you might have grown fond of him. I thought you might have been upset."

"Oh, that," I said, going to make the tea. I decided to offer him a cup, it might seem more normal. My parents were always eager for me to appear normal. "Well, it was a bit unexpected, obviously. Actually, strictly speaking, he died today. The police came in the night to tell me. They were a strange couple." I described them, telling him how one was very thin, looked positively anorexic, perhaps being in the force didn't pay very well.

He didn't laugh. He didn't even smile (and it was quite a funny description, actually). He took the mug of tea I put in front of him and sipped it.

"Have you got any sugar?" he asked.

He always had sugar in his tea. There was some in the cupboard, but I'd already sat down with my own cup.

"No, sorry, I don't take it," I said.

We sat there, drinking tea, not speaking. I was wondering how long he'd stay for, if he would want to look round the house.

"The police came to me after they'd been here," he said at last. "It was a shock, of course, I still can't really believe it. He hadn't even retired…"

He paused. I wondered for a horrible moment if he was going to cry. He didn't even like Uncle William. I couldn't understand him at all, why all this emotion?

"There's some admin that needs to be done," he said at last. "I'll look for a few papers while I'm here – his passport, drivers licence, things like that. And I have to register his death."

He stopped again, like he was fighting to keep something down, as if his own words were making him think about things he didn't want to face. He coughed, sipped his tea, wiped his mouth.

"I think I go to the registry office," he said, not really talking to me any more, more thinking aloud. "William sorted all that when Mum and Father died, but I seem to remember he said you have to go to the office in person, you can't just phone them. And I think I have to cancel all his documents, notify the bank, things like that.

123

I'll phone the undertakers again tomorrow, they might have a list I can use, of things that need to be done."

I wondered why he hadn't got on to it already, he'd known all day. Perhaps he'd been busy with other things, it's not like any of us were expecting Uncle to suddenly die. I decided not to ask, he was in a strangely vulnerable mood. I cleared the mugs and put them in the sink. I could wash them later. I wanted him to go now, I was planning to go out and I wanted to shower and change. He didn't seem in a hurry.

"It's strange being back here without William," he said, looking round the kitchen.

I could tell he was remembering, noticing the things that had changed since he'd lived there as a child. "I think I'll look around," he said, pushing on the table as he rose to his feet. He seemed older, as if he was moving into his elder sibling's place. "I suppose it's my house now, after all," he said, confirming my thoughts.

I opened my mouth, ready to contradict him. Then closed it again. That was nearly a bad mistake. No, I needed to wait, to let him think he was going to get everything, until the Will was found. Perhaps he'd find it today, if he was going to start going through papers. However long it took, I needed to be patient. It was interesting that he too was discounting Alexsander – clearly neither of us thought he was still alive.

"I'll start in the study," he said and left.

I watched him walk out. He even walked differently, with a slight stoop as if all his energy was gone. Perhaps the disturbed night had knocked him a bit. I washed the mugs, then went to my room. I heard him, rummaging through drawers in Uncle's desk, then I heard doors open, as he walked through the house, looking at everything I suppose. Perhaps planning what he'd change when he lived there. I heard him come upstairs, open Uncle's wardrobe, the clink of hangars. Then he went back downstairs, slowly, as if carrying something.

I was applying makeup when he shouted up the stairs, telling me he was leaving. I went down, I wanted to know if he'd found the Will.

"How did you get on?" I said. "Find everything you need?"

He patted a bulging briefcase. "I think so, thanks," he said. "I found some papers, I can check those. And the undertaker asked for some clothes. Ready for when the police have… finished. With the body." He waved the other arm at me, laden with a suit-carrier.

"Have you got a spare key? So I can come back when I need to?"

I wasn't having that, him invading my privacy, coming and going when I wasn't here to keep an eye on things.

"No, sorry," I said, "I'll have to get one cut."

"Well, could I have your current mobile number? So I can check when you're in?" he said. "The one I have doesn't seem to reach you – have you changed phones?"

I had actually changed phones several times since I'd given my parents the number. I don't need to hear from them. There was no way to avoid giving it though, so I went into the study and wrote it on a scrap of paper. He had opened the door when I got back, letting cold air flood into the hallway.

"Well, it was nice to see you," he said, as if he wanted to say something but wasn't sure how. "I'm glad you're holding up okay. Your mother is upset, of course, but the twins didn't really know William, so they're not really affected."

I was interested by this. Why would my mother be upset? She didn't like him, she never had as far as I could tell. Perhaps it was the suddenness that had shocked them. He was still speaking, droning on, letting the cold air into the house.

"If you want to talk, you know where we are. We can sort out where you'll live a bit later. Unless you don't want to stay here on your own tonight? Do you want to come back with me?"

I shook my head, managed to not raise my eyebrows. Honestly!

It was like his whole world had changed, everything tipped upside down. It's not like he saw his brother very often. I couldn't see why he wasn't just getting on with life; sorting out the admin wouldn't take him very long, it needn't disturb his routine too much.

"Bye then," he said at last, "thanks for the tea."

As soon as he was outside I shut the door. Then I went upstairs to continue getting ready. I was meeting friends at the pub. I could do with a drink and a laugh after all that heaviness.

Chapter Eleven

I quickly picked up that people expected me to be upset by Uncle William's death. I began to see that I could use this to my advantage.

The next day was Wednesday, I decided to attend the music practice. I had spent the day at home, told work I was too upset to do anything, and was pleasantly surprised this was acceptable, people expected me to be distraught. I told them he had died 'yesterday' and didn't elaborate, so of course they assumed it had happened in the evening, not before I had worked the previous day.

I popped to the chemist and bought some makeup, a pink kohl pencil to make my eyes look red, a lighter foundation than my complexion, so I would look both pale and like I had tried, was trying to look normal.

I arrived at the church slightly late, so everyone was already there. I could hear them playing as I negotiated the side passage and opened the door. They were mid song when I opened the door to the sanctuary. Sadie looked up, and stopped playing.

"Well, look who's arrived."

She considered for a minute. Obviously, I might have come out of a sense of guilt, had realised she was right and I needed to be part of the team. Like I said before, churches love to help people who think they're wrong and want to change. I watched her face as her expression changed from hard to doubtful.

"Right, hello Clara. Nice you could join us. Have you come to practise?" she asked.

"Yes," I said, but quietly, so they could hardly hear. I kept my head bent low and walked over to a spare chair, started to assemble my clarinet. I gave a loud sniff.

"Say, are you alright?" said Melissa, who was standing nearest. She lowered her violin slightly and looked at me.

"No, not really," I croaked, putting down my instrument and giving a shudder. (I hope you're impressed by all this. I should've been on the stage!)

"Right," said Sadie, annoyed her rehearsal was being disturbed but wanting to look sympathetic. "What's the problem then? Anything we can help with?"

It was perfect. There she was, struggling between irritation and trying to appear caring, and it made her look completely hard and nasty.

"No, not really. I'm fine, sorry, I didn't mean to disturb things. It's just that…just that." I paused for effect. "You see," I whispered, "Uncle William died yesterday."

"Oh Clara!" said Melissa. She put down her violin and came to hug me. I dislike being hugged, but forced myself to keep still. The others were coming closer too, gathering round to comfort me.

"Why ever are you here?" asked Kimberley. "You should be at home, taking it easy."

"I had to come," I said. "Sadie said I can't play in church any more if I don't attend the practices. And I love to play, it's the only thing I feel I can do for the Lord. So I had to come. But it's so hard…" I let my voice trail away.

Sadie was squirming. She had come nearer too, was standing at the back of the group, looking uncomfortable. I gambled on her not calling me out, telling them she had told me that weeks ago and it hadn't made me come before. To start a defence would do her no good at all, it would just make her look even worse.

"Right…" she began. But the others were already talking, telling me that of course I could still play in church, my abilities were much

128

better than theirs and of course I didn't need to rehearse if I was too busy. And when had my uncle died, and what had happened, and how could they help? They all spoke at once, eager to reassure me and offer comfort.

I kept my head down, fiddling with my scarf. I was waiting for Rob to take the lead, to come closer. It was his job, he couldn't keep his distance now. I ignored the others and looked straight at him.

"I'm in such a muddle," I said. "I know I should try to carry on, but it's been such a shock..."

"Clara," he said, his voice full of concern, "I don't think you should be here. Not to practise music anyway. You need to take some time to adjust to this. Would you like us to pray with you?"

Of course I wouldn't. But I couldn't say that, it would blow my cover. So I nodded, and sat there while they said their prayers. One of them even touched me, put their grubby hands right on my head, spoiling my hair. But I sat there, pretending it was all helping, whispering, "Yes Lord, yes Lord," as they prayed. It showed them how spiritual I was, how sincere. Even Sadie said a prayer, but it wouldn't help her position at all. They all knew she'd been harsh and uncaring, that little speck of mud would stick very nicely.

"Now, I really think perhaps you should go home," said Rob, being all fatherly and caring. "Do you feel alright to drive?"

"I'm not sure..." I said. This could work well, if he was offering to take me.

"I can drive you," said Kimberley. "I'm sure Sadie won't miss my playing for once."

Not what I was hoping.

"No, I said, standing and repacking my clarinet. "I'll be fine, really. I'm probably better on my own."

I grabbed my coat and walked to the door. Rob followed me. When we were in the hall, before I opened the outside door, he spoke.

"Clara, have you thought about the funeral at all? Would you like me to call round, have a chat?

"It's a difficult time, you will be coping with all sorts of feelings. I might be able to help. You must remember that everyone grieves differently, there is no right or wrong way to feel right now." He stood there, his face full of concern, wanting to help.

I nodded, managing to not smile. Glee was not the response he was expecting.

He passed me his card. "My number's there, call me any time. How about if I pop in Friday? Would that suit you? I could come in the evening, say about seven?"

I nodded. "That would be great, thanks," I said. I walked out, flicking his card with my thumb. The evening had been very worthwhile.

***

By the time Friday came, I was ready. I had done a little Google research on bereavement, and had decided how to behave. I figured that part of Rob's ministerial training would include some kind of counselling course, and I wanted to appear as if I really was bereaved. I had to research it, because actually I wasn't too bothered by Uncle's death. To be honest, I'm not sure I would be upset by *anyone's* death – I guess I just hadn't yet found the right person.

I decided to go for the 'disbelief, confusion' stage, mixed in with a little anger. I could direct the anger towards my family, which would allow me to prepare Rob for anything they might decide to tell him about me. I thought it was likely they would decide to have the funeral at the church, and I was concerned their version of my life might not tally so well with what I had told people. I needed to raise a few doubts about their integrity, just in case.

I was pleased to read that crying was not always part of grief, and that some people worried that they weren't able to cry. This was good, it would save me having to generate tears for effect, which was a lot of effort. I could tell Rob I couldn't cry, and let him reassure me that this was normal. (Have you noticed how people are so keen for things to be 'normal', and tend to worry if they don't fit into the category? It's weird.)

I would have to see how things developed in terms of my long-term plan. If I looked upset enough, I might manage to entice Rob into physical contact, perhaps he would put his arm round me or something. That might lead to an opening to take things further. But I knew I should be careful, any hint of flirting and he'd back off and refer me to one of his deacons.

Rob arrived exactly at seven. I heard his car pulling into the driveway, the crunch of gravel as he walked to the front door. I switched on the light in the porch and opened the door with a 'sad but brave' smile.

"Hello Rob, nice of you to come."

"Hi Clara, lovely spot this. How are you doing?"

I offered him wine, but he settled for coffee and followed me into the kitchen. I poured fresh coffee into a couple of mugs, then suggested we took them into the lounge, as it was more comfortable. I had lit a fire, so it was cosy – and it was much cleaner these days, you didn't choke on dust every time you disturbed a cushion.

I sat on the sofa and curled up. I had worn a tight skirt for the occasion, which looked as if I had hurried home from work, and gave him a quick glimpse of my legs when I lifted them beneath me. He didn't react, and chose to sit in the armchair next to me, with a small table between us. He took a sip of coffee, which was strong and hot, then placed it on the coaster. He turned to face me.

"So Clara, how are you feeling? Bereavement can be such a difficult time."

"I don't know, to be honest," I said, giving him the brave smile again. "It's almost like it isn't real. Some mornings I wake up and I've forgotten he's dead, I expect to see him sitting in the kitchen drinking his tea, same as usual. I walk in, and wait to hear his jolly, 'Morning Clara, how did you sleep?' But instead, it's empty." I paused, trying to remember what else I had read online.

"And I feel so angry," I continued. "It doesn't seem fair for him to be taken so soon. And I'm angry with my parents. They should have noticed he had heart problems, they should've insisted he went to a doctor. He was my dad's brother, but Dad didn't care about him at all. It's very weird, I even find I look for him, when I'm in town or in a shop, I keep glancing at people and thinking for a second that it's him, that he's not dead."

Rob was nodding.

"That's all very normal Clara, but don't worry, it will pass.

"There are different stages of bereavement you see, and you might find that you pass through all of them, or just some of them. There's no 'right' way to mourn for someone you've lost, and different people behave in different ways. You must try not to worry. Or to let other people make you feel you are wrong in some way.

"It is normal for the first stage to include disbelief, it can be hard to accept someone we loved has gone. Gradually you will accept that William has gone, but it might take time."

I nodded, pretended I was relieved to hear I was normal. I wondered how to encourage him to share the sofa with me. He was still talking.

"The next stage usually involves grief – lots of sorrow, but not always tears – some people find they can't cry, even if they would like to."

"That's me!" I said, glad he had raised it. "I'm chewed up inside," I said, copying a phrase I'd heard at work, "but I don't seem able to cry. The tears just won't come. Kinda eye-constipation!"

132

He didn't laugh, didn't even smile. He nodded, full of sympathy.

"Poor you, that must be very hard. But try not to worry. And don't worry if the tears do come, but at an unexpected moment. Sometimes people will lose someone close to them and not shed a tear, then months later, something minor happens and they cry buckets. It's like the body suspends emotion sometimes, holds it in until it's ready to come out.

"The same can happen with anger. You might feel anger towards your parents, or the medics who found your uncle, or the police for the road conditions. But often that is simply anger at the death working its way out. It usually passes."

He leaned forwards, put his hands on his knees. I looked at them, noticed the hairs on his wrists where his cuffs were rolled back. I thought about touching the hand nearest me, stroking the dark skin, pulling him towards me. But he'd probably just get up and leave. This had to be subtle. I tried to listen to what he was saying.

"Have they confirmed the cause of death? You said on Wednesday they suspected it was a heart attack? I know a post-mortem can sometimes take a couple of weeks – have you heard anything yet?"

I nodded. "Yes. It's been done already – they must be having a quiet patch." I smiled, a joke at the ready, then remembered I was supposed to be looking sad. "They think it happened while he was driving, and he lost control and hit a tree. Apparently he was already dead when he made impact, they can tell that from their tests I think. I don't know how. But they said he'd had a heart attack while driving.

"They asked me why he was out, where he was going. But as I told the police, sometimes he just went for a drive, he said it helped him to think. Perhaps he was having trouble at work – I know he was thinking of retiring."

Rob was nodding, taking it all in.

"It will be better when you've sorted out a few details, having things left hanging is never easy. I'm sure he didn't suffer at all, it sounds as if it was very fast, so that must be a comfort. And of course Clara, you can be sure of where he is now. Only his body has died Clara, your uncle is safely with his Heavenly Father now. You can be sure of that…"

Actually, I didn't much care what he had died of, so long as it could be classed as 'natural causes' and not hold up the house going through. But I nodded back and gave a big sigh, so he would think I would be crying if it weren't for the whole shocked-no-tears thing. He asked, very cautiously, about the funeral. I guess it was all business for him, a nice little earner on the side. But he couldn't look too eager. Wouldn't be professional.

"Have you and your parents had time to discuss it at all? Do you know what William would have wanted?" he said.

"Well," I said, "my parents are a big problem. You see, they didn't like Uncle, and they didn't like that he went to church. Of course, I expect they'll try to hide that, they'll want to appear all loving and upset, but it will be an act." I shifted slightly, so I was facing him, looking full into his face.

"I had to move out Rob, they were too difficult to live with. My mother has a problem with lying, you can't believe anything she says, and Dad won't ever criticise her, it's like she has a hold over him. I came to Uncle William, and he insisted I move in with him, got away from them. Then I started coming to the church with him, and it changed everything. I've put my parents behind me, and I'm not looking forward to having to deal with them again. Sometimes I think I hate them."

Rob was looking concerned. "How are they since your uncle died? Are they upset? Sometimes a death can make people re-evaluate, think about their priorities. You should try to give them a chance Clara, ask God to help you forgive them. It can be impossible by ourselves, but God can help you with this, and you'll feel better if you do. Anger and hatred can eat us up inside if we let it."

I nodded, let him think I was taking it all in. "I'll try," I said, "but it won't be easy. After I moved out, I tried to persuade my brothers to move in here too, to escape from my parents. But my mum wouldn't let them. She's very controlling." I began to warm to my theme. "Like I said, she lies. I'm worried if we have the funeral at the church that she'll tell people lies about me, and people will believe her. I don't want to lose my friends there, they're very precious to me…"

Rob was nodding, full of sympathy. If he was wondering who exactly those precious friends were, he didn't say so. I tended to flit in and out a bit, but he wasn't to know that I wasn't seeing people outside of the church. I could've been meeting Melissa or Kimberley every week for coffee and a chat. I thought it was a safe enough thing to say. He tried to reassure me.

"Clara, people in the church are very fond of you." (I doubted that was true, they hardly knew me, but I didn't correct him. People believe their own lies even more than they believe yours, so if he was going to say things to make me feel better, that would only be helpful in the long run.)

"Whatever your parents might tell people," he continued, "I'm sure it won't influence what others think. You must trust us to not be easily led, we'll know they're lying." (Which was hard to resist smiling at. But I didn't. It's important to be consistent with gullible people, and to let them think they're right.)

We briefly discussed the funeral. I told him I hadn't talked to my parents yet, so couldn't say what they would want to do. As Uncle was Dad's brother, I assumed he would have the last word in what happened. None of us knew where Alexsander was, so there was no hope of contacting him. Rob gave a possible outline to the sort of service the church could provide – all very religious and long-winded. But apparently, because Uncle had been a member there, it would be free, so that made it quite attractive.

I thought there might be the chance to play a solo too, if I phrased it right, which would be good. It would be nice to get a little admiration from the audience.

Eventually Rob stood, ready to leave. He'd said the obligatory prayer, but not made any attempt to touch me, not even a hand on my shoulder. I decided to take the lead. As we stood in the dim hallway, him fastening his coat while I moved towards the door, I reached for his hand. He looked surprised, but didn't snatch it away. I held it in both my hands and looked into his eyes.

"Thank you so much for coming Rob," I said. "It has been such a comfort. I feel so… I don't know, sort of lost." I paused. Was he going to reach out with the other hand, touch my face, tell me I wasn't alone? Was he going to squeeze my hand with his, hold it for a little longer?

No. He gently extracted his hand and gave me an awkward smile.

"I'm glad I could help Clara," he said. Then he reached for the door and opened it. "You have my number, if you or your family want to talk more."

He left.

Perhaps he was gay.

Chapter Twelve

I expect you're wondering about the Will – whether it had been found and how my family reacted. I'll tell you about it. I also want to tell you about Rob, and how I managed to explode that situation. Of course, at the time, I didn't realise the repercussions of either event. We never do, do we? We go through life, making the best decisions we can at the time, leaping at opportunities when they arrive, and then wham. Big change. All very unexpected.

First the Will. Dad visited in a fury. He had found the Will amongst the papers of course, and very properly passed it straight to his lawyer. Or at least, that's what he told me. I expect he had a quick peek first, then sent it to his lawyer to find out what could be done. But by the time he came to me, he was pretending the Will had been read to him by the executor, and he was challenging the contents. Which was exactly what I'd expected.

The Will was all legally correct, of course. It was written in the legal jargon, "The Last Will and Testament of William Arthur Oakes... etc., etc." I had used a friend's computer and we'd found an online 'write your own Will' website, which was very helpful and basically did everything for me. It clearly revoked any previous Wills, and given the timing, he wouldn't have had time to write one that revoked mine. The only slightly dodgy part was the date, which of course was all back-dated to just a few months ago. I had thought it wouldn't be needed for a few years, otherwise I might've considered making it earlier. I knew the counter-signatories were safe enough. They were real people, happy to sign and date for a few quid, and unlikely to be found because both had moved house recently. They would be easy to persuade to lie for me, if they were found and it became necessary, but I thought that was unlikely. I had made a few receipts too, showing how one worked in the garden and the other was a builder, which they had signed, as if signing to show they'd been paid. It would look like Uncle had written his Will, then called in a couple of blokes who happened to be working in the garden at the time, to witness his signature.

Of course, Dad was furious. I think he must've rushed round right after he spoke to his lawyer. I arrived home from work, hoping for a quiet evening in, and there he was; marching up and down the drive, too angry to sit in his car. He practically wrenched the door off the hinges when I parked – I thought he was going to grab my arm and drag me out of the car.

"It won't work Clara. You've gone too far this time."

I smiled up at him, copied my mother's frown-smile, like I was a bit confused.

"What's the matter Dad? Are you alright?" I said. I reached for my bag and climbed from the car, as slowly as was possible. I knew it would infuriate him to be kept waiting, and I wanted him livid. Angry people don't think, they react, and I wanted him to be all emotional reaction for this conversation. Too much logic might ruin my plans.

"You know exactly what the matter is Clara, don't think you can fool me with your little act. I know you too well. My solicitor has read William's Will and I don't know what you hope to gain from it, but it won't be the money. This house belongs to me now, and I want you out.

"Are you listening to me?"

I was searching in my bag for my keys. The car beeped as it locked and I walked to the front door, keys in hand, head held high.

"I think you need to calm down a bit Dad," I said, "especially as weak hearts seem to be in the family. Why don't you come in and tell me what's bothering you?"

I opened the door, hung my coat on the hook in the corner and walked down the hallway into the kitchen. I could hear him breathing behind me, like I was being followed by a great bull gearing up for a charge. I thought my heart comment might not be so far off the mark if he carried on like this.

"Tea?" I said, waving the kettle at him.

He shook his head, and continued his pacing, from one side of the kitchen to the other. I ignored him, filled the kettle, pulled out a cup, then sat at the table. I sat at the head, in the chair Uncle had always used. Silently stating my position. Dad on the other hand, was not silent. He was ranting.

"You've always been difficult Clara, never one to return affection or be well behaved. But you've pushed it too far this time. You're not going to get away with it. You've crossed a line. I'll be involving the police, whoever's necessary. We'll stop you. Even if it means they lock you up. I will not let you get away with this."

He was standing over me now, shouting into my face.

"Excuse me," I said, keeping my voice low and quiet. "I think the kettle's boiled. Are you sure you don't want a cup?"

I thought for a moment he was going to hit me. But he didn't. He thumped the table. One hard fist, banged on the oak top. It must've hurt him.

I ignored him and poured water over a tea bag, leaning forwards so the steam swirled up, warming my face. Wet and hot, smelling of tea. I mashed the teabag with a spoon and flipped it into the bin before splashing milk into the mug. When I was ready, I sat back down and took a sip. All unruffled and calm. The mature one.

"Dad, what, exactly, is the problem?"

He growled. Honestly, he did – a deep guttural noise in his throat. I considered barking back. Instead I smiled and repeated myself.

"What's the problem? I can see you're a bit upset. Do you want to tell me what it's about?"

He still didn't sit, not properly. He leant against the work surface and glared down at me.

"Stop pretending Clara. The Will. I know you had a hand in it. I don't know how you persuaded William to change it, I imagine he'd left everything to that loser son of his, but it won't work."

He kept repeating that. I wasn't sure if he was convincing himself or trying to tell me. He hadn't *actually* said the words. Hadn't actually voiced that I was sole beneficiary, that all the money, all the assets, were now mine. I wasn't sure I could be bothered to play this game any longer, to keep pretending I didn't know what was in the Will.

"Did it not say what you'd hoped then Dad?" I said, "Did Uncle not give you back the family house that you felt he owed you?"

His colour changed from red to puce. When he spoke, flecks of spittle flew out, catching the light as they sprayed the floor.

"You are not having it Clara. My solicitor assures me I have a good case. The Will has been passed to McDuff, William's solicitor, who is named as executor – but it won't work. I will fight it. And I will fight you. Every inch of the way if needs be."

He leaned forwards, towering over me, trying to dominate me with his size and intensity.

"You have gone too far this time. The legal people won't let you get away with it, and nor will I. I will involve the police if necessary."

I sipped my tea. It was hot, strong, how I like it. I raised an eyebrow and smiled. Nothing infuriates an angry person as much as being smiled at when they want to be taken seriously.

I had known about McDuff, of course. When I'd written the Will, I had used the one I'd found in the filing cabinet as a template. As expected, everything had been left to Alexsander, and it named McDuff as the executor. I hadn't been sure if they had some

140

arrangement, if the lawyer knew he would be sorting out Uncle's estate, so I'd left things as they stood. I'd only changed the beneficiary – to myself – and the counter-signatories. Everything else was the same, copied from the old Will to the new one. Although I obviously hadn't known the timing of events when I wrote it, they now worked in my favour. I suspected the lawyer kept a copy of the previous Will at his office. He would now assume that Uncle had changed his mind, written the new Will, and been planning to take a copy to McDuff. But the heart attack had prevented him, which explained why there was only one copy of the new Will. Dad was still ranting.

"Even if the Will turns out to be legitimate, which I doubt, I will still fight you Clara. This house belongs to me. If William had left it to Alexsander, I would have contested it on the grounds that the boy is dead. It would've been a hassle, might have held things up for years, but eventually it would have been mine. But you? You don't deserve anything."

He paused, like he was just remembering that I was his daughter, that perhaps I did have some rights.

"You would receive your share, your third, when your mother and I die, not before. Not now. I grew up in this house. I should've contested the Will when my parents left everything to William, but it was a less strong case, my solicitor told me I would probably lose. But not this time. This time I will win. This house belongs to me."

He was just repeating himself now, and it was getting boring. I wanted to get on with my evening, not listen to an old man crying over spilt milk. I decided I would correct him on a couple of points and then let him storm out.

"Well, Dad," I said, "I expect you're disappointed. I can understand that. But Uncle William had every right to leave his stuff to whoever he wanted, and we became very close over the last few months. Very close."

I paused. He could add whatever connotations he wanted. It might make him less keen to rush off to court. I turned to him and stood up. He was taller than me, so I was still looking up at him, which I didn't like, so I crossed to the sink. I leaned back and looked at him across the length of the kitchen.

"I *will* inherit this house Dad, and I will sell it. You can buy it if it means so much to you, but the money is mine, you can be sure of that. And you won't contest a thing. Not unless you want the family secret to be aired. You see, I know about Joanna, I know about Mum's past. And I want what's due to me. If Mum had gone to the papers, told them her story, she'd have earned a nice little nest egg, we'd all have been more comfortable the last few years. But she didn't. She was selfish, decided to keep her secret to herself. Well, I'm not so inward looking. I'm quite prepared to tell everyone what I know. I'll let a few tabloids know where we live, tell them about how Mum raised us, make an interesting story.

"Not because I want to," I added, "but because I need the money. If you hold things up with the house, then I'll need some cash to tide me over won't I? So, it would be fair to use Mum's story to compensate me, seeing as how it's you who's making things difficult.

"And don't think I won't get the house eventually," I said. "Because I will. You can make a fuss, whine to a few lawyers, get your day in court. But it will cost you, and in the end, I will win. Uncle loved me, and he wanted me to have this house. And nothing you can say will change that, you'll just slow things down a bit."

I smiled, let him see I wasn't bothered. "Now, was there anything else?"

He opened his mouth, then shut it. For a moment he just stared at me. I think, if he'd had a gun, he'd have shot me. But he had nothing, and he knew it. He turned and walked out. The bang of the front door echoed through the house. By the time his car roared

142

down the driveway I was on my way upstairs. I thought I might go out for the evening after all.

***

I went out the following Monday too. With Rob. It wasn't exactly a date, but I figured I could make things look a little hazy, mix the facts up a bit. Sometimes if you put a spin on things, people come to their own conclusions. Everyone likes to think the worst, you just have to point the way.

I knew his day off was Monday – it was written on the inside cover of the notices sheet they gave out every Sunday, I guess so we could read along while all the activities were announced again by the town crier. Anyway, I figured that this meant two things. Firstly, Rob would be free of meetings and church commitments on that day and secondly, if someone were to have an emergency, he would ditch his day-off and come running. Christians are meant to put their own needs behind other people's, and I thought a day-off was one of those unnecessary things that could easily be discarded if you were the minister.

So, Monday morning, I phoned his mobile, said I was in a bad way, was there any chance he could pop in. Initially, he tried to fob me off with someone else, suggested he could call one of the deacons for me. But I was persistent and sniffed a lot (easier to cry when you're on the phone) and of course, he agreed to come.

I was waiting when he arrived.

"Hi Rob, this is very kind of you," I said. "Were you busy? I know it's your day off, but this couldn't wait."

"No, no, that's fine Clara," he said, keen to pretend he didn't mind. "Esther was just doing some housework before we went out for the day, so I can spare an hour."

I grinned, full of gratitude, and showed him straight into the kitchen. Everything was prepared. I'd had the ovens on their highest setting all night, and it was like a sauna in there. Rob walked in and turned, shocked, to ask why it was so hot. I told him I hadn't been able to sleep and had been making bread. Shutting the kitchen door behind me (didn't want to waste all that heat) I went to the kettle and asked if he'd like tea or coffee. I didn't bother to offer wine, I knew he'd refuse. As I filled the kettle, Rob removed his jacket and hung it on the back of the chair. I smiled.

I then put the next part of the plan into action. I explained how I wasn't sleeping, I still kept expecting to see Uncle sitting in the kitchen, I just couldn't accept he was dead.

"I've been thinking," I said. "In fact, I was up all night thinking, which is why I was in bit of a state this morning. I think if I could actually see him, see his body, then I would feel better. It would seem more real, and I could start to move on. They've released the body now. It's at the undertaker's."

Rob was nodding.

"But I don't want to go on my own," I said, "I might be upset. So, I thought you could come with me? I phoned the undertaker and we can go this morning, would that be okay?"

Rob looked surprised.

"Now? Er, I suppose so. It's quite short notice though… it might be better to–".

"No," I said. "I want to go now. And I've made the appointment. Here's your tea," I said, plonking a mug on the table. "I'll just pop to the loo before we go. And I'll hang up your jacket for you," I said, picking up his coat and hurrying from the room as if I was bursting for the toilet.

He probably thought it was extremely strange that I should hang up his jacket right before we were about to leave to visit the undertaker. But people do behave strangely, don't they? Especially if they are recently bereaved and worried about seeing their dead uncle in the flesh. And I hadn't given him chance to react, to stop me. I had whisked it away while talking at ninety miles an hour, there was no time to respond.

I took his jacket upstairs with me. His mobile was in the inside pocket, where I had seen him put it a few times when he took calls during the music practices. I grabbed my phone from next to my bed and took both phones into the bathroom, locking the door behind me. Now for some fun.

You see, I had more or less given up on the big seduction. Rob was too frigid, too scared to take chances, he obeyed too many rules. But things might change if I could weaken the security of his home life a little. And if not, I would throw enough mud that some would stick, just to punish him for resisting all my attempts at a little intimacy. I needed to shake up Esther a bit, turn her into the suspicious wife. People hate to be checked up on, even if they've done nothing wrong. It makes them want to be cagey, to avoid saying what they're doing, to resist being monitored. I should know, my parents have always tried to control my life, and nothing makes me more inclined to shun their rules than constant checking.

I turned on his mobile. The password was easy : 3164. I had watched him type it in more than once. People are very careless. I then scrolled through the texts sent to his wife. I wanted to send her a message, and I needed to copy his style, or she would suspect that he hadn't sent it. I considered sending a lewd comment, something that would leave her in no doubt we were having an affair. But his texts to her were all very boring, the sort of thing a child might have sent. I worried that she would know at once if it was completely out of character. I settled on something safe but suggestive.

I typed: "Clara, missing you already. Esther busy with housework, and I've finished what I needed to do in town. Can I pop in? Right now? Crazy to see you."

I signed it "Rxxx", because that's how he finished texts to her. Then I sent it to her phone, like he had meant to send it to me but had got in a muddle.

I added my phone number to his address book, then changed the time and date on both phones. I spent a few minutes typing messages back and forth between his phone and mine, which would appear backdated due to my changing of the settings. I'd already planned them, so it didn't take long. They were nicely intimate. I also removed a few clothes and took some revealing photos – some on his phone, and some on mine which I sent him. I put them all into his 'saved photos' folder. They should help things along if he protested his innocence and showed wifey his phone to prove there was nothing to worry about. Even if he found and deleted the text conversations, I thought there was a good chance he wouldn't check the photos, so they'd be ready and waiting to shock someone in the future. It made me giggle to think about it.

I now needed to get him out of the house before suspicious wife turned up. I went back to the kitchen, told him I was ready to leave. He looked like he was going to refuse, suggest we went another day, so I started to talk very fast, saying how I couldn't rely on anyone else, I was so alone, if it wasn't for the church I didn't know what I'd do, I really felt that God had sent Rob to help me. That shut him up. He wasn't going to argue if it had come from God. He picked up his jacket and followed me out. He didn't seem to notice it was lighter than before – I slid his mobile into a corner of the kitchen, so it would look like it had fallen there when he took off his jacket. I didn't want him seeing my additions too soon.

We left the house and I locked the door. A light was on in the bedroom, but he didn't notice. Why would he? It was morning, dull but not dark. Only if someone was actively checking the house would they see the light, assume someone was upstairs.

I said I would drive. He started to protest, to say he was happy to drive me, but I told him it would keep me calm if I had to drive. Then he suggested we could go independently, saying he would follow me there in his car. I knew he was thinking about his day-off, deciding that he could zoom home quickly after we'd seen the corpse if he was in his own car. Incredibly selfish of him. I made a little plea, to please not be left on my own afterwards, it would help me so much if he was in the car with me. That settled it. Off we drove, leaving his car parked in my driveway.

Esther struck me as someone who wouldn't mess about. If she suspected Rob was fooling around, she would go and see for herself. When she arrived, she would find his car, sitting in my driveway. She would knock on the door, but no one would answer. If she opened the letterbox for a snoop, she might hear the music I'd left playing in the upstairs room. She might notice the light on in the bedroom at the front. I hoped she would wait for a bit and then go home.

She would confront him as soon as he returned. Of course, he would deny everything, tell her the truth. But I thought there'd be an element of doubt. She would always wonder. If she looked at his phone before he did, that would all add to her suspicions. Especially if she deleted the texts, if Rob never saw them, and therefore couldn't explain that I must have added them myself. Even if she was still there when we got back to the house, she would always wonder. Things like that ferment in the brain, they never go away. One day, even if she thought it had all been sorted and put away, it would come back and bite. Those things we think we've moved on from, the things in the past, they still lurk there, waiting.

We drove to the centre of Marksbridge and I parked behind the supermarket. It was for customers only, but they never checked. I told Rob I didn't like parking in the High Street, it was too difficult. He smiled in sympathy but didn't comment. I knew he was thinking that all this was taking much longer than he'd hoped. He'd noticed in the car that his phone was missing, and had tried to think when he'd last had it. I could tell it was bothering him.

We walked up to the undertaker's shop. Is it called a shop? Makes it sound like they sell the bodies. Anyway, it looked like a normal shop, double-fronted, with a gravestone in the window on one side and lots of flowers in the other. It was all quite smart. Perhaps Macket and Macket were doing rather well. Perhaps death was a good business to be in these days.

We went in and a little bell trilled above our heads. A man appeared, Mr Macket I assume. He was wearing black and was short, as if carrying all those coffins on his shoulder had squashed him a bit. I wondered if he was lopsided, but you couldn't tell because he was a twitchy sort of man, didn't keep still for more than a second.

I introduced myself, explained I had come to see Uncle.

"Ah yes, Miss Oakes," he said, checking his large desk diary and blinking repeatedly, "we are expecting you. Do come this way, I will show you into the chapel. Does your friend wish to accompany you? Or he can wait here if you would prefer to be alone with your uncle…" He pointed to a sofa in the corner, a place where mourners could rest in comfort.

I explained Rob was my minister and would be coming with me, and we both followed Mr. Macket through the door at the back of the shop. It was all rather nice, sunny and clean. Felt more like visiting a friend for tea than a funeral director. We walked along a short corridor which smelled of perfume, and into another room. It was just a room, though Mr Macket had called it a chapel. I guess it sounded better than saying, "We've got the body in the back room". There were a few chairs to one side, a small table with a box of tissues, some flowers in a vase. On the wall was a shelf, like a mantelpiece, with a cross in the centre and candles either side. It was the candles which were providing the scent. But the only thing you really noticed was the coffin, a cloth draped over it, in the centre of the room. I had a sudden memory of all those horror films where the body slowly rises from the depths, arms outstretched, eyes unseeing. I felt a giggle rise and turned it into a cough.

Mr. Macket went and stood to the side, solemn, offering to lift the cloth so I could view the grim remains in detail (the cloth itself was more like a net curtain, you could see the body, see it was Uncle.) I nodded and he peeled back the cloth. I peered in, looked at the body – waxy, powder on his cheeks where they'd tried to make him look less dead. Which seems like a silly idea to me – how is pretending someone is just asleep helpful? He was wearing his best suit, but his tie wasn't straight, one side was hanging down. He'd have hated that if he'd known, he was fastidious in how he dressed. He also looked like he needed a shave.

I wanted to touch him, I've never touched a dead body before. But I thought it might appear odd, so I nodded again and went to one of the chairs, sat with my head bowed, like I was praying. I was trying to decide how long I could wait, could keep Rob with me. He wouldn't want to rush me, but I could tell he was anxious to leave, to get home to his possessive wife. There was some music playing, the sort that sounds like it's been packaged in a tin. Tinny and mournful. Music for the dead. I sat for as long as I could bear, then I raised my head and looked at Rob. He looked miserable.

I wandered around the room for a bit, looked at the flowers, took a tissue and pretended to blow my nose. I looked at the cross on the little shelf – it was double-sided, with a crucifix on the back, I guess they'd turn it around if they had a Catholic body staying.

I couldn't think of a way to delay Rob any longer, so I nodded and we both walked out, Rob thanking Mr. Macket as we passed, me trying to look forlorn.

We walked to the car in silence. As we drove back, Rob tried to ask how I was, to do his caring minister thing. But I couldn't be bothered to talk by then. I'd kept him away from home for a couple of hours, now I could release him and get on with my day. He didn't seem very open to affection of any kind and I wasn't going to keep being rebuffed. He started to talk about the funeral. Apparently Dad had contacted him, and they had set the date for the following week. I told him my parents hadn't told me yet, which surprised him. I expect they were hoping I wouldn't be there, but I didn't mention why.

I turned into my driveway at speed, splattering the gravel. At the top of the drive, next to the house, I could see two cars. One must be Esther's. That made me smile. Rob was sounding worried.

"That's Esther's car. I wonder what's happened. She must've been trying to phone me."

He leapt from the car as it stopped and ran towards his wife.

"Esther, what's happened? Why are you here?"

She stood very still. I think she'd been crying, her cheeks looked wet and her nose was red. She obviously wasn't one of those heroines who cry well, she was one of the swollen nosed blotchy ones. He was trying to put his arm round her, but she was moving away.

As I went to join them, I heard Rob explain that we'd been to the undertaker's.

"Clara asked me to accompany her, to see her uncle's body," he said.

I did my 'surprised but recovering quickly' face, as if this was all news to me but I was catching on fast.

"Oh, the undertakers... yes, that's right. We went to the undertakers... to see the corpse..."

Rob was looking surprised. Esther was looking angry. She pulled out her phone, showed him the screen. I assumed my text was on there. Rob frowned, completely confused.

"But, I didn't send that," he said. "Clara phoned me, asked if I would visit. You know that... you were there..."

"I know what you told me," said Esther. "But I don't know what this is about," she nodded at her phone again. "It looks a bit weird Rob."

I moved to the front door.

"Do you two want to come in to discuss this?" I asked, holding open the door.

"No," said Esther, "I think we need to discuss it at home."

Rob nodded, then remembered his phone. "I've lost my phone," he told Esther. "Let me just have a quick look inside, in case I lost it there. Then we can sort this out. It's very odd, I don't know who can have sent that text..." His eyes told me he was beginning to suspect exactly who had sent it, but he wasn't willing to have that conversation. Not yet. Not while he was still off guard, and not until he had sorted out his wife.

They both went inside, Rob marching to the kitchen, Esther following. I think she just wanted to be there, to not leave us alone together. It didn't matter. This would play out, one way or the other. It was vaguely interesting, but of no importance, the fun had been in setting it up. I didn't bother to follow them, and they emerged almost immediately. Rob was holding his phone.

"Found it," he said. "It must have fallen out of my pocket earlier."

"Okay," I murmured.

They left, muttering goodbyes, saying they would be in touch, but mainly anxious to be gone. Back to their marital home, back to safety where they could try to work out what had happened and why. They would never fathom why – there was no reason other than amusement. I wondered, briefly, when I would next hear from them. Then I set about organising the rest of my day.

Chapter Thirteen

I didn't see Rob again until the funeral. That was a bizarre event, I can tell you.

The hearse was already approaching when I arrived, gliding down the road towards the church. The undertakers had offered a car for the family, but my parents were too mean to stretch to that, and I sure wasn't going to pay, so we'd all driven ourselves.

We met outside the church. I think my father would've preferred a simple burning at the crematorium, but Rob had probably done a hard sell on him, convinced him there should be some kind of service at Uncle's church. It looked good to the rest of the congregation, churches are meant to be there for *'hatches, matches and dispatches'*. It's how they make their money.

My parents, dressed in black, were standing together. The twins were both in suits that were too big, I suspect they'd been bought for the occasion and were going to double up as suits for interviews when they needed them later. Everyone looked tense. Hair combed, shoes polished, faces blank. They were standing with Rob, who nodded when I approached and then moved away. Like I might contaminate him.

We walked in, a unit of mourners. Our faces were grim, but anyone watching would've thought that was due to the occasion, not because we hated each other. My mother had phoned me repeatedly, trying to persuade me to change my mind, to let Dad have what was 'rightfully his'. Sometimes those calls ended with her spitting that I was "just like Joanna." Sometimes they ended with her sobbing. It didn't matter, there was nothing she could do.

My brothers had also done their best. Michael had visited, banging on the door Saturday morning, trying to be all pally, on my side, let's be civilised and sort this out. I didn't even bother to invite him inside. Edward had met me at work, tried to take me out for coffee. He was trying the 'two adults having a sensible chat' routine. I told him I was too busy for coffee, didn't bother to explain further. I didn't have time for any of them.

We all sat in the front row. The church was packed, I suppose Christians like to show support for one of their own. Most of their theology seems bound up with the afterlife, so I guess it perpetuates the myth when someone actually dies. Important not to let the cracks show, to talk all about 'being in Heaven' and 'still alive' even though there's a sodding great box right in front of them with a very dead corpse inside which does rather ruin the cosy pretence.

Rob led the service, not looking at me once. Esther was there, I'd seen the back of her head as I walked in. She had come to see me earlier in the week, at the house. She came with another woman, for support I guess. They stood on my doorstep, looking like Jehovah Witnesses but without the suits.

Esther was fighting hard to remain composed, but she held herself together, I'll give her that. She explained that her and Rob had seen the texts, and knew that I had entered them myself. I shrugged at that, told her she could believe that if she wanted.

But I could tell that she *did* believe it, she didn't actually doubt Rob at all. Perhaps he really was gay.

She tried to offer me some kind of help, said I was obviously having trouble accepting things as they were, and she was ready to offer me support if I wanted counselling. Her and this other woman – I was obviously deemed too dangerous for her to be alone with me. I didn't even bother to respond, just repeated that she could believe what she liked, and closed the door on them.

So, there I was, sitting with my family, who all wished it was me in the coffin, in front of Uncle William, who definitely would've switched places with me given the chance. And behind me was Esther, who would deny it if asked, but was certainly wishing I was dead, as much as everyone else. All made for interesting dynamics.

Midway through the service, I played my solo. My family had made a fuss, of course, told me I should sit there like the rest of them, only my father would be taking part, when he stood up to spout lies about what a great brother William had been. But I wasn't taking any notice, I wanted to play. They didn't want me to make a fuss during the actual service, so they capitulated. I played Bach, a nice piece that displayed my talent. I played with my eyes closed, swaying as if lost in the music, full of passion. When I opened my eyes, several people were crying, which was very pleasing. I like to control the emotion in a room. Esther and my family stared at me with stony eyes, but everyone else was moved.

***

Of course, my little game with Rob's phone didn't end there. I think they left things for a few weeks out of respect, in case it was a mad blip caused by Uncle's death. But within the month, I was visited again, this time by two deacons.

I had continued to play my clarinet on Sundays, though hadn't bothered to attend the practices of course. I like to play, and there was no reason to stop just because Esther avoided looking at me whenever we were in the same room. I often stepped forwards, after a song had finished, and played it through again, adding twiddly flourishes to show off my ability. I always played with my eyes closed, which meant no one could indicate that I should stop, and most of the audience thought I was 'lost in the emotion of the Spirit'. Sometimes I would speak, finishing the last note and then on the same breath saying that I wanted to explain why that song was so special to me. I spoke with a low voice, like I was humble, staring at the floor like I was shy (but really so no one could indicate that I should stop!) I would use lots of religious phrases, like how blessed I was, how humble, how the Lord really spoke to me. People never clapped, I'd given up on trying to make them do that, but I would get little noises of appreciation, I knew I was pressing the right buttons. I'm good at that.

It did tend to lengthen the services by quite a lot, which meant sometimes the sermon part overran the time allocation. During coffee, people would mutter about how late everything had ended. I always joined in of course, agreeing it made things difficult for families who needed to get home and feed their children lunch.

"Someone should have a word with Rob," I would say, "It's not very honouring to God to keep talking for so long. It shows a lack of discipline."

It never seemed to occur to anyone that actually, it was due to my lengthy playing that the timing had gone awry.

Anyway, as I said, I was visited at home. Twice actually, but I'll tell you about the church one first, as I need to work myself up to tell you about the second one. The deacons arranged a time for their visit one Sunday, and arrived the following Tuesday evening. A couple of grey-haired men in jeans and sweaters, tired from their day at work, uncertain about how to fulfil their role. I could almost smell the fear on them when I opened the door.

They were amateurs, chosen by the church to organise the cleaners, to arrange social events, and to decide how the money should be spent. So I was far beyond their area of expertise, and they knew it. I expect they had initially become deacons happily, seeing it as a sort of promotion above the rank of normal members: spiritual leaders of a community. But they had never anticipated sorting out the nitty-gritty of real life, the problems of a world far removed from the image presented in the Sunday Schools of their past. They talked about things like 'fornication' and 'adultery', never dreaming that one day they might have to tackle issues like 'a bit on the side' or 'getting laid'. Now they had been sent to sort me out. I could imagine the meetings where my actions had been discussed, the worry about how to appear 'loving' when it was flaming obvious that I was upsetting things and needed to be stopped.

I decided not to make things easy for them. I had only agreed to the meeting because it gave opportunity to further my game a little, sow some doubt into a few more minds. I opened the door and let them talk for a while on the doorstep. They muttered about it being kind of me to see them, there were some issues they needed to discuss, they hoped I was well. Then one of them, Kevin Matthews, was brave enough to suggest I should invite them in. I decided they might take a while and I would be more comfortable sitting down, so I opened the door wider and pointed to the lounge, said they could go in there if they wanted, take off their shoes on the mat first.

They sat on chairs, facing me, stiff in their coats, awkward in socks. I didn't usually bother about taking off shoes, but I was wearing slippers myself, and I thought it would unsettle them to have cold feet. They looked miserable. Kevin wore green socks, with a hole in them. The other deacon, Scott Downey, reached down and pulled up his black socks, stretching them across his shins like a school boy. I smiled.

"Clara," said Scott, and swallowed. "We need to discuss some sensitive issues with you, some things have come to our attention and we don't feel we can ignore them. You see, belonging to the church involves some commitment, there are some codes of behaviour, laid down in the Bible, that we expect people to adhere to. Shall we start with a prayer?" he added, as if he had just remembered it, had meant to begin the session with prayer but nerves had gotten the better of him and he had launched into the main issue straight off.

"No," I said. "Just say what you want to say. I would assume we all prayed before we met? I don't expect God has forgotten and needs reminding. I think we can assume he will guide our discussion." I decided I would talk in churchy language for a bit longer, so they weren't quite sure which side of the fence I was on. Good to keep them uncertain.

Kevin coughed and took the lead. "Yes, of course. We have spent a considerable amount of time in prayer, seeking the Lord's guidance. Now we need to resolve some issues." He coughed again, like the words were causing him trouble.

"Clara, we believe you sent some inappropriate texts to Esther, using Rob's mobile phone, suggesting that you were involved romantically?"

He didn't mention the photos. I wondered if that was because he didn't know, or if they had decided to focus on one thing at a time. There was also the possibility that Rob and Esther themselves hadn't discovered them yet, which was funny. I smiled again.

"It depends what you mean by 'inappropriate'," I said. "Surely we have all done things that are 'inappropriate' at one time or another? Doesn't the Bible teach that even thoughts can be seen as 'inappropriate', that what we think matters, and is a sin? Tell me Kevin, have you never had 'inappropriate' thoughts?"

"Well, yes," he said, "but that's not what we're discussing here."

"Well, is that fair?" I said. "Should you be mentioning things you feel I have done which are inappropriate, when you admit that you yourself have thought things that are inappropriate? Doesn't the Bible teach that they are equal? Both sinful? Yet you are trying to condemn me and look innocent yourself."

"That's not the point," said Scott, rescuing Kevin who was

floundering, knowing I was wrong but unable to articulate it. "The point is, that you sent texts to Esther, suggesting Rob had committed adultery. We have discussed this with both of them, and we believe what you wrote to be a lie. This cannot be left unresolved. The diaconate have discussed and prayed about the matter, and we feel you should resign your membership. You have acted wrongly and there must be discipline."

I started to object, but he ignored me and continued speaking. I think it was a prepared speech, possibly written out and practised beforehand. He was keen to deliver it before I muddled them again.

"You may, of course, continue to attend Sunday services, as we hope you will come to a point of repentance. However, we would recommend that it would be better for you to attend a different church, at least for the time being. We are happy to help you find a suitable church, if you want us to.

"We have also decided that should you decide to still attend our church, you can no longer play the clarinet during services. We are grateful for your input, and appreciate the expertise you have brought to the music group. But we feel that it is seen as a leadership role, that by being at the front people will consider you to be part of the fellowship. And for now, we are asking you to relinquish that role."

"Okay," I said.

That confused them even more. I think they had been expecting a defence, perhaps even tears. Or maybe that I would fall to my knees, plead for forgiveness, another chance.

I thought for a moment, then asked, "Can I give my side? Can I be allowed a chance to speak at a church meeting, to give my side of things?"

They looked at each other. Kevin shook his head.

"No. You may tell us now, if you have anything to say in

response, and we will convey that message to the meeting. But you are no longer able to speak in meetings."

"So, I am not to be allowed to defend myself? That hardly seems fair."

"You can tell us now," said Scott. "What do you want to say Clara?"

But I didn't want to tell them, there was no fun in that. I wanted to talk to all the membership. I hadn't quite decided what I would say, whether I would suggest Rob had led me astray, used my bereavement to take advantage of me. Or perhaps I would say it was my fault, in the turmoil of emotion at losing my dear uncle I had flung myself at Rob, and he had been unable to resist, and now I was sorry, I wanted to repent.

But neither story would have any traction with Kevin and Scott. Even if they believed me, they would report back to the deacons, who would chant their prayers, invoke their spirits. Then they would speak again to Rob and Esther, who although weak did not strike me as stupid. They would quickly dispel any doubts, my story would fall on deaf ears.

The membership was different though. I had once attended a meeting, just to see what they were like. They were boring, long-winded, and mostly pointless. The membership however was quite big and very varied. There were old ladies and tired mothers and stressed business men straight from the office. Some of them would be gullible, some of them would let my words sink home, to be remembered in the future. They were the ones I wanted in my audience. Those were the people I wanted to play my game with, the ones I could influence, persuade with clever words and displays of emotion.

I stood, our discussion was ended. As I opened the front door, watching them struggle to put on their shoes while standing in the hallway, I told them I would be attending the next meeting.

"I understand what you have said, but I feel I have the right to a fair trial," I said. "I've decided that I will attend the next church meeting – it's on the 23rd isn't it?"

Scott nodded. "Yes, but…"

They had both moved outside, were standing again on the doorstep.

"No," I said, "no buts. I will attend and I will speak. I have the right to be heard. If you refuse to let me come, I shall turn up every Sunday morning and make a fuss until you let me speak. And you don't want that, you don't want me disrupting the time of worship, do you? So please tell the diaconate to expect me on the 23rd. You can add me to the agenda if you want."

"Clara, please, can we not sort this out now?" said Kevin. "None of us wants a fuss, we all want to seek the Lord's will in this and move forwards. We're not condemning you, all of us are sinners, but there has to be discipline. Why don't we go back into the lounge and discuss everything now? There's no need for this to involve everyone else."

"Yes," I said, "there is. I will be there on the 23rd."

I shut the door.

They stood for a few minutes, I could hear them talking in low voices. Then one of them rang the bell. I ignored them, went back into the lounge and turned on the telly. I was looking forward to the 23rd, it would be fun.

***

I heard nothing further. The day before the church meeting, I was ready. I had planned a little speech, had decided to go for the 'Rob took advantage of the poor bereaved niece' angle. I knew they wouldn't accept that their hero was bad, so I would portray him as weak. We had been alone, I had been crying, he had moved to comfort me, one thing had led to another. It was easy to explain how it had happened, an attractive young woman and a red-blooded male.

The texts were slightly harder to explain, so I'd decided that being distraught by our sinful actions, I had wanted to tell someone, to confess. I wasn't sure how to do this, so had sent the texts to Esther as a sort of cry for help. I knew she would come, and had hoped that it would force Rob to admit what we'd done, and together we could come to the church, ask for forgiveness and move on.

It was a good story, and if I told it well, as least a few people would believe me. Actually, I expected most people would start to doubt Rob's version.

It was late when I finally turned off the television and went to bed. The next day, I would go to work as normal, but finish early to prepare for the meeting. I would have a nice long bath, spend some time on my makeup. I needed to look sad but pretty, so people would understand how irresistible I had been, how easily Rob had slipped into my arms, how passion had taken over. I washed my face and cleaned my teeth, ready for the next day. When I climbed into bed I realised how tired I was, must be all the brain exercise with planning everything. I fell asleep almost as soon as the light went out.

Chapter Fourteen

I woke with a start. My heart was thumping, although I didn't realise why. Not at first. I just lay there, frightened. I had never been frightened before, not once in my whole life. My throat was dry, but I couldn't swallow, and it was hard to breathe, like I had a lump in my chest. I could feel my heart racing, the blood rushing through my veins, and I was listening, straining to hear. Something bad was going to happen.

The fear grew, the tension more than I could bear, so I lifted my head, looked at the end of the bed. There was someone – *not* a man, but the shape of a man. He was sitting there. That's all, sitting. Not moving, not speaking.

But I knew who he was, who he represented. I knew at once. Knew and was terrified. The very air was different, warm, electric, wrapping around me like cotton wool, suffocating. If I hadn't been already lying, I would have fallen. My body had no strength left, my bones had dissolved.

I was frightened because I saw, for the first time ever, *who I was*. It wasn't a pretty picture. I was aware of every tiny thing that I had ever done wrong, every person I had hurt, every upset I had caused. And I knew that he knew too. For the first time, it mattered. I cared what he thought. I knew, absolutely, that he loved me. Which in itself is hard to believe, because I thought I was incapable of love, of either giving or receiving it. But this love was stronger even than my inability. He knew everything, and yet, had come because he loved me.

I couldn't speak, couldn't move. I lay there, half sitting, heart thumping like it would burst, mouth dry. I felt like I might melt, right there in the bed, simply cease to be. More than dying. Worse, somehow. I wanted to cry, but there was too much sadness for that, the tears had evaporated in the hotness of understanding.

Then he turned, looked at me. I hadn't thought it could get worse, but this was. Much worse. The knowledge of who I was shot through me like a physical pain. It was too much. More than I could bear. He didn't speak, but he *saw*.

When he nodded, I knew I had a choice. I could feel like this forever, this agony, this dissolved personality, this never dying death. Knowing his love but pushing it away. Or I could change.

I chose change. Who wouldn't? He still didn't speak, didn't leave. But he knew. I was aware of that, my decision was known and sealed. He would not allow me to change my mind. There was no going back.

For a while I did nothing. I felt like I was sort of absorbing him, and being absorbed in return. The warm was comfortable now, a cocoon. The fear was still there, but somehow it had changed. A good fear. Is such a thing possible? I could have been anywhere, the whole room, everything around me, the bed below me, the covers over me, had become indistinct. I could have been floating. Everything physical, including my body, had become irrelevant. There was only *him*. Nothing else mattered.

I still don't know why I did it. Even today, I feel so stupid when I think about it. It was the worst thing I have ever done. But I had to know, some part of my brain wanted proof. So I pushed myself up, nearer, and slowly, cautiously, I reached out, to touch him.

Imagine touching fire, hotter than that. Putting your hand through white hot flames, molten iron. That's what it felt like. Agony too great to even scream. The skin melted and shrunk, drew back to expose flesh that spat and sizzled.

I pulled back my hand in a flash. Intense pain, everything focussed on that cooked skin, burnt flesh, screaming nerves. My body went into shock and I vomited, all over the bed. When I looked up, he had gone.

Chapter Fifteen

Okay, we have to stop there.

Even later, sitting in the airport lounge, surrounded by all the luxury an airline can muster, the memory of it shook me. The rest is easy to tell, I reviewed it in minutes. But that night, that pivotal point which changed everything, that needs some reflection time. It demands it. The game ended.

There I was, living my life exactly how I wanted, and it was like an ice bucket thrown unexpectedly. Suddenly, without warning, I was not the centre of the universe, the most important thing. In fact, in the grand scheme of things, it turned out I was rather small and insignificant; and I needed to change. For the first time, ever, I had felt loved and accepted. It made me *want* to alter my plans, to try and live up to that acceptance. That would shock anyone I reckon.

Later, waiting for my flight, sipping gin and thinking about it all, I began to wonder. Do you think it was all planned? Things like going to live with Uncle, starting to attend church and hearing enough to recognise who came to me. Even the discovery about Joanna, realising that we were similar, had a place. It felt as if in some way, I had inherited the essence of her, I was made in the same mould, but instead of being allowed to be destructive, perhaps I was being prepared for something better. I like to be the best. Maybe those traits which had allowed her to destroy, were going to be used as a strength, perhaps there was something that needed to be done, and I was uniquely designed to accomplish it.

There was nothing random about all this. I had been chosen.

When, in church, Rob had been doing his impression of a Punch and Judy show, when I had wanted to shout, "He's behind you," I would, actually, have been correct. I had only seen the people, but there had been far more going on than I had noticed.

***

I had sat in bed for a few minutes, then I went to shower. I cleaned myself without letting the water touch my hand. By the time I was clean, I was starting to doubt what I'd seen, what I'd known. I tried to tell myself it was a dream, those prawns I'd eaten for lunch must be doing weird things to my brain. That's me all over – a bit fickle at times. But I couldn't ignore my hand, and I wasn't dreaming that. It was agony. It even smelt horrid, cooked flesh. I don't think I will ever be able to eat barbecued food again. It hurt too much even to bandage, the thought of cotton touching the raw flesh made me shudder. I wrapped it in clingfilm in the kitchen, because I'd read somewhere that that was what you did with burns. It felt slightly better when the air couldn't get to it.

I went to check, of course, looked all round the bed for something hot that I might have touched in my sleep, a radiator pipe overheating, an electrical wire going wrong, anything. But there was nothing. The throb in my hand couldn't be explained away. It was excruciating evidence that not even I could ignore. I cleaned up my bed using only my right hand. It wasn't easy. Or pleasant. I wasn't going to fuss around with washing disgusting bedding, so I sealed the lot into a black bag and put it out with the bins.

Then I sat, in the lounge, on Uncle's gold chairs, and had a think. My feet were bare, which reminded me of the deacons with their socks. But I didn't feel like smiling. I was still feeling slightly queasy to be honest. If it wasn't for my hand I would've put the whole thing down to a hallucination due to a stomach bug. But I couldn't ignore that hand. It wasn't a dream. Which meant it was real. Which also meant I had agreed to change, things had to be different. So, sitting there, I made a plan. It didn't include a visit to the church meeting; I didn't dare to do that now.

I decided on a few things I *would* do, to sort of show willing, start to live differently. Not that I especially wanted to, but I wasn't stupid, I knew when I was beat. I decided I would read the Bible that Uncle had given me, just to find out what it was all these religious people made a fuss about. I thought the whole church, religion thing had missed the point rather – there was certainly nothing in the church that had prepared me for actually meeting *him*. But perhaps they'd diluted things, perhaps the secret was found in their book, so I'd have a look.

I also thought I probably did need to go back to church. That's what you're supposed to do, isn't it? The person I had met was far removed from the God they claimed to be worshipping, with their songs centred on themselves, the social focus and the traditions. But perhaps I had missed something. Perhaps, if you looked deep enough, God was there, sitting at the back, waiting to be noticed.

The problem was, I didn't think they'd let me. I know the deacons had made all those 'you can still attend on a Sunday' noises, but I didn't honestly think they'd be welcoming me with open arms. Especially after all my threats to stand up and have my say. I would probably be escorted from the premises as soon as I turned up. And I couldn't phone Rob, explain what had happened and ask him to tell them to let me in. They would all just think it was part of the game, a ploy to make more trouble. What I needed was someone to speak for me. Someone who had some credibility in the church, who would be listened to if they spoke for me, explained that I wanted to start again, not make any trouble.

Hence I thought of Sam Whittaker. You remember him? The old fossil who sometimes led prayers. He was old, past it really, but for some reason, those church people still respected him. You could tell. If he spoke for me, they would listen, give me another chance. I decided to pay him a visit. I would go Wednesday afternoon, when I'd sorted out a few things in my head. I thought, to be honest, that probably *he* would sort things for me. The whole deciding to go to church in the first place, noticing Sam Whittaker on that first Sunday, being given the Bible - all that would help now, help to sort out what I was supposed to do next. If things had happened for a reason, if there really was a plan, then I figured he would sort the next bit too. Who knows, perhaps he had already prepared Sam, maybe he would be expecting my visit.

I waited until it was late enough for the rest of the world to be awake (no way was I going to be getting back to sleep), then phoned work. I told them I'd had an accident, burnt my hand, needed to take a few days off and would tell them more after I'd visited the hospital. Then I rang the doctor's. Always a gamble getting an appointment, but I managed to convince the dragon on reception that I had a medical emergency and was told to arrive at 10.30. I wasn't sure about driving with one hand, so ordered a taxi. I could've asked Rory to take me, of course, or Bill, who I had been with a couple of nights ago, but I wasn't keen on them asking questions. The doctor would be easier to fob off I thought.

The taxi arrived on time and I was waiting, not wanting to miss the appointment. An Asian chap was driving, his identity badge swinging from the clip in front of me said his name was Rakesh Patel, though I think the photo was an old one, as it showed a man with a beard and he was clean shaven. Either that or he'd borrowed it from a mate. The radio was on, set to some foreign channel, playing Indian music – the sort of rubbish you get on those Bollywood movies you occasionally see advertised. I wasn't in the mood, and told him to turn it off. He didn't speak, nodded and switched it off. We drove the rest of the way in silence.

The surgery had one of those 'self-check-in' screens, where you have to enter your date of birth and name and they tell you sit in the waiting room. Cheaper than a person I guess. I sat in the corner, watching a woman who was struggling to keep a runny-nosed brat quiet. I hoped the germs couldn't reach across the room, I had enough to worry about without being ill. A few old people were there as well, stagnating on uncomfortable chairs while they waited. There was a rack of pamphlets stuck on the wall, telling you how to cope with various illnesses. On a small table was a stack of greasy magazines, old and tired, carrying the germs from previous patients. The top one was a travel guide, a shiny photograph of the Taj Mahal, hiding the tabloid-snapped face of a hungover Royal on the cover of the magazine below. I moved it and stared at the familiar face.

'Strange to be famous,' I thought, 'it might seem glamorous at the time, but then your face – rarely the one you wanted people to see – ended up in some doctor's waiting room being sneezed over.'

I sat there for about three years. The sun streamed through a side window, reflecting from the Taj photo, straight into my eye. It was annoying, so I angled the magazine slightly to stop the glint, then sat there, staring at the white domes, not thinking.

At one point a doctor called for the next patient over the intercom, then forgot to turn it off. We heard the door open, Mr Green being welcomed, and directed to a chair.

"Ah, hello Mr Green. Take a seat, what seems to be the problem?"

"Well Doctor, I've had awful trouble with me…"

Unfortunately one of the receptionists had noticed and rushed in, so the next thing we heard was her interrupting and reminding the doctor to turn it off. I thought it was funny, but the other patients all turned shocked faces to each other and tutted.

Eventually I was seen. Dr Mubashira turned out to be a girl, hardly older than me, brown skin, straight backed, and with smooth black hair tucked into a pony-tail. I explained I had burnt my hand in a bonfire, didn't give any more details. The doctor looked suspicious, tried asking other questions, but I just shrugged, asked if she was qualified to sort it out. I knew that would annoy her, she would think I was rude and presumptuous, which would distract her from asking too many questions. To be honest, it already seemed a lot better. It was agony, I'm not saying it wasn't, but it looked less raw than I remembered it being. She told me it wasn't serious and would heal in a couple of weeks, though was deep enough that it would probably blister. She sent me off to a nurse for a dressing and bandage, which made it hurt even more, and gave me some antiseptic cream for the blisters. I could take paracetamol for the pain. She also gave me a lecture about sunburn, as if that was likely in England.

"When the new skin grows, it will be very sensitive," she said, reciting some info from when she was training I expect. "You will need to protect it, especially from sunburn. Wear a glove if necessary, and use a high-factor sunblock cream."

She looked at me, checking I was listening. "Your hand will become sunburnt very easily."

I nodded, but I wasn't really listening. I had no plans to travel anywhere sunny.

***

That evening there was a pub quiz at The Bull. Tony, a bloke from work who fancied me, had asked if I'd join their team last week, and I'd just laughed, told him I didn't know what I'd be doing. But I quite fancied going out, when it came to it, so I changed into decent clothes – not easy with one hand the size of a loaf of bread, and drove myself there. Driving was a bit dodgy too, the bandage made changing gear and steering a bit inaccurate, but I managed it. I did clip a wing-mirror on a Mini when I parked, dented the casing, but I didn't think the owner would notice, there wasn't much lighting in the carpark. They had parked right on the edge of their space anyway, were asking for trouble.

I went in and joined Tony's team. There were six of them, squashed around a sticky table in the corner. I'd met them all before, so they just nodded when I arrived, Tony grinning because he thought it meant I liked him. A bloke called Simon sat up a bit straighter too, thinking I might like a change I expect; Tony wasn't the most exciting bloke in the world. I let him buy me a gin.

There were a couple of girls: Jessica and Ashley. They smiled when I arrived, but neither seemed very inclined to welcome me. Perhaps they were reserving judgement until they knew how useful I would be with the questions. Jessica had blonde hair and shiny fingernails, square ended and painted pale pink to match her lipstick. Very 1960s. I wondered if they were false, but the light wasn't good enough to tell. Ashley was dressed entirely in black. When she lifted her beer I noticed her wrists and hands were decorated with a henna tattoo. An intricate design of flowers and leaves laced from one finger across her hand and around her wrist. Which meant her ginger hair must be natural, as I'm sure I'd read somewhere that you can't use henna on your skin if you dye your hair. Not quite sure why you would want a henna tattoo anyway, unless you're Indian and getting married.

But there was something about the pattern that got into my brain. Every time I closed my eyes, I could see that design, imprinted on my mind. Flowers intertwined, leaves creeping forwards, symmetrical curves and petals traced along her wrists, stretching towards her finger tips.

The quiz, like all pub quizzes, was suited only to people who actually like these things and bother to do some research before they arrive. Be honest, do you know the names of Vietnamese presidents or random roads in Australia? Not really the sort of knowledge one acquires naturally is it? The four blokes were intense, the girls were quietly knowledgeable.

Simon and Ashley were both rather adept at answering, muttering together about the names of G K Chesterton (who I didn't even know was a novelist before the evening began), then deciding on "Gerald Keith", which was wrong. (He was called Gilbert, if you're interested – I wasn't.) The only answer I knew was to the question about a film which had 300,000 extras in it. I guessed it was *Gandhi* – just because it was a film I knew had massive crowd scenes. I managed to answer a few others by listening to the general mutterings and then saying aloud what someone else had been considering, making it look like my idea. I don't think they noticed. It worked especially well for the question about Vivien Leigh's birthplace. I wasn't quite sure who Vivien Leigh was, but an older woman on the adjacent table was whispering that it was India, so I in turn hissed "India – she was born in India" to my team. It turned out to be right, which impressed them all.

It was a boring evening, and I left before the end. The two girls scowled when I said I needed to leave, Jessica saying that it probably wouldn't make any difference anyway, which was bitchy of her. Tony offered to come with me, but I wasn't having that. I'd thought the evening might be fun, and it had just been boring, he wasn't going to get any favours from me for that.

I picked up dinner from the Indian takeaway on my way home, carrying the greasy bag in my good hand. I ate it in front of the telly. There was an old film on, *Slumdog Millionaire*, so I watched that for a bit. I must've fallen asleep in front of the telly, because when I woke up it was cold and I was uncomfortable. I had been dreaming about those henna patterns, seeing them traced onto the furniture and walls, stretching out across the whole house. Delicate red-brown lines decorating the gold furniture and white walls.

I left the dirty containers where they were and dragged myself to bed. I lay there, waiting, wondering if he would come again, tell me more of the plan.

**

When I woke the next day, everything stank of curry. Even after I'd washed my hair and chucked out last night's rubbish; it lingered, a sweet spice that clung to my clothes and seemed part of everything I breathed. It must have been repeating in my guts or something.

I started to read that Bible. I started at the beginning, and ploughed through all the fantasy bits about giants and floods, and the boring bits about who was related to who. As I turned those thin pages, skimming through books of history and poems and story, I could smell curry. After a while, I decided the Bible itself must have been near enough to the korma while I ate, so the pages had absorbed some of the steam.

It was a weird experience, reading something I'd heard quoted so many times, something I knew snippets of, yet had never actually read for myself. Much of it was boring, or illogical, or completely unbelievable. I began to wish I had listened to more of those boring sermons I'd sat through, I could've used a few explanations.

But pervading it all (as well as the smell of last night's dinner) was a sense of God – omnipotent, beyond reach, above all, yet reaching down, touching people, guiding events. I didn't understand it, most of it washed over me and was instantly forgotten, but something of the essence of the book was absorbed by me. It was as if reading it affected me, like the house being affected by the curry. I recognised the God who was described, and was aware of how insignificant, how fleeting, were the lives of the human actors. Tiny specks in time, yet he chose to use them, to work through them, to make them part of *his* plan. When they listened to him, whatever snippet of time they happened to be living in, if they followed his plan, what they did mattered, was significant. He gave their lives worth, simply because *he* had worth.

And so I visited Sam Whittaker. He was the only person I could think of who was respected and might listen to me. I have already told you how that went. He listened, believed me, told me to leave. When he said those words : "Do you know where you'll go?" India was obvious. All those Indian references, people, smells. It was like they were clues along the way, a bizarre map that I was bound to follow until I made the correct decision. It made sense. I had the money, thanks to Uncle William, and I was pretty much done with my current life. My game had ended, there was no one and nothing I especially wanted to stay for, so why not leave? India was an odd choice, but it would be different, exciting. And perhaps there was a bigger reason, one I didn't know yet.

The next few weeks were bit of a whirlwind. The probate came through without hitch, and I put the house on the market at once. My family had phoned and written and visited numerous times, but when it came to the crunch, they didn't contest anything. I assume the threat of having all the Joanna history revealed was too great for them. I heard later that Dad had spent a fortune trying to find Alexsander. I guess he thought if he could produce a more plausible heir, I would be bumped and he would get a second shot at inheriting the house later – we all knew that if Alexsander was alive, he was unlikely to last long. But he drew a blank. He traced his nephew to a squat in a derelict factory near the Thames, but no one knew where he went after that. I'm guessing in the river itself, especially if he was still using, which seems likely.

The money went straight into my bank account, the house

contents were sold through an agent – I didn't even bother to attend the house-clearing sale. There was nothing there I wanted. I rented a flat and moved out. By the time I was boarding the plane at Heathrow, the house sale was just being finalised. I heard nothing from my family, nor did I expect to. It didn't matter. I was moving on.

***

My flight was announced over the tannoy, and I gathered my bags. I decided to use the washroom one last time before leaving – even in Upper Class it's like peeing in a tiny cupboard on the plane. The loos in the lounge had cloth hand towels and soft music and seemed clean. I washed my face before leaving, and used the hand lotion, still being gentle with my injured hand. By the time I left they were calling my name. That didn't matter, they wouldn't leave without me, too much bother to find the bags I'd checked in.

The woman at the gate gave a forced smile and tried to hurry me. But I was enjoying myself, so I feigned a limp and made my way very slowly down the ramps towards the plane. I was shown to my seat and offered a drink. Then I sat there, trying not to think about how many hours my bum would be on that seat for. Even with the ability to turn it into a flat bed, it wasn't exactly comfortable. The seatbelt sign lit up, the stewards did their safety drill, and we began to taxi from the stand. I wondered what was waiting for me when we landed. I wondered what the plan was.

Chapter Sixteen

The flight arrived on time. I gathered my belongings from the overhead bins as soon as the seatbelt light went out. Everyone was tired. However big your seat might be, being in the same clothes, breathing the same air, regurgitated from the belly of the plane for nine hours, makes you feel stale. I ignored the voice telling me to remain seated with my phone off and took it off 'airplane' mode. I wasn't expecting any messages, but you never know. I was ready and waiting, so as soon as the door was opened, I walked smartly past everyone else and was first off. I had been on that plane for quite long enough.

The walk through the airport was uninformative. People followed signs to luggage or onward flights, everyone felt fuzzy, you could tell. Airports are always like that – too much static electricity and too many overtired people. Everything is over used, worn out and germ ridden.

Immigration took forever. They had some weird system that didn't really work properly, I assume to check fingerprints. We all had to put our hands on a screen, but it didn't work. I'm not sure the border guards themselves knew the science behind it. They kept telling people to wipe their fingers with cleaning gel, then try again. Over and over, while everyone else waited. They didn't let anyone through, were trying to be thorough, but it just wasn't working.

I scanned the hall, wondering if there was a way to jump the queue. I considered fainting or pretending to be unwell. But there was a woman to our left in a wheelchair, and she was no further ahead than the rest of us. Plus there was always the possibility they might refuse entry if I was considered a health risk. I waited.

I had applied for a tourist visa. This was not strictly accurate, but I figured it would get me into the country with the minimum of fuss. If I decided I needed different papers, it should be easy enough to bribe someone now I was here.

Finally I made it to the front of the line – a cursory glance at the passport, a stupidly long wait at the fingerprint machine, then into the country. I followed signs to the luggage hall and rescued my bags from their loop around the belt. They were new, I'd splashed out on something decent for the trip. One was scratched, which was annoying. I don't like when my things are spoilt.

I had avoided a final trip to the airplane toilet, and now needed a washroom. There was one in the corner, so I wheeled my bags over, bracing myself for an unpleasant experience.

The washroom was clean. Unexpected. A woman stood at one end, and she smiled when I entered, and ushered me into a cubicle. The woman came in with me, to wipe the seat – also unexpected. We danced around each other for an awkward moment as I tried to fit my bags in with me and she tried to leave. Eventually we were sorted, with her on the correct side of the locked door. When I had finished, she turned on the tap so I could wash my hands and showed me where to dry them. She then stood there, waiting. If she thought I might tip her she was wrong. Tips are for people who might be helpful in the future.

I pushed my luggage, through the green customs door, and out.

Beyond customs was a whole new world, I should describe it for you, this was so not Marksbridge. Everything was strange. Accents, heat, smells. People were milling around, offering taxis, trying to exchange money, advertising hotels. I searched for my name on the hundreds of pieces of card being held up for inspection, and felt some relief when I found it. Booking a hotel car had been a good bit of planning, I certainly didn't have the energy for taxi negotiations.

The driver collected the car – a rather smart Mercedes – and helped me with my luggage. I noticed a sign in the carpark : *No sitting. No spitting. No cooking.* Below it, a group of three men sat, long backs in crumpled cotton shirts, cooking something on a tiny stove. I smiled. I might fit into this country rather well.

I eased back, stretching my back against the seat, glad to be out of the stale air of the airport. I might not know exactly why I had come, but I had arrived. I watched India as it passed my window, looking for clues.

The roads were full. Really, completely, no room for another vehicle sort of full. Most cars were white (though my Merc was black – I like that, being a bit special). We threaded through the traffic, moving into gaps, honking frequently, passing other vehicles and being overtaken on both sides. It wasn't just cars and vans. Men strained to pedal bikes, some were precariously loaded with goods, others were pulling trailers, stacked high with gas canisters, or plants, or firewood. If we paused, even for a second, women would thread their way through the traffic, knocking on windows with the back of their knuckles, holding a cupped hand towards me, pleading for money. Their clothes were bright but worn, as if washed many times. Their hair was matted, and their eyes stared in at me, persistent. I turned away. I had nothing for them, and I found their gaze intrusive.

We passed an area of scrubland, filled with makeshift tents blowing in the breeze. Women were hanging washing on gnarled branches, their skin dark against the garish brightness of their clothes.

Green and yellow auto-rickshaws edged between the cars, their drivers squinting at the world between hanging beads and tiny gods stuck to the steering wheels. My driver pointed at one, told me it

177

was a 'tuk-tuk'. The name stuck in my head, and that's what I called them from then on.

We passed smarter buildings. There were guards, leaning bored against walls, guns slung across their backs, crumpled khaki trousers.

You might be wondering how I felt. Would you be nervous, if it was you? I don't get nervous, mostly I am either bored or excited. I wasn't really thinking anything, to be honest. It was all too new, I was just watching it all, like a movie, through the window. I think the last few weeks had been such a roller coaster of admin and organisation, and the journey so long, that I was now feeling numb. I was in survival mode, forcing myself from one essential step to the next, and anything creative was beyond me at this point. I somehow thought that tomorrow, after a decent night's sleep in a comfortable bed, I would be able to make some decisions.

Did you expect me to be thinking about Rob and Esther, my family, Uncle William? Ah, that shows that you're not really keeping up. I had moved on you see. That's what people like me do. We appear to be involved, part of other people's lives, then when it's time to leave, we leave. They don't matter anymore, they're not thought about. It's simple. I had had my fun, played my games, then my plans had been stopped. Now I was here – waiting for someone else to direct me. I wondered what, exactly, my role would be. What was it in this country that my unique talents were designed to achieve?

The driver was talking, and I let his words wash over me. He pointed out the army base, and the people taking advantage of the cooler winter weather to get married, and the president's residence with 300 rooms for just one person. I knew I should respond, chat to the driver and form a connection. A driver would be a useful person to know. But I was too tired. I just couldn't be bothered.

We soon neared the broad road that stretched from India Gate to Government House. We passed within sight of India Gate, inscribed with the names of martyrs – though it was barely visible through the pollution haze. There were grass verges, and fountains, and beds of flowers. It was possible, for a moment, to think this was England at the end of a sunny spell. The round parliament building loomed to our left, then we spun round a roundabout and along a wide tree lined avenue. The trees were mature and shady, their blossoms covered in dust. Everything was covered in dust. This was not a clean city.

The car arrived at the hotel. Or, to be more accurate, it arrived in the driveway. Two guards stepped forward and the driver popped open the bonnet and boot. The guards peered in – I have no idea if they were checking for bombs or bodies. Perhaps both. We were waved on and drove a hundred yards further. The boot was opened again and a man leapt forward to open my door. I was keen to take control of my bags, but I was too late. They had been hauled from the car and put on a conveyor belt, like at airport security. Everything was scanned, and I was directed through a metal detector while a woman waved some rod across me. It was unexpected and strangely annoying. I thought I had finished with all the security, I wanted to relax now, be treated like a guest. Snatching my hand luggage from the tray, I marched towards the reception desk.

The air in the hotel lobby was cool. It was also quiet compared to the noise of the street. People spoke in lowered voices, and there were smells of flowers, and candles, with an undercurrent of cumin. A man followed me, my cases in a precarious stack on his trolley. I told him I wanted my luggage to stay with me – I have been in these hotels before, they try to deliver your bags directly to your room, but in fact there is often a delay, leaving you without clean clothes for an annoying hour while they sort out their muddled procedures. He stuck doggedly to my heels.

The reception was busy, there were a few people checking in. I couldn't see an opening to get to the desk, so I inched to just behind a loud tourist with a lot of luggage and a large wife. They didn't look comfortable travellers, the sort of people who want everything to be exactly like everything at home, but with an accent. I didn't think they would enjoy India. The man was speaking, checking his room booking, checking the price, asking when the restaurant would be open and could they get a beer and a burger and someone to press their clothes?

I watched the man behind the desk. He wore a very white shirt and his mouth smiled while his eyes watched. He assured the couple the room was "no problem," the meal was "no problem," the service was their "absolute pleasure." All the while he was signalling to his colleagues, assigning tasks, typing. When the guest proffered a tip, it disappeared as if by magic. This was someone who would be useful, who spoke the same language as me.

I turned to my worried looking porter, who was attempting to stand as near as possible to where I'd edged into the queue. I ignored all the people glaring at me and asked where the washroom was. Peeling a note from my purse, I left him in the lobby with strict instructions to NOT take my bags anywhere, and walked quickly in the direction he had pointed.

The washroom was clean and thankfully empty. There was an assortment of combs and lotions and tissues for use, wide marble tops and well-lit mirrors. My reflection was stale, lank hair and smudged eyes. I set to work with eyeliner and lip gloss and tidied my hair. I wasn't willing to risk the water in my mouth, so my teeth remained dirty. Also nothing I could do about my clothes, though I used the perfume spray and washed my hands. I didn't want to look as awful as I felt. Whatever my role here was going to be, I would need people to help me, and I'm not one to procrastinate, I may as well start cultivating a relationship from the beginning. Feeling marginally better, I returned to the lobby with a sense of purpose.

When the receptionist was free, I gave him my full smile and tried not to look as if I had spent the last day travelling. I was grateful for all his care, listened patiently to his spiel about the facilities, told him how excited I was to be in India. He told me his name was Malik, and I took care to use it frequently, making our conversation personal. Lots of eye-contact and big smiles. I'm good at manipulating people, and I had a feeling Malik would prove useful in the future.

When he took my passport to be photocopied, he found a large rupee note sandwiched between the pages. When the passport was returned, I didn't bother to check if it was missing. I recognise a kindred spirit when I see one.

Then I asked who I should speak to if I needed things – a car, or a guide. He assured me that he was my man, anything I might require he could help me with. I asked about staying for longer, was informed this was, "Not a problem". I asked if it was possible to extend one's visa, he told me it was, "Not a problem." I asked if it was possible to pay for new papers, again, "Not a problem." He was leaning forwards now, his eyes keen. We were understanding each other. When the formalities were finished, he signalled for someone to take his place, and stood. He would show me to my room himself, the porter scurrying behind.

It seemed to take forever for them to leave. They wanted to bring my bags into the room, wanted to tell me about the hotel facilities, show me the complimentary water bottles and minibar and a thousand other inconsequential details. I just wanted them to leave me alone, but I couldn't be rude, I might need them. I smiled and listened and willed them to leave. Eventually, I was able to tip them (again) and shut the door behind them.

I was tired. The room was comfortable and clean enough, I had no energy for more than a shower before I fell into bed. I set an alarm for a couple of hours, then slept. Not well, of course, I hadn't slept well since the visit. I wondered if *he* would come again, if I was still getting things wrong, needed another shock. So whenever I started to fall asleep, I would get this sort of excited feeling, right in the centre of my stomach. Which doesn't do much to relax a person, as you can imagine.

Of course, feeling nervous was the right emotion, considering what would happen. I had no inkling then, of quite how big the plan would be.

***

When I woke, the daylight was beginning to fade. It was still light, but the sun had lost something of its urgency. I forced myself out of bed and into clean clothes. I needed to go to the bank to check on my money, and I wanted to walk before it was dark, to help myself adjust to the time change. I grabbed a bottle of water to clean my teeth, then drank the rest before setting out.

Malik was still at reception, and he gave me directions and a map. My bank had a branch nearby, it was one of my reasons for choosing the hotel. He told me the area was safe enough, I could go on my own, though should try to return before it was dark. He tried to order a car for me, but I wanted to walk. That was not as easy as I had thought, and it will show you something of India, so I'll explain:

There was no pedestrian route from the hotel, so to leave I had to dodge incoming cars on the driveway. When I joined the road, a line of tuk-tuk drivers smiled happily and began to offer their services. I wanted to walk. This was not something they understood. They suggested places I might like to visit. They tried to agree a low fare. They followed me along the road, asking where I was going, how much I would like to pay. I tried ignoring them, then telling them to go away, wished I knew how to swear in Hindi.

You had to admire their persistence, but I was too tired to be bothered with them. After a few hundred yards they seemed to get the message and returned to their spot near the hotel.

However, I was not to be left alone. As I walked, several people stopped to ask where I was going and to offer directions. More tuk-tuk drivers passed me, doubling back to offer their services. I was very foreign and very much a target. I realised that my linen trousers, blouse and sunhat – bought for the trip – made me very noticeable. I needed to buy some ethnic clothing, something so I wouldn't be quite so obvious. Remember what I've already told you? Much easier to change things from the inside, and to do that you need to blend in. I wanted to be prepared, ready to act when the plan was revealed.

Most people on the street were men. I was watching, noticing, learning. You have to understand people before you can persuade them. I knew from my time in the US that even cultures which appeared similar often had underlying differences which altered how people thought and reacted. There wasn't much that appeared similar here, but I wasn't worried. I would watch and learn and then use my skills to acquire what I needed.

I should also tell you about the roads – they were a whole adventure on their own. When I reached the first road junction, I just stood there, watching. Tuk-tuks and cars (mainly white) flowed continually along the roads while bikes wound between them. There was no pause to the flow. None. I watched other pedestrians as they crossed. They waited until a vehicle came which was moving slow enough to avoid them, then they walked out, waving a hand up and down. They walked a few paces, while the car swung round them, then waited for another gap, walked a few more steps, edging their way between the traffic, gradually moving across the multilane road. After a few minutes of watching, I was ready to brave it myself, slipping through the torrent without disturbing the flow.

There was something unreal about my walk. Perhaps because I was so very tired, but I think it was because *everything* was different. Everyone was brown skinned, I didn't see any other white people. There was a constant noise from horns, and people shouting, and loud music coming from temples. The air was thick with pollution and incense and spices. It was like wading through a dream. I wasn't worried, not at all, but I could feel a new tension in my stomach, like a cat stalking new territory. I didn't know this place. I didn't know what was expected, or what was safe, or how to avoid being scammed. Were people being helpful to an obvious tourist, or were they hoping to entice me into danger, to remove my valuables? I needed to learn quickly, so I could start to influence things to how I wanted them. It was exhilarating.

I arrived at the bank. There were guards at the gate, and I was directed up some steps, past more guards at the door, into a cool sanctuary of calm. The inside of the bank could almost have been the one in Marksbridge High Street. People spoke in quiet voices, the air conditioning was ferocious and everything was glass fixtures and shiny fittings.

I spoke to a woman at the desk. I didn't have an appointment, but I figured I was foreign and looked rich, which meant I was important. They could rearrange their schedule for me. I didn't say that, I simply acted as if I expected them to. They did; I was shown into a room.

There was a thorough identity check, so I was glad I had brought all my papers, and then they explained how I could access my money, and made arrangements for me to have funds available when I needed them.

I didn't want to carry too much cash, planned to mainly use cards, but they told me India was a cash economy. Everyone used hard currency, and relatively few people even had bank accounts. Cheques and credit cards had limited use, other than in large hotels, and shops designed for tourists. Apparently, even house buying was often at least partly done in cash. I listened carefully – not something I was used to doing, but I needed to learn how things worked here. I decided to withdraw some more rupees. There had been limits on how much I could bring into the country, and although I had largely ignored this, there hadn't been time to obtain much currency beforehand.

I was taken down some stairs, so I could withdraw cash from the teller. I was now in the regular part of the bank, where everyone came to sort their money. The queue of customers from outside the bank had been paused, and watchful faces peered at me through glass doors.

There were five men in the line inside, waiting, silent. They were a pretty good example of the people I'd seen on the street. One had an injured leg, one wore pointed shoes and narrow trousers and looked round as though accusing people. An old man in dirty tunic and too-short trousers, fresh from the mosque, stood with his hands folded in front. Two men in jeans and tee-shirts, nondescript, standing as if to attention. They all waited, with contained anxiety and hard eyes, like they weren't comfortable being there. A young guard watched on, fiddling with the stick in his hand, moving them back if they moved too near the counters, anxious himself. It made me wonder how often there was trouble in banks, if most people used them regularly.

There was a clerk behind a screen, counting out rupees and passing them to the customers. Each person stood slightly to one side when they had collected their money, not causing a delay, but checking. Every note was recounted, double-checked. Every single 100 rupee note, not even enough to buy a cup of coffee, checked and accounted for. Then they left, through the doors, past those waiting outside, back to their lives.

I reached the front of the queue and withdrew my money. I

watched as the clerk counted it into piles, then I pushed it deep into my purse. First step complete.

I walked back to the hotel, passing all the same scenes as before. Most shops had men outside, chatting and looking for customers. I avoided eye-contact, but they still spoke, tried to entice me inside or asked where I was going. I didn't feel personal space was much respected here, even my fast pace and scowls didn't deter them. I made a note to buy some ethnic clothes as a priority, I felt way too conspicuous. I hurried past a mosque, and a hotel, and some kind of park. As I approached my hotel, the buildings were big, government owned houses I guessed, with guard houses at the gates. I was already getting used to the traffic, and meandered across the roads with wary confidence. If I hadn't been so tired it would've been fun.

Arriving back at the hotel was something of a relief. The sky was noticeably darker now, already dusk. Perhaps nightfall happened faster this side of the world. I slowed as I walked through the lobby, taking care to walk near the reception desk so I could catch the eye of my contact, Malik, and smile. I felt having some help here was going to be invaluable and I wanted to remind him of my existence, to remember my tip.

I shed my shoes at the door of my room – goodness knows what they had walked through. The tiredness swamped me as I began to relax. Gulping water from a bottle, I scanned the room service menu. I decided I had been adventurous enough for one day, a curry and sleep were all I wanted. I chose a dish with no meat, because I was worried about the hygiene standards. Whilst the hotel might, or might not, be clean, there was no telling the condition the meat had been kept and transported in. I was cautious, there were some seriously nasty bugs out there. I wanted hot food, freshly cooked.

I was almost asleep by the time my food arrived. I shovelled in a few mouthfuls of hot food, avoiding the chillies placed as a garnish. Then I stretched out on the bed, every bone aching. It was enough. I had arrived. Perhaps tomorrow I would learn what the plan was. But tomorrow was another day.

Chapter Seventeen

I woke twice during the night, both times feeling completely refreshed and ready for the day – once at midnight and again at 2 am. I ate some cold rice left over from room service, drank some water, then forced myself to go back to bed and stay there. Jet-lag was something to be mastered (I'd read that somewhere, and I'm a strong person). When my phone showed 7 am, I hauled myself out of bed and into the shower.

I was already finding this country a hard place to relax, the people here didn't seem to bother to keep anything clean. Even in the shower, I was very aware of all the bacteria that were probably floating in the water. I didn't want to be ill, that would be unpleasant, so concentrated on keeping my lips pursed shut, and as soon as I was clean, I dried my face, then rinsed my mouth in bottled water. It seemed slightly OCD, but I would worry about that later. I needed to look out for number one.

When I was clean and dressed I wandered up to the hotel restaurant for breakfast. It all looked great – fancy pastries on silver platters, large tureens of hot food, fresh fruit arranged in patterns on a tray of ice. But you have to remember my training, because I wasn't sure I wanted to eat any of it. The pastries were uncovered – so what bugs had crawled across them while they sat there? They could be smothered in salmonella from a wandering cockroach. The hot food was covered, but how hot was it? Had it been heated initially to at least 75°C, then hot held for a maximum of two hours at 65°C? There was no telling how long it had sat there, below the required heat for killing bacteria and above the coolness needed to prevent it multiplying. The fruit was all peeled – possibly by someone with dirty hands, probably washed in water that would make me sick. I settled on toast I could make myself in the toaster provided and ordered a boiled egg and coffee (black – no idea if the milk was pasteurised). I left the dining room less hungry, but certainly not full.

When I got back to my room, I grabbed a bottle of water and sat on the bed, leaning against a stack of pillows with my knees pulled up to my chin. I needed a plan. I was here, because it had seemed obvious to come and I needed to go somewhere. But now I wanted to know what to do next. I'm not a great long-term planner, I tend to decide things as they happen, but I had met bit of a lull. I had to do *something*.

You might be thinking, given my recent encounter, that I would pray, ask for guidance, something like that. Not really me. I figured I would be put right if I went off in the wrong direction, but otherwise, I had a brain, I should use it.

When you think of India, what comes to mind? Bollywood? Curry? Elephants? Poor people? There were a lot of poor people. I had already seen them, even on my ride from the airport, you couldn't help but notice that some people were struggling to survive, that this country had poor that were in a different class to the so-called 'poor' in England. I decided that I would do something to help them. I liked the idea, the prestige of heading up a major charity, being sent money from the rich West, being revered as a saint. Yep, it had appeal, perhaps that was the plan. I thought charity leaders probably had rather a high status, they would hobnob with the rich and powerful (all in the name of raising funds for those they were helping, of course).

The only problem was how to get started. I grabbed my laptop and balanced it on my knees, took another swig from my water bottle, and started to do an online search. I found a list of charities working in the city, and looked on their websites to find one that was respected but would be interested in a large donation from a new supporter. I could look at their accounts (all on public record) to work out which ones were worth approaching. A plan was beginning to form. I would phone a charity, explain that I had recently come into some money and happened to be visiting India. I hoped to make a sizeable donation, but first would like to see some of the work, first hand, that the charity was involved in. This would give me some idea of what the needs were, what I could actually do here. I wouldn't mention my own plans, they didn't need to know that. I simply needed a way in, some introductions, someone to pave the way. I could make up the rest myself.

I began to have this vision of myself, perceived as a saint by people in England (who I would, of course, be contacting for funds). People love a good story of a sinner turned saint, beggar made into a princess, stuff like that. I was good at influencing others, I would use this enthusiasm to raise funds, build projects, change laws. I would be the helper of people, the one who sorted out the mess this country had got itself into. I would be famous, the public would want to see me, thank me, help me. I would be the charitable equivalent of a film star.

I found a charity I could use. They were well established, seemed to be very active and it was run by local people. That appealed to me. The thing with benevolence, it tended to also breed power. If a hospital was built through generous donations from rich well-wishers, then those who ran the hospital also kept the power. The poor, although now able to get medical help, were still dependent. They were still in a position of accepting what was offered, they didn't have any 'right' to change the hospital at all. Perhaps, in order to have any 'power', you needed to be the one giving. For a relationship to exist, both sides needed to give *and* take. The trouble with charities set up in the rich West, was they did all the giving, the relationship was very unbalanced. I liked the idea of working with local people. When I struck out on my own (I hadn't quite decided what form that would take, I would make it up as I went along) the poor people could help me. That would make them feel there was a fair balance of power. There wouldn't be, of course, I would be in charge. But they would *feel* equal, and it would look good to my prospective donors.

I phoned the charity at once. I explained my position, laid it on thick about having inherited lots of money, had come to India (I didn't say why, none of their business) and seen so much poverty already. I was looking for a way to help, but wanted to direct the funds towards something specific. Could they show me some projects? Take me out into the field so I could see for myself? (You'll be impressed with how much jargon I had picked up in just a couple of hours of reading.)

Of course, they were a bit surprised by the immediacy of it all. I was passed to several different people before I reached someone who seemed to have a brain. They were polite – I was offering them money. But they didn't exactly jump straight into helping me. They said they needed to refer up the chain of command, to speak to supervisors, rubbish like that. I told them I was only available for a very short time, if they wanted to work with me it would have to be quick. They didn't want to lose the chance of some money, so they agreed to try and put something in place for the next day, and someone would contact me later that day to discuss it further.

I ended the call and packed away my computer, squeezing it into the tiny room safe with my passport and cash. I had the day to either relax, or to see some more of the country. Now I had a plan, I was keen to get on with it. The delay from the charity was frustrating. I decided I would go out, buy some ethnic clothing and see more of this strange culture I had landed in. I rang reception and asked for a car.

I left my room. Usually, I would have stayed in my room, doing what I wanted until someone called to say the car was waiting. I was still learning how this country worked though. I didn't know if they would reserve the car, or if, when I didn't appear, they would send the driver out with someone else. So I went down at the appointed time. Malik was behind the desk.

"Good morning Miss Oakes." He looked down, checking, then smiled, "Yes, you have a car today. You are wanting to visit the shops. Very good. It is ready."

"That's good, shall I wait outside?"

"Please have a seat." He gestured towards some sofas clustered near the reception desk.

I was confused. "But I thought you said it was ready?"

"Yes," he nodded, "Completely ready. Please take a seat."

I decided to clarify where I wanted to go. It was confusing enough communicating with Malik, who actually had very good English. I wasn't sure how I would get on with a driver. Some people here had very strong accents, it was hard to understand them.

"I would like to buy some clothes. Some normal Indian clothes, like people who live here wear. Please could you tell the driver for me? Can he take me to some suitable shops?"

Malik smiled, and did a strange sort of head wobble. I wasn't sure if that meant yes or no or something in-between.

"Of course Miss Oakes, no problem. Please take a seat."

I sat. I had no idea if Malik had understood. Nor did I know where my car was. My inclination was to simply go out to the road and hail a taxi, if the driver was late then he would find himself without a passenger. But again, I was held back by my need to learn this country. I might need a driver in the future, I wanted to begin fostering a relationship that would be useful to me. I waited for twenty minutes before my car which had been 'completely ready' arrived in the drive and a man I didn't recognise hurried in to find me.

Malik came over to where I was sitting and led me out to the car. I wasn't sure if he expected another tip. I decided he could manage with a smile this time, so I beamed my thanks to him and struggled to find the seatbelt, which had slipped into the depths below the seat cushion. I was secure by the time the car moved away, though I guessed few passengers bothered with belts. Foolhardy, I felt.

We travelled at speed through the city. It was like dancing a tango – lots of near misses and tension, but everyone seemed to know the steps and we got to where we wanted to be.

We parked next to a shop in a busy street. I asked the driver if he would wait and he assured me he would. Stepping out was a harsh contrast to the cool quiet of the car; thick, hot air surrounded me. Unfiltered by windows, the noise was like an assault – car horns, people shouting, chanting from a nearby temple. Cars and motorbikes and tuk-tuks and people and, unexpectedly, cows, all shared the road space, almost colliding but somehow managing not to. People stared as I walked towards the shop. They didn't avert their gaze when I saw them watching, but looked openly, their brown eyes following me with interest.

The shop was peaceful. Fans stirred the air, and there were a few women looking at samples of material, served by men in suits. Both sides of the shop had long counters, with the walls shelved to the ceiling. Bolts of cloth were lying on the counters, the women choosing the quality and colours of silk they desired.

All the customers were women. They stood in groups, chatting and discussing the fabric. I saw manicured hands and silky hair cascading down their backs. Designer handbags rested in the crooks of arms and gold jewellery weighed down their wrists and necks. This was a shop for the wealthy. I was in the wrong place.

I wasted a few minutes discussing what I wanted with the sales assistant. He was keen to sell me a sari, assured me his was the finest silk, that he could give me a good price, that the quality would not be matched elsewhere. He thrust some samples towards me, and even I could see they were beautiful. Rainbows of silk, waiting to be cut and hemmed and pleated into saris. But I would have been just as conspicuous walking in the street in these clothes as I was in my own. I would also have felt ridiculous, as I wasn't at all sure I would manage to wear a sari without it slipping from my shoulder and coming unwrapped.

I didn't bother to thank him or make excuses. I nodded, turned, and left.

My driver was surprised to see me again so quickly. I think he might have been sleeping. I was going to have to attempt a conversation. This would not be easy.

"This was not the sort of shop I wanted," I began.

"You not wanted clothes shop?" he said.

"Yes. But not expensive clothes. I want cheap clothes. The sort of clothes people who live here wear."

He frowned. "This shop sells very good quality clothes. They will give you very good price."

I wasn't managing to explain this properly. I would start again, try to give more information.

"I am not a tourist. I have come to work with a charity." This wasn't strictly true, but I hoped it would give the right flavour. "Tomorrow I am going to visit some projects. I am going to be with poor people, people who have no money. I want to look the same as them. I want clothes that are not expensive."

There was a pause while he worked out what I meant. I imagine he found my accent as difficult as I found his. I smiled at him, tried to look friendly.

"Can you help me?"

194

He smiled back and did the same funny head wobble I had seen Malik do.

"Yes, no problem. I drive you now?"

"Yes, please. To a shop that sells cheap clothes."

We pulled back out into the traffic and drove away. I might need a driver in the future, so I struck up a conversation.

"Have you always lived here?"

"Yes sir."

I was slightly surprised by the 'sir' but perhaps it was just habit. I was taller than the women here, but was fairly confident my gender was obvious.

"How do I say 'thank you' in Hindi?"

He said something that sounded like *"Tannibad."* Warming to his theme, he began to tell me that most people spoke Hindi, but a few spoke Punjabi. Immigrants, and his voice darkened as he said this, so I could tell he disapproved, spoke Bengali. He decided to teach me some Hindi. To say "Hello" I should say *"Namaste"* and bow slightly. He then told me how to say "How are you?" and a variety of replies. I watched the world stream past the window as the words washed over me, every so often I repeated a word, made it look like I was listening.

The car stopped. It had not parked, as the curb was already crowded with vehicles. Cars and bikes swung around us, honking but not angry. This happened, no one cared. My driver told me this was the shop. I was worried about where he would wait.

"I will wait here."

"But what if the police come? Are you allowed to wait here? Where shall I meet you if you need to move?"

"No problem. I will wait here. You go and buy your clothes," followed by another one of those head wobbles.

I was not at all certain that this was a good idea, but I didn't have a better option. I scrambled from the car and went into the shop.

As the door closed behind me, I caught sight of my car drawing away. Bother. Nothing I could do now.

This shop differed from the previous one. It was busier, more people and more noise. It was arranged more like a department store, with bays of different things and people walking around. They sold a few ornaments and cushions, as well as clothes.

A woman approached and asked if she could help. I smiled and tried to explain what I wanted. She looked worried, but led me over to an area of shelves and began to pull packets down to show me. She said she wasn't sure if she had anything suitable, but she thought I should try *salwar kameez*. This turned out to be the tunic and trousers that most women seemed to wear. She gave me a couple to try on, and directed me to a changing cubicle.

I looked at the trousers first. She had called these *salwar*. They were very long. I went to tell her she had made a mistake, these were much too long for my legs. In fact, they were too long for anyone's legs. Perhaps there was a manufacturing fault.

She smiled and shook her head. They were not too long. I should try them on. I did. They were narrow over the ankle, and this held them in place. The great lengths of material then hung loosely over my legs, and a pull-string fastened the waist. The top was huge, it would have fitted a tremendously large bottom. But when they were fastened they seemed to fit. Actually, they were very comfortable. When the tunic, the *kameez*, was on, it covered the excess material at the top. I rather liked it. It felt a practical outfit and easy to wear. It also had a pocket, somewhere I could keep the knife I had brought from England. In case of emergencies.

I emerged from the fitting room and my assistant smiled, satisfied with the result. I dressed in my own clothes and joined her back at the shelves.

"You need a *dupatta*, a veil," she said.

I had a choice. Some were cotton, others were chiffon or silk.

They were long and thin and every colour you could imagine. Indians wore very bright clothes. I decided to buy one silk and one cotton *dupatta*, and a couple of *salwar kameez* in contrasting colours. I was directed over to a grill, where a man sat, taking the money. I paid and was given a receipt, then went to collect my clothes, which had been wrapped in paper and tied with string. I felt pleased with myself, I was achieving things already. Now I just needed to find my car again.

I left the shop and stood for a moment on the street. Cars and tuk-tuks danced past. A skinny child carrying a large baby walked between them, knocking on windows and asking for food. The baby was almost as big as the child and I wondered if she would drop it. A man spat in the gutter. Birds argued over a forgotten core. There was so much colour and noise and heat. It was exhausting, even for me. I decided to try and phone the hotel, and was in the process of pulling out my mobile when the car arrived. It dodged a motorbike and narrowly missed a cyclist who was straining to pull a trailer of gas canisters, coming to a stop right in front of me. The driver grinned up at me. I smiled back. There was something urgent about this country, everything was busy. I liked it.

I told the driver to return to the hotel. Another head wobble, and we were off. Our progress was slow, often stopping as someone stepped in front of us or something drove towards us, going against the flow of traffic, in the wrong direction. But it was comfortable and cool, and the driver seemed in no hurry. I have never seen a less angry driver, he was used to the world getting in his way.

I watched a market through the window. People and vehicles and cows, all entwined. There were food stands, cucumbers peeled and sliced lengthways; lemons, squeezed and served with mint (which looked enticing, but who knows where the water they were mixed with came from); pomegranates cut into gleaming stars. It was all beautiful. Many of the stands had incense sticks burning, perhaps to deter the flies.

Some people were collecting plates of food, some kind of curry I think. They ate off paper plates, which they then threw into the street. There was a gaunt cow, licking the remains and a thousand flies buzzed in the air. At one point, a girl walked beside the car, peering in, trying to make eye-contact. I ignored her, waited to speed up slightly and leave her behind.

Some children ran amongst the crowd. A man in a turban carried a plastic carrier bag. An old woman was selling apples. A young man vomited as he walked, bright pink fluid flowing from his mouth onto the road. Worshippers removed their shoes before entering a temple.

The women in the street were well covered – either in black burka and hijab, or bright in silks and cottons, or modern in western dress. But no skin on display, no shoulders or legs, and necklines were high. The men mostly wore western trousers and shirts. A million flip-flops on dusty feet. Everyone was brown, and I felt very pale, very foreign, very special.

Chapter Eighteen

I decided to use the hotel car to travel to the charity office. When I had contacted them, they offered to send a car. But I prefer to be independent. It would also be good to spend more time with my driver, to form some kind of bond with him, to add him as another ingredient to the mix. Just in case.

I phoned reception and asked who had driven me the day before. I didn't quite catch the name, it sounded like 'Karan'. I think it was Malik I spoke to, so I practiced my Hindi, said *"Tannibad"* when we finished talking. Later, he told me that actually he speaks Punjabi. That shows what this place is like – a whole mishmash of people and cultures and languages. Hard to keep up when you first arrive.

Now, I expect you might be wondering about the house money, about why I went ahead with accepting Uncle's inheritance, when I clearly wasn't entitled, whichever way you look at it. But here's the thing. *I was still me.* Yes, I had encountered someone who shook the very depths of me, who turned me around and showed me which way to walk. But *I was still me.* I figured if there was a reason I needed to be in India, then I was likely to need some cash. It had obviously come my way for a reason, and I was not going to be handing it to my father. His need was not greater than mine. I had a use for it – I just didn't know *what* at that point in time.

I had the money from my savings all accessible in my bank account. I should receive the rest of the money from Uncle's estate in a few months, though I was a bit shocked by how much tax I needed to pay. I figured the money would last a few years if I wasn't too extravagant. There had been some initial expenses, but I viewed these as set-up costs. Things like my ticket (an open return), clothes, some decent luggage. I had promised a big donation to the charity, told them my finances were tied up until the inheritance came through. Whether or not they actually received any cash was at this point undecided, but they didn't know that, and they would help me on the strength of a pledge. They weren't to know that my pledges weren't exactly reliable.

I dressed for my charity visit. Long sleeves and high neck, I didn't want to be disapproved of. I decided on European clothes, because I wanted them to take me seriously and I wanted to look obviously wealthy. I looked at my shoes: Gucci, classy – with goodness knows how many germs on their undersides. Walking boots would be a better option. I was glad I had packed them – they took up lots of room in my suitcase, but I had been unsure about the weather and terrain I might encounter, and they were good boots. I didn't like thinking about all the muck I had seen on the streets so far, and I had only visited relatively 'safe' areas. The charity was not going to be working in places that tourists usually visit. I wondered if it would be dangerous.

I waited in my room, reading, until I was called to say the car was waiting, did I still require it? I assured them I did and went down to the lobby. My driver was waiting, and I greeted him with a smile. I considered asking if I could sit in the front of the car, try to increase our familiarity a bit. He was a bloke, I'm good at charming blokes (unless they're frigid church leaders). But I wasn't quite sure yet of what was appropriate in India, what the normal male/female relationship was, and Karan might be useful later, I didn't want to offend him, so I played safe and sat in the back. I did chat all the way there though, was friendly and entertaining, as we dodged cars and motorbikes and men on pedal bikes, in the dance that was Indian driving.

We arrived at the charity office. I don't know what you were expecting, but it looked like a house. It was a three-storey building in a residential road, with a parking place out front and a garden to the side. A man met the car in the street, introduced himself as Ranveer Shah, and led me inside. We passed a guard in a shed next to the door, who smiled, showing missing teeth. I ignored him.

I was led along a hallway and up a flight of stairs, and I was shown into an office. A woman rose from the desk and came to greet me. Her name was Lily.

Lily was shorter than me (everyone in this country was shorter than me). She was very elegant with thick black hair and careful makeup. Although she wore *salwar* and *kameez* they were better quality than the ones I had bought; a silk scarf was draped over her shoulders. When she spoke her English was good. This was an educated woman. She might be useful.

"Miss Oakes, it is lovely to meet you," she said, bowing at the waist. "Please? Will you sit? May I offer you some tea?"

"Thank you," I said, perching on the hard chair opposite her. "Black tea please." (Never risk the milk unless you know for sure it's been pasteurised.)

Lily explained how the charity worked. They had set up community centres in the resettlement districts, and were teaching people what their rights were, so they could claim them. This sounded unimpressive, so I asked for more details.

Lily told me what it meant to be poor in India. I sat on the hard chair, sipping tea, while a ceiling fan stirred the air above me. I heard that when the government decided to update the central parts of the city, putting in those wide roads and parks I had seen, they needed to relocate all the poor who'd been living there. So they built housing, away from the centre, often away from where people worked, and resettled the poor there. They were given land to build on, or a government sanctioned home, and told to continue their lives from this new location.

I listened to the traffic, a continual buzz through the picture window from the street below. Lily was serious, keen for me to understand how people could no longer reach their jobs easily, how families had been uprooted. I glanced at her, then scanned the room.

There was a desk in one corner, and a dusty plant wilted next to the window. It was warm, and Lily's voice rose and fell in a sing-song manner, mesmerising.

"Many of the people we work with are Dalits. You know about Dalit people?"

I nodded, I'd heard of them, had heard them called 'untouchables' before, I think in a movie or something. The Hindu faith had a caste system, people were designated a place in life when they were born. The Dalits carried the weight of their ancestor's guilt – or something; I didn't exactly know. They were the lowest of the low, only allowed certain work, unable to improve their position in life.

I was trying to understand. You see, when I'd been visited back in England, although I had known terror, and the horrible realisation that I was nothing special, a mere speck of failed humanity, I had also felt accepted. For the first time I had met someone who honestly knew what I was, and yet still wanted to be with me. Which left me with this unexpected desire to try and please him. You need to understand, I hadn't changed, *I was still me*. But my motives had turned 180°. I wanted to know what this plan was that I was meant to be a part of, and I had a feeling Lily might provide the key. So as I sat in that stuffy office, fighting the urge to sleep, I was trying to listen, to learn about this place.

Lily rose, straightening her scarf.

"Come, we can talk more in the car," she said. "I will show you the areas we are working in. If you would like to see?"

I would. Listening was not something I enjoyed, seeing was better. I asked Lily if I could take photographs.

"Yes, that will be fine. You should ask permission first, that is polite. But people are used to us taking their photograph, they know it will be used to help improve their situation. They will not mind."

I nodded, as if I would follow her advice.

Lily wanted us to travel in the charity car. I wasn't having that. It was a pokey little thing, looked very uncomfortable. I told her Karan would take us.

As we drove, Lily continued her talk. I watched as we passed a park, tall trees and fountains, then a street of shops, each one narrow, with a bright sign above it and tables outside covered in vegetables. The sun shone through the pollution haze, muted but still bright, still hot. We turned and drove along a street of shops selling car parts, then a road where each shop sold tyres, great rims of rubber for big trucks, smaller tyres for bikes, all stacked next to the shops. People here seemed to group all the similar shops together, perhaps it made bartering easier. I realised Lily was still talking, and forced myself to listen.

"Some of our work is concerned with ensuring people have identity cards," said Lily. "The government will provide food and education for the poor, but to access it, they must have identity cards. Many of them do not, which is a big problem."

I nodded, trying to look interested. It didn't sound very exciting.

"People need to be informed of their rights," she continued. "They have the right to clean water, the right to not be abused, the right to life. This is particularly important to teach the girls. In India, girls and women have very few rights. Having a girl baby is very sad, it means the family will need to pay a dowry if she is to marry, and this can be expensive. So if an ultrasound scan shows a baby is a girl, the mother will abort it. This is illegal, it is not allowed, but – it happens. We are becoming a society of males, in some areas this will be a big problem. There are not enough girls." She licked her lips, waiting for a response.

I nodded. We were passing poorer areas now. There were more people, the traffic was slower. We stopped more frequently, edged around obstacles.

When we arrived at the edge of the resettlement area, Karan turned to speak to Lily. He spoke Hindi, but I could tell he was unhappy about something. Lily told me he was unable to drive any further.

"The road ahead is very rough," she said, "there isn't room for a car. We will need to walk. Is that okay? You don't mind walking?"

As we waited, a car overtook us, honking, turning into the side road. Clearly some cars found room. Perhaps there was another reason the driver was unwilling to go any further. I was already removing the seatbelt and opening the door. I spoke to the driver.

"You will wait here for us? Or shall I phone you when we need collecting?"

"Better if you phone," he said.

I took his number, adding it to my list of contacts as 'Driver, Karan'. A good move for the future I thought. Then I climbed out and nodded at Lily. We set off up the side road.

There were buildings on either side, but the road was wide. The problem was the stalls, which people had set up alongside the road, and the tarmac itself, which was pitted and rough and covered with litter. There *was* traffic – small cars and tuk-tuks and many motorbikes, but I understood why the driver had been unhappy about going further. The chance of a tyre burst on shards of metal abandoned in the road, or scraping the sides on the shacks and stalls, would deter anyone in a decent car. Some areas of the road were burnt, as if someone had started a fire right there in the street. There were piles of tarmac, perhaps left over from when the road was built. Piles of all sorts of things actually, litter, and rotting vegetables, and even excrement (which I hoped was from an animal). I was glad to be in boots, even if my feet were sweating. I might be clomping next to Lily's delicate stride, but at least I was protected.

We picked our way around the rubbish and potholes, keeping an eye on the traffic that came within inches of us as we walked. A whole family perched on a motorbike, the youngest balanced at the front, an old woman clinging on at the back. I watched, absorbed, noticed everything. My eyes were hungry.

There was the constant honking of horns, shouts from people, music, the odd bark from a dog. I could see into shops. Open doors into small rooms shelved from floor to ceiling, stacked with goods, or open fronts with tubs heaped next to the road and stock hanging from strings above the entrance. The store owner perched on a stool in the doorway, watching the world as it passed; or standing, bartering with a customer, eager to get the best price.

Painted signs lined the street. Even the ones written in English were weird, unfamiliar. Jaiswal Trading Co., Kumar Hardware, Gupter Digital Studio, Guruji Sports, Mindworkzz. Most I couldn't read, as they were written in curly Hindi, brightly coloured, dusty, ignored.

Washing hung on lines strung between houses, or on the many balconies that rose above the rectangular buildings. Tiers of living spaces. The windows were unglazed, and when I looked up I glimpsed plants, people leaning out while they smoked. But mostly washing. There was a lot of washing.

We stopped at a small building, and Lily led me up the tall steps.

"This is our community centre," she said, sounding proud.

It was basically a room, scarred pink paint and plastic chairs. Not much to be proud of, I thought.

"The women can come here, we can educate them, tell them their rights. It is difficult for some of them to complete the paperwork necessary for an identity card, so we can help with that," she said.

I handed her my phone, asked her to take photos of me. You never know, the bleakness of it all might inspire someone to donate.

Some children had started to follow us, grubby faces and dusty feet. They were perfect for some photographs that would make me look good, the altruistic foreigner caring for the poor. I posed, kneeling beside them, careful to choose backgrounds that showed the litter strewn ground, the broken buildings, a gaunt cow. The children grinned, and laughed and made victory signs. This was slightly disappointing, as 'sad and hungry' would've been a better look. I couldn't see anything about their lives that was worth smiling about. Rubbish tips were their playgrounds, or sitting on hard ground next to an open sewer, the slick grey liquid oozing past as they played with a broken toy or a stick. I tried to pose in front while they played, but they were too conscious of the camera, they always smiled, laughed, posed. Never mind. Perhaps we would find a dying baby or something later, something I could use to tug at the hearts back in England.

Although I was in each photo, looking caring and sad, I was careful not to actually touch any of the children. They didn't look very clean. It was possible to position myself slightly in the foreground, balanced on my big boots, hair flowing to one side. I wanted to look nice.

Lily took me to a school next. We went through the metal gates, across a veranda, to a doorway. A woman greeted Lily, welcomed me, and led us back into her office. She was the head teacher.

The office was big, but not exactly grand. There was a long desk, which she sat behind, and a couple of dirty plastic chairs had been placed in front, for us to sit on. I sat carefully, aware of the rats that had scuttled under a cupboard when we entered. Other than the cupboard, there was a table, stacked high with what looked like books and papers and junk. That was it. A couple of high windows, walls that had at one time been white, a concrete floor where mice and rats ran when they thought it was safe. Like I said, not luxurious.

The head teacher was tiny and efficient. I listened, waiting to hear something I could use. Perhaps I could link the school with some English ones, start a sort of 'education swap' charity. That might work, people like to think their money is helping children, and education would appeal to them. I could probably manage to do very little work, once I had set it up, it would basically just need me to put headteachers in touch with each other. Then the school in England could raise the funds, send the money to me. I could remove some (for 'administrative' costs) and give the rest to the Indian school to use as they wanted.

"This school building has two thousand pupils," the headteacher said. "They arrive in three shifts, two in the morning, and the last one in the afternoon. Each shift has its own staff, pupils, and resources." She shook her head, frowning. "This causes big problem with the budget. If the building needs repair, who pays? The first morning shift says it doesn't need to pay, so does the afternoon shift. Sometimes communication is not good.

"I also have problem with my staff," she continued, keen to let me know the problems she faced.

A rat had decided it was safe, and had ventured out from under the table. I shifted my feet, and it darted back out of sight. Somewhat distracting.

"My teachers are demotivated. They have too much paperwork to complete and there is no time to actually teach the children during the lessons, because they are too busy completing applications for identity cards. The government say we must do this. But we have many pupils. This takes too long. There is no time for teaching." She sighed.

She then spoke at length about the budget – I assume she

thought I might be a means of expanding it. She would be disappointed, I wasn't finding this a very stimulating visit. One of her snippets of information was that most children were still fairly illiterate when they graduated, aged ten. So I couldn't see that this was an organisation worth investing in. If people in England knew that, they were unlikely to send money. I didn't want to be involved in something that was failing.

I stifled a yawn and wished the seat was more comfortable. The rats were now quite openly darting across the floor, hurrying from one corner to the next, sometimes stopping in the middle of the room, as if in conversation. No one reacted. This was obviously normal. I stood, I had been there long enough.

The head teacher stopped mid-sentence and stood too, looking surprised. I smiled but decided not to shake her hand.

"Thank you so much for your time," I said, "it has been very interesting to hear about the school. I expect we'll be in touch."

Lily too stood. I could see she was perturbed by the abrupt curtailing of the visit, but frankly, I'd had enough. This place was hopeless, the people living there were hopeless, and I had seen enough dirt and poverty to last me a lifetime.

Lily did the whole hands-together-slight-bow thing that seemed to serve as a thank you, but I was already walking out the doorway. She caught me up and we walked towards the gate. We passed some open doors and I glanced in. Children were sitting in rows, while teachers either stood at the front of the class or wandered down the aisles. Some children had books open on their desks, others stared ahead. In one room, a boy had his head resting on his arms on the desk, he appeared to be asleep while the teacher sauntered around the room. I didn't count, but there appeared to be less than seventy kids in the rooms. The headteacher had definitely told me that the teacher to pupil ratio was one to seventy. Maybe some kids didn't turn up. Or maybe she had lied. That was the trouble, you never knew who to trust. A ceiling fan lazily stroked the air. Flies quarrelled at the windows. We left.

I turned to Lily. "I think I have seen enough now, so could you take me back to the main road? I'll phone for my driver."

Lily agreed, though seemed hesitant, nearly saying something then deciding not to. As we walked through the resettlement area, through the areas of unfinished housing, back to a main road, she stopped, suggested a detour. There was someone else she wanted me to meet. I'd had enough frankly, but said I would, as long as it was quick. I was still hoping to see something I could use for my idea.

Cars were parked along the length of the road, some under plastic covers, a few under precarious shelters made from scaffolding with corrugated iron roofs. Cables snaked between tall poles, sometimes knotted in great tangles, sometimes dipping to almost head height. We passed dusty trees, and overflowing skips, and doorways with tall steps that jutted into the road ready to trip us.

She led me along a narrow path between buildings. We had left the main street, if it could be called that, and were walking on a stony pathway up the hill. There wasn't room here for food stalls, and I realised the road we had left was the market area. There had been plenty of food being sold, well-stocked shops. If people had money, they could eat. The piles of litter continued, blowing in the breeze, caught against fences, piled in corners. There was a duck, searching through one heap of rubbish, seeking food. I hadn't seen any water, a dismal life for a duck. Actually, a dismal life for most creatures. I was glad I had money, wasn't part of the squalor. As we walked, Lily pointed to a narrow lane leading away from the path we were on.

"That is an entrance to the slum," she said, "it's where the illegals live. We have many people here from Bangladesh. They do not have papers, they cannot live in the resettlement area, so they build houses there, on the waste land. We are trying to help them, but it is not easy. There is much hardship."

The people we passed stared at us, but I was used to that now and barely even noticed. There didn't seem to be any malice in their watching eyes. I was simply different, interesting, something to change the monotony of the day.

Most people here seemed to be sitting, not doing anything. They had sat behind stalls in the main street, or on tall stools in the few tiny shops we had passed. Now, in the lane, people sat on walls and steps and in groups on the floor. If they walked, they moved slowly, as if to conserve energy. If this was due to heat or malnutrition or simply because there was no enthusiasm left for life, I couldn't say. Not yet.

Lily stopped. There was a building with an open door. We climbed the two tall steps.

"The high steps are very necessary," said Lily, pointing. "At the moment it is warm and dry, but when the rains come it is very different. People will be needing to have high houses. The sewers here are open drains, the rain will wash them into the pathways, sometimes into the houses, especially in the slum houses. This is very bad, very bad indeed."

I nodded, trying not to think about it, stepping up into the room. There was no furniture, just a worn rug on the concrete floor. A woman came to greet us. She was very tall, almost manly, with narrow shoulders and skinny arms. She wore a sari, though it wasn't silk and looked old, worn. She smiled. She had a good smile.

"You must be Clara," she said, "I am so pleased you have come to see us. My name is Kavita. Please, come and meet the others."

There was a staircase in one corner, and she led us up. These steps were steep, at least a foot high and less than a foot wide. In my walking boots they were very narrow. I concentrated on not falling backwards as I followed Kavita up the winding stairs. Round and round we went, it was like climbing stairs in a castle. We reached another landing, another room, another concrete floor. There was a family hanging washing, building something, reading, living out their lives. We walked along one wall – everyone ignoring the fact we were there and us pretending we were invisible – to where the stairs continued in the far corner. Then up again, winding round, steep narrow steps, up to the next floor.

At this floor we stopped. Kavita slipped off her flip-flops, and Lily removed her shoes. It would've been a hassle to untie my laces, and the floor wasn't exactly a clean carpet. I kept my boots on. Both women paused, waiting for me to remove my shoes, then decided not to suggest I should. I was foreign, it was expected that I would be different.

The room had a concrete floor and doorways. No furniture. The staircase continued in the far corner, and as we stood there a man passed us and continued upwards. Presumably he lived up there. Not much in the way of privacy then.

They took me through a wooden door, into a room. There was a single cupboard with a large bolt on the outside, and a table. A circle of women sat on the floor. I clomped my way inside, and someone brought me a chair, so I sat, near the door, and hoped this wouldn't take too long. It didn't.

They offered me tea, which I refused, then asked if I would like to hear their stories. I looked at Lily, told her that I had an important phone call, and I needed to get back to the hotel. Normally I would have just refused to stay, not bothered with an excuse, but there was something about Kavita, some strength that I recognised. I felt drawn to her, thought she would be useful. But I was tired and uncomfortable and I'd had enough. I could do more charity stuff another day, when I wasn't so tired. I stood.

I saw disappointment in the women's faces, they had been waiting for me, had wanted to tell their stories. Probably hoping to get some money. But they were an unattractive lot, chubby arms and dirty hair. They weren't suitable for my photographs, they had nothing I could use. Except for Kavita. Like I said, there was something about her, some magnetic quality that made me think she would be useful. Lily was standing, resigned now to my abrupt behaviour. She thanked the women on my behalf, but I was already leaving, making my way down those winding stairs. At the bottom, I turned. Kavita had followed us out, and I did the hands-together-bow thing I'd seen other people do.

"Thank you Kavita," I said, being my most charming self. "I am terribly sorry to have to leave, but I had explained to Lily that I was expecting an important phone call, and she unfortunately didn't allow enough time for this part of my tour."

Kavita nodded, but didn't speak. Lily moved, as if to say something, but I turned slightly, hiding her from sight.

"I am though, extremely interested in your work here," I said. "Perhaps you would allow me to visit again? When I have more time? I would love to see more of what you're doing."

Kavita smiled that smile again. It was a good smile, I would photograph it when I came back, people would respond well to it. I don't know why I was drawn to her. Usually I look for the weak, those easy to mould. This woman had strength, but there was something, something intangible, that I wanted and thought she could give me. She had a certain assurance, almost a power; a power that I hoped to direct to my advantage.

"Of course Clara," she said, "I would be delighted."

I nodded. Then turned back to Lily. "To the car now?"

We walked through the traffic, followed by tuk-tuks and skimmed by motorbikes and cars. People wandered through the traffic, we were back in noise and chaos and busyness. I was trying to phone my driver, shouting to him that we were returning to where he had dropped us, how long would he be, could he hear me? All the time vehicles buzzed past and horns honked in my ear. No longer new and interesting, simply annoying.

I wasn't sure if Karan had heard me, but as we turned the corner and came to the junction where he had left me, I saw the car come to a stop. A man was frying potatoes in a large metal bowl. He held the potato on one hand, a knife in the other, and as he sliced, cubes of potato fell into the sizzling hot oil. I paused for a moment, watching. They smelt delicious. But I wasn't going to risk it. I turned back to Lily.

"Thank you again," I said, opening the car door. "That was very kind of you." I slid onto the back seat. "I'll be in touch," I called, shutting the door before she could answer. I waved through the window at her, smiling like a satisfied but exhausted altruist.

"Take me to the hotel please," I instructed my driver, and we set off. I waved to Lily until she became part of the blur of people and cows and traffic behind us. Her eyes were confused. Perhaps she had assumed I would give her a lift back to the charity office. Oh well, it didn't matter. I wouldn't be needing her again.

Chapter Nineteen

I decided to visit Kavita on my own. After a day at the hotel, using the spa, relaxing, recovering from all the squalor I'd seen, I thought I would go back, see if I could further my plan a little. I had emailed various churches in England, attaching the photos I'd already taken, explaining that I was working with the poor in India, and seeking prayer support. I didn't mention money, not initially. They wouldn't like that. But someone doing good work, doing things they wouldn't fancy doing themselves, that was something they could talk about. If I asked them to support me in prayer, it looked humble and they would like that. Later, when they were committed, I could let some of the specific needs be known and ask for some cash. Later.

I was confident I could find Kavita's house again, if not from the road then certainly from the school, and it would be easy enough to get directions to the school.

I realised I would stand out, it wasn't exactly a tourist spot, but I knew how to handle myself, I'm good at reading people, and I had a knife in case things got nasty. I removed all my jewellery and left it in the safe, taking only my phone. I decided to wear smaller shoes, as the boots would be too obvious. I managed to buy some slip-on shoes in the hotel lobby. They weren't cheap, but neither did they look obviously expensive, and I figured they would be covered in dust soon enough. I then dressed in my ethnic clothing, hiding my hair under the *dupatta*. It was wide enough that I could hide my arms and face too, so I hoped to pass relatively unnoticed through the resettlement area. It was a vain hope, and nearly cost me my life.

I asked driver Karan to drop me at the same place as the day before. He was unhappy about me being on my own, made all sorts of fuss about me needing to be accompanied by someone from the charity, a tourist wasn't safe in this area, there were better places he could take me.

I ignored him and insisted. Told him I was being met by an official. This wasn't true, and I could see he was still unhappy, but he stopped arguing and drove me. When he stopped, he checked I still had his number, told me to be careful. I think he was worried he might get into trouble, perhaps lose his job if anything happened to me. Maybe next time I would use a taxi. I don't like restraints, never have.

I walked away quickly, trying to retrace my steps from the previous day. It wasn't very easy because when I was following Lily, I had concentrated more on not stepping in something unpleasant or tripping, than I had on where we were going. I managed to find the lane that wound up, away from the main shopping area.

As I walked, eyes watched me. A few people approached, looked as though they were going to speak then changed their minds and followed at a distance. I was aware I had a tail of people, an ever-growing crowd a few yards back. I felt in my pocket, found the knife I had brought with me, wondered how effective it would be. Walking on my own was very different to being escorted. I wasn't frightened, I was alert, aware of the danger and trying to avoid it. I wasn't sure I was in the right lane, and decided I would need to ask for directions.

I glanced back again. From the crowd following me, a young man emerged. He walked with a swagger, tight jeans on narrow hips, slim body well-muscled. Shorter than me, but not unattractive. I was wary, especially as he smiled.

"Hello Mrs, are you lost?" he said.

"No. Thank you," I said. Best to keep things polite while I could. I gave him my 'get lost' smile, not that I'd had much success with it in India. It worked no better now, and he kept coming towards me.

"Where are you going? I live here, I can help you. I am thinking you are in wrong place. Where do you want to go?" He smiled, but his tone was commanding, expecting a reply.

I considered ignoring him, walking away. But too many people were watching. Next to us, seated on the ground, was a small group. They were surrounded by rubbish, more was stored in fat white sacks, from which they were pulling items, sorting them into piles. They paused in their work, watching us. We were providing entertainment. Their faces showed they recognised the man, their eyes showed – I don't know, not fear exactly. Concern perhaps. I didn't know who he was, but he had some authority here. I wondered how many of the people following were connected to him, most were young men, a few girls. He also looked strong and fast – I didn't think I stood much chance if I tried to outrun him, especially in this warren of half-built houses and litter strewn pathways. I decided to play his game, see where it got me.

"I am working here," I lied, "and need to return to the school I visited yesterday as I am working with the head teacher. Thank you for your offer of help, but I can manage on my own. I know the way."

I turned, started to walk away.

"You are going the wrong way Mrs," he shouted after me. "This place very dangerous. I will take you safe way. Take you to school by a better route. You come with me."

I had slowed while he spoke, and he was level with me now. I realised he was taller than I'd thought, about my height and he stood very close, blocking my path, staring into my face with his black eyes, challenging me to refuse, to try to get away. Although

216

he appeared to be acting alone, I felt surrounded. Several people were watching, but I didn't think any would come to my aid should he try to force me to go with him.

I felt again for my knife, found it in my pocket. His eyes followed my hand and he shook his head, eyebrows raised, letting me know he knew what I was thinking and he would be faster, surer, more adept. This was his territory, his rules. If it came to any sort of a struggle, the odds were on his side. We were being polite but that was for show, a thin veneer which we both understood meant nothing.

I was thinking fast, weighing up the odds. I had few choices. I could try and run, but he would catch me. He was stronger than me, if we fought, he would win. I didn't know what he wanted – my valuables? To keep me as a hostage to try and extort money? To simply dispose of me as a lesson to those watching, showing that he was boss?

I could follow him, hope for a chance to escape later. But he wasn't stupid, my chances would decrease as time went on. I looked around. Those watching avoided my eyes, the people sorting rubbish suddenly busy with their chore. Black windows in surrounded houses stared down at us, the occupants hidden. I could feel the tension thick in the air.

Then suddenly, things changed.

There was a shout, the watching crowd parted and a woman approached. Not running, but hurrying towards us.

"Teacher, you are coming back," she shouted, "you not wait for me."

I didn't recognise her, but she spoke as if she knew me. She must be one of the women we had met yesterday. She joined us, flicked intelligent eyes towards me, then staring at the young man, spoke in what I assumed was Hindi or Bengali, or something. Some fast flowing language that sounded cross, like there was some plan which he had misunderstood, and she was in charge. He shouted back a bit, there seemed to be some heated discussion going on. Then she reached out, took my arm in her strong brown hand, started to lead me away.

I had no idea if I was a prize being bartered over, if she was as much a threat as he had been. But I figured I had more chance of escaping her than him, I allowed myself to be pulled away. The young man stood there, watching us. I heard him hoick a glob of spittle, expel it to the ground as we hurried away.

The woman was gripping my arm, the one nearest my knife, rushing me towards a narrow gap between the buildings. I recognised it as an entrance to the slum. It wasn't the safest place to be taken, but nor was staying on the main lane, where the man and the crowd waited. I realised that if she planned to rob me (not that I was carrying anything of value other than my phone) then I had little chance of escape. This might be a well-designed scam, an oft repeated routine that enticed naive wanderers into an inescapable lair.

Without warning, she dropped my arm and moved slightly ahead, waving at me to follow. I did. There were houses, towering on both sides, rough brickwork, inexpertly laid, a narrow pathway between them. They reached up, many storeys high, filtering the light so it was like entering a tunnel, bleak and grey.

My guide was ahead, and I hurried to keep up with her. Heavy black wires were knotted above us, at one point a single wire dangled, as if cut, possibly live. I ducked beneath it. Beside the pathway was a gutter, oozing with sewage. Stray bricks littered the path as if abandoned, or fallen from the haphazard walls that stretched above us, cutting out the light, sealing off fresh air. My every sense was on full alert, avoiding debris on the path, ducking under protruding brickwork, keeping away from the open sewer. My guide hurried me forwards.

She was running now, her flip-flops tapping the concrete as we hurried along the narrow walkway. I concentrated on keeping up, not tripping, the grey sewage slick beside us, the housing leaning overhead, the light grey and dim. Then the walkway narrowed even further, became almost dark. A grey tunnel. I could make out wires snaking above my head, and the buildings jutted out in places, so I had to be careful not to bump my head. It felt damp, as if the walls were sweating.

My breath was coming in short gasps, the air thick and hard to breathe. I was clutching my *dupatta* trying to keep it from falling. My new shoes were rubbing, but she was quick, I concentrated on keeping up. Our feet beat the floor, fast, erratic as we dodged a stone or jumped over a gap where the gutter dissected the path. Forwards, deeper, faster.

Every few yards we passed an open doorway. The interiors were too dark to see, though I was aware of shadows, moving. No time to wonder who was watching us, how safe we were. We rushed around corners, at one point she lifted a curtain, ran through a home, exited the other side. I followed her, glimpsing a threadbare carpet, past an old lady seated in a doorway, beating wet washing with a stick, then back to the alley. Grey concrete, uneven brickwork, feet slapping the ground. My damp fingers clasped my shawl, my feet sore, my breath ragged. I was completely lost now. Should the woman desert me I would have no idea how to get back to the main streets. But she didn't. She checked behind us once more, then slowed, walked a few paces, ducked into a doorway. I followed.

We were standing in a room. No furniture. A concrete floor, a stairway, a plastic bag in one corner. The woman faced me, frowning. I felt for my knife, glanced at the doorway, measuring the distance. We were both breathing fast, I could feel my lungs as they attempted to suck the bitter air inside, expelled it as a pant.

"Why are you coming back?" she said between breaths. "This not safe place. Why are you here?"

"I want to see Kavita," I managed to say, before shaking my head. It was too soon for talking, I had no breath. I lowered my hands to my knees, stayed there, bent over, waiting for the dizzy airlessness to pass. I had no idea if she would know who I meant, I couldn't remember where I had seen her before. But she seemed to have rescued me, was making no move to harm me, I began to relax a little.

The woman frowned, thinking, waiting for her breath to steady. I could hear a radio, an engine roaring, people talking – all the sounds of the slum creeping through the thin walls, mingling to a buzz of constant noise; above it all, our breath, short and harsh.

"I take you," she said at last, when finally our breath was more even. "You will please be following me. Next time, you not come alone."

She set off immediately, taking me back to the pathway. We were walking now. I was aware of faces, watching from doorways, sounds of life from within the buildings. I looked inside as we passed doorways, and saw people sitting, sometimes cooking on a small stove, squatting next to it; sometimes sleeping, stretched out on the hard floor, an arm for a pillow. No one seemed to have furniture. Old rugs were strewn on the concrete, a few possessions were stacked in corners.

I suddenly felt very angry. Perhaps it was the release of tension that did it, made me more aware of what I was seeing, made me notice. How could people be this poor today? How could a world that had space travel and computers and mobile phones allow people to live in this state?

I also felt angry with the English. Why the hell did we have food banks in England, where we had a system of benefits to help the poor? In fact, how could anyone in England even claim to be poor, as they sat on their sofa, watching their television, chatting on their mobile phone? Perhaps they needed to get off their arses and sell some of their stuff and stop whingeing! They owned more than these people could even aspire to own. I was ranting inside my head, a politician making a speech, trying to make sense of the poverty I was seeing.

As we walked children began to appear. They watched us pass, then slid from doorways and followed us, silent, watching. Sometimes we passed a chicken, or a thin dog wandering, aimless. A rat scurried in front of us and dropped into the wet gutter.

The grey air thinned, more light filtered down, the pathway widened. We stepped out between the final two houses and stood on the wider lane again. I recognised the more organised buildings of the resettlement area. Our tail of children melted away, and we walked a few more yards then turned into a lane I recognised. Kavita's house was on my left, I could see her sitting on the threadbare rug, talking to someone. My guide pointed, nodded, and walked away, keen to be rid of the inept stranger. I climbed the two fat steps up to the house and walked into the room I'd entered yesterday.

Chapter Twenty

We talked. Kavita was easy to talk to. Her English was good, accented but clear. As I grew to know her better, in the months that followed, I noticed that whenever she spoke, she moved her hands. Sometimes smoothing her dress, sometimes twisting material, knotting it to make rag rugs, sometimes sitting on an old sack in the sunshine, helping a woman sort nuts from husks. That first day, when I climbed the steps into her house, she was threading beads onto a long piece of yarn. The beads were plastic, snipped from a hollow wire, multicoloured and shiny. They would become part of a bracelet to be sold on a table in the market.

Later, I would think about how she had risen to meet me when I arrived. How she had accepted me without question, had settled back on that thin rug to hear my story and to tell hers. Later, I would understand that in this place, one learned to accept things as they happened, to quickly grasp new situations, to either bend to them or flee. Poverty does not allow one time to ponder, you learn to respond instantly or opportunities slip away and danger seeps in. Later, I would understand these things.

I told Kavita very little about myself, only my name, and that I was looking for an investment in India, a way to use my uncle's money. She didn't ask more, and it seemed unnecessary to lie, so I didn't offer anything further. Mainly I listened. I wanted to know what this strong woman with the coal black eyes was doing in the resettlement area. She belonged there as much as I did.

I learned that until a few years ago, Kavita had been a senior nurse in a big hospital. She had trained in spite of her parents' wishes. They were wealthy, and wanted her to marry well and produce heirs. She ignored them and followed her own plan. Then, one day, she became part of a mobile medical centre, going into the poorer area of the city, offering free medical care to those who couldn't afford it. It was while she was there, a nurse in a caravan accompanying an ancient doctor who weighed babies and dispensed pills, that she met the women. I met one of them, Rashi, that first day. She was living upstairs.

"Come," said Kavita, after we had talked for about half an hour, had introduced ourselves and touched on why we were there. "Come upstairs. To properly understand my work, you should meet Rashi. She can explain so much better than me. She has lived it you see, I have merely seen it."

We climbed those steep castle-like steps to a floor above. A door opened as we arrived, and a woman stepped forwards. Kavita removed her shoes at the top of the stairs, and after a pause, I did too. I told myself it was because it was easier today, as I wasn't in boots, and there was no point in making them hostile if I might need them later. I'm not sure that was the whole reason though.

In the room was a bed, against one wall, and a cupboard with shelves above it. We sat, cross-legged, on the rug. I leaned back, resting on the wall. It was not exactly comfortable, but I would cope. Rashi offered tea, which I refused, then settled next to me. There was something bird like about her, especially next to Kavita, who again struck me as manly, though I couldn't have said why. A fan circled above us and there was a window, unglazed but latticed, letting light and the sounds from the street float inside.

"I came to the city when I was a girl," said Rashi, folding her thin hands, sparrow-claws, in her lap. Her voice was quiet but clear, her words sure. She had told her story many times, you could tell; the emotion was gone out of it, but the sentences were easier to say. Below us, in the street, someone was laughing.

"I lived in a rural community, my parents grew crops and raised animals. We didn't starve, but some days we were hungry.

"I helped my mother in the home. Even as a little girl, I knew they had been disappointed when I was born, that they had hoped and prayed to the gods that I would be a boy. But I was a girl. They named me Rashi. My father called me Abla Rashi. I remember his voice: 'Abla Rashi, boil the water. Abla Rashi, feed the goat. Abla Rashi, bring me a drink.'"

I glanced at Kavita. "Abla?" I said, "Does that mean 'Miss'? 'Little'?"

She shook her head and patted my hand.

"No, it means 'Worthless'. There is a story, told to little children – Abla Nari was a weak, useless woman… Abla is often used as a way to address children. Girl children."

Rashi was still talking.

"One day, a man came from the city. He was very tall, and he wore a hat. He said he was looking for girls to work in his factory. He would pay a wage, teach me a skill and pay for me to attend school. He said he could see I was a good girl, and that he would educate me, improve my chances in life so I would make a good marriage. He told my mother to think about it, and to meet him the following day at the railway station if she was willing for me to leave. He said he wanted good workers, and he knew that my parents would miss my help, so he would pay them 8,000 rupee. At the end of the year, if I was unhappy, I could return home and they could give back the money."

I quickly did the maths – a child was worth about a £100. Rashi was still talking.

"Eight thousand rupee was a lot of money. The harvest had been bad that year, my parents were worried how to feed me and my brother. For my father, the choice was easy." She paused, stared unseeing at the window for a second. "Perhaps for my mother too, she liked the idea that I would be schooled, taught a skill.

"So they sold me." Her voice was flat, no emotion. "My mother walked me to the station, and I caught the train with the tall man. There were two other girls with him. He fed us chapati on the journey, the train was slow and stopped many times. I was frightened, I had never travelled before, but mainly I was excited, looking ahead, keen to do well.

"When we arrived in the city, there was no factory. There was a house. We were set to work, cleaning and washing and preparing food for the workers. We were not sent to school, we were taught to dance, and how to smile and move. Mostly the workers were kind to us, but they were tired. Always tired. So if we made a mistake, spilt something or forgot to clean their room, they were angry."

She paused, and looked again towards the window. I could hear an engine in the street below, and children shouting. A mosquito hovered in the window, then floated inside, landed on the wall above Kavita's head. Rashi licked her lips and continued.

"When I was older, after a few years, they told me to dance for the customers. At first I thought this was exciting, a promotion. I still didn't really understand you see, I didn't know what the workers did. I knew they worked at night, I knew they had visitors because we heard them. Our whole world had narrowed to that house, we were never allowed outside, we never saw the sun. When it was dusk we were shut into our room, we couldn't leave until it was light again. If we needed to make water we used a bucket. It wasn't until we were old enough to dance that we were allowed out. By then it was too late, of course. By then we had no choice…"

She stopped. Kavita spoke for her.

"The girls were trapped, you see. They had to service the men, but the money was paid to their owners, not to the girls themselves. So they couldn't escape. Where would they go anyway? They had no money for train fares, no relatives within reach – even supposing those relatives would take them back and give them shelter. Who wants a used woman, a woman no man will ever marry? They really had become like Abla Nari, they really were worthless."

For some reason, my mind went to Aunt Susan. She would never have welcomed me back in the same position, she had barely tolerated me as it was. Yet her hardness was nothing compared to what I was hearing. I looked at Rashi. I wondered if I could use her story to stir some interest back in England, if when people heard they would give money to save other women. Perhaps I could take her, pay for papers and take her back with me, parade her around the churches – churches are an easy touch for raising money – let her tell her story. We could embellish it slightly, add a few dramatic details. It might work. I shifted on the hard floor and stretched my back.

"So, what happened?" I asked. "How did she escape?"

"Kavita helped me," said Rashi. "We met during a health inspection."

"Yes," added Kavita, explaining. "The house owners, they like to say their girls are clean, they can charge more money, get a better price. So they let them come out once a month to the medical van. We check their health, do tests for diseases, and for a few minutes, we are alone with the women, we can speak to them. Always we ask the girls, are they happy, is there anything we can do for them? Most are too frightened to speak, they are afraid they will be punished if they complain.

"Some are unwilling to leave, they have chosen their profession themselves, as adults. Perhaps they were child brides, or came to the city looking for employment. It pays better than construction work and is easier. Once they have lost their reputation, what else can they lose? They would rather stay, continue to earn.

"But Rashi told us that she wanted to leave, though she had nowhere to go. I told her I would meet her, take her somewhere safe."

226

"One day, they forgot to lock my door," said Rashi. "I left, walked to the corner and met Kavita. She brought me here."

Kavita nodded. "I waited at that corner every day for three weeks, hoping she would have a chance to escape. We had no time to plan properly you see, we had to make it up at the time, while she was being examined."

I imagined the scene. A whispered conversation while the nurse checked her pulse, took swabs, felt her abdomen. Rashi speaking in snatches, afraid she would be overheard, Kavita thinking fast, devising a plan while they had time, not sure if the young woman would be brave enough to go through with it, even if she had opportunity. I nodded. Yes, there wouldn't have been time for a better plan.

Then the wait. Every evening, every morning, walking to the corner, watching. Not knowing if today would be the day the woman would arrive. If she would ever arrive. But being there anyway, just in case.

"I brought her here," said Kavita. "I had rented these rooms, to use as a base. My own home is in a better area, and I wanted to be able to stay near the people, to be part of this community. But they're not very safe, there is no privacy."

She looked at me. That's all. She didn't ask, didn't suggest, didn't hint. She just looked, and waited.

But I understood. Rashi was owned and had escaped. Her owners would be keen to recover their investment and to use her as a warning to others. Escaping must not be an option for the other women. If Rashi stayed here, in this building, she would be seen by the people who walked through it to the homes above, or spotted through a window, or discussed on the street. She would be found, and taken back.

Now, this didn't bother me overly of course. A sad story and all that, but not really my concern. It wasn't my fault that life was nasty sometimes was it? There are some evil people in the world, and that was how it was. But, as I was about to shrug, to agree it was impossible, something stopped me.

Perhaps it was the challenge of the whole thing. Those men I was hearing about – the drug dealers and pimps – they had it pretty good in the slums I reckoned. They had lots of power. I like to challenge powerful people, and I'm good at it. Why should they get away with what they're doing? Why shouldn't anyone stand up to them? It would be exciting to change the odds a little, a game much more thrilling than winding up a little minister and his church. This would be a game with high stakes and big risks – and that appealed to me. I could pitch my wits against these people, these kings of the slums, and I would win.

So, instead of the shrug and change of conversation, I nodded.

"Yes," I said, "she should come with me."

That was it. No planning involved. Though to be honest, most of my schemes involve very little planning, I was good at making things up as I went.

Afterwards, when I thought about it, I was surprised that Kavita had agreed. Why would she trust me? But she had, something had made her trust me. Or use me. But I didn't like to think about that, didn't like to acknowledge that maybe this woman was better at manipulating people than even me.

So, that was how it started. I took Rashi back to the hotel with me. Karan met me at the corner, and I told him to drive to some shops, because I was not going to walk through the hotel lobby with some hooker from the slums next to me. So we went shopping, dressed her up a bit. She still smelt of course, but we walked quickly to my room and I shoved her in the shower while I went to find Malik, negotiated another room. It was only temporary, only a start. But everything has to begin somewhere, doesn't it. And at the time, it was fun, exciting.

It made me laugh to be in that posh hotel restaurant, surrounded by businessmen from around the world, while some poor tart from the slums sat next to me, and no one knew. We walked together across those shiny floors, sat in alcoves and sipped tea, and no one gave us a second glance. The waiters and cleaning staff and receptionists buzzed around her, just because they thought she had money, was somebody. It just goes to show, put people into different wrappers and they become something new. For a few days, Rashi dressed and ate and was served like a rich bitch. It made me laugh.

Of course, that was only the beginning. It could never have continued, not that I ever thought it would. But enjoy the moment with me for a minute. Watch those posh people eating next to Rashi, listen to the staff treat her with respect; and have a laugh with me. It's fun to mix things up a bit isn't it? Fun to break the rules, especially the unwritten ones.

Chapter Twenty-One

Taking Rashi away from the slums was the beginning. I began to work with Kavita, going every day back to the resettlement area, walking with her through the slums. I learned the area, the people, the lifestyle.

Of course, Rashi couldn't have stayed in the hotel for long – I wasn't willing to stretch my funds to two people living there, and really it was too good for her. So I went back to Malik, told him I needed to buy or rent somewhere, some kind of house, where a few friends could stay. Kavita came too, for the negotiations. We had tea down in the hotel lobby, surrounded by carved lattice, wicker furniture and bowls of exotic flowers. While we sipped tea – me, Kavita, Rashi and Malik – Kavita and Malik planned where and what we needed. I listened to the music and enjoyed the draft from the fan, the gurgle from a fountain. Rashi sat big-eyed, absorbing the splendour of it all.

I let Kavita and Malik work out what was needed and how to procure it. We spent a few days driving to different areas, looking at properties, and eventually found something suitable. I'm not keen on paperwork, dealing with big institutions, things with rules and procedures. It was easier to put Kavita's name on the paperwork, and my cash joined her deposit into the owner's pocket. But that was okay, it was still my game, money is meant to be spent.

Did I trust her? Was I happy to sign so much over to Kavita, this woman who I hardly knew? Happy – no, but I couldn't be bothered to think of a better option. Worried? Not really. You see, I still felt in control. I am good at people, at reading them, manipulating them. I could tell that Kavita wasn't really interested in wealth, not for its own sake. It was something to be used, to further her plan. It happened that her plan and mine had converged, we wanted the same things. Sort of. She wanted to rescue the women, I wanted to stick it to the pimps, and look like a hero.

That made us partners, but I still felt in control. I could use what she was doing as a basis for my own charity. She would do the work, but once it got going, it would be my name in the title. I would be the person the world saw, the one who'd set up this charity, the person doing all the good work. It would bring me a little fame, eventually. It was like baking cookies, this was the stage where I collected all the ingredients.

The house was in a safe place, away from the resettlement area. It had several rooms, most as yet unfurnished, and a garden of mature trees and lawns. The few rooms we did furnish were clean and uncluttered. It was easy to buy lots of heavy wooden furniture, reminiscent of colonial times. The walls were white and the floors were tiled. Every ceiling had a fan, and although it was never cool, it wasn't too bad when the air was stirred.

There was a guard at the gate. All the houses in the road hired guards, they were cheap and effective, and this was an expensive area. They lounged in khaki trousers in a small shed next to the gate, carrying a gun and looking bored. No one unexpected could pass through the tall gate. Other than monkeys. They were a pain, sitting on the high fence with their yellow-brown fur and calculating eyes. I didn't trust them at all, and avoided walking near them when I was outside. One day I would borrow the gun and shoot them all. The house was a good place though, a haven to visit when I'd had enough of the hotel, much nicer than Uncle William's house. I had done well, and my only regret with having cut all ties to my family was that they would never see it, never know I had done so much better than them.

The future didn't worry me. It never does. If at some point I needed more money, some extra cash to continue living comfortably, then I could use the respectability of Kavita to open the tap of the English churches. No one had responded to my initial emails, though I was continuing to send them out, because they were easy, and you never know, do you? Probably they were going straight into the church's spam box, if they had such a thing. But I was confident they would respond, in time. Even if I had to drag Rashi or Kavita back with me, parade them at the front of congregations and make them recite their horrific experiences to strangers. I was sure we could manage to get finance from somewhere. We just needed to put the right spin on it. But all that was far in the future. I'm someone who lives from day to day, and my days were full and exciting.

Even while still living at the hotel, I had abandoned Karan and his fussy ways and bought myself a motorbike. It was small and old, because I didn't want it stolen, but it got me from place to place with no fuss and a lot of excitement. Indian driving is all about watching your left-hand side. Whatever the driver on your left does, you must avoid them. If you swerve suddenly to avoid them, then the driver on your right has to avoid you. For the most part, it works. Driving that bike, avoiding cows and potholes and tuk-tuks was huge fun. It was also fast, I don't know why everyone doesn't get one.

***

It was a few months later that I met Shan. Or 'Mr Shan' as he was known.

I met Kavita at the house in the resettlement area. I was still living in the hotel at the time, but she had moved by then, was living with Rashi in our new house. She still used the old place as a base and stayed there sometimes if she was working in the area. She said it made her more accessible, the same as the people she was trying to help. I think she had the same notion as me – that if you never receive anything from the people you want to help, the relationship is too uneven, the charity has all the power. Staying in the resettlement area meant Kavita needed help from poor people. She needed them to help her carry gas cylinders, and to tell her when the water was turned on, things like that. It wasn't comfortable though.

I parked the bike next to the step and climbed up, into the first room. She wasn't there, so I called upstairs and went to find her. She was sitting on her bed, tousled hair and crumpled clothes. I had woken her, even though it was late, almost midday. Kavita didn't speak much in the mornings, I'd already learnt that. She waved in my direction, heaved herself off the bed, walked, tall and thin, through the main room.

"Tea?" she said.

I nodded, slipped off my shoes and followed her into the kitchen. I use the term 'kitchen' loosely. There was no door, just a doorway off the main room. There was a work surface on two sides, and a fat gas bottle sat on the floor, below a double ringed burner. The gas was bought from the market and hauled up the stairs. It was heavy, and I had once followed Kavita when she was replacing it, she and another woman struggled to get it up the steps and I worried it might fall on me. In the corner was a bowl, for washing up. There was no tap. I avoided eating anything prepared there, and only occasionally drank tea. This room had so many hygiene issues it couldn't even be classed as a food preparation area.

Kavita filled a battered kettle with water from a plastic container and put it on to boil, then walked past me and down the stairs. I assumed she was going to use the communal toilets in the street below. The house had no plumbing, other than a long hose which could be connected to the tap in the street. It reached up to the 'wet room', which was next to the balcony, so slops could be brushed into a pipe that led to the sewers. On one occasion when I was in there, I had seen rats slide from the pipe and scuttle across the floor. It wasn't a place I would want to wash in, though most people had clean clothes. It was only really in the slums that people actually looked dirty. They smelt of course, I had noticed that a lot when I first arrived, until the constant pollution blocked my nasal ducts and my brain got used to the general aroma. By this time, I noticed only the most stinky of body odours (and assumed that should I return to England, my own personal hygiene might need extra attention).

I sat on the balcony while I waited for Kavita to return. It wasn't unpleasant, with plants in big pots, washing draped across a rope, and an old rocking chair. I sat on the rocker and waited, listening to the sounds from below. India is noisy – you notice it when you first arrive, but after a while it becomes background noise you never notice. Kavita joined me, placing a china cup in my hand. It had no handle, and I held it by the rim so it wouldn't burn me. For a while we sat in silence, sipping hot tea, stupefied by the midday sun. I'm not a person who has friends really, but Kavita was alright. Apart from the fact that she still reminded me of a man, she was turning out to be useful and very little hassle. She understood about letting people be, she never tried to change me, never expected me to behave in a certain way. Perhaps because I was foreign, perhaps it meant normal rules didn't apply. Whatever the reason, she was easy to be around.

Kavita yawned.

"Excuse me. I am very tired. I was late to bed last night, I sat up with Rashi for as long as I could. I didn't come back here until late."

I nodded. Rashi was now living in the new house, but was having trouble shifting her clock. Since childhood, she had been trained to sleep during the day and work all night. It was now proving difficult to change that, but she couldn't apply for work until she did. I knew Kavita was often there, chatting until the middle of the night, then having to wake the next day so she could attend the clinics in the slums. It explained why the women, when they came to the medical caravan, often appeared almost drugged they were so drowsy, squinting in the sunlight. Years spent in only darkness changed your perception of daylight.

"I'm glad you came," she said. "I want you to meet Kamala. She came to me yesterday. She wants us to help her sister."

I frowned. I wasn't keen on that, on our work being known. If it became too public, the people I was working against would be warned and start to retaliate. It was better to keep things low key, stay under the radar until we were better organised. Like I told you before, you have to prepare all the ingredients before you can bake a cake. I didn't want people rushing ahead before we were ready, spoiling everything.

"Kamala?" I said, "Who's she?"

"I will show you, on the way to the van," said Kavita, not wanting to chat.

We finished our tea, and I waited while Kavita went off to the bedroom again. When she emerged she looked almost exactly the same, except her hair was twisted into a knot and hidden under a *dupatta*.

We set off, walking through the resettlement area towards the slum. We would meet the health van at the corner, near where the rag pickers sorted the rubbish, searching for things they could sell or recycle. It took us a while, because as we walked, people called to Kavita, told her a baby was due or a wedding arranged, or that someone had recovered from an illness. She would stop, stand fidgeting with her scarf as she listened or gave advice, before moving on, tall and thin, gliding over rubble and debris. I walked beside her, understanding very little as most people spoke in local languages, watching and learning and looking for danger. Kavita would translate, try to include me in the conversations, but I wasn't too interested to be honest.

"That's Kamala," said Kavita after a while, pointing to a woman draping wet clothes on a rope. We climbed the steps to the first floor and joined the woman on the balcony.

Kamala nodded when we arrived and pointed to a chair. I sat in it, Kavita curled her long legs beneath her and sat on the floor. Kamala squatted next to her. She was a chubby woman in a faded yellow sari, her head and shoulders almost completely hidden under her scarf. She spoke a few sentences to Kavita, then turned to me.

"You must help Laxmi," she said. "She is not safe."

Kavita put her hand on the woman's arm, silencing her, and began to explain.

"Laxmi is Kamala's younger sister, so she feels responsible for her. Both women came recently from a rural area, married to men who had been recommended to their parents. They belong to the Vaishya caste, so are tradesmen, the match was a good one. But the dowries promised were unrealistic. This happens sometimes, people agree to pay more than they can afford, hoping to borrow the money. Kamala was married first, and her parents paid the dowry as agreed. But now Laxmi has arrived. Her husband is demanding the dowry but their parents have not been able to raise the money, they have paid less than agreed. He is very angry. Kamala wants us to help."

Kamala nodded throughout Kavita's explanation, though how much she understood I wasn't sure. I had grown better at understanding some pretty bad accents, but even so, I had struggled to follow Kamala's few words. She was obviously uneducated, a poor girl who'd grown up on a farm. Her parents must have called in a few favours to arrange the marriages, and now it had all gone wrong.

"It is very rare for a rural family to have two daughters," explained Kavita. "Usually the mothers have a scan while pregnant, and if the baby is a girl, they abort it. In some areas, there are very few girls being born, it will be a problem in a few years time."

I nodded, I'd heard this before, from Lily.

"The dowries are often expensive. Originally, they were designed to protect the woman, they were a gift from her parents when she married, so she had some money of her own. But today it is very different." She paused, shaking her head, in despair at how her country had changed. "Today, the money is promised directly to the husband. Girls are seen as too expensive, a burden. People do not want them, and will mourn if a girl is born. Here, in the resettlement area, a woman who delivers a girl will be expected to stay inside the house, to hide her shame for a few months. Everyone is disappointed, they all know that to be female is a shameful thing..."

I shuffled, keen to leave. We were meant to be meeting the health bus, seeing a few patients, making a few contacts. This was delaying us and I couldn't see that it was our concern.

"Well," I said, "that's all very sad I'm sure. But it isn't really something we can get involved with. Not in this case." I looked hard at Kavita, hoping she would agree and we could leave. "We don't have the resources to get involved," I said, "she'll just have to go back to her parents or something."

Kavita was twisting a loose thread in her hands, thinking. She didn't look at me, and instead turned to Kamala.

"Laxmi is married to Mr Shan?" she asked.

Kamala nodded. Kavita turned to me.

"Mr Shan runs one of the houses," she said. "Perhaps you should see him."

This made the conversation more interesting. The 'houses' were the brothels we were planning to empty. Some of the brothels were run by the women themselves, they had organised themselves into groups and might even live elsewhere, arriving for work like any other job. They worked two shifts, some during the day, others at night. This was a lifestyle choice, the women wanted to work there and were free to leave if they wanted to.

But we were interested in the other brothels, those often owned by men, where we suspected the women working had little choice and were in fact owned, often trafficked when young like Rashi, working almost as slaves. It seemed odd to me that the men running them should bother with wives, but perhaps they planned to produce sons and didn't sully themselves with the girls they owned. I was surprised one of them had agreed to marry a girl from outside the city – perhaps they were seen as pure in some way. It also meant that her parents must have done a good job at the deception, he would've demanded a high dowry I expect, as a man with power and influence.

"Often marriages are arranged with distant family," said Kavita, "Mr Shan's own family probably came from the same area as the girls. That is the tradition here."

I stood, keen to leave.

"Okay," I said, "we can visit him. When I've met him, I'll decide if we can help." I leaned towards Kavita, who had also stood. "But I doubt we'll get involved." I said, my voice soft but certain. "We don't need the hassle at the moment."

"We will see," said Kavita, unperturbed. She spoke a few words to Kamala, who bowed towards me, and we left.

We met Shan in his shop. Yes, that's right, as well as one of the brothels, he owned a shop. It was narrow fronted, a tall step up into a dark doorway. Near the entrance there was a high four-legged stool and a fat policeman sat there, scowling at the world. On the way there, Kavita had explained that in addition to the brothel, and the grocery shop, Shan sold drugs. He saw himself as a cut above the dealers who strolled the slums persuading teenagers to try their wares. He sold directly to customers from his shop. There were several such shops in the city, and each one had a policeman on their staff. Surprised? Yeah, so was I. Apparently they are there 'to keep the peace' but in reality, they take a cut of everything sold and are in effect bodyguards for the dealer. Everyone knows this, no one does anything about it. The authorities would deny all knowledge, but I think they like that people are controlled and orderly. In a city with this many poor, the last thing you need is any kind of instability or rioting. You have to admire their gall really, I rather wish I had thought of it.

The shop was dim and smelled musty. Kavita had suggested that we should go there to buy groceries. It would avoid confrontation, and allow me to see Shan, to get a feel for the situation. Shan would, of course, know exactly who we were and why we were there, but we would all pretend otherwise for now. It gave everyone a chance to decide on their plans, to see who would make the first move. Sort of sizing up the enemy. I was discovering that everything within this area was known about, secrets were whispered, information traded. There was an undercurrent of organised crime, though quite *how* organised it was, was uncertain.

So we climbed the step into the dull-lit shop and looked around as if searching for produce. Not that anyone in their right mind would want to buy any of the limp vegetables rotting in crates along the wall.

Shan was shiny. No, that's the wrong word. Greasy? It's hard to find a single word so you can picture him. There was something polished about him, the way his thick black hair was smoothed back from his forehead, his jeans had been ironed (honestly, who irons jeans?) and his shoes were shiny and pointed. He was a slippery character, reptilian, but in a tidy, western way. He stared at us when we went in, made no move to greet us as customers, to try and sell us anything. Just stared. Black eyes, hard, appraising, above a lipless mouth, sharp folds in his cheeks, a dimple in the square chin. On the front of a magazine, you would think him handsome, but in that shop, he seemed predatory. I saw Kavita shiver beside me, as if infected by him. I stared back, challenging him to speak first. But he didn't.

"We need some okra," Kavita was saying, beginning to rummage in one of the crates. Still he made no move towards us, no attempt to play the shopkeeper. The policeman had turned slightly on his stool, was facing us, wary. He didn't want trouble and had detected something in Shan's attitude that worried him. We ignored him. Kavita continued turning the vegetables, talking all the while about food and prices and it being too dark to find what she wanted. Shan staring, me staring back, sneering, daring him to make a move. I thought about saying something, mentioning Laxmi, simply to get a reaction, to provoke some kind of action. Not that I cared one way or the other about the girl, I just wanted to win a fight. I felt myself squaring up to him, glaring back, my hands forming fists. But Kavita had given up on the vegetable hunt, was pulling on my arm, telling me she knew a better place to shop, we could try the stall at the market. Still he stared, no expression but somehow mocking us. As we left he spat, I heard the glob smack against the step after us, but I couldn't turn, Kavita was hurrying me away.

"What was that?" she said, cross. "You must not challenge these people. We agreed, we go and look, you would see Mr Shan, we would leave. I did not expect that, that... You made him angry," she finished.

I shrugged.

"I didn't like him," I said.

But she was right, of course she was, I knew that. Shan was not an enemy we wanted to tackle before we were ready. And as we walked away, my desire for confrontation faded. I decided Laxmi would have to take her chances, we weren't equipped to get involved in a marriage dispute. Helping her would jeopardise what we were trying to set up. Let her family help her, they were the ones who'd caused her problems.

***

I met Laxmi, just the once, about a week later. I had joined Kavita on the medical bus, was helping her to organise the women who gathered into some kind of order, sorting through health records written on slices of coloured card, when Laxmi arrived. She had completely covered her head and shoulders with her scarf, not removing it until she was inside the bus. Perhaps she was hiding from the eyes of men. Perhaps she was just hiding. I looked at her.

Her black plait hung straight down her back, reaching beyond her waist, looking almost too heavy for her slim frame. She had huge eyes and hands that trembled as she removed her clothes, went to be examined. I heard her whispering to Kavita, but couldn't decipher the words.

Kamala arrived at the same time, they must have had some prearranged agreement. When Laxmi emerged Kamala pulled her towards me, made me look at her again. Laxmi was slimmer than Kamala, and she leant towards her sister, dependent and desperate.

"You must help us," Kamala said, her voice low and urgent. "There is not much time. Things are very bad now."

I looked at them, the older sister keen to protect her younger sibling, probably continuing to fulfil a maternal role that had begun when they were children.

I shook my head. "No," I said.

I didn't bother to explain why, to say that helping her sister would handicap us, give us an enemy we weren't ready to fight. I didn't tell her about our plans, the purchase of the house, the hope

241

we could get more girls there, could break the cycle of rule that the pimps held in the area. I simply shook my head. I didn't have to explain myself, not to them.

Laxmi reached out, touched my hand. Her hand was warm, surprisingly soft for someone who'd grown up on a farm, and as her fingers clasped mine I saw her nails were clean and shaped. She said nothing, but that warm hand holding my own, those big eyes full of trust – well, I guess someone more emotional would've been moved. She had a childlike quality about her, a sort of innocence.

Kamala whispered to her sister, shaking her head. I saw the despair in her eyes, knew we were their last hope, knew we were crushing that, leaving her with no place to go. It was tough for them. But like I said before, life here *is* tough. Not my problem. And she was pretty, even I could see that, with her liquid velvet eyes surrounded by thick lashes. I figured her chances were good, Shan wouldn't want to damage that perfect coffee skin, he was unlikely to hurt her.

***

I was, by then, beginning to find my way around the culture. I had two main roles in the slums. Sometimes I went with Kavita to the medical bus, and helped with the admin. I organised the women, made contact cards for them, tried to chat a little. We wanted to learn about their past, why they were there, whether they wanted to leave. It involved gaining their trust, which as a foreigner was almost impossible, but I could help by organising the paperwork, leaving Kavita free to chat. She befriended them, learned who had come to the slum as a child, who had grown up there, who had arrived as an adult searching for work.

I was taller than almost everyone, and my natural confidence gave me authority. I had become Kavita's bodyguard. If there was any sign of trouble, women squabbling over who should be seen first, or a man escorting someone and demanding to be allowed to attend the consultation, I simply had to move forwards, shout something, wave them back. Even without a weapon I seemed to be able to control them, which made Kavita's role easier and more efficient.

A few of the women spoke good English – good enough for me to understand them anyway. They would come to the van, watch while I filled out cards of details, smile. It surprised me how cheerful they seemed, how they accepted their role in life, it was normal. Kavita explained their attitude to me.

"Many of these women will have arrived when they were girls," she said, reaching for the next card. "Like Vani," she said, waving the card at me as if it was a fan. "Her mother sold her when she was about eight years old. Though that won't be her exact age probably, people here are often vague on age…

"But anyway, she arrived as a young girl, her family told she would have a job and training. Since then, she has been a sex worker in one form or another. It is all she knows, all she remembers. There is no shame in it anymore, it's just how life is. She has friends, food, shelter – why worry?"

She slid the card back into the index box and stood there, frowning.

"They have no choices, these women," said Kavita, "their lives are decided by others. But the real problem, is that it self-perpetuates. Because these women accept it as normal, they don't fight to change anything, and they don't do what is necessary for their children to have different choices."

"Do many have children?" I asked, moving the cards further from her, before her restless hands started to shred the corners.

"Oh yes," said Kavita, picking up a pen and clicking the top. "Some will have been child brides, now deserted. Some will have not taken precautions when working. Usually the children are sent back to their village, to live with their own mothers. The sex workers are never visited by their families, they have lost their reputations. But they can keep in contact by phone, if the village has signal.

"And some keep their children with them, they live with their mothers, usually in a room not far from the brothels. But the care they receive is sporadic, especially if their mother works a day shift. It's easy for them to fall prey to a pimp themselves, even though the law is tough on underage sex selling. It happens." She sighed, her whole face sad. "Here, too much happens. Too much is accepted as normal. No one is willing to change anything..."

She sighed, gave a small shake of her narrow shoulders, and went to find the next patient.

I also helped at the slum school. It wasn't called that – they called it 'the reading room', but basically it was an informal school, run in one of the houses in the slum, for the kids who couldn't attend the proper school for one reason or another. Perhaps their parents were illegal immigrants, or criminals or something. I do know that sometimes the problem was finding transport costs, or the uniform. Although the government provided uniforms and satchels for certain children, life in the slums was hard on clothes. There were no cupboards to store clothes, no machines to wash them gently. The whole 'dunk in water and bash with a stick until clean' method has never been printed on any care label that I've seen! So clothes didn't last long, within a few months they were worn out, scuffed from sitting on concrete, never hung, as uncared for as the wearer. No uniform meant no school.

These kids were taught by one of the women, Seema, who lived in the slum, and I went twice a week to help her. I read stories and taught them English nursery rhymes.

Actually, the kids spoke quite good English – better than most of the adults, including some of their teachers. I suspect it was because some of the shops had televisions, and the kids would loiter in the doorways, watching cartoons and assimilating the language. They couldn't read or write it, of course, so the school was trying to help with that, which is where I came in. They listened, I think because I was foreign, bit of a novelty. To be honest, I found I quite enjoyed it, I like an audience. The kids themselves weren't too bad either. They didn't exactly obey rules, but I could relate to that. I had a couple of favourites: Raj, who had the scruffiest hair you've ever seen, and Chutki. Chutki had one of those minds that bounced from topic to topic, and she spoke very fast with no pauses, like there was no filter between what she thought and what she said. She had the biggest smile ever, with a gap between her front teeth. There was something unstoppable about her, a bubble of energy.

Most children arrived more or less on time, others drifted in while we taught. Kavita told me that knowing the time was not a problem in the slum, a family was more likely to have a mobile phone than a toilet. Plus, time mattered. The water pipes had water twice a day, for an hour in the morning and another in the evening. During that time, people attached their hoses, filled their water butts, so they could have water throughout the day. All the houses were very close together, so one person using water would alert all the neighbours, no one would miss the hours of water. Children would know when, in relation to the water, they needed to go to school. Mothers would leave to work as maids in the wealthier houses. Fathers would go to their stalls in the market, or jobs as construction workers, or tuk-tuk drivers.

Many of these jobs had risks. Health and safety was not overly emphasised on construction sites, in factories. Even the women working as maids faced risk – a wealthy home with a guard on the gate could abuse their domestic worker and who would know? Who would care?

So as I said, I was finding my way, learning the culture and how things worked. I thought I was doing pretty well. Until the Laxmi incident.

It was soon after this that Kavita suggested we try to raise some more money. I still had lots left in my account, of course, but she didn't know that, and we wanted to take our plan a step further. We planned to bring some more women to the house, but we needed to furnish the remaining rooms and know we could provide enough food until they were self-sufficient and could get employment. The aim of the house was to provide a safe refuge, somewhere for women to escape to after leaving the brothels. They could stay while they changed their body clocks, recovered their health (which included their mental health) and were fit enough to leave. Kavita talked a lot about repairing their self-esteem, teaching them they had value, were significant. I didn't know about any of that, I've never been into emotional crap, but I was keen to prove I could beat the pimps. Toppling empires appeals to me, and since *that* night, when *he* visited, I had switched to toppling empires that were evil.

We were sitting in a children's play area when she raised the subject. I say 'play area' because that's what it was called, but really it was an area of hard mud and broken bottles and litter, with a single climbing frame, provided by the government, in one corner. A boy was swinging on it, upside down, watching us. We were sitting on an old rug, with Deepa, shelling nuts. Deepa was a woman from the slums. She was fat, and sat solidly on the rug, her stomach spreading across her legs, her bulky arms moving, grabbing nuts, sorting them, her great bosom wobbling at every move.

A large sack was open between us, and we were sorting the nuts from the husks. Deepa had bought the sack from the market for 300 rupees. When the nuts were sorted, she would take the sack back to the market, where she could sell it for 400 rupees. She spent 50 rupee transporting it. It would take all day for her to sort it, which meant she was earning about the equivalent of 60 pence for a day's work. It wasn't worth doing, in my opinion, so although I sat with them, I wasn't helping. I've never been one to get my hands dirty. Not in the physical sense anyway. The sun was relentless, beating down on the back of my head, and I adjusted my *dupatta*, trying to get some shade.

Deepa and Kavita were busy sorting. Their fingers were dusty, stained brown by the dirty nuts. I was sitting next to them. The rug was dirty, covered with strands of husk and dust. An insect crawled along one edge. It was most unpleasant. I watched the boy on the climbing frame, his hair hung towards the hard packed mud, his eyes strangely oval shaped as he stared at us.

"We need to find some money," said Kavita, pulling a handful of nuts from the sack.

I liked that about Kavita, she didn't mess around, she said what she thought.

"Well," I said, watching her fingers as they picked at the first nut, "as I told you, I've emailed the churches I have links with. I'm waiting for them to reply."

Kavita shook her head. "They won't reply," she said. "No one reads emails, they are easy to delete, and I think you did not have many friends in those churches. You must write a letter, to the man who told you to come here. He will help you I think."

I was annoyed at that. I'd never told her that Sam Whittaker had 'told me to come', only that he suggested I moved away. I hadn't told her why, obviously, but she'd asked once, why I had come to India, and I'd made something up about an old man giving me advice. People in India like the old, they think they're wise, so I thought it might have some traction. But I didn't want her thinking he was my boss or something.

The pile of husks was growing bigger and a breeze moved them slightly, spreading them across the rug. Some landed on me, and I brushed them off, irritable.

"He's too old to help," I said.

I was sure she was wrong, didn't know what she was talking about. But later, when I was back in the hotel room, after I'd showered away the filth of the day, I thought about it some more.

Kavita was right about the emails, they were too easy to delete. If we needed money, I still reckoned churches were the best place to start. Think about it, all those people meeting every week, emotionally receptive as they arrive ready to listen. All they need is some prompting, someone to suggest that there are people in the world needing their help, some photographs of children looking sad, and they're happy to open their purses. It makes them feel better about the things they can't change I guess. Plus, I am now forced to admit, perhaps they are more open to God using them to balance things up a bit. They are more likely to listen.

Perhaps I should write. The room had a supply of stationary in the desk, I pulled out a couple of pieces of creamy paper and an envelope and wrote a letter. I think it may have been the first letter I have written as an adult. I described what was happening, how I had met Kavita, that we were trying to provide a safe place for the women, that we'd bought the house. I told Sam that we now felt we needed some support, and I asked if he would help, if he would take my news to the church and present it for me.

I asked reception to print off a few photos for me, and enclosed them with the letter, then left it at the desk to be posted. I didn't expect to hear anything, but you never know, was worth a try.

***

I was still waiting for a reply when I heard about Laxmi. Kamala

248

came to us. We were at the house in the resettlement area. It was morning, and Kavita was pouring tea from the pot, wearing her 'morning face'. I was the only one who was properly awake, so she wasn't very good company, and I was pleased when I heard the shout that we had a visitor. I wasn't pleased when I saw who it was.

Kamala rushed into the room. Her eyes were wild, and her hair had escaped from its plait and was tangled across her shoulders.

"Laxmi," she said, and dissolved in a heap on the floor, sobbing.

Kavita went to her, held her tight, rocking her, smoothing her hair, waiting for the sobs to subside, for her to calm down enough to speak. She put her hands on the woman's chubby arms, stroking her, offering comfort. When Kamala could speak, she spat the words in hiccups of spittle and anger and despair. She told us about her sister.

He had killed her. Burnt her, to be exact, but I don't like to offend your western sensibilities, so I'll spare you the details. I will leave you to imagine the stench, the crisp flesh, the horror.

I felt sick when I heard, because I remembered my burnt hand, imagined the agony of that being over my whole body.

It was a harsh lesson. I learned that things here are tough and unforgiving, that I needed to move with care. The stakes here were high, I was going to be challenging people's livelihoods, their means of survival. Which meant they would fight hard to stop me. This was a game where the losers might not survive – which was exciting but I now realised I needed to be wary.

It also made me direct my plan very much towards Shan. Up until then, I had an unfocussed desire to beat the pimps, to give the women somewhere they could flee to, to make a name for myself as a hero. But now it felt personal. Now I wanted to beat Shan, to close down his business, to force the authorities to act. I had met Laxmi; okay, I had decided not to help her, but the fact that she had

249

come to me, touched me, gave me a link to her. Shan had destroyed her, which was an insult to me.

We listened to Kamala, Kavita comforted her, gave her tea, tried to persuade her to stay. But she needed to get back to her husband, was too frightened to stay for more than about an hour. I took her on the bike, weaving through the traffic while she clung to my back, hot and damp. When I got back to the house, I asked Kavita if she had known it might happen.

"You didn't seem surprised," I said, carrying more tea onto the balcony. "Did you know he might kill her?"

Kavita shook her head. "Not for sure – I hoped not. But, it happens," she said. "And burnings are not uncommon. It is easily denied, can be passed off as an accident while cooking. A domestic incident, not a murder. The authorities rarely investigate very thoroughly, not when the victim is a woman."

She looked up at me, resting her cup on her knees.

"I think it would have made no difference to your decision," she said, her voice soft. "I think you would still have refused to take Laxmi."

I thought about that for a minute, then decided to be honest.

"No, you're right. It was the right decision. We aren't ready to defeat Shan yet, it would be too soon."

Which is true, can you see that? Yes, it was all very sad about Laxmi, horrifying actually, in its way. But if we had helped her, brought her to the house, then we would've been targets too. Who knows what Shan might have done, possibly burned down the whole house, killed all of us and stopped our plans before they had even got started.

I felt cross though. My hand was hurting, it did occasionally, though I don't know why.

"We need to stop Shan," I said. "He has way too much power."

Kavita nodded and sipped her tea.

"Isn't there any way we can get the authorities to do something?"

I asked. "If all this is illegal, can't we make them look into it? Wouldn't they listen to someone rich and foreign?"

Kavita shook her head and smiled. "The days of the British being in charge are over. You have no influence here," she said.

She thought for a moment, tapping her nails against her cup, frowning at the ceiling fan as it turned the air.

"The authorities will only act if they have evidence of children being in the brothels, or women being forced to work there against their will," she said. "We need to find out when new children have been brought from the countryside, then go to the police, ask them to do a raid. If they find children, then they will act."

"Okay," I said, pleased. That didn't sound very difficult, did it?

Chapter Twenty-Two

My next surprise was an email. Well, not so much the email, as who it was from. It must have been about two weeks later. I had moved into the house by that time. It was cheaper than the hotel, and Rashi had adjusted sufficiently to be useful. She now cleaned and cooked for us, helped by a woman brought in by Kavita. The house was comfortable and with an extra guard on the door, it felt more secure than the hotel, I didn't have to put everything in the safe whenever I left the room.

I had just returned from the slums when I read the email. It had been a busy day, we'd had some new women at the van and I'd made contact cards for them and stood waiting while they were examined by Kavita and the doctor. Dr Chande he was called, a tiny, thin, man, with a lined face and white hair. I was tired when I got back, I showered and made some tea, then sat on the bed with my computer. There it was, an email from Esther. Now that was a surprise!

```
Dear Clara,
```

(I very much doubted that she thought of me as 'dear' Clara, so that made me smile.)

```
I am writing with some sad news. I
understand that you and Sam Whittaker
were friends, and I am very sorry to
have to inform you that he has passed
away.
```

(Funny how she said 'passed away'. People never said 'died' any more. Like it would soften the finality of it somehow if they used different words. Maybe she thought I'd be upset. But I don't get upset by things like that. It was bit of a blow, because I'd hoped Sam would be useful, but that was all. There was nothing personal involved.)

Rob was named as Sam's executor, so
he needed to look though his things,
and came across the letter you sent.
We have discussed it, and I felt that
I should write.
Obviously, we don't feel it would be
appropriate to bring your work to the
church as a whole for support.
However, I have spent time praying
about your situation, and I think I
should help. I cannot ignore what you
did Clara, but I am meant to forgive
you, and that involves moving on. I
am therefore sending you the contact
details of some people who might be
able to help. They raise money here
in the UK, and use it to fund projects
they feel are worthwhile. If you
contact them, they might be able to
help you.
I hope and pray you are now using your
talents in the way God intended for
them to be used.

Best Wishes,
Esther

The bottom of the email had the details of the charity, an online link, and some contact details. Interesting. Interesting that she would have written, and interesting that she had been willing to help.

I went to find Kavita. She was in her room, damp from the shower, combing her hair. All the women in this country seemed to have long black hair, sometimes it reached their waists. Kavita wore hers plaited and folded up into a fat bun. She was combing it with a wooden comb when I went in, sitting cross-legged on the end of her bed. I told her about the email.

"You must write to them at once," she said, pulling the comb through her hair. Water sprayed from the ends, puddling the tiles. "We need more money before the other girls come. When Shan's house is raided, we must have somewhere for the girls to go, otherwise they will be taken straight into another house, put to work for another boss. They have no skills beyond entertaining men, no money, no family willing to help. We must be ready."

So I wrote. I explained what we planned, and wrote clearly how the money would be spent – to finish furnishing the house, to pay for the guards and groundsmen, to feed the women while they learned new skills.

I wasn't sure I expected to hear anything, but within a week the charity replied, saying they would like someone to visit. They came, inspected our facilities, offered some advice. They spent a long time talking to Kavita. The people who came were Indian themselves, so they understood the situation. They liaised with their staff in the UK, providing local expertise. They told us that if we were to be supported financially, we would have to be checked regularly, that our accounts must be in order, it must be clear there was no scam taking place. I resented the intrusion, the rules, the authority of the whole thing. But Kavita was adamant that we needed the money, that she would deal with all the formalities, so I agreed. It was another step along the way you see, it took our plans just a little bit further. Another ingredient to add to the bowl. Soon we could start mixing.

***

Chutki was tiny. Her dark hair fell in rats tails to her shoulders and when she smiled she showed yellow teeth with a gap, and a lot of gum. I guessed her age to be about ten, because although she was tiny, I had learned by then that children in the slums looked a lot younger than they were. As I have told you, she came to the ad hoc school in the slums, and always wore the same dark blue *salwar kameez*. If it was ever washed, it must have been when she was sleeping.

It was Chutki who told us about the children. We were squashed into the downstairs room of Seema's house. There were about twenty children seated around us, their crossed legs touching the back of the child in front, their papers balanced on their knees. Seema had given them all a pencil, and was showing them how to write and say the letters of the English alphabet. I was meant to provide a suitable word for each letter, the aim being that they would hear and copy my accent. Most of them were scribbling and chatting, and the boy nearest to me was having great fun sticking the point of the pencil through the paper, making a hundred tiny holes. It was hot, even the mosquitoes couldn't be bothered to fly, and floated above us on waves of warm air. We had dragged ourselves to 'G'.

"'G' is for girl," I said, every bit as bored and hot as the children looked.

"There are new *girls* at Mr Shan's house," said Chutki, drawing the straight lines of an 'H'. She had moved ahead of us with her alphabet, and was cheerfully matching the wrong letter with every sound we explained.

"How do you know?" challenged the boy making holes. "You're not allowed to play near Mr Shan's house, he chases people away if they do."

"I know, because I saw them," said Chutki, showing her gums in a smile of triumph. "They came in the morning, very early. I saw them. With my own eyes I saw them. There were three." She looked at me and frowned. "Will they come here, Miss Clara? Will they come here or go to the big school?"

A boy walked past the open door. He glanced inside, kicked at one of the shoes that were scattered around the step, continued walking. One of our pupils sighed and got up to collect the shoe and replace it next to its pair. They all shed their shoes when entering the house, but they couldn't afford to lose one – who knew when they might happen on some that fitted, when next sorting through the rubbish. Chutki was watching me, her eyes huge.

"Will they?" she repeated.

"I don't know," I said. But I did. Shan would never allow the girls to attend school. They weren't even allowed to leave the house, they wouldn't be seen again until they were older, had lost all contact with their previous lives and were big enough to dance, to start to earn their keep.

"'H' is for house," I said, thinking. We hadn't known there would be new girls arriving, they tended to arrive in secret, smuggled through the slum unseen. It was unlikely Chutki would have invented the story, so I was inclined to believe her. Which meant, if we could persuade the police to raid the house in the next few days, they were likely to find the girls. If they found children, they would close down the brothel. It was one of the laws they actually adhered to.

But we would have to be careful. If we went to the police at the wrong time, Shan would be warned, the girls would be hidden elsewhere until the raid had happened. If no children were found, there would be no reason to close the house, Shan would continue as before and we'd look stupid. We might even be sued for wasting police time. We certainly wouldn't get a second chance.

"'I' is for igloo," I said. Twenty faces looked up, bemused. I guessed India wasn't big on igloos. "'I' is for India," I corrected. 'And idiot,' I thought.

"Did Mr Shan see you?" I said. If he'd noticed Chutki, he might decide it would be safer to keep the girls in a different house for a while. Or he might decide to hurt the child, give her a warning so she didn't pass on information in future. I hadn't forgotten my lesson with Laxmi.

Chutki pressed her lips together and shook her head. She had written a large 'L' on her paper, the lines wobbling as the child next to her joggled her arm. She poked him with her pencil, then turned back to me.

"I was on the outside steps, up high," she said.

I knew the steps she meant. Near Shan's house was a pile of bricks, probably scavenged from a nearby building site and being kept for an extension to his house. They were high, higher than my height, and looked insecure, as if they might tumble on top of a careless passer-by. Behind them, were some steps, wrought iron, which led to the second storey of the house opposite. I had seen children sitting there before, partly hidden, above the walkway, watching as people passed. It didn't look a safe perch, but not much about growing up in the slums was safe. I could see why they liked it, it would be as close to hiding in a treehouse as these kids would get.

I had walked past Shan's house many times. He didn't live there, he lived above his shop, but it was where he ran his business from. Where he kept the girls. It was in one of the narrow lanes, too small for a vehicle, but near the wider road where the medical van stopped. The lane was strewn with rubbish, the houses almost touching in places where the walls bulged towards each other. I sometimes wondered who had built them – no one with building experience, that was for sure.

Shan's house was only noticeable if you happened to look up. It was made with the same shambolic brickwork as the other houses, the same big step up to the door, the same gaping windows above the gulley carrying sewage. But there was a lamppost outside – I guessed it had been stolen from a street at one point – hooked up to one of the tangled wires that ran throughout the slum, carrying electricity from the main network. There was also a satellite dish, and an air-conditioning unit, both perched high on the outside wall. I wasn't sure if either worked, or what point there would be to running an air conditioning unit in a room with unglazed windows, but they spoke of a certain status. They told anyone who cared to look that this house had 'luxuries'. It was all about advertising, showing a good front, looking better than the competition.

Seema was watching me. I wasn't always sure how much she understood when I chatted to the children. I think her written English was better than her spoken language. She didn't spend time watching Western cartoons like her class did. I smiled at her and continued the lesson.

"'J' is for jump," I said.

The boy next to me had completely shredded his paper now. Chutki was laboriously copying the 'M' from the paper Seema was holding. Several other children were laughing as a boy slipped an insect onto the shoulder of a girl who had torn her paper and was trying to swap with the girl next to her. It was hot and I was tired. I wanted to go home, tell Kavita about the children at Shan's house and make a plan. Teaching was dull and tedious, but for now, I needed to be here.

"'K'" is for kick," I said, wishing the time away…

***

258

I met Kavita as my bike drew up at the house. She had also just returned and she waited while I rolled the bike into the driveway. The guard saw us and opened the gate, giving us a yellow-toothed smile. We walked past him and up to the house.

Rashi had prepared food. I told Kavita we needed to talk afterwards, then followed her to the kitchen. I didn't want to discuss the situation in front of Rashi, you can never be sure who to trust, so there was a frustrating wait while we ate. The food was the usual over-spiced mush that people eat in this country. I trusted it was safe though, because I'd spent many hours with Rashi, teaching her to wash her hands, keep perishables cool, wipe surfaces, wash cloths, not store raw meat and dairy products in the same space. We'd battled over the apparent waste of water when something looked clean and I insisted it should be washed again (like her hands) or the waste of food when I decided it should be thrown away, and not simply have the mould removed. But now I trusted her, she was reliably hygienic.

Eventually the meal was finished, and we left Rashi to clean up while we went into the living room. I sat in the rocking chair, pushing my back against the padded back, setting the rockers in motion. Kavita sat opposite me on a long dark wood chair scattered with cushions. I told her what Chutki had told me.

"Do you think she's right?" said Kavita.

I nodded. "It sounded likely. I asked her where she was, and I know the place, she could easily have watched unnoticed. And you know how those kids live, they wander free for most of the day and night, they're more like animals than children."

"Animals with keen eyes," said Kavita. She was holding a cushion, picking at a loose thread. She realised what she was doing and placed it next to her, reaching instead for the bag of knitting that was on the low table between us. She pulled out the needles and began to wind the thread.

259

"This might be the best chance we get," I said. "I think we should go to the police. Shall I go this afternoon?"

Kavita was shaking her head. "Always you want to rush," she said.

"Like I said, this might be the best chance we get," I repeated.

For a while, neither of us spoke. Kavita knitted and I sat, rocking in the chair, impatient for her decision but knowing she wouldn't be hurried. I could've gone to the police on my own, was considering the possibility. But it would be better if we both agreed, we'd be more likely to succeed.

"Very well," said Kavita. "We need to make a plan. If the police visit, the girls inside can leave. I think we are ready."

I nodded. We had furnished the remaining rooms and hired another guard for the back of the house. Stocking the cupboards with food would be easy enough, and for a few weeks the girls would stay on the premises, building their strength, changing their clocks, learning how to make decisions again.

"First, we need to warn the girls," said Kavita.

I shook my head. "The more people we tell, the more likely it is that Shan will hear."

"Then how will they know where to come?" said Kavita. "We can have the medical van nearby, but how will they know to look for it? We need to warn them, to tell them to be ready to leave, that when the police arrive they should slip outside, come to us and we will bring them here.

"Otherwise they will be taken to a government safe house. But they are more like prisons, the women are not free to leave, they are treated like criminals. When they are finally set free, most return to the slums, continue as prostitutes. It is better if they come here. Here they will have choices, we can care for them, teach them new skills."

She had put down the needles, was tugging at the wool,

attempting to undo a knot. It was large, hidden by the rest of the wool in the ball. She must have bought it like that, the problem hidden inside, unnoticed until she started to unwind the layers. She tugged at the edges, trying to loosen a thread.

"Yes," she said, "it is complicated. Some of the women will still wish to return to the brothel. It is all they have ever known, the way of life is their normality."

"One of us must be there," I insisted, "but they must not be told beforehand. When the police arrive, we can wait outside, usher the girls away. It can be done quickly. Shan will see us, but he'll know it was us anyway. He might come here, try to get them back, but we'll be ready for that."

Kavita nodded. "Yes, our home is outside of his territory, I do not think he will cause trouble here, once the girls have arrived, even if he manages to find us." She thought for a moment, picking at the tangled wool.

"It should be me who goes to the police," I said. "They'll listen to me, being foreign."

Kavita smiled. "No Clara, they will not. You seem to think that being British is a good thing, but here, it is not always so. I will go to the police, I will give my family name, it will have influence, they will listen."

I couldn't see a problem with that. Plus it meant I would be free to go to Shan's house, I could be there waiting, watching in case he somehow heard, tried to move the new girls away before the police arrived.

"Which police station will you go to?" I said. There were over a hundred in the city, dotted around every district with their khaki clothed officers. "Will you go to the headquarters, near the Bengali Market?" I assumed that would be the biggest, and we wanted to be taken seriously, to get some muscle involved.

"I think not," said Kavita. "I am not sure how urgent the police will think this matter. I think the station in Connaught Place will be better. It is closer to here, we would have more influence I think."

I knew the building. It was an imposing structure, with a flag outside, built of sandy stone. I nodded.

"And the children inside Shan's house?" I asked. "Will they come here too?"

Kavita frowned. "I think the police will take them," she said. "In India we have many lost children – children with no homes, and many families looking for children who have been lost. It must take up very much time for the police. I think they will have a system, a way of dealing with such things. I expect they will take the children and send them back to where they came from."

"Will the parents want them back?" I asked, thinking of Rashi, of how her parents had been keen to sell her, her father happy to be rid of the burden of a daughter.

"This we cannot know," said Kavita. The knot was gone, and she began to wind the wool back into a ball. "Sometimes the problem is too big, we can only tackle one part at a time. For now, we want to remove those young women from Shan's house, to let them have a chance at normal life. The new children, I do not know what will happen to them. It is possible they will return to their parents, only to be sold to someone else. Yes, it is very possible. But we cannot deal with that. Not today. Today Mr Shan is our problem, and that is the problem we will deal with."

I wasn't altogether happy with that. I didn't particularly care about the children one way or the other, but for me to feel like I had won, they should be removed from the control of the pimps. I decided I would bring them to our home. Kavita didn't need to know in advance, we could sort out practicalities as they arose.

I rather liked the idea of waiting near Shan's house while Kavita went to the police. There was no way of knowing when the police would decide to act, so it might be a long wait, possibly several days. But potentially, things would happen very fast, and I wanted to be where the action was. When the police arrived, I guessed there would be some chaos, I could probably manage to slip inside Shan's house unnoticed. I could then smuggle the women and girls out, even if the raid proved fruitless. I could get the girls to the van and bring them here, to safety. Shan would've lost his employees, even if the police didn't arrest him. I would have won a small victory. The more I considered it, the more I liked it. The person who went to the police station had a tedious role, involving paperwork and waiting and speaking to the right people. Afterwards, they could say they had told the police. That's all. Very uninspiring. I however, would have a story to tell. It would be exciting, something to talk about later when I was explaining how I set up the charity. I would be a hero.

We discussed timings, and Kavita agreed we should act quickly. It would be best if the police raided while the house was open for business, during the night, though as I said, we had no influence over that part. We could do our best though, so we decided that Kavita would go to the police that evening, about 8 pm. I found I was excited, looking forward to it. Which shows how little I had actually learned.

Chapter Twenty-Three

By the time 8 pm arrived, I was ready. I had dressed in dark clothes, with a black *dupatta* to cover as much of my pale skin as I could. The medical van was parked in the lane as near to Shan's house as I could get it. Driving it there had been something of an adventure in itself, as it was somewhat bigger than my bike.

In case you're wondering, no, we didn't actually have permission to use the van. And certainly I, with no valid driver's licence, had no right to drive it. But we had decided the medical charity wouldn't notice it was missing until the following day, Kavita knew where the keys were kept, and it was the best vehicle to use because, if people saw it, they wouldn't think it especially odd as they were used to seeing it in the area, if not at that time.

I had driven my bike to the charity headquarters, told the guard at the gate I was doing an errand for Kavita, and let myself into the office with her keys. It was easy enough to find the key in the middle drawer of the desk in the third office. I also picked up a file, which I waved at the guard when I left. I told him I was taking the van to meet Kavita and Dr Chande for an emergency appointment, and would be returning it later that night. I spoke quickly but with authority. If you behave as if what you are doing is legitimate, people rarely question it. Especially people as far down the pecking order as a bored guard on a gate, and especially when you are leaving. I have noticed they are more fussy when you arrive, that's when you need your cover story nice and simple. But once they see you are leaving, even with something like a vehicle, they don't really question it. He had my bike, so he knew I'd be returning. He was a guard, not a brain surgeon…

I then drove to the resettlement area. The van arrived with a few more scratches than when I'd set out, but I don't think I actually killed anyone even if there were a few scrapes along the way, so we'll leave it there. You don't need details.

I parked fairly near to the tiny lane that wound its way up to Shan's house. There was a sort of garage. It was a space adjoining a house, uneven brick walls and a rough cement driveway, covered with corrugated iron, which happened to be empty. I decided to borrow it for a few hours. If the owner returned he would be angry, but I had cash, he could be paid off, and the van was safer out of sight. I had been worrying about that, wondering if I'd return to find no wheels or the windows smashed as someone searched for drugs if it was parked in the street. So I reversed into the space, touching the walls of the house as I did so, but they didn't collapse, so that was good. I left the doors unlocked, and a note inside, explaining to the owner of the garage that I would pay him for the use of his garage when I returned if the van was untouched. It might help, you never know with these things.

I walked up towards Shan's house, keeping as much in the shadows as I could. There were a few children still wandering, like sewer rats with black eyes, but I ignored them and headed for the steps where Chutki had hidden. If the wait was too long, if it looked as if the police weren't coming that day, I would pay a kid to wait as lookout and go somewhere more comfortable. But for a few hours, it was fine. I grasped the metal handrail and climbed the steps, which swayed with each footstep. It was an iron stairway, made elsewhere and moved to position after the house was built. Possibly stolen from a building site. The steps led to a door – an outside access for a second floor living space. I hoped no one would arrive to disturb me, and settled down to wait.

It was a long wait. I was perched at the top of the metal steps, with nothing to rest my back against. Every time I moved, the steps twanged loudly, as if they weren't strong enough for my weight, weren't properly secured to the wall. The noise didn't much matter, the slum was never quiet, there were always voices and motors and music, even at night. I was well hidden. The lamppost outside Shan's house was indeed attached to an electricity source, and pale yellow light oozed through the night, leaving me covered by shadow.

As the night crept closer, fewer people passed below me, and by the time it was properly dark, only stray dogs and rats scurried along the footpath. Plus the occasional man, customers for Shan, stinking of beer and body odour as they staggered beneath me. At one point, a man fell against the steps and they swayed away from the wall, hovered mid-air for a moment, before crashing back against the house they were supposedly attached to. I clung on, wondering if I would crash to the ground, but other than a scraped shoulder when the steps returned to position, I was fine, and the man was too drunk to notice the extra weight. I watched as he turned into Shan's house.

I was at the point of leaving when they arrived. I'd sat there for long enough, I'd decided the girls could take their chances and we could think of a less uncomfortable plan. But before I could stand up and return to the van, I heard them. Sirens cutting through the general din. They weren't exactly stealthy.

They must have abandoned their cars in the lane where I'd parked, because I heard doors slam, and shouts as they came nearer. Then they appeared, six men pushing a seventh ahead of them. It was Shan – they must've collected him from his home on the way. I watched as the police followed him. They came towards me, then turned into his house.

I was already standing, creeping down the rickety steps, though it wouldn't have mattered if I'd stomped, with all the noise they were making. My legs were stiff, the blood bubbling back into my limbs, fizzing painfully as I ignored it, forced myself to keep walking. I didn't know how long I would have, but I knew I needed to be quick, to collect as many women as I could during the initial confusion of the raid.

The door of the house was open, a policeman standing behind it. He was probably guarding the exit, but was watching for people leaving, not entering. His back was towards me. I noticed the bulge of his sides over the leather belt of his trousers, the gun in the holster, the black shoes planted on the cement floor. Then I was past him, sliding along a wall towards a stairway. There was a shoe in the corner, which I threw towards the doorway. It fell just beyond, in the lane, falling with a clatter. Enough to distract the man, make him glance outside, while I raced for the steps. I started from behind him, sprinted to just inside his line of sight, so to catch me would've involved effort and he wasn't built for speed. He must have caught sight of my feet as I jumped up the steps, but not enough to alarm him. His job was to contain things inside, and I wasn't leaving. He didn't even bother to shout, probably assumed I worked there.

At the top of the stairs was a corridor, strewn with rugs, doorways leading off on both sides. The corridor seemed too long, much longer than the room downstairs, which ran the length of the whole house. There was shouting from the floor above. Not completely certain whether or not the policeman would follow me, I opened the first door, and walked into the room.

It wasn't luxurious. There was a dirty rug on the floor, strewn with clothes, a blanket hanging across the window. An oil lamp spluttered on a low table (probably to add 'atmosphere', because I was sure the house had electricity) and a bed. As I entered, a man and woman rose from beneath the dirty bed cover. She looked worried, he looked confused, then angry. He opened his mouth to object.

"Out!" I said, "Police!" (Yes, I know I wasn't police, but he didn't know that. The less you say, the less likely people are to argue with you.)

His mouth closed, opened, closed. Then he flung back the cover (I won't describe the view, it wasn't pleasant), grabbed his clothes from the floor and left. I heard him storm down the stairs as I turned to the woman.

"We must leave quickly," I said, hearing shouts from below as the man was prevented from leaving by the policeman at the door. "I work with Kavita, at the medical van. We can help you to leave Shan, if you want to?"

She was staring at me, not moving, I wasn't sure for a moment if she understood English. Then she bowed her head, one elegant movement, and looked back at me.

"I can leave?" she said, "Not have to work here anymore?"

"Yes, that's right," I said. "But we have to hurry. Can you help me to get the other women? Anyone who wants to leave? We need to be gone before Shan realises what's happening, he might be able to stop us…"

She had climbed down from the bed, was kneeling on the floor and was lifting the cover, reaching underneath the bed.

"You don't have time to pack," I said. Honestly, what could she possibly own that was worth delaying her escape for?

Then I saw, and stopped.

From under the bed peered two eyes, round and black. The woman gently extracted a tiny girl, pulling her out, whispering, smoothing her hair.

"Your daughter?" I said.

She nodded.

"She hides under the bed while you – work?" I said.

She nodded. The girl was standing now, her mother kneeling beside her, pulling some sort of dress over her head, explaining something in some language I couldn't follow.

"Can you help me get the other women?" I said again. "I can look after your daughter," I added, not wanting her to delay.

She looked uncertain, so I moved across the dirty rug, picked up the child and balanced her on my hip. She weighed nothing, a doll with bones. The child stared up at me, her whole face dominated by huge eyes that watched, silent. I guessed she had learnt to be silent early on in life. I also guessed she might have nits, so I held her loosely, kept my head away from the tangle of dark hair that shrouded the little face.

The woman was beginning to understand.

"Wait," she said, pulling on some clothes. Then she slipped from the room.

I waited. It felt like hours, but was probably only a few minutes. From other rooms I could hear shouts, men arguing, women screaming, children crying. The police had obviously started at the top of the house, on the third floor, and were barging into rooms, disturbing business, demanding to search the whole house. I stood, holding the child, considering options, what I should do if the police arrived before the woman returned. All the time I was aware of the child on my hip watching me, it felt like she never blinked. At one point she put out a hand and touched me, very lightly, with one finger, on my nose. As if she was checking, trying to determine if this strange coloured woman was real.

The woman eventually returned – with one other woman. One. What had taken her so long?

"Where're the others?" I said, "Didn't they want to come?"

"I have been to Priya," said the woman, "I told her we could leave."

All that time – for one woman? What had she been doing, giving her my CV? Honestly, you would think these women didn't want to escape! I realised I would have to be more forceful, they seemed half asleep. I wondered briefly if they could be using drugs, if Shan kept them doped to make them compliant.

"Okay," I said, you wait here, "I'll get the others. What room is this? Yours? Or does it have a number? Where do I tell them to come?"

"I am Vani," said the woman, giving a small bow. Like this was an introduction at a tea party or something!

I didn't wait to hear more. Telling the two women to stay where they were, I left. I was still carrying the child on my hip. This was intentional. Women are funny about their children, it would make the hooker obedient, she would wait, obey me while I held her child.

It did rather blow my 'I am a policewoman' act though. Not that it was really necessary. The noise from upstairs was obvious now, if they'd started quietly, hoping to catch people before the whole house was disturbed, it hadn't worked for long. There were already doors opening, men pulling on clothes as they made for the stairs. They didn't even glance in my direction, intent on leaving, on not being involved in whatever was causing the disturbance. I walked past them as they headed down, to the waiting policeman. I wondered how many he'd actually manage to stop leaving. Probably not many, unless he waved his gun around.

I pushed past the man leaving the next room and rushed inside. There was a woman standing in the middle of the room, looking confused.

"Put on some clothes and go to Vani's room," I told her. I could explain more later. I left.

Running along the corridor, I entered each room in turn, shouted the same instruction, left. I wouldn't have long before the main of body of police started to come down to this floor, and I wanted to be out of there before then.

In the last room, there was a surprise – another stairway. That

270

explained the length of the corridor, it must run across the length of two houses, with stairs down to the second one from this room. I wondered if the police knew the layout, thought they probably didn't, and decided it would be a possible exit route for us.

I took the woman sitting on the bed back to the first room with me. There were seven women in all, and three tiny children. Three! Can you imagine: three babies smuggled under beds every night while their mothers worked, three toddlers who learned never to make a noise at night, then three children who had grown up thinking this was normal. Three! These were not the children we'd been told about, these were the results of hidden pregnancies, determined mothers.

There was no time to explain things properly, so I shouted the basics. It was necessary to shout by now because it seemed everyone else in the neighbourhood was shouting. There were yells from below us, as the customers tried to leave and argued with the policemen, and noise from above as the police raided the rooms and searched for children. Doors being kicked open, furniture being knocked over, people crying in anger and alarm. I told the women that IF they wanted to leave, I could take them somewhere safe. But they wouldn't be able to return to Shan, ever, and they didn't have time to take anything with them.

Then I asked Vani if the room at the end led to the outside. There was a pause while she considered what I'd said, a pause when I congratulated myself on not shaking her or punching her. Honestly! She moved in slow motion that one. When she finally nodded, I told them to follow and led the way, running along the worn rugs, ignoring the noise from above and below, passing the doors which had all been flung open, gaping doorways showing abandoned rooms with tousled beds and discarded clothing. Back to the room at the end, past the bed and the knocked over chair, down a wooden staircase that wobbled as we ran down it, into a tiny room. There was no guard, and the doorway opened onto the lane a couple of doors up from Shan's door, near the metal steps where I'd hidden. I led the women out, took them back to the main lane, past the crowd that had gathered to watch the commotion in Shan's house. Some people pointed as we ran past, perhaps they recognised the women. We didn't pause, raced down the lane, round the corner, and back to the van.

The van was still there. That was a relief. I told the women to get inside, then climbed up after the last one and sat for a moment. I hadn't counted them, but they seemed to all be there. I was still holding the kid, so I handed her back to her mother. All the kids were silent, it was a bit eerie, unnatural.

I had a decision to make. I had seven women who were safe. I could drive the van back to our home, away from the muddle in the slums, start to help them rebuild their lives. But there were more women in that upper floor. I'd heard them shouting, knew the police had started up there because there were women and clients on that third floor. So, should I just abandon them, take the ones I'd already rescued and call it quits? Or did I go back, try to persuade the police to let me have the others, or see if I could get them away from the police so they could escape too? I didn't think they'd be watched very closely, they weren't the target of the raid – Shan was, and the children he'd brought in. And that was the other thing, where were those children? Should I really leave them as Kavita had suggested, allow them to be sold again to a different Shan? Or should I try to rescue them too? It seemed we had children anyway, nothing I could do about that.

My inclination was to go back, to see what was happening and look for a chance to collect more women. But my problem was the women I already had. They followed me out of the house easily enough. As I've said before, in the slums you learn to make decisions quickly, and these women had probably been waiting most of their lives for a chance to escape, a way out of the near slavery they found themselves in. So, a few shouted instructions, the obvious disruption of the house by police, and they were willing to follow. But they didn't know me. A few possibly recognised me from consultations at the van (I was foreign, makes me noticeable) but not all of them would. And recognising someone didn't necessarily mean you would trust them. Not long term. Not once the initial aim of escaping had been accomplished.

Which added to my dilemma. If I left the van, went back to the house, it was quite likely that at least some of the women wouldn't be there when I returned. They would decide to take their chances elsewhere, to possibly try to simply disappear into the slum, or to beg on the streets until they had enough money to return home.

I looked at them. They were still tense, sitting on the floor of the van or on the few seats around the edges. Not talking, but alert, watching. They didn't exactly look in a listening mood, if I tried a lengthy explanation, if I told them we could keep them safe, but wandering the streets would mean Shan's colleagues would find them, claim ownership, send them back to work. I could explain our plan, to give them a safe place to learn new skills until they were capable of independence, getting a job, living as they chose. But I doubted they would listen, not without having seen our house first.

It was a pain. I wanted to go back to Shan's house, finish what I'd started, remove all of them. But I knew it wasn't sensible, that Shan would reclaim some of those I'd already collected. Reluctantly, I put the key in the ignition and edged the van out from the makeshift garage. We would go home.

Chapter Twenty-Four

I drove into our driveway and parked the van. The guard frowned when he saw my passengers, but said nothing. He valued his job. Rashi came out to greet us. She went to each woman in turn, bowed, said something foreign. It seemed to settle them. Then we took them into our house.

By the time Kavita arrived, everyone had eaten, and been allocated a room, and we had a sort of rota going for the shower.

Kavita looked exhausted – that grey drawn look with sunken eyes that stares out of the mirror after a couple of nights partying. I made her tea, because I didn't want her disappearing off to bed before she'd told me what had happened, and sat opposite her at the dark wood table. She sipped her tea, then rested her head on her elbows.

As I'd suspected, the police had collected Shan before going to the brothel. The houses in the slums didn't exactly have postal codes, so they'd been worried about raiding the wrong house. Kavita had waited at the police station, and they had told her about it when they returned, so I was hearing it third hand. They had entered the house, and taken Shan and the woman who stayed in the reception area (that must be the downstairs room I'd entered) upstairs. They'd then systematically searched each room. (It sounded much more organised than the chaos I'd witnessed.) They had arrested Shan and several women. No men, so they had either shouted their case satisfactorily, or managed to barge past the guard at the door. Or slipped out via the alternate exit. They had not found any young girls. Kavita thought they would keep Shan and the women overnight for questioning, then release them tomorrow.

It was a blow, I can tell you. I still tended to trust what Chutki had told me, so someone must've tipped off Shan and he'd had time to move the young girls to a different location. He would carry on as before.

Kavita didn't mention any children being found upstairs. It seemed unlikely the police would neglect to look under beds, so they must have only been on the lower floor. She was tired. She finished her tea, then excused herself and began to drag her body off to bed. As she left the kitchen she paused, then turned to me.

"We will need to find other safe houses," she said, "they can't all stay here."

I was surprised. "Why?" I said, aware I was frowning. It had been a long day. "It might not be perfect, but it's more comfortable than where they've come from, surely? You think they're going to start complaining at having to share rooms or something?"

Kavita shook her head, came back to the table and sank back into the chair.

"We can talk more tomorrow, I'm too tired now. But no, we need to split up the women, so the ones who go back can't tell the brothel owners where we are. We want to avoid trouble, and we want to stop the ones who don't stay from persuading the others…"

"Go back?" I repeated. "You think some will go back?"

Kavita nodded. "Clara, some of these will women will be like Rashi. They will have been bought as young girls, taken to the brothels, more or less forced into prostitution. But not all of them. Some of them will have chosen it. We cannot force them to change careers, we can only offer them a choice. Some will decide to return."

"Return?" I was finding this hard to believe. "Why would anyone choose to make money like that?"

"Ah Clara, you still have lots to learn," said Kavita, shaking her head. "Being poor in India is very hard. If you are a Dalit, you have very few rights, it is easy for people to abuse you, to work very, very hard in extremely tough conditions, for very little pay. It does not matter that we will teach the women to sew, or hairdressing, or to make things to sell. The work will be hard. For some, they would rather work in the brothels. They have already lost their reputation, everyone knows what they have done. So where is the shame in returning to it? Why not work less hard to earn money?"

I opened my mouth to object. Then closed it. "But surely, they would rather do something else?" I said, feeling less sure.

"Some will want to stay," agreed Kavita. "But remember, some of these women have grown into adults living in the brothels. For them, the way of life is normal.

"Now, I am exhausted. We can talk more tomorrow. Today needs to end now, so I can sleep."

I watched her walk from the kitchen, slowly, as if her bones were tired.

The women were sorted for the night. Some would need to sleep on blankets on the floor, but we could make better arrangements tomorrow. I picked up the keys to the van, and went to return it to the charity office.

Returning the van was as easy as taking it had been. I drove straight into the short driveway, and when the guard appeared, I explained I didn't need the van anymore and was returning it. I asked him if he would take the keys. He could return them to Chande tomorrow. Which would raise eyebrows, but I was beyond caring. I felt so deflated, so angry with the situation. Yes, I know we had rescued some women, but I didn't care about that, I cared that Shan was undefeated.

I picked up my bike, and started to drive home. The roads were still busy, they tended to have less traffic after nightfall, but not significantly so. You actually needed to be more alert, as it was harder to see the animals that wandered into the road, and several vehicles didn't bother with lights.

I drove through the dark streets, my hair streaming out behind me, my eyes searching the road ahead, my brain going over possibilities.

On impulse, I turned the bike, narrowly missing a man straining to pull a cart of milk churns. Instead of heading home, I drove towards the police station. Perhaps there was something I could do.

The police station was in a wide avenue, lots of police and military and smart white cars. There was nowhere obvious to park, so I turned the bike onto the verge, left it next to a gum tree. It wouldn't be long before it was spotted, but I didn't need long. I strode towards the police station. It was well lit, and I saw people emerging. As I got nearer, I could see it was a group of women. The chances were high that these were the women from the house. I trotted towards them, keen to catch up as they began to meander down the street. They looked aimless, as if unsure where to go.

As I got nearer, I recognised one of them and called out. She turned, then stopped the group. They all faced me, surprised to see me there.

"You are from Shan's house?" I said, not bothering with introductions. I was tired, wanted to find out what was happening.

"Yes. I am knowing you. You help at the medical van. Why are you being here?" said the woman I recognised. She wore a blue sari and no shoes. I guessed she'd forgotten them in the chaos, and no one would bother about a woman not wearing shoes, it was her own problem.

"Where are you going?" I said. "I'd heard the police had arrested you."

"Yes, but they had an emergency, something more important.

They have sent us back. They do not wish to hold us overnight. Tomorrow we must report back. But…" she smiled.

I knew what that meant. Once they were back in the rabbit warren of a slum, they would never be seen again. These were not women who were likely to report back to a police station. They lived under the scope of the law, no rights but also no obligations. Which the police also knew. But it would save them taking space in one of the government safe houses, which I understood to be little more than reform homes, where the women had no freedom and were treated like criminals while costing the tax payer. Their situation must have been deemed too petty to be worth the paperwork. They were free. So they were mine – if I could persuade them not to return to the slum.

"Do you want to go back?" I said. "There is another option, if you want."

The woman was looking confused, not following my accent. Another woman tugged her arm, they needed to be moving on, to be somewhere else before they were caught with a new violation, someone else complained about them. The woman began to turn away.

"No! Don't go," I said. "Listen first. You know Kavita? Kavita – the nurse? She has a house, a safe house, away from Shan. The other women are there, you can come, you will be safe." I was garbling now, desperate to stop them walking away but with no influence over them, nothing to threaten or entice them with. They had to choose to come, to take a risk on me, and they hardly knew me, and they knew how dangerous trust could be.

"Please believe me," I said (Yes, I know it sounded lame. But honestly, what would you have said?) "We can help. It is a safe place, a secret place. You can stay, be free. We can teach you how to be independent, to be able to work in a better job. Won't you come? The others are there," I finished, "and the children."

Perhaps it was the mention of the children that did it. I don't know. But they stopped walking away. They looked at me properly.

"We can't pay," said the woman, the spokesperson.

"No, we have money," I said. "Will you come?"

They turned towards each other, making a huddle, hands on arms, heads touching. I worried about how long this was taking. I glanced towards my bike – it was still there but lots of people were milling about, it wouldn't be long before someone in authority saw it, had it impounded. The women were talking, discussing. Low voices, urgent tones. The night had already been a bizarre one, did they want to prolong it? Take a chance on a stranger? But what were their other options?

At last they turned back. The woman looked at me.

"We will come," she said.

Great, now to get them there. In India, it's not uncommon to see several people sharing a motorbike. But there were six of them, and my bike wasn't big to start with. I told them to follow me, and walked across the grass to where the bike was waiting. A man was approaching from the other side, I think he had spotted it, was planning to investigate. I gave him a wave, then scooted it back to the road. I looked around for a taxi. If I could squeeze most of them inside, it could follow me back to our house. But the few that passed were not going to stop for a gaggle of poorly dressed women.

I gave up, and pulled out my phone. Kavita was too exhausted to come, and she wouldn't want to leave the women alone in the house (Rashi didn't count).

Karan. I still had his number, hopefully he wasn't working, and would come. I thought he would, he knew I would pay. He answered on the third ring.

"Hello, Mr Karan? This is Clara Oakes, from the hotel – you remember me? You used to drive me to….yes, that's right. Please, are you free? Could you do a job for me? Drive some friends? I will pay you, of course, and a little extra for the late time. You can? That's great. Can you come now? Wonderful…"

I gave him our location. I told the women we needed to wait, a car was coming. They looked worried, so I told them it was a friend, he would follow my bike, who wanted to travel with me? The woman with no shoes opted to ride behind me, the others squeezed into Karan's car when he arrived. He looked unhappy, but I told him to follow me and set off. He didn't have time to argue. I led them to our house, paid Karan well for his trouble (I might need him again one day) and took them inside.

Rashi was looking tired, but I told her we needed more food. She dipped her head and started cooking again. I figured it would be good for her – when she realised how many people now needed to be fed, she'd soon start to teach the other women. They could all learn a few basic food hygiene facts, then help with the cooking.

Kavita hadn't emerged, so I started to reorganise the bedroom arrangements. We didn't have enough rooms, several women now would have to share rooms, with some sleeping on the floor. But we did have sufficient bedding, and I could go furniture shopping the following day. Or so I thought.

What we really needed was a bigger house. After rattling around as a threesome for a few months, we were now bursting at the seams. I didn't know how long the women would need to stay for – that was Kavita's department. But I did think that now was a good time for those charity people to come back and do an audit. When they saw what we were doing, it might motivate them to raise some cash for us.

I began to plan names for the charity. I quite liked 'The Clara Trust'. I would have to tell that to Kavita when she woke up. I was feeling cheerful now. I had beaten Shan. He would return tomorrow to his empty brothel, all his workers safely hidden with me. I had won the first round, and it was a pleasing thought.

Then Crowny ruined it. Crowny was the woman with no shoes. Well, she had some by the time we ate, I think Rashi had found some flip-flops for her. But anyway, she was one of the second lot of hookers that came to live with us. She spoke to me while she ate, scooping great spoonfuls of spicy slop into her mouth with a piece of pita bread. Watching them eat wasn't pleasant, and I was about to leave, when she looked up, saw me watching, and lowered her food.

"It was kind of you to come for us," she said. "Thank you."

I shrugged, it was no big deal.

"It's a shame I didn't manage to collect you at Shan's house," I said. Then, thinking, I added, "Or the young girls – the children. Were they there somewhere? Did the police miss them?"

Crowny shook her head and narrowed her eyes. "You knew about them? They were gone, moved to another house. Mr Shan had heard they had been seen, he didn't want to risk them being found. I do not know where they are now," she said, as if worried I might blame her somehow.

"He knew?" I said, "How? How did he know?" I couldn't think who could've told him. I had only told Kavita, I wasn't sure even Rashi knew. We'd done our best to keep it secret. Had one of the police tipped him off?

"A boy," said Crowny. "He came to the house and told Mr Shan. There was much shouting, then the girls were moved. Four girls. I do not know where they are now."

"A boy?" I said, "What boy?"

"From the school. He said a girl at school had told everyone she had seen the girls. He said the teachers were listening."

I had a sudden image of Chutki, drawing the wrong letters on her paper, chatting about what she'd seen. All of us had heard – I had done nothing to keep her quiet, hadn't asked her to tell me later, in private. I had simply asked my questions, learned the facts. And so had everyone else in the room.

Something in my stomach dropped, leaving a cold stone of dread. Don't ask me why, why I would even care about the slum brat. But I did. Maybe it's because I saw her as one of mine, part of my property, and I didn't want Shan to destroy that. Or maybe I was changing; being changed.

"Does Shan know who?" I said, not sure if I wanted to know the answer.

"He does," said the woman, "I think he does. The boy said her name. I do not remember it now. Perhaps Mr Shan too has forgotten."

But we both knew that he wouldn't have. That name would now be indelibly written in his brain, unfinished business. He wouldn't want others to know he'd been caught out by a child. He would make an example of her. A terrible warning to others in the neighbourhood. If he could burn his wife, who knows what he would do to a child, a slum rat.

I went to my room. I told myself this wasn't my concern, I had done what I could to help these people. One child, one dirty, uneducated child, wasn't worth the risk was she? What would she become anyway? If she grew up, she was destined to follow the women into a brothel, or to beg on the street. She would produce more slum rats, continue the cycle of poverty. She was never going to amount to anything, she couldn't even match the correct sound to a letter. Perhaps it was better that she should end her wretched life now, shorten the time suffering, scrabbling for existence amongst rubbish and sewage...

I stopped. I wasn't managing to convince myself. And I knew that she mattered to *him*. I knew that *he* wanted me to go back for her. Don't ask me how I knew, I just did. Like you know not to slap the child screaming in the supermarket, not to pinch the purse from the old lady in front of you, or that you should kiss your mum occasionally. You just know. Even if you ignore it, do what you feel like, you still know, somewhere inside, you can't help it. So I knew, even though I didn't want to, even though I tried to persuade myself otherwise, I knew.

I went back to the kitchen.

"Is Shan still with the police?" I asked.

"Yes, I think so," said Crowny. "We did not see him. But when we arrived, they took him away. They said they would release him tomorrow. I do not know if that is still true."

I decided to believe it was. That gave me some time. I could arrive at the slum in the morning, find Chutki (don't ask me how) and bring her to the house. After that, I didn't know. I assumed she had a mother somewhere, we would have to contact her, try to arrange for her to be sent somewhere safe. But for now, she could wait at our house, perhaps her mother could come too. It would look good when the charity visited, I told myself. They'd move us up their list to needing emergency help. Yes, I'd go tomorrow, in the morning.

I stretched out on the bed. I was so tired. The day had been busy, full of unexpected decisions and excitement. I was dirty, needed to shower. In a minute, I thought, feeling the pillow, soft under my head. The energy drained out of me, my limbs were heavy, the bed comfortable, safe, supporting. I slept.

Chapter Twenty-Five

I woke with the light. Daytime streamed into the room, demanding a response, harsh and impossible to ignore. I put an arm across my eyes, tried to sink back into sleep, but I was awake, the threads of sleep had evaporated.

For a while I lay still, reliving the events of yesterday, remembering. The thought of Chutki nagged at me, and although I tried to ignore it, tried to make lists of things we needed to buy, people who could be informed, photographs I could use for marketing, Chutki was there. I couldn't ignore her and the danger she might be in.

I hauled myself from the bed and into the shower. The floor was damp and stained, and all the towels were heaped in a mouldering pile in the corner. It was not a good start. We needed to get organised, sort a rota for housework, possibly hire a maid until the women were able to be useful. I washed away the grime and stink of yesterday and walked wet to my room. I had to rub myself dry with my bed sheet, which I then dumped by the door ready to be washed. It wasn't a good start to the day, I hoped things would improve.

I dressed and ate, then walked into the garden. No one else seemed to be awake, and I wondered what time they had all gone to bed. Kavita wouldn't stir until midday unless disturbed, the women would be in their nocturnal cycle. The day was bright and unusually clear, the pollution had cleared slightly overnight, and the air felt fresh, almost clean. Such mornings were rare in India, and I lifted my face, feeling the sun on my cheeks, listening to birds squabble in a bush. It was a good morning to be alive.

Back in my room, I stuffed my phone and some money into my bag and slung it across my body. Then I grabbed my keys and went to my bike. The guard waved when he saw me (I never did learn his name, I knew him by his yellow teeth). He opened the gate and I drove away, heading for the slums.

I went to the house that Kavita used and parked the bike off the road, near to the steps. I looped chains around the wheels, but if someone decided to steal it, they would cut through them like butter, so it was fairly pointless, more a deterrent for bored kids than a serious thief. Then I started to walk, up to the slum school, looking for Chutki. I had no idea where she lived or what her full name was. My plan was to wander around and hope I got lucky, asking anyone I recognised if they knew her.

I had spoken to three people, with no luck, as I approached the lane where Kamala lived. I hadn't seen her since the day Laxmi died, had no idea how she was, if she had recovered. But she might be useful, so I climbed the steps into her house and called her name. She shouted back, from the wet room. I went in, avoiding the water that was creeping to the edges. Kamala was sitting on the floor, wet washing between her splayed knees, beating it with a stick. Water and suds leaped into the air with each bang of the stick. It was the slum equivalent of a washing machine.

"*Namaste,*" I said, bowing slightly. I wasn't sure how she would greet me, if I would become a target for the beating stick. I didn't know if she blamed me for her sister's death, or if I was viewed as an innocent, if unhelpful, bystander.

"Why are you being here?" she said. Which was rude, but not particularly aggressive.

"I am looking for a girl, Chutki," I said. "Or Seema, the teacher," I added. Possibly the teacher knew where the pupils lived. "It is important," I added, "she might be in danger."

Kamala paused, considering. Then she pushed away the stick

285

and the wet cloth and stood. Water dripped down her legs from her soaked skirt. She bent, squeezed out the washing and added it to a heap of sodden material in the corner.

"Wait. I take you," she said, walking past me into the main room.

I followed her wet footprints. It took her seconds to change into dry clothes, to pull a *dupatta* over her head, slide her feet into plastic flip-flops.

Then we set off, through the winding lanes, under the overhanging buildings, past the rag pickers with their white sacks of rubbish. I stepped over stray bricks, dodged hanging wires, avoided the evil gutter that sweated beside the path. Rats scuttled before us, dogs shied to one side, the odd chicken watched from a perch on a broken wall.

We arrived at a doorway, and Kamala called out. A woman appeared and there was a shouted exchange. The woman then ducked back inside, there were voices, and Chutki appeared. She was chewing a piece of bread, clutching it with dirty fingers, and when she smiled the crumbs clung to her teeth. The woman stood behind her, slim and frail, barely old enough to be a mother, though I assumed that's who she was.

"Chutki," I said, "you need to come with me."

"More lessons?" she said, about to refuse.

"No, Mr Shan knows you told me about the girls in his house. He is angry."

Chutki stopped chewing, her face froze.

"I can keep you safe," I said, "but we need to leave quickly, before he comes back. Your mother can come too," I added, not sure of the protocol here. The slum kids seemed pretty unsupervised, but I wasn't sure that necessarily meant the parents didn't keep some kind of a track on them.

Chutki turned to her mother and spoke rapidly, one word flowing over the next, the volume rising as her mother answered, angry, confused. She ducked as her mother put out her hand and whacked her on the side of the head, then more shouting, more anger, hotter and louder, more urgent.

They stopped. Both turned to me.

"Yes, that's fine," said Chutki. "My mother thanks you for your help. She will stay here."

I nearly laughed. That had so *not* been the exchange.

Chutki grinned at me. "Where are we going?" she said.

"It's best if you don't know. Tell your mother I will keep you safe, but you need to come now, and I don't know when it will be safe for you to come back." Maybe never, I thought. But I didn't say that, we could figure that out later. For now, Chutki needed to be hidden, somewhere safe.

I turned to Kamala. "Thank you," I said. Then I bowed to Chutki's mother. She bowed back, then reached out, hugged me. It was short, unexpected, and tight. I didn't flinch as her soft brown arms pressed against me. I understood; she was thanking me. She trusted me to keep her child safe. I just hoped that I could.

We left. Chutki walked away from her home, just like that. She didn't bring anything, didn't say anything. She hugged her mother and was almost drowned in the strong tight embrace, her little face smiling up at me over her mother's shoulder. Then off we went, back through the lanes and pathways, between the leaning houses that filtered the light. We ran past the oozing grey sewage, sluggish in the ditch beside the path, ignored the people who stared as we hurried past their gaping doorways; a million unseen eyes, watching.

I slowed, and reached for Chutki's hand. Whilst my main concern had been speed, to reach her before Shan, I now felt more cautious. I was consumed by a new feeling, not fear exactly, but an overwhelming sense of danger. Something bad was going to happen.

We continued at a fast walk, my senses straining to predict what

287

was around every corner, who was watching from dark doorways. I kept close to the walls, hoping to hide in the shadow of brickwork.

As we neared a corner, I heard someone stumble, and I leaned into the wall, pulling Chutki behind me. There was a curse, the sound of heavy footsteps coming nearer, then the unmistakable rustle of clothing as someone marched towards us. I waited, wished I'd had a weapon, searched the narrow lane for an escape route.

A man rounded the corner. His tee-shirt was rolled up, his swollen belly sweaty in the heat. He barely glanced at us, hurried past, leaving a wake of whiskey fumes.

I exhaled, and continued to walk. Chutki glanced up at me. She sensed my tension and was silent, walking close. Every darting rat made me jump, my ears straining to hear through the general rumbles of the slum, my eyes peering into the shadows. Every doorway was a threat, every corner hid danger.

We reached the end of Kavita's lane, and I could see my bike, leaning against the step. With a sudden release of tension, I started to run. Faster and faster, avoiding debris and potholes, straight down the lane to safety, practically dragging the child behind me.

When we reached Kavita's house, I began to unwind the chains from my bike. My breath was short, coming in urgent bursts, as I tried to explain to Chutki that we would go to the house, she could stay there and we could send messages to her mother until we found somewhere better, perhaps a relative. Or until Shan was finally stopped or dead – then I stopped.

Shan was still winning. Yes, I had removed the women. And yes, I now had Chutki. But he still had those girls and he was still out there, free. He was still conniving, using his influence, trying to reinstate himself. We hadn't stopped him, we had only dented his empire. It wasn't enough.

I decided I would go after him. I would find him, force him to tell me where those girls were. I wasn't afraid of him, he was a rabid dog, wild but insignificant. I would stop him.

I knew it was wrong. That feeling, the one that had told me I should rescue Chutki, was just as strongly telling me that I should return with her to the home, that this wasn't a fight I would win. But I ignored it. I have spent a lifetime ignoring that voice, those feelings that would guide me if I would let them. I didn't want to listen. I wanted to do it my way.

It's important that you take note of that. Afterwards, when Kavita told the world that I was a hero, that I'd done what I had to save Chutki, you must remember this. I was doing what I wanted and was ignoring what I knew to be right. Ah, how we want our heroes to be perfect, those who give to society to be well motivated and pure. But I doubt if any of them really are. Who really knows the heart of people? Who can really judge motives and separate them from outcome? Good things happen for the wrong reasons, and bad things are often the result of honourable intentions. So remember please, because I want you, at least, to understand. I wanted to beat Shan.

I pulled out my phone, called Karan. He would be happy with my generosity, keen to do further work for me. I arranged where to meet him, then took Chutki to the corner of the resettlement area where Karan used to drop me. As we walked there, past the coloured billboards and washing strewn balconies, I watched all the time for Shan. I didn't know where he was, when he would be released, which way he would decide to go. I wanted Chutki well away before he arrived.

Karan arrived at the corner soon after we did. He must have left the hotel immediately when I called. That was pleasing, I like efficient staff. I pulled out some money and leaned into the car.

"This is Chutki," I said, nodding towards the girl. She grinned back at me. "Please take her to the house we went to yesterday.

You remember it? Great. Please go straight there. I'll pay you now. I have my bike, so will follow on later, when I've finished here…" I gave him a wedge of rupees.

I turned to Chutki, opening the door. "Go to the house and go inside, ask for Kavita," I said as she scooted across the seat and sat upright. She looked delighted, I wondered if she had ever been in a car before. Certainly not one like this. She sat very straight, her legs trailing towards the floor, her face glowing, her hands splayed on the seat next to her. She nodded.

"Do you have paper? And a pen?" I asked Karan. He scrabbled in the glovebox, and held them out to me. I wrote a note, first to the guard, giving permission for him to let the car pass. I didn't know if he could read, but it was the best I could do. Then I wrote another note, for Kavita, explaining the situation.

I would phone her too, but this would cover any problems, if she didn't listen to her messages. I knew she wouldn't be awake, she didn't enjoy mornings. I handed the notes to Karan, shut the door, stepped back. They drove away, Chutki waving madly. It was done.

Chapter Twenty-Six

I left my bike where it was and made my way back towards the slums. I passed the garage I'd used yesterday to park the van, turned up the narrow lane towards the metal steps and the brothel. I didn't know where Shan would go, whether he would head back to the house he used for business, in the hope some of the women were there, or if he'd go straight to his home above the shop in the resettlement area. Or neither of course – perhaps he would go straight to wherever he was hiding the new girls. I didn't know, so was making it up as I went.

My bag was light at my side, bumping against my hip as I walked. I wished I had a gun, or at least a knife. If the opportunity presented itself, I knew I would kill Shan. He deserved it, it would be justice. I also knew I had no right to mete out that justice, I was not the wronged party, but I felt those who had the right were too timid, too bound by laws and fear to do what should be done. And I was encumbered with neither.

I could see the metal steps now. I walked up the litter-strewn lane, watchful, alert. There was the general hum of noise that never left the slums, and for once I was aware of it. I heard the men laughing in a doorway, the racing motor as two teenagers tried to repair a bike, the crying of a baby. I walked up to Shan's house, and paused.

The door was still open, the lock damaged from where the police had flung it open. It swayed slightly, opened into the room, then swung back with a thump as a breeze caught it. The hinges were damaged, so it was no longer aligned with the doorframe, and it again began to open. Like a child playing peek-a-boo, uncovering its face.

I stepped forwards, pushed it open. Gradually the interior of the house was revealed. First the stone step, then the dusty rug, rucked up where feet had scuffed over it. I could see the chairs, their backs to the door, then the narrow table at the back of the room. Along the wall there still lay shoes, in a muddle, as if hurriedly picked over, then abandoned. But no people.

I walked into the room and listened. The door behind me swung shut. No sound from within. I walked to the stairs, peered up. Grey light filtered down, and the smell of tired air. But no sound. No footsteps, no music, no voices. I paused, wondering whether to climb them, to look in other rooms, or whether to leave, try Shan's home. There was no time for either.

The door crashed open. Light screamed through the gap, blocked by a figure, tall, thin. I couldn't see his face, only his silhouette. But that was enough, I could see the aggression in his stance, the threat in the weapon in his hand.

I opened my mouth, ready to speak, to ask questions, demand answers, drew a breath –

"For you, bitch," he said.

Something exploded inside me as the floor rushed up to slam into my face.

"It's what you deserve," he said, as a second bullet propelled into my stomach.

I lay there, knowing I had been shot but not quite able to process it. My mind was working, but in staccato, not linking events with logical effects. When the pain hit, it consumed me, fuzzing everything else, reaching into the far parts of me.

Yet I was still awake, still able to see and hear. He came into the room, walked to where I lay. For some reason, I focussed on his shoes, brown, long, well-polished. I saw the glint of reflected light as they approached, watched their black underside as they stepped over me. The sound of them, tapping on the concrete, muted by the rug, seemed unnaturally loud. I wondered if he would kick me, wondered how personal this was. But he turned, was leaving, I was a job, now completed.

"That's the end of you," he called, even as he walked through the door, back into a world that was surely continuing. A world that would impossibly still function, still appear normal, even though my own part of it had shattered.

I stared at the doorway in front of me, as it mingled with stars and fireworks and an ever-growing fuzziness. The floor beneath me was hard, the grit scratching my face as I tried to turn, attempted to pull my legs up towards me, to ease the pressure, quench some of the blood.

I knew I was dying. I could smell death in the blackness of the blood spreading from me. Though my brain was still able to think, which was surprising. My thoughts were disjointed, blotted by pain. But I could still think. I did know what was happening.

Images rather than words flooded my head. I didn't think of my family at all, they were no longer part of my life as it seeped away. Nor did I think about the church, of England, of Rob and Esther and their cosy religion. I thought briefly of Kavita, of her strength and the way she moved and spoke. A strong woman. I knew I could trust her, she would help those women, build them up, help them to be free. And part of me knew that Esther would help, would be a liaison in England. Without me on the scene to cause awkwardness, she would embrace the work, keep the funds arriving. But mostly, I thought of Chutki. That smile, that zest for life, that eagerness to grasp opportunities. I knew I had done the right thing in saving her, even if my next decision was folly. Shan was lost to me. But even if I'd found him, destroyed his reign in some way, in reality it would change very little. Someone else would rise up, take his place, continue to oppress. And the missing girls? Very likely, they would remain missing, along with thousands of others.

Do you care? Do you feel the story hasn't finished properly? Feel cheated? We care about those we've heard about, those with whom we have a link.

But realistically, those girls too would've been replaced by others. I was never going to win, not really. All I could ever have hoped was to save the few that I could. And I had. The poor will always be with us, we can only help some of them.

As I lay there in agony – and it *was* agony, my pain receptors work just as well as yours. But, as I lay there, did I have regrets? Would I have chosen differently? I don't think so. Because you see, although the pain was almost all consuming, although rational thought was beginning to drift into a muddle of images, Chutki, Kavita, the child under the bed, Karan and Malik, my family... although I was beyond any kind of action other than the careful intake of shallow breaths, part of me was free. Some corner of my mind, my spirit if you like, was at peace.

No, I would not have done it differently, because actually, I don't think it would have been possible. Don't forget, even with everything that happened, even with this all-encompassing pain which was now beginning to make everything else fade, even as my world started to slip away and become dark, I knew. I knew beyond doubt. In spite of it all, I was better off. Simply because *he* was worth it.

Do you doubt it? Do you fear that Dickens' Sydney Carton might not have faced the guillotine? That Hugo's Valjean may have deserted Cosette? Ah, you either have no faith, or have never encountered something of true value. You should read the theatre that is the Book of Job, then you would understand. This was never about wealth or health or prestige or safety for loved ones. This was about *him*. One who is worth everything. Real life doesn't produce happy endings, surely you know that much.

"End of you," my executioner had said. End of me? I wanted to shout after him, to laugh or smile at the irony – though actually I think my face was more contorted into a grimace. Not the end. We all have a 'use-by' date, a time to die. But this wasn't the end of me. I knew that, knew what he didn't. Not the end. The start of something new.

The pain was intense, even breathing was becoming difficult. I lay there, on my side, warm stickiness gradually surrounding me. And I waited. It wouldn't be long, I knew that as sure as anything. It wouldn't be long, and then he would come for me. The one who was worth it...

Afterword

Imagine for a moment that you can see through time. Pretend that you can see through the curtain separating your past and future, and consider what that might mean. Maybe nothing...

There are some events in life which are more important than others. You would agree? So, I have a question for you: If you could look ahead, to the consequences, do you think it would change your actions? Ah no, we have considered that already – the events of the future would not warn sufficiently to alter our course.

So instead, consider another question. If you saw something, experienced something, precious – a treasure with more value than any other, would *that* alter your course? I believe it would. And that, really, is the point.

To glimpse something beyond compare, to taste something you would desire above all else, to find that which is truly worthy....that, my friend, would drive us, alter us, steer us. That would decide our behaviour, our actions, our aims. And that, really, *is* the question. Have you found one who is worth it?

The End

Sold

By Anne E. Thompson

I held you,
Your weight light on my hip
As I touched your button nose
With mine,
Peered deep into
Shining eyes,
Because you are my world.

We held hands
As we walked to the station.
And you skipped beside me
Trusting
While my heart
Became still,
Because you were my world.

I sold you
To the man whose words
Promised me,
That you would be schooled
And be fed
And have chances in life,
Beyond my reach.
And I walked away,
With breaking heart
And one hundred pounds
And the prayer you would be safe.
Because you were my world.

Acknowledgements

Writing a book always involves several people, and Clara is no different.

I have been privileged to visit the work taking place amongst the poor in India, by both Actionaid and Tearfund. Both organisations have my greatest respect, and I should clearly state that Clara Oakes is a completely fictitious character, and resembles no one I met. The other characters and events too are works of fiction, created in my imagination.

The needs illustrated in the story, however, are very real. Even today, people are living in real poverty, girls are being trafficked, women are denied choices. I will never forget sitting in a home in a resettlement area in India, listening to a group of strong women talking about their lives. Or listening to sex-workers in the red light district, as they explained why they worked there. I was touched by their stories, and I hope that in reading Clara, you will glimpse something of the struggle they face.

Several people have been involved with helping me sort out facts regarding things of which I had no previous knowledge. Anything that is correct is due to them - any mistakes are all mine.

Thank you to Dr Poppy Hatfield for advice on medical issues.

Thank you to Loretta Simpson Cert.FAA for her help with the scene with the funeral director.

Thank you to my friends in India who advised me on names and culture.

Thank you to Michelle Scriminger for her help regarding the training and work of a food hygiene officer.

Especially thank you to my family, who cheer me on at every stage, and have spent many hours listening to interesting facts about psychopaths.

Also by Anne E. Thompson

Fiction

Hidden Faces
Invisible Jane
Counting Stars
JOANNA

Non-Fiction
How to Have a Brain Tumour

Published in 2019
Ellen

Anne E. Thompson also writes a weekly blog at:
anneethompson.com

Chapter One

My Story

I first saw them on the bus. They got on after me, the mother helping the toddler up the big step, holding the baby on her hip while she juggled change, paid the driver. I wondered why she hadn't got her money ready, been prepared so we didn't all have to wait. I watched as she swung her way to a seat, leaning against the post for support, heaving the toddler onto the chair by his shoulder.

Then they sat, a happy family unit, the boy chattering in his high-pitched voice, the mother barely listening, watching the town speed past the window, smiling every so often so he knew he had her attention. Knew he was loved. Cared for. They had everything I didn't have but I didn't hate them. That would have involved feelings and I tended to not be bothered by those. No, I just watched, knew that those children had all the things, all the mothering, that had passed me by. Knew they were happy. Decided to change things a little. Even up the score, make society a little fairer, more equal.

Following them was easy. The mother made a great deal about collecting up their bags, warning the boy that theirs was the next stop. She grasped the baby in one hand, bus pole in the other and stood, swaying as we lurched from side to side. She let the boy press the bell button, his chubby fingers reaching up. Almost too high for him. Old ladies in the adjoining seats smiled. Such a cosy scene, a little family returning from a trip to the town. They waited until the bus had swung into the stop, was stationary, before they made their way to the door. I was already standing, waiting behind them.

The mother glanced behind and I twisted my mouth into a smile, showed my teeth to the boy who hid his face in his mother's jeans, pressing against her as if scared. That was rude. Nothing to be frightened of. Not yet.

The family jumped from the bus and I stepped down. As the bus left I turned away, walked the opposite direction from the family. In case someone was watching, noticing, would remember later. Not that that was a possibility but it didn't do to take chances. I strode to the corner, turned it, then made as if I had forgotten something. Searched pockets, glanced at watch, then turned and hurried back. The family was still in sight, further down the road but not too far. She had spent time unfolding the buggy, securing the baby, arranging her shopping. All the time in the world.

I walked behind, gazing into shop windows, keeping a distance between us. They left the main street and began to walk along a road lined with houses, smart semi-detached homes with neat square gardens. Some had extended; built ugly extra bedrooms that loomed above the house, changing the face, destroying the symmetry. There were some smaller houses stuffed by greedy builders into empty plots, a short terrace in red brick. It was just after this the family stopped.

The mother scrabbled in her bag, retrieved her key. The boy had skipped down the path, was standing by the door. The mother began to follow but I was already turning away. I would remember the house, could come back later, when it was dark. I would only do it if it was easy, if there was no risk. If she was foolish enough to leave the back door unlocked. No point in going to any effort, it wasn't as if they meant anything to me. There would be easier options if it didn't work out. But I thought it probably would. There was something casual about her, about the way she looked so relaxed, unfussy. I thought locking the back door would be low on her priorities until she went to bed herself. People were so complacent, assumed the world was made up of clones of themselves. Which was convenient, often worked to my advantage. As I walked back, towards the bus stop, I realised I was smiling.

***

Other People

She realised she was pregnant on Tuesday. She should have known before, of course she should, but she hadn't thought it was possible. No one ever thinks they will be the 'one percent' who gets unlucky, that is just some mathematical myth printed on the packets of birth control paraphernalia.

She stared at the blue line of the pregnancy test and threw it into the small shiny bin with the other four. They sat there, accusing her of stupidity for not believing the obvious. She snapped down the round lid on top of them, hiding them from view. She wished she could hide the truth as easily.

She washed her hands, letting them stay under the running warm water for longer than was necessary, her mind blank. Then she went to her bed, lay there staring at the ceiling, hands on her stomach. Inside, a life fluttered, swam, fought to survive. As yet unfelt but now very real. Now she knew, she felt very pregnant. The world was different. She was different. Could she do this? Could she allow the sorrows of the past to continue? Could she protect her baby from the things that had happened? Her baby. There, she had said it. It was hers. Perhaps the hormones were already starting to build, to gang up on her, to warp her mind so that everything rational was put aside and only the baby mattered. Protecting the baby. But could she? Could she protect this new life? Did she even have the right to try?

She rolled onto her side, eyes shut, mind whirling. She needed to move, it was her turn to cook dinner. Josh would be home in an hour and then she would have to tell him, to share her secret, which would make it even more real. What should she do? Josh, she thought, would be excited. Once the shock had passed, the unexpectedness of it all, he would be pleased. He had wanted children, been disappointed when she told him she would never have any, that wasn't part of her life plan. He loved her enough to marry her anyway, harbouring the thought she might change her mind, caring enough to take the risk that she might not. It was too soon, too early in their life together but it was what he wanted. She knew that. Which made it harder, more difficult to know what to do. Josh didn't understand, not really. She had never told him the truth, the life she had built was too precious, too precarious.

She glanced at the clock. Seven o'clock. She would move in a minute, the bed was comfortable, like a cocoon. She decided she would tell Josh later, after she had spoken to Margaret. Margaret would know what to do. Perhaps it was time to grow up a bit she decided, to face a few things that she had buried long ago, to learn a few more facts. It was so much easier to hide though, to pretend that she was normal, that her life was the same as everyone else's, that she was the same. To ignore those nagging doubts, those fears.

She pulled herself to a sitting position, pressing her hands on the soft mattress, snagging the duvet with her slipper. She would cook sausages for supper. Her default meal, they were easy.

She wandered into the kitchen and pulled open the freezer, pulling out meat and vegetables, setting the temperature of the oven, clattering tins onto the work surface, filling saucepans with water. Her mind was in the past, remembering.

***

JOANNA by Anne E. Thompson
Published by The Cobweb Press
ISBN 978-0-9954632-2-6